RUINING HATTIE

P. RAYNE

ABOUT RUINING HATTIE

A man with no limits is the most dangerous kind of threat.

When Trent Clarke caught me picking pockets at eleven, he didn't turn me in. Instead, he took me under his wing and taught me that in this world, you take what you want and never look back.

He might have shaped me, but *I* built my empire of the most successful string of strip clubs on the West Coast.

Now that I have everything, it's time to track down my deadbeat mother and remind her who she left behind. That is if the drugs didn't kill her already.

But I don't find the worn-down shell of the woman I remember. Instead, she has all the things she never managed to give me—the white picket fence, a family dog, even church on Sunday mornings.

The real kicker? She replaced me and raised the perfect daughter with all the care and love she never gave me.

A twisted need for revenge roars to life inside me, and I aim it at my mother's precious stepdaughter—sweet, sheltered Hattie Sinclair.

At first, it's purely about vengeance, pulling Hattie into the darkness to watch her innocence unravel piece by piece. But she becomes something more. Something dangerous. Something I can't resist.

Until she becomes my obsession.

ruining hattie

TRIGGER WARNINGS

Trigger warnings can be found on our website if you want to
check them out.

PLEASE NOTE:

These warnings contain major spoilers.

www.prayneauthor.com/extras/content-warnings

PROLOGUE
TWENTY-SIX YEARS AGO...

The little boy's stomach grumbles and twists with hunger pains. He can't remember a day, an hour, or a minute when it didn't feel as if his stomach was eating itself away. Although starvation has been present most of his life, it never gets easier.

His mom doesn't even notice her own hunger pains anymore, let alone the way her son's cheeks have sunken in or his hollowed-out eyes.

His mom, with her mouth hanging open, is still slumped in a half-upright position on the couch, one of the two furniture pieces left in their tiny one-bedroom apartment. Slowly, things have disappeared. His bed. The kitchen table. The small number of toys he'd accumulated from his mom's visitors to keep him quiet and away. She told him it was to pay rent and keep a roof over their head, but he knew they were lies.

On the third time the landlord came to collect the rent, his mom told the boy to go for a walk. Which turned out to be a regular thing every time the landlord came over. He'd always be gone when the boy got back, but every first of the month, he'd show back up, and the boy would leave the only safe haven he knew, if you could call it that.

He doesn't know or care how she convinces the landlord to let them stay, he's just happy to still have somewhere to sleep at night. Once when he was nine, they lived outside for six months until one of his mom's friends offered to let them stay with her. It was the most miserable time of his life. Adding the cold to the hunger had been far worse than now.

A lot of guys come around these days. Sometimes they get mad and scream at him if they can't wake her up, but it's not his fault. She can't even wake up when her own child begs and cries for her that he's hungry.

But he's grown tired of begging. It makes him feel so helpless. And nothing changes from day to day anyway.

Another pain twists his stomach, and he turns back toward the fuzzy TV, barely able to make out the picture on the screen. It used to work okay, but one of his mom's guy friends ripped off one of the rabbit's ears.

Climbing off the dirty floor, he walks over and stands in front of his mom. His hands are fisted at his sides as he stares at her. Seeing her like this used to make him sad. He used to worry that she was dead. Now it only makes him angry.

He watches the other moms outside of their crappy apartment through the dirty glass, holding the hands of their children, walking along the sidewalk. The way they smile down at their kids makes his heart constrict. His mom has never looked at him like that.

He nudges her shoulder, but she barely moves. He pushes a little harder.

"Mom, wake up. I'm hungry." He despises the note of pleading in his voice, but he doesn't have much of a choice. He's too hungry. Too starved. The nausea and the cramping have started.

She doesn't react.

"Mom," he says a little louder. When she still doesn't move, he shakes her shoulders with both of his little hands.

She groans. "What?" Her face screws up and she pushes him back, not bothering to open her eyes.

"I'm hungry."

"Go away." She swats her hand in the air and lies across the couch.

"I need something to eat." He wants to stomp his feet, but he knows only little kids do that.

"So get something." She lifts one skinny arm and motions in the general direction of the kitchen.

Does she really not know the cabinets are empty?

"Mom, wake up." His voice hitches at her disregard for his well-being.

When her breathing evens out again, he knows trying to wake her is a lost cause. His hands squeeze into fists, and he lets out an angry grunt before stomping off to the small bathroom.

The little boy can't wait for the day when he doesn't have to rely on anyone to take care of him. When he's an adult like his mom, he'll take care of himself no matter what.

He stares at himself in the cracked mirror and turns on the water, saying a small prayer that water will come out of the tap. It does, and he splashes water on his face and arms, then a small amount to stick his hair down.

He figured out quickly that if he's dirty or smelly, his marks are more likely to see him coming. But if he takes the time to clean himself, they usually think he's just like any other kid his age. No one immediately notices his worn clothes and the dirty shoes with holes. Most people are too busy with their own lives to really pay much attention to him.

He leaves the apartment with one thing on his mind—pickpocket someone with enough cash in their wallet to buy himself a meal at the family diner down the street. The waitress there is nice, and sometimes she sneaks him a piece of pie.

Two hours later, the boy returns to the apartment with a full belly, worried that maybe he ate too much. He's eaten too fast or too much before and thrown it up only for the hunger to come on faster again, which means everything he did to get food was for naught.

The moment he closes the apartment door behind him, a shiver runs up his spine, and his muscles tense.

He's here.

Of all the men who come to visit his mom, Stan is the absolute worst.

He always looks at the boy in a way that makes the eleven-year-old want to crawl out of his skin. He doesn't know what Stan wants to do to him, but he knows it isn't good. Knows he won't like it.

Stan walks out of the bedroom down the hall, and a smarmy grin spreads across his face when he spots the boy. The sound of him closing the bedroom door booms through the small apartment. "Glad you're here, Ty. Thinking maybe you can help your mom out."

A fission of fear rushes through the boy, but he locks it down, not about to let Stan see it. Showing this man any fear will only lead to his doom.

Stan makes quick work of the hallway, peering down. "Cat got your tongue?" He arches an eyebrow, but the boy still doesn't say anything. "Seems your mom is down for the count, so I came here for nothing."

"What'd you want me to do about it?" The boy's vile comeback is instinctual, and he regrets allowing his anger and fear to rule him. Deep down, he knows that he's outmatched.

"I know your mom needs some money, and since she can't give me what I want, thought maybe you could."

The little boy's stomach pitches, and he has to bite back the bile racing up his throat. "No." Though he doesn't even know what Stan is asking, he knows enough that he doesn't want whatever he's offering.

Stan grips him at the back of the neck and tilts his face up so the boy can smell the booze on his breath. "C'mon now.

After all I do for you and your mom? You can't give a little to get a little?"

At the glint in Stan's eyes, the boy screams for his mother over and over while Stan laughs in his face. When she doesn't appear, the fracture in the little boy's heart cracks into shards, ripping at his flesh.

"She's never coming to save you, boy, haven't you figured that out yet?" The grip on the back of his neck grows tighter, and Stan runs his hand down the boy's side to his waist.

Whatever is going to happen next, the boy knows with every fiber of his small being that he needs to leave one of the only homes he's known and never come back.

He brings his knee up and nails Stan in the groin. The boy flies out of the apartment, down the stairs, and across the parking lot. He continues to run. And run. And run.

When he can barely breathe, he stops and finds himself in a part of town he's not familiar with. Staring around, that fear to escape shifts, and he grows scared. But it's a different kind of scared than the one he felt at home with his mom. He whispers that he can do this. He's grown enough to live on his own. She wasn't doing anything for him anyway. He's no stranger to having to survive alone.

A few weeks later, the weather is starting to turn, and he needs to steal enough money to get a jacket and better shoes from the secondhand shop down the street. He has managed to feed himself and found a place in the park he can hide out and sleep at night without anyone bothering him.

On his quest to find someone to steal from, the boy loiters on the sidewalk that edges along the park. If he gets caught, the park will give him a better chance of getting away, what with all its winding paths and vegetation and his speed.

He waits until a man walking his dog stops to let the dog sniff at one of the bushes beside the sidewalk. It's always easier when the person is distracted—people with their dogs, teenagers with their friends, women with lots of shopping bags in hand.

The boy leisurely walks by the man. Sometimes he pretends to bump into people, but other times, like this one, it's not necessary, because the corner of the man's wallet is visible in the pocket of his coat. With a quick reach, the boy grabs and tucks the wallet into his waistband and keeps walking, the man none the wiser as he attempts to pull the dog away from the bush.

He's just about to walk into the park and his hiding spot to see how much he scored when someone grips his upper arm, forcing him to keep walking ahead.

"Hey!" The boy looks up at the stranger and tries to yank his arm out of his hold, but the man only squeezes harder. "Let me go."

"You're coming with me, kid. We're gonna have a little chat."

His heartbeat hammers. He's not afraid of getting caught and getting in trouble with the police. He's only eleven, what could they really do? Put him in some foster home that he can escape from the first night? But he's terrified of them tracking down his mom and forcing him to live with her. He yanks his arm again, but the man's fingers press into his arm harder.

Once they get behind the jungle gym, the man releases him, keeping the boy's back to the rock climbing wall and standing wide in front of him with his arms crossed.

"Relax, kid, you're not in trouble." The man flicks his gaze down at him, and for some reason, the boy believes him.

It wasn't until years later that the boy realized just how much that meeting set his life on a path that he never could have predicted.

1

BASTION

The bass from the music at the front of the house thumps through my office at the back of the club. The Black Orchid has more than twenty locations in four different states, but I run the business out of the first club I started in Seattle.

A decade ago, when my sister married billionaire Obsidian Voss and a bunch of fucked-up shit went down, I made a promise to my sister, Arlana, that I'd get myself on the straight and narrow. So did our dad, but I knew if we were together, we'd likely revert to our old ways at some point.

So I moved far enough away that he wasn't in my life every day. He's used the past decade to moderately straighten himself out, even got married five years ago. I used the time, and some seed money from my brother-in-law, to build the most successful chain of elite membership strip clubs throughout the West Coast. I wonder what that scrawny, frail kid would think of himself now.

What makes my strip clubs different isn't the lush interiors or the top-of-the-line talent, but the fact that the women who dance here want to be here.

Too many strip clubs take advantage of the women who are the sole reason they have customers. I take care of my girls, giving them a more-than-healthy living wage, health benefits, and they keep all their tips. And if they offer extra services in the VIP rooms, that's their decision and their earnings.

I only have one rule. No drug or alcohol use on the premises. My patrons don't want to see some glazed-eyed woman give a half-assed effort when she's shaking her tits and ass in his face. My girls sell the fantasy. Every man in my club better feel as though they're the one the dancer desires—whether it's because she's grinding her pussy on his lap and her tits in his face, or because she throws him a look from the stage that reads "I need you and only you."

I sell the make-believe fairy tale, but the man's version. That they're the hottest, wealthiest, biggest alpha dog in the room. Men are such simple creatures that they buy into the illusion without question. As a result, they pay the ridiculous membership charge to get in here and the inflated price of the drinks, and they stay longer than the average consumer at a club like mine. They don't even balk at the upcharge for a lap dance or a visit to the VIP room.

Everyone benefits—me, the dancer, and the clientele— which has been the key to a long-lasting, successful enterprise. And it's made me filthy rich. Which is all I've ever wanted, but somehow, there's still an emptiness inside me.

I push away the uncomfortable gnawing feeling and shake my head. Now that I've had time to calm down after nonstop building the business, the past has been creeping into my psyche more and more, which is probably why, during a weak moment last week, I did something so fucking stupid. I still can't believe I did it.

There's a knock on my office door and I say, "Come in." I'm thankful for the interruption.

The door swings open, and my right-hand woman, Steph, struts in. She's worked for me for five years now, and once I knew I could trust her, I assigned her the task of traveling to all the different Black Orchid locations to make sure things are running smoothly.

I used to do it myself, but I don't enjoy traveling from place to place all the time. Maybe it's from never having a solid home growing up—at first because my mom didn't pay the rent, and then with Trent and Ariana because we'd done enough damage in one town that we had to get out before we caught any heat. Either way, I quite like having a home these days.

Sure, I still visit all the locations, but it's more of a biannual thing than a monthly thing at this point.

Steph smiles and sits in the plush leather chair opposite my desk. Her tight-fitting skirt cuts off mid-thigh, and her blouse has the top three buttons undone, revealing her considerable assets. It's an outfit that would never be accepted in corporate America, but in a strip club, she somehow manages to look demure.

"You're back. How'd everything go?" I lean back in my chair and steeple my hands in front of me.

"Everything's in order, though the Sacramento club is going to need a new manager. Riley put his notice in while I was there."

I frown. "Where's he going?"

Steph rolls her eyes. "Said his wife is on him to quit. She doesn't like that he works around half-naked women all day."

My lips press together. "Happy wife, happy life, huh?"

"It's bullshit. If a man wants to cheat, he will. Simple as that. Doesn't matter if he's around naked women or not."

I shrug, not entirely agreeing. Desire and proximity together can be a potent cocktail.

"Do you want me to make him an offer he can't refuse? He's a decent manager."

She's not wrong, and I don't want to lose him, but if he doesn't want to be there, what's the point in trying to convince him otherwise? We'll just end up back here at some point.

She crosses her legs slowly, and my gaze drags across the movement. Steph has a great set of legs.

I shake my head. "No, let him go. But once you've picked someone to fill his position, I want to do the final interview."

She smirks. "Don't trust me?"

Tilting my head down, I look at her from under my brows. "You know I do, but I get the final say."

She nods before filling me in on some more details from the California clubs. I give her a few tasks, and when we're done, she stands and walks over to the office door, then flips the lock.

Like some Pavlovian response, my dick twitches. Steph saunters to my desk, squeezing herself between where I sit in my chair and the desk.

I don't fuck the dancers, and truth be told, I shouldn't fuck Steph either since she works for me. But she understands the deal, and she's never tried to make it anything more than it is—two adults getting their rocks off when the mood strikes.

"Something I can help you with?" I arch an eyebrow.

"The business stuff is over now. Time for a more pleasurable experience." She sets her hands on the armrests of my chair and pushes it backward, making room for her to drop onto her knees in front of me.

I groan low in my throat. "What did you have in mind?"

The corners of her lips tilt up. "You're a smart man." Steph runs both hands up my thighs until she covers my now hard-as-a-rock dick with her hand. She squeezes my length, eliciting another groan from me.

"Do your worst."

Always loving a challenge, she smiles up at me while unfastening my belt. As I'm admiring her with my dress pants splayed open and my zipper down, my phone buzzes on my desk with a text. Unable to stop working, I glance at the screen. When I see who's texted me, my entire body stiffens.

Steph tugs my cock out and is stroking it as I reach for my phone.

1 new message from Mr. Smith

My chest grows tight, and that familiar nausea churns in my stomach. Cursing my impulsive decision weeks prior, I open the message as Steph wraps her lips around the tip of me. I'm not even enjoying her blow job. That's how fucked up this situation is.

> I located the individual. I've sent a report to your email along with my invoice. Let me know if you need anything else.

Sitting up straight, I push Steph's shoulders, and her mouth pops off my cock.

"What the hell, Bastion?" Her lipstick is smeared, and her eyes are narrowed.

"Something's come up."

"I'm aware." She reaches for my dick, but I push her hand away.

"You need to leave, Steph. I have something I have to deal with privately."

Her cheeks redden, and her jaw clenches. She's about to argue but seems to think better of it when she takes in my expression. "Fine."

She stands and tugs her skirt down, trying to muster up some kind of dignity, but that's hard to do when you just had your mouth wrapped around your boss's cock and he abruptly called things off. I hate doing that to her or making her feel that way.

"I'll be in the Nevada clubs next week. I'll let you know if there's anything pressing that needs your attention," she says.

I nod, not bothering to look at her. There's probably confusion written all over her face, and I can't blame her. I don't even understand myself these days. After the door shuts behind her, I stare at my phone's screen, unsure if I want to go through with this or not.

When I reached out to Mr. Smith and asked him to track down my mother, I genuinely thought he would report back with a death certificate. That she'd passed away from a drug overdose at some point in the twenty-six years since I left her in that filthy apartment. The box would be sealed, and I could move on. Even then, I knew it would bring up a bunch of shit, but I never expected her to be alive.

Where is she? What is she doing? Is she still an addict and living on the streets? Is she in jail? I thought that was the most likely possibility and probably the only way she was still alive—she wouldn't have the ability to constantly feed her demons like she would out on the street.

I push my hand through my hair, then set down my phone and pull my laptop toward me, clicking on my email. The report is there, just as Mr. Smith said it would be. My heart hammers as I hover the cursor over the email, warning alarms blaring in my head.

Once I click, there's no going back.

Who the hell am I kidding? There's already no going back just from the mere fact that I know my mother somehow managed to beat the odds.

"Fuck!" I slam my fist down on the desk beside my computer. I've fucking opened Pandora's box.

Hiring Mr. Smith to track her down was a stupid decision. It was a weak moment. I'd just returned from visiting my sister at Midnight Manor for my niece and nephew's seventh birthday. Every time I'm around my sister and her family, it feels surreal. She grew up the same way I did—with her father, my pseudofather, running cons on people—and somehow, she's managed to have a normal relationship and family of her own.

Granted, she missed out on experiencing eleven years with a neglectful addict for a mother, but Arlana's birth mother ran away from her and Trent early on, so she hasn't had it easy either.

I hate to admit that I was jealous on the plane home, and that lingered the following weeks. I don't begrudge my sister's happiness, she deserves it, but I found myself wishing I could have a slice of it for myself. The past came haunting, and I wondered where my mother ended up, so I called my brother-in-law, Obsidian. He connected me with his brother Kol, who led me to Mr. Smith. I didn't tell Obsidian who I was looking for, instead saying that I needed to track someone down for business purposes. That way he wouldn't share my call with Ariana. The last thing I needed was for her to be all over me about this.

Since she's met Obsidian, she's become so fucking into

discussing feelings it makes me want to pierce my eardrums with a knife most times.

Who am I kidding? There's no turning back now.

After taking a deep breath, I press on the email, then click on the report attached.

The words "Carla Lynn Sinclair (nee Blake), 57" are printed at the top of the report, and I squeeze my eyes shut to push back the swell of emotion at seeing her full name.

It takes me a couple minutes, but I dig into the report. Interesting. Mommy Dearest lives in Wisconsin now and has been married for seventeen years to a guy named Robert Sinclair, who came into the marriage with a seven-year-old daughter, Hattie.

I'm in a state of disbelief as I read. She's a religious churchgoer every Sunday and works as a hairdresser at a local salon. She's had no speeding tickets or arrests since she got married and, by the looks of it, is now a fucking model citizen.

What the actual fuck?

The pit of rage inside of me burns hotter the further I read.

When I was around, she could barely function, but after I leave, she somehow manages to get her fucking shit together? And she doesn't bother to try to find me?

I grip the edges of my computer and toss it off my desk. It crashes against the wall and falls to the floor. I push back from my desk, my chair pinging off the wall and to the side. My chest heaves as I stare at my computer, cursing it for this oily feeling mixed with rage rushing through my veins.

I thought when I received this report, I'd get some measure of closure at the certainty that my mother had passed away. Instead, I've stirred up a hornet's nest of emotions I'm not nearly equipped to deal with.

No matter what, the question remains. What am I going to do about it?

2

HATTIE

"Bye, Hattie. Have a good night." My coworker Marwa passes my desk.

I smile and wave, watching her meet our other coworker, Tiffany, at the door. Disappointment mixed with envy invades my chest.

Given that it's Friday night, they're probably going for dinner and drinks. I've been invited many times and turned them down each time, so I have no one but myself to blame for the fact that they no longer ask me to join them.

A few years ago, I moved to this medium-sized town in Wisconsin with my parents after I finished college because my dad got a new job here. I've found it hard to make friends. As a kid, it was so much easier than as an adult. Probably because I don't do what most other twenty-four-year-olds do. I don't dress in tight outfits and go carousing at the bar. I don't drink except for maybe a glass of wine at Christmas and Easter, and I spend most of my evenings at church or volunteering somewhere with people from church.

Sure, I was raised by strict parents under the influence of religion, but that's not why I do it. It's mostly because I'm afraid. Afraid of what will happen if I let go and experience some of the things I'm curious about. Would one risky decision lead to another and then another until I no longer recognized myself?

It doesn't matter. I'm never going to be a crazy risk-taker who drinks and parties and sleeps around. Just imagining it, I can see the look of disappointment on my dad's face, and it feels as if someone dug a knife into my chest, twisting it around.

Ever since my mom passed away when I was six years old, I've done everything I can not to cause him any trouble. I'm still haunted by the memory of how distraught he was right after it happened. Even the smallest thing—like burning dinner or me messing up tying my shoes—would put him over the edge. He never ranted or raved. That wasn't my dad's style. But I could see the profound frustration and weariness in his eyes, as though this small thing might be what sent him spiraling into the abyss of his grief.

I promised myself I would never be the cause of stress in his life. I would only better the situations. It's a habit and a mantra I still live by today.

When he married Carla a year after my mom's death, I was unsure how I felt about the quick relationship, but when I saw the light back in his eyes and how she made him happy, I decided to give her a chance. She's been a wonderful parent to me, and I think of her as my mother, not my step-mother. Unfortunately, the memories of my mom are blurry at best and seem to fade more with each passing year.

After I shut down my computer, I pack up my things and walk to my car to head over to my parents' house. I always have dinner with them on Friday nights before I go to the church for a women's ministry meeting. It's not exactly how I want to spend my Friday night, but it's better than sitting in my apartment alone, which is what I'll be doing by default tomorrow night.

Once I'm on the road, I call my friend, Taylor, from back home.

She picks up on the first ring. "Your ears must be burning. I was just thinking about you."

"All good things, I hope." I smile and stop at a red light.

"I was wondering if you'd worked up the nerve to talk to that hottie in your office yet."

Even though I'm by myself, I feel my cheeks heat. "I should have never told you about him."

She laughs. "Oh yes, you should've. Because I'm going to harass you about it until you do something and your life turns infinitely more interesting."

She means well, I know she does, but her words are like an arrow hitting a bull's-eye because she's not wrong—my life is boring.

"We can't all go off to college, denounce religion, and sow our wild oats like you did." The light turns green, and I ease on the gas.

"I know better than to try to get you to give up on church, Hattie, but just because you believe in a higher power doesn't mean you have to live like a nun. Newsflash, you are not in a convent."

A laugh escapes me as I pull into the left-hand turn lane. "I'm fully aware of that. And it has nothing to do with my religion anyway, I'm just shy."

"God, I wish you hadn't moved so far away. If we were still in the same town, I'd make it happen for you one way or the other."

"I appreciate that, and I miss you too. Now fill me in on the hot dates you have planned for the weekend."

Sadly, I live vicariously through Taylor's stories. She always has something new and exciting going on. When we were growing up, she was just like me. But while I chose to go to a Christian college, she attended a state school, which is where she tells me she got a *real* education. Since then, we're practically polar opposites. But just because our beliefs are different doesn't change the fact that I love her and the kind of person she is to her core.

By the time she's done telling me about the date she went on earlier this week and the "total fucking hottie" she's going out with tomorrow night, I'm pulling onto my parents' street.

"Well, good luck, and let me know how it goes," I say as I park in their driveway.

"I don't need luck. I just got a new pair of four-inch heels, and they make my legs look a mile long."

We both laugh and, for not the first time, I wonder if I had opted to go to the state school, would my life be different? Would I even want it to be like Taylor's?

"Give me a call Sunday afternoon and tell me all about it." I don't have to bother telling her I'll be busy at church on Sunday morning—she knows.

"Will do. Try to have some fun this weekend, okay?"

I blow out a breath. "Goodbye, Taylor."

Her laughter rings until she ends the call. Shaking my head, I turn the car off and pull the key from the ignition, tossing it into my purse that sits on the passenger seat.

As I exit the car, my mom pops out onto the porch with a wide smile and a wave. I return both, and when I reach the porch, she pulls me into a tight hug. When I inhale the scent of the perfume she's worn since she came into my life, a feeling of safety and security wraps around me.

For all my secret ambitions of being a more adventurous person, the truth is I love this feeling right here.

"How was your day?" she asks as she pulls away and runs her palm down my cheek as always.

"It was good. Same old." Since we moved here, I've worked as a bookkeeper and administrator for a manufacturing company in town.

"That's great, honey."

She looks more tired and worn down than usual, and I hope she isn't working too hard. Lately, her hours have increased from building up a large client list over the years. I guess that's what happens when you're a talented hair stylist.

"How are you? You look tired. Spending too much time at the salon?" I arch an eyebrow in question. She's been known to overdo it sometimes when she's booked up and someone wants her to squeeze them in. She's never been able to say no.

She gives my shoulder a squeeze and opens the door to the house, motioning for me to go first. "No."

I give her a look.

She giggles. "I promise. I just don't have the same kind of stamina I used to. Guess that's getting old."

"Fifty-seven is not old." I shake my head and go inside, setting my purse on the wooden table inside the door.

"Thought I heard your voice. Hey, sweet pea, how are ya?" My dad walks up from the back of the house.

My chest warms at the moniker my dad has called me since I was little.

He uses his cane for extra support, one arm out and ready to pull me in for a hug as soon as he reaches me.

My dad was in a car accident a few years back, and since then, he's had to walk with a cane. He went through a couple of surgeries and physical therapy but never fully recovered—physically or financially. Which is why I use a chunk of my salary to help pay down the medical debt. They both hate accepting my help, but the truth is, it's necessary if they want to be able to retire any time in the next decade.

I don't mind. They spent so much time and effort raising me, and my religion has always taught me to help others.

Who better to help than the two people I love most in this world?

"I'm good, Dad, how are you feeling?"

He envelops me in a one-armed hug, and I wrap my arms around him and squeeze. "Feeling good. Don't worry about me."

I roll my eyes as I pull away. He knows I'm going to worry about him no matter what he says. Some days he's in quite a bit of pain. Depending on the weather, his joints may bother him, but today is a sunny June day with no clouds in the sky, so as expected, it seems like a good day for him.

"I'm just about to take the steak off the grill. Why don't you go help your mom get everything else on the table outside?"

"Will do." I kiss his cheek and head to the kitchen to bring out the side dishes.

Once we have the garden salad, corn on the cob, asparagus, and scalloped potatoes (my dad's favorite) on the table, we all sit and join hands.

"You want to do the honors, sweet pea?" my dad asks.

I nod. "Heavenly Father, please bless this food and our bodies. Thank you for these gifts we are about to receive from your bounty. In Jesus's name we pray. Amen."

"Amen," my parents say in unison.

We all smile around the table, and I settle in for my usual Friday night—predictable, unexciting, and a little boring. But I chose this life. This is what I want, so I can't complain.

3

BASTION

I pull up in front of the address typed on the report and stare at the house. I wasn't sure what I was going to find, but this perfect slice of Americana wasn't it.

The home isn't huge by any means, but it's well cared for with a red brick path leading to the white-sided two-story with black shutters. A generous porch runs across the front of the house, and the hedges that line the walkway to the house from the sidewalk are perfectly manicured.

It's about as far as you can get from the dilapidated apartment I escaped from when I was eleven.

My hands wrap around the steering wheel of my rental car until my knuckles turn white.

What the hell am I even doing here?

It's a good question and one I still can't answer. When I woke up the day after reading the report, I knew I had to come see with my own eyes that my mother is still alive. I booked a last-minute flight for some reason. Maybe it's the disbelief that my mom is actually still alive after the way I left her. Maybe someone stole her identity after they found her dead in her own vomit. It's not like there was anyone who would report her missing. Then there's the final theory —maybe Mr. Smith is really shitty at his job, and he has the wrong person, who knows? There has to be a more logical explanation than the fact that my mom cleaned herself up and got her shit together but never came looking for her only child.

I don't even know why the fuck I care. I'm thirty-seven years old, not a child anymore, and I made it on my own without her.

But the fact is, something inside me needs to know. So I continue down the street, parking on the other side of the road. Far enough down that I can see the house and its comings and goings, but not close enough to draw the attention of the residents.

I grip the steering wheel for about a half an hour before a modest sedan pulls into the driveway. Cursing the way my heart beats faster at the possibility that the car could hold my mother, I try to see who is driving, but the tinted windows don't allow it.

When the driver's door opens, my throat constricts that this could be the moment. A second later, a wash of relief floods through me. Yeah, either Mr. Smith got it all wrong or this is just a friend. It's not my mother, but a woman in her early twenties with long dark hair, dressed as though she's just come from some boring office job. The front door of the house opens, and an older woman steps out onto the porch.

A rush of air leaves my lungs, and I gasp because there's no doubt this woman is indeed my mother. Though she's much older than the last time I saw her, and it's hard to tell with her healthy weight and glowing skin, it's her.

Her hair, now gray, is cut in a bob to her shoulders, and she's wearing a pair of beige capris and a light blue T-shirt. She's no longer gaunt with deep, dark grooves under her eyes and no meat on her bones. It's obvious she's healthy and taking care of herself. Which for some reason pisses me off.

The way she smiles at the young woman making her way around her vehicle and up to the porch makes me feel as if there's a volcano in my chest ready to erupt.

"Well, well, well, hello, Hattie," I say to myself.

My mom brings her in for a hug and closes her eyes as though she's savoring the moment. My hand falls to the door handle, but I stop myself from opening the car door and hurling myself at them. Instead, I swallow down the bile rising up my throat and blow out a breath.

As if the tender hug wasn't enough, my mom pulls back and runs her palm down Hattie's innocent face, and I break out into a cold sweat. I don't know if it's anger or shock, probably a little of both.

Over the years, I'd forgotten about her running her palm down my face. Probably because they were rare moments when she was lucid and looking at me with apology for being a shitty mom who couldn't get clean. She did it a lot in the early years of her addiction, but by the end, before I ran away, those moments never came, no matter how much I wished for her to just see me and what she was putting me through.

And seeing her do the same thing to someone who isn't even her real daughter...

My hands squeeze into fists so tight that I have no choice but to release the tension. I'm surprised my teeth don't turn to dust with how hard I'm clenching them.

Un-fucking-believable.

She can't even take care of her own son, but here she is, looking adoringly into this young woman's eyes like she means the fucking world to her?

Thank goodness for Trent, who taught me the self-control needed for patience because had he not, I'd already have rushed the front porch. Instead, I watch as they go inside, and I ponder my next move.

And there will be a next move because one thing is for certain—it's time Carla Sinclair pays for her sins.

A couple of hours later, the darling stepdaughter walks toward her car. There's no sign of Carla anywhere. I refuse to think of her as my mother now that I know she's been alive all this time. She's simply Carla to me now.

I don't know what possesses me to follow who I presume is Hattie, but five minutes after she leaves Carla's, she pulls into a church parking lot.

Who the fuck spends their Friday night at church? Sunday mornings I get. You want to believe in a higher power so you can feel better about the fucked-up shit you do? By all means, go for it. But a Friday night? This woman must be innocence and purity personified. Either that or an idiot.

I scowl as I watch her leave the car and make her way into the church.

Within a minute, I pull away. She can spend her night here, but I'm not going to spend my entire Friday night in a goddamn church parking lot. Instead, I go find a hotel to check into and raid the minibar and stew over what I want to do, if anything.

I don't bother to leave my room until Sunday morning, spending Friday night and all day Saturday tying one on and attempting to push away the memories of the past that seem determined to haunt me since I started this stupid quest.

I've always been willing to drink, but not generally to excess—likely a by-product of growing up with an addict for a mother. But I was desperate to get rid of the oily feeling slinking through my veins. It's like I'm right back there as a little boy who just wants his mom to love him.

My head is pounding as I pull into the church parking lot, knowing, based on Mr. Smith's report, that Carla, her husband, and Hattie will be in attendance.

I'm still not sure whether I want to confront Carla or not.

I chuckle, thinking that causing a scene in the middle of a church service might be the most punishing way to get back at her. To ruin the perfect life she's made for herself. Expose her for what she is and reveal to all the other parishioners exactly the kind of woman who has been hiding in their midst.

But my thirst for revenge demands more.

Church has already begun, and the parking lot is nearly full. No one is leaving their cars or exiting the building. Curious to see if Carla can indeed really be inside a church and not burst into flames, I exit the rental vehicle and head inside.

The door to the sanctuary is open to the foyer, so I can hear the minister speaking as I head in. Once I'm inside, I stop at the back and look around the pews, stopping on Carla and her family. The back few pews are empty, so I slide into one that affords me the opportunity to watch them.

Of course, nothing much happens during the service, but once they're done, I watch as the three of them stand and speak with the people around them. Even from back here, it's clear from Carla and her husband's body language that Hattie is their pride and joy. Whatever they're talking to the people about, it must be about Hattie with the way they gesture to her as if she's a crown jewel with their chests puffed out.

I clench my hands in my lap when Carla wraps an arm around Hattie's shoulders and squeezes her into her side.

Then an idea comes to mind.

An idea of how I can get back at my mother for what she did.

Little, sweet Hattie might just need a little corrupting.

It's almost too brilliant. I'm surprised the idea didn't come to me sooner. Ruin Hattie and then reveal to Carla that I'm the one who corrupted her innocent stepdaughter. And she'll only have herself to blame—if she hadn't raised me the way she did and decided not to find me once she was sober, I wouldn't have the capacity to ruin an innocent young woman. But our predicament is Carla's fault, and it's time she knows what she did.

With a smile, I rise up from the pew and walk toward the exit.

I'll be back, and by then, I'll be ready and armed to do some damage.

4

HATTIE

The bell rings above me as I step through the door. The coffee shop is only half full, typical for a Tuesday evening after working hours. The odd time I've been here during the day, this place is bustling.

I come here after work about once a week. Not because I'm meeting a date or anything, but because I don't want to go home and sit alone in my apartment. Sure, I may only curl up with a book on the couch in the lounge area at the back, but I'm still out in the world. Even if I'm out in the world alone.

I carry my hot chocolate to the lounge area in the back of the café. It's my favorite place, complete with an electric fireplace, a pair of couches, and a couple of chairs. It's cozy even though summer is almost here.

Once I'm settled, I open my book, losing myself in the world between the pages. I'm unsure how much time passes before I hear, "Evening."

The deep male voice draws my attention, and I look up to a handsome man seated in one of the chairs opposite me.

I'm not unaccustomed to other people sitting in the lounge area, but I'm not at all used to them engaging me. Especially someone who looks like this man. He definitely doesn't seem like he's from around here.

For some reason, my cheeks heat, and my breath grows shallow. "Hey," I squeak and dip my face back to the pages of my book.

God, no wonder I never have a date. Look at my reaction to when the opposite sex talks to me! Especially a man as good-looking as him. He has shoulder-length brown hair with a glint of highlights that fall in light waves, but it's his eyes. The deep blue eyes that draw me in. The jeans and deep green Henley he's wearing leave no doubt that underneath is a fit and lean, muscled body.

"I'm sorry, have I made you uncomfortable? Would you prefer for me to sit somewhere else?" he asks.

My eyes widen at my book, and I slowly look up. "Of course not."

It's not that I don't get approached now and then, but I'm not used to complete strangers making small talk with me, let alone a man this attractive and much older than me. If I had to guess, he's probably in his mid-thirties.

"You sure? You seem like you might be more comfortable if I sat farther away." His gaze is intent on my face.

Though being under the weight of his stare does make me uncomfortable, he's done nothing wrong, and I'd never want him to feel bad. "I just thought you were being polite in saying hello, that's all. I didn't realize you wanted to have a conversation."

One corner of his lips tips up in a wry smile. "When doesn't a man want to speak with a beautiful woman?" He winks.

My face is like an inferno now, ready to erupt in flames. "Oh, well... thank you for the compliment."

He doesn't respond, instead glancing at the book splayed open on my lap. "What are you reading?"

My lips press together. "It's a book about a family of nine siblings in Alaska who were orphaned when their parents died in a snowmobile accident." There's no way I'm going to tell him it's a romance and a steamy one at that.

He nods, and from the glint in his eye, he knows I'm leaving out the best part of the book.

"Do you read?" I ask quickly, before he can question me further about my book.

He shakes his head. "Don't have a lot of time for it, unfortunately."

An awkward silence descends between us, and I curse myself for letting my nerves get in my way. Taylor would be so disappointed. I always get too in my head when I'm around people I don't know. It takes me a long time to get comfortable with new people, which made the move here a few years ago more difficult than it needed to be.

He's just a person, Hattie. An attractive one, sure, but still just a person, and he approached you first.

I swallow past my dry mouth and force myself to talk. "What keeps you so busy?"

A look of satisfaction crosses his face as if he's happy I'm talking to him. "I own my own business. It keeps me pretty occupied."

I shift my book off my lap and reach over to the table beside me to grab my hot chocolate. "What industry are you in?" When I blow lightly on my steaming mug, I notice his eyes dart to my lips, and my face heats again. Is this flirting?

"I'm in the entertainment industry." He stands abruptly, and I'm irritated with myself for the disappointment in my chest that he's about to leave. But instead, he leans forward with his hand held out. "I'm Bastion."

I quickly set my hot chocolate back down and accept his hand. "Hattie. Nice to meet you."

When our palms meet, the heat from his seems to seep into mine. A pleasurable buzz travels up my arm when his middle finger skims down the center of my palm as he pulls away.

"Believe me, the pleasure's all mine, Hattie."

I suppress the shiver that races up my spine, afraid he'll realize how much he affects me. I don't even know where my reaction is coming from. It's never happened before.

He sits back in his seat and plucks a coffee cup off the side table and brings it to his lips, maintaining eye contact with me the entire time he sips. Something about his gaze feels intimate, so I glance away toward the fireplace that is on but doesn't have any heat being forced out because of the time of year. Regardless, my body temperature rises.

"What do you do for a living, Hattie?"

The way my name tumbles off his lips does something to me, which is ridiculous. This man is much older than me and hasn't given any overt signals that he's interested. He's just being polite and making conversation. Maybe he's as lonely as I am, given that he's not in his hometown. I can certainly relate.

"I do bookkeeping and other administrative tasks for a manufacturing company in town."

He nods and sets his coffee on the table. Despite not wanting to, I notice how large his hands are and how they dwarf the mug when his fingers are wrapped around it.

"I'm envious. I've never been great with numbers."

I can't help but smile. "I've always liked numbers. They just make sense to me. I like that math has one answer and it's straightforward. You just follow a series of steps to find it. There's little room for error."

"I'm more of a people person myself."

A small laugh slips from my lips. "Now that's something I've never been good at."

Bastion tilts his head. "What?"

"People. I've never been good at figuring them out, their motivations. I tend to take people at face value." I shrug. "It's burned me before." I swallow back the shame when Rich's face flashes in my mind.

Bastion leans back in his seat and crosses his legs so that his ankle rests on his opposite knee. "Do tell."

My eyes widen. Not a chance am I telling this stranger about

Rich. The only person in this world I ever told about what went down was Taylor. "I'd rather not."

He raises both hands. "Fair enough." Bastion reaches for his coffee again. "So what passes for fun around here?"

I shift uncomfortably and reach for my own drink, just to give my hands something to do. "I'm not sure I'm the best judge of that."

After he sips his coffee, he sets it down again, while I continue to hold my mug with both hands in front of me.

"Why do you say that? You're what..." His eyes rake up and down me, and I glance away. "In your early twenties?"

"Twenty-four," I say, mustering the courage to meet his gaze again.

"I'd think you'd know where all the fun places are around here."

I wish my chest didn't pinch at the reminder of how empty certain parts of my life are. Bastion has unknowingly shot an arrow right at the tender part of me.

"Remember the part about me not being good with people?"

He nods.

"A by-product of that is me not having much of a social life," I say.

He nods knowingly, lips pressed together. "Most people are overrated anyway."

When he winks at me, rather than looking away this time, I smile.

"What exactly brings you to Wisconsin?" I lean back into the couch and shift to my side, tucking my legs up on the cushion, but I still momentarily when something like anger flashes in his eyes. It's only for the briefest of moments, there and gone so quickly I'm not even certain I saw it in the first place.

"I'm considering some investment options in the area." Before I can dig any further into what that means, he says, "I've seen a bunch of advertisements around town for some Lake..." He shakes his head as though he can't remember the name.

I fill in the blank for him and tell him what the tourist destination has to offer. We chat for a while longer about nothing of much consequence, but I notice that the more we talk, the less awkward I grow. I'm sure that's not uncommon, but it's unusual for me to be this comfortable, this fast.

Maybe there's hope for me yet.

Bastion finishes his coffee and picks the empty mug up off the table and shifts to the edge of his seat. I try to ignore the disappointment pushing against the inside of my rib cage at his impending departure.

"I need to be going, but I'll be in town again next week. Would you care to meet up?"

Something in my subconscious screams at me to say no even though I've enjoyed our conversation. But at the same time, the flicker of excitement that rushes through my veins every time I cause his lips to lift in a small smile feels somehow addicting.

When I don't immediately answer, he says, "If the idea makes you uncomfortable, I apologize. It's just that it can be lonely being away from home. I thought we had some good conversation, that's all."

He understands what it feels like to be alone too. My chest squeezes.

We're in public at a coffee shop. It's not as though he's asking me to meet him in his hotel room. There's no danger here. What's the harm in enjoying this small amount of spontaneous adventure life has thrown my way?

I can meet him again, enjoy his company, and once he's left for good, it will just be a nice memory for me to revisit from time to time. It's not even like he's asked me on an official date or anything. It would just be two people meeting to share some platonic time together.

My mom has long been encouraging me to date. A handful of eligible men at church have made their interest known, but none of them are very interesting to me. After what happened in college with my one and only boyfriend, I haven't been able to work up the nerve. I don't ever want to feel that way again. My parents don't understand my hesitance, but I'm too ashamed to explain to them what happened all those years ago.

"Okay, we can meet again."

Bastion gives me a pleased grin. It's the first time I've seen a full smile on his face, and the effect is overwhelming. A set of perfectly white teeth lights up his entire face, more beautiful than I thought possible since he's very much the best-looking guy I've ever seen in person.

"Wonderful. Same time, same place?" He arches an eyebrow.

I nod. "Sure." My voice comes out reedy and thin.

He stands from the chair and towers over me, looking down at me. "I'll see you then."

Without another word, he turns on his heel and leaves without a backward glance, which disappoints me more than it should.

No matter, I'm excited to have news to tell Taylor. Bit by bit, I just need to put myself out there a little more.

5

BASTION

I wake up and roll onto my back, whipping the scratchy sheets off my body. I might be staying at the best hotel in town, but it's a far cry from what I'm used to these days. There was a time in my life when I would've thought this place was the Four Seasons, but those days are long behind me, and I swore to myself that I'd never go back.

Getting out of bed, I walk the short distance to the bathroom and turn on the shower. It takes a whole ten minutes for the damn thing to warm up before I step under the spray. Tilting my head back, I close my eyes as the warm water washes over my face and picture Hattie sitting on the couch in that café last night.

She has the street smarts of a baby kitten. She didn't even know a predator was in her midst. The woman is naïve at best, stupid at worst.

Just the thought of her is triggering, though. Being in her company, it was a struggle to keep myself together. Every glance at her healthy demeanor, clean clothes, and the way she presents herself to the world—it all screams well-adjusted. A typical, normal upbringing. Something I was never afforded.

My hand grips the wet strands of my hair until my skull aches. It took everything in me not to unleash the toxic fury brewing inside me when I was around her last night.

One thing about Hattie—she's lonely. It was obvious in the way she sucked up my attention. Sure, she was fidgety at first, but she reminded me of a helpless puppy, panting with its tongue hanging out, sitting at your feet just begging for attention. And every time I gave it to her, she lapped it up, wanting more.

The best thing, though, is I'm pretty sure she's attracted to me, which makes all of this easier.

You don't spend twenty-plus years scamming people and not get good at reading them. Reading the subtext of their words, their body language, and the things they're not saying but wish they could ask for.

My laugh echoes off the shower tiles around me. What a stupid cunt. This con will surely be the easiest I've ever encountered.

After my shower, I get dressed and grab something to eat at a shitty diner down the street. I glance at my phone as I'm leaving, satisfied with my perfect timing.

When I pull up to the curb in front of the triplex where Hattie rents an apartment, she's leaving the building and heading to her car. She's wearing a pair of billowy white dress pants and a light blue blouse that's practically buttoned up to her neck and covers her arms.

I wait twenty minutes before I approach the building.

Mr. Smith's report let me know that she lives on the ground floor of her building—never a good idea for a single woman. Derelicts like me will only use it to their advantage, and that's exactly what I'm doing with a reflective vest and base-ball cap on. With my blue pants and matching polo, I look official, as though I'm here to take a meter reading or check out the building's landscaping. I even have a clipboard and pen in hand as I round the back of the building to figure out what my best point of entry will be.

It doesn't take long for me to figure out that the west side of the building is where I need to be. It separates the building from the house on the street behind it, and lucky me, there's a fence and tall cedars that run along it. Unless someone comes around the corner, I'm practically undetectable.

With one final check that no one is around, I toss the clip-board and pen on the small round table Hattie's set up on her back patio.

These sliding glass doors will do just fine. Pulling the screw-driver I brought with me from my back pocket, I approach the door, then get down on my haunches in front of it. It takes me longer than I'd like to get the door to jump its tracks—which I attribute to how long it's been since I had to do something like this. I'm out of practice. But when I'm finally successful, the blast of adrenaline that pours through my veins is the rush I forgot. God, I've missed it.

It's not like I've been a saint for the past decade, but I haven't had to resort to doing shit like this.

I make my way into Hattie's apartment and secure the door behind me, then I take a moment to look around. It's pretty much what I expected—clean and tidy without a whole lot of stuff lying around. The furniture looks as though it may have been passed down to her. Though it's dated, it's been taken care of, and there's a crochet blanket folded neatly and draped across the armrest of the couch. Her TV isn't oversized, and in the corner of the room is a large basket.

Slipping the latex gloves from my pocket, I slide them on as I step over to the basket and look inside. It holds a bunch of yarn.

I thumb through a few books stacked on the coffee table. The first two don't elicit much interest from me, but when I leaf through the last one, the word cock jumps out at me. I start reading, the grin on my face growing with every sentence I finish.

So little Miss Perfect isn't as perfect as she appears. She likes her smut. Noted.

Maybe there's more to Hattie than meets the eye. I dislike the way that thought intrigues me, so I set the books back down as I found them and continue.

The kitchen doesn't hold anything of interest, unless you consider that she appears to eat like a college student based on the amount of mac and cheese and ramen noodles in her cupboard.

A quick search through the bathroom tells me she owns little, if any, makeup, but she has a whole skin routine she must follow. There's a plethora of lotions and scrubs and serums littering the counter. The medicine cabinet yields nothing, so finally I make my way into her bedroom.

If there's anything interesting to be found, I'm sure this is where I'll find it.

The first thing I notice is how different the space feels from the rest of her apartment. It's not as well-kept and put together. Whereas the rest of the apartment holds very few personal mementos, this room is filled with them.

Pictures of Hattie and another woman her age make up a collage on a bulletin board. Some are from when they're very young and others from their teen and college years. In one, the girls are in what I'd guess is their early twenties, and they're standing on the end of a dock with their arms wrapped around each other's shoulders, big grins on their faces.

My gaze snags on the swell of Hattie's breasts under her one-piece swimsuit.

She's got a banging little body under those baggy clothes she wears, that's for sure. Maybe I'll be able to convince her to get on stage. I laugh at the thought.

Perhaps she'll actually enjoy male attention at some point, and I can use that to my advantage. Imagine what Mommy Dearest would think if her precious little girl danced on stage and let men slide dollar bills into her G-string.

A feral smile spreads across my face.

There's nothing interesting hiding under the clothes in her dresser, and when I open the top drawer of her nightstand, I half expect to find her sex toy collection, but all I discover is her sock drawer. Maybe she is as repressed as I thought. What single twenty-something woman doesn't have at least one sex toy?

But then I open the next drawer to find her bras and underwear and am surprised they're all made with lace. I figured Hattie for a white cotton panty kind of girl, but under those oversized clothes, she wears pretty, if not sexy, lingerie.

The dichotomy of this woman grows more interesting every minute.

I continue to her closet, taking a picture of how it's arranged before I search through it. There are a couple of fancy boxes on the shelf at the top, and I pull those out to go through them.

The first one seems to be a memory box of sorts. It's filled with old movie stubs and concert tickets, greeting cards, most of which are dated from a few years ago. When I get further down in the box, I find some pictures of her and a guy with blond hair and bright blue eyes—Mr. All American himself. Go figure. It's clear they were in a relationship. Though there are no intimate pictures of the two of them, they're holding hands in one, and in another, he has his arm draped around her shoulders as he kisses her cheek.

Based on the dates on the things in the box and the fact that his picture is nowhere on display in the apartment, I'm going to assume the relationship is long over. Is this what women do? They hold on to all this shit? To what? Feel the heartbreak all over again? I'll never understand them.

I put the lid back on the box and look into the next box. It's filled with mementos from school—report cards, awards, participation ribbons. I'm not surprised that little Hattie was quite the student.

I put the boxes back where I found them and search the bottom of the closet, where I find several photo albums. I still for a moment with my hand on them before I pull them out.

My chest is tight as I slowly pull back the cover of the first one and am greeted with a picture of Hattie—probably ten years old or so—and her parents at an amusement park. All three of them have the kinds of smiles that would let anyone looking at them know that they've never been happier. This is a family who truly loves each other and looks out for each other.

My eyes focus on my mother as I flip through each page, the rest of the people in the photos becoming a blur. I don't remember ever seeing her smile like that. Not once in my eleven years with her. All I remember is the dead look in her eyes or the disappointment and regret she always had when she looked at me. Whether it was about our situation or directed at me specifically, I could never tell.

Fuck this.

I slam the front of the photo album closed and shove them all back in the bottom of the closet. I've seen enough to know who Hattie is and how I might manipulate her for my gain.

Pulling my phone from my pocket, I check how the closet looks compared to the image on my screen and find they look nearly identical.

I don't know why, but before I put my phone away, I snap a photo of Hattie's collage board with all the photos of her over the years.

After one final check that everything appears to be how it should be, I make my way to the sliding glass door. I plan to leave it unlocked and hope that Hattie thinks she forgot to lock it before she went to work. Either way, she'll never suspect me.

I suppress the urge to hurry away from the building. That's the kind of thing that gets people's attention. Instead, I leisurely walk back to my car, my mind spinning with all the images of my mother in those pictures.

My phone vibrates in my pocket as I approach my vehicle, and Steph's name lights up the screen. Once I'm seated inside the vehicle, I accept her call, putting it on speaker-phone as I start the car.

"What's up?" My voice is clipped.

"Well, good morning to you too."

I roll my eyes and start the car. "What do you need, Steph?"

The call clicks over to the Bluetooth in the car as I pull away from the curb.

"Who pissed in your Corn Flakes this morning?"

Granted, I'm being a prick, which I rarely am. I've always found it's easier to get people onside with honey rather than vinegar, but after that trip down memory lane, I can't put on a front.

"I'm going to hang up now." My hand moves toward the screen on the dash to end the call.

"Wait! I wanted to let you know that Sean was in here last night looking for you. Ray just told me."

Ray is the head of security at our Seattle club. Since I'm away, I asked Steph to have a bigger presence at the main club and told the rest of the staff to go to her for anything that came up. But since I'm the only one who deals with Sean directly, I understand why she's calling me.

"It will have to wait until I get back." I turn right off Hattie's street and find myself heading in the direction of Carla's hair salon.

"Where are you anyway?"

"None of your business."

"Whatever." Steph's voice sours at my tone. "When can we expect you back?"

"Friday. Not sure what time, though. Tell Sean to come to the club on Saturday night, and we can talk."

"Fine. I'm going to be at the Sacramento club this weekend, so I'll see you next week I guess."

I make another turn that brings me closer to the salon. "We may have to do our check-in on a video call. I have to be back here next week too."

There's a slight pause. "Bastion, what's going on?"

"If there's something you need to know, I'll tell you." I press End on the call.

I consider Steph a friend, and yeah, we're fuck buddies, but I'm still her boss. We're not in a relationship, nor does she know anything about my upbringing. So she needs to back off when I tell her to.

I'm curious what the hell Sean wants. I allow his gang, the Reavers, to run drugs through my club in exchange for a cut.

We've had an arrangement for the past few years, and it's been lucrative for the both of us.

Whatever. He can wait.

I pull into a parking spot on Main Street directly adjacent to the hair salon. There's a large window at the front so I can see inside, no problem. And there's Carla, working on a client—all smiles as though she doesn't have a worry in the world. As though she doesn't have a son she abandoned sitting right outside her window. A son who has bided his time until he can ruin her perfect snow globe life.

I unclench my hands off the steering wheel, freeing the tension ache.

"Fuck this." I put the vehicle in drive and pull out of the spot.

A horn honks and tires screech on the pavement. I flip them off in the rearview mirror, getting the hell of Dodge, before my patience dies.

6

BASTION

I’ve been back in Seattle for a day, and already the urge to return to Wisconsin presses against me. I’m anxious to get my plan underway. I’ve always been this way. Trent would calm me, tell me not to rush. To always be prepared. Every time I think of the photo albums I found at the bottom of Hattie’s closet, it’s as if my insides turn to oil, and I want to punish someone.

Sure, I could show up on Carla’s doorstep and give her a piece of my mind, but the satisfaction I’ll gain from that will only be temporary. Slowly deconstructing her pride and joy, peeling away the layers of naïveté and innocence that cocoon Hattie, will be much more satisfying. Carla will never be able to look at her little angel the same, and for the rest of her life, she’ll know it’s her fault that I went after her precious daughter. She’ll have no one to blame but herself. Let her live with the shame of ruining her daughter since she seems to feel nothing for ruining her son.

There’s a knock on my office door, and I sigh. “What?”

Ray pops his head in. "Sean is here to see you, boss."

I nod. "Any of the VIP rooms free?"

I've never invited Sean into my office. The last thing I need is someone like him snooping around in here. We may have a mutually beneficial business relationship, but he's not to be trusted.

The only person I truly trust in this world is my sister, Ariana. I can't even say that I wholly trust Trent. Sure, he raised me as his own, but he loves nothing more than a con, and I've never felt entirely confident that he wouldn't throw me to the wolves if it benefited him in some way. Everyone has their price—except my sister. She never has.

"Yeah, one of them is open," Ray says.

"Put him in there. I'll be out in a few minutes."

Ray nods and closes the door behind him.

There's nothing I can't get up and walk away from right now, but I'm not going to let it appear that I'm at Sean's beck and call. He's in my place of business, not the other way around. So I take a few minutes to check Hattie's social media profiles to see if she's posted anything today—she hasn't. In fact, her profiles are boring as shit. The last time she even posted was six months ago, and it was a picture of her and some other church members at a soup kitchen.

Finally, I stand from my desk and throw on my suit jacket before leaving my office, locking it, and heading toward the front of the house. It's Saturday night, so the place is packed. Music pumps through the large room, and the men seated at the stage's edge wave dollar bills, desperate for the atten-tion of the girl dancing on stage.

I'm not surprised since it's Paige, a.k.a. Amethyst. She's one of the more popular dancers, hence the Saturday night shift.

She catches my eye as I walk through the room and gives me a quick smile, which I return. Paige is a good employee. Shows up for her shifts, doesn't cause any drama, and always has requests for lap dances or visits to the VIP room.

Ray is posted at the entrance to the hallway that houses the VIP rooms, and he gives me a nod as I approach. "Five."

"Thanks, Ray." I smooth my tie down my chest and pass him.

The door to room number two opens as I walk by, and one of the dancers, Renee, a.k.a. Blaze, walks out, closing the door behind her. I'm sure her client is probably taking a moment to clean himself.

Her eyes widen when she sees me, and she reaches for my wrist. "Can I talk to you for a second?"

I frown in concern. Something is clearly wrong, and it makes me wonder what just went down in the VIP room. I really don't want to deal with a shitty customer tonight.

"Sure." I lead her over to the wall, putting myself between her and the room she just vacated. "What's going on?"

"I'm scheduled for next Tuesday afternoon, but I have to take my kid to the doctor. It's the only time I could get an appointment." Her eyes glitter with unshed tears.

I know her four-year-old son has been having some ongoing health issues lately, and she's been trying to get to the bottom of it.

I give her shoulder a reassuring squeeze. "Tell Emma I'd like her to try to switch you out with one of the other dancers if possible. If not, we'll have to be short-staffed. You need to take care of your little guy."

Emma does the schedule for all the dancers, and we have a rule that there's no changing shifts. Before we instituted the rule, everyone was always complaining about who got what shift, swapping shifts with each other. It was too chaotic, so we had to put a stop to it. We lost a couple of good dancers who needed more flexibility, but overall, it's worked well for us.

A wide smile transforms the concerned look on her face. "You're the best. Thanks, boss!" She gets up on her tiptoes and kisses my cheek before rushing down the hall.

Relieved it's not something worse, I proceed to door number five. When I open it, I find Sean bent over the table, doing a line of his own product.

I close the door with a slam, and Sean's head whips up, white dust falling from his nose. He smiles when he sees me and holds out the rolled-up bill he's using to snort the powder off the table toward me.

My hands fist at my sides. I've never loved letting this little shit run drugs through my clubs, not after how I grew up, but it's a means to an end—money. Besides, there's this little thing called free will. People have to make their own choices. If they end up fucking up their lives from using, that's on them.

"I'm good."

Sean shakes his head. "I'm gonna get you to give it a go one of these days."

No, he won't. But it's not a point worth arguing.

"Why are you here?" I sit at the far end of the built-in couch that runs like a U around the small room.

Sean rubs his nose and sniffs. "My bosses have been running some numbers, and they think we're handing too much over to you. They want to reduce your cut by ten percent."

I unbutton my suit coat and casually cross my legs. "Tell your bosses no. Anything else?" I arch an eyebrow.

Sean chuckles low. "Yeah, I don't think they're going to like that answer."

My head tilts. "I thought you were the big boss man?"

He scowls and shifts in his seat. "Everyone has someone above them."

I shrug. "I don't. Unless it's some woman riding my dick."

The way his nostrils flare, he doesn't like that. "Regardless, all this shit"—he gestures to the powder on the table—"comes from somewhere. There's always someone further up the line calling the shots."

"What message did you come here to deliver, since you're making it clear that you're just the errand boy?"

"Like I said. They're cutting your take by ten percent."

I stand and fasten the button on my suit jacket closed. "No, they won't, and if they try, they won't be running anything through my clubs anymore. You're not the only piece of shit who slings dope, you know."

Sean stands too. "I told them you'd say no."

"Good. Then they won't be surprised." Without waiting for him to respond, I make my way to the door. Once my hand is on the knob, I turn and look at him over my shoulder. "Make sure that shit is off my table before you leave this room."

Then I head back to my office. No one stops me, as I'm sure my mood is written all over my face.

This shit with Sean is a problem. I'll be surprised if whoever Sean's dealing with accepts my no. Which means I'm going to have to come up with a contingency plan.

Shouldn't be that hard. As I told Sean, he's not the only player in town.

The biggest challenge will be doing so while I'm spending half my time in Wisconsin.

I wanted to move things along with Hattie slowly so that I don't spook her. So that when all the pieces are in place, she's primed and ready to accept my offer. Instead, as I reach my office, I pull my phone from my pocket and pull up my lawyer's number. I don't give a shit if it's Saturday night. He always answers my calls.

Of course, he answers on the first ring. "Saturday night? Really, Bastion?"

"I want the timeline moved up. Make them an offer they can't refuse. I want this deal closed in the next three weeks max." I hang up and slam my office door shut behind me.

Just like when she was in my life, Carla's reappearance has meant nothing but emotional turmoil for me.

I flew back into Wisconsin last night. I hadn't planned to be here until Tuesday morning so that I'd meet Hattie at the café that evening, but I changed my mind last minute on Sunday afternoon. I want to spend today and tomorrow trailing Hattie. I need to really know this woman if I'm going to be able to manipulate her.

She leaves for work at the exact same time as she did the day I broke into her apartment last week. Creature of habit. No big surprise. She's a con artist's dream.

Hattie drives straight to work in her shitty little sedan—no stops for breakfast or coffee. When lunch rolls around, a bunch of her colleagues leave to grab something, but not Hattie. She must pack a lunch or not eat at all. I should've guessed that Hattie's a brown bagger.

At the end of the day, she appears a little bit after the majority of her coworkers have already departed, and I sink down in my seat when she pulls out of the parking lot. Once she's passed me, I start the car and follow her. She heads to Carla's salon.

Seeing the two of them together through the front window makes my chest tighten, squeezing the breath from my lungs. They laugh as if they don't have a care in the world, and I grit my teeth. Then Carla takes Hattie to the back of the salon, but when they return, Hattie's hair is wet, and it's clear that she's here for a haircut.

I hope Hattie doesn't cut her long, dark hair too much.

What the fuck is that thought about?

The steering wheel creaks as my hands tighten around it. I force myself to let go and shake out my aching hands. That's a habit I need to stop.

Nothing eventful happens while Hattie gets her hair cut, and she gives Carla a long embrace before she leaves. *Relax, ladies, you'll see each other soon.* Carla runs her palm down Hattie's cheek, and my nostrils flare.

I follow Hattie back to her apartment, where she stays for the rest of the night.

The next morning, I trail her to work. Once again, she leaves at the exact same time and doesn't deviate from her route to work, nor does she leave at lunch.

I abandon my post mid-afternoon to prepare for our meeting that evening.

Once I've showered and shaved, I style my hair, leaving it more mussed than I normally would. I'm going for open and approachable. With that in mind, I decide on a pair of black jeans and a light gray T-shirt. It's more undone than my usual style, but I'm not looking to highlight our age difference or the difference in our financial situations. I need her to remain open and welcoming to me.

Now, the question is... will she show?

And what will I do if she doesn't?

7

HATTIE

*A*s I walk toward the entrance of the café, I second-guess myself for probably the thousandth time. Should I be here? I don't even know this man.

Then I remember how he said it was lonely being in a town that wasn't his own, and I get that feeling in my chest because I know that exact feeling. Still do, if I'm honest.

So here I am, going to meet a man I had a brief encounter with last week and don't really know much about.

But we're meeting in public, so really, there's no harm.

I walk in five minutes early and find Bastion already seated in the lounge area. He spots me as soon as I enter, and the look of relief on his face when he raises his hand in hello lets me know I wasn't the only one who was nervous the other might not show up.

I gesture to the counter, indicating that I'm going to order my drink, but he holds up a steaming mug. With a smile, I approach him.

He looks more at ease than he did last week. His hair is a little messy and his clothes show off that he must work out every day. He's so attractive, and I hate that I wonder what he wants with me.

"I grabbed your drink already. Figured since I invited you here to meet me, the least I could do is pay for your hot chocolate."

I sit across from him and set my purse next to me. "You remembered what I drink?"

He shrugs. "I remembered thinking how interesting it was that you had a hot chocolate this time of year, when most people would be drinking a coffee or tea. Or maybe an iced coffee."

"I don't like coffee." I scrunch up my nose at the thought of sipping the bitter drink.

Bastion smiles and raises his glass. "Thankfully, I don't suffer from the same affliction."

I chuckle and lean forward to pick up the hot chocolate. "Thank you for the hot chocolate."

"My pleasure."

There's a beat of awkward silence. As always with someone I don't know well, I'm not sure how to fill it. Thankfully, Bastion saves me from having to figure it out.

"How was your day at work?" He brings his coffee to his lips and sips.

"Nothing exciting." I shrug. "The usual."

"Is that how you like it?" He tilts his head, and it causes a lock of his hair to fall down over his forehead.

"What do you mean?"

"Not exciting."

"Oh, um... I've never really thought about it. I suppose I'm a bit of a creature of habit. What about you?"

He thinks my question over, and I like that he doesn't just give me some pat answer. "My life was very eventful for many years. These days, I prefer most things to be predictable and easy. I think there's still room for some excitement, though." He winks.

It takes me a moment to understand his innuendo, and when I do, my eyes widen and I feel my face heat. "How... how about you? How are things going here in town? What exactly is it you're doing again?"

He leans back in his seat and crosses his legs, resting his ankle on his opposite knee. "I won't bore you with the details, but essentially I'm looking for somewhere to invest my money."

I get the sense that whatever reason he's here in town is private. I certainly don't want to pry and have him thinking that I'm trying to figure out his financial situation.

"Did you grow up here in town?" Bastion asks before I can respond.

I shake my head and set the mug down when it grows too hot against my palm. "No, I grew up in Tennessee."

"What made you move here?"

My mouth twists as I consider how much to tell him, but there's no harm in him knowing all of it. It's not a secret or anything. "My dad was in a car accident about four years ago, and though he's okay now, it took a long time for him to recover. He still walks with a cane as a result of his injuries."

Bastion frowns. "I'm sorry."

That old familiar ache in my chest when I remember that night returns—when I wasn't sure that he'd make it, and then when I knew he'd survive, listening to the doctor describe the extent of his injuries.

"He worked really hard to recover, but it took a long hospital stay and a lot of surgeries and rehab afterward. Once he had the all-clear to return to work, he started looking for a new job that paid more than the one he had." When Bastion gives me a questioning look, I explain. "My parents were left with a lot of medical debt as a result of the accident. So when he was offered a good job here, it just made sense for them to relocate."

"And you followed?" He lifts the mug to his lips.

"That probably makes me sound like a child, doesn't it? I'd finished college by then." I look down at my hands on my lap.

"It makes you sound like a woman who loves her parents very much." There's a slight edge to his voice. Maybe he doesn't have a good relationship with his parents.

I meet his gaze. "They're the most important thing in the world to me, so yeah, I followed. Got a job here, and I do what I can to help them pay the bills." I shrug.

He blinks several times, almost as though he's surprised. "That's very generous of you."

"I do what I can."

Bastion nods slowly.

"So all that to say, I've only lived here for a few years myself." I take a sip of my hot chocolate, cradling it between my hands.

"Do you like it here?"

I sigh because I'm not sure I know the answer to that question.

"I take it that's a no?" He arches an eyebrow, which I've found is something he does quite often.

"It's not that, it's just..." Do I explain to this man, whom I enjoy talking to, how awkward I can be? Is that going to ruin the entire thing that's happening between us? Is there something happening? I inwardly sigh. I'm not meant to do things like I am right now. Then I remember Taylor telling me to own who I am and not pretend to be someone I'm not, so I do. "I'm sure you've noticed that I can be a little socially awkward."

He shakes his head. "No. You've been great company both times we've chatted."

My face heats again, and I say a small prayer that Bastion can't tell that I'm blushing. "I don't make friends easily, so moving here has been somewhat... isolating." I shrug, not wanting to make it a big deal.

"I find that surprising," he says. "Have you tried joining any clubs or community organizations? What about church?"

I bring my mug to my mouth and take a sip. "I do attend church, have most of my life, but if I'm honest, I miss my old church. The people at my current church are wonderful," I'm quick to add, "but most of them have been here their whole lives. I can't help but feel a little like I don't belong, no matter how nice they are to me."

"What about dating apps?"

I give him a horrified look. "I've seen enough videos online to know they're not for me."

"I probably shouldn't have assumed that you don't have a boyfriend. It's just that you mentioned feeling isolated, so if you do... I have to say, I don't think he's a very good one."

We both laugh. It's on the tip of my tongue to ask him if he has a girlfriend, but I can't bring myself to do it.

"No, no boyfriend." Rich's face flashes through my mind, and I push away the mental image. "Anyway, suffice to say this town is lovely. I think I would just enjoy it more if I could get out of my head and find a group of friends to enjoy it with."

"Makes sense. Do you follow football?"

His sharp change in topic jars me for a moment, but I appreciate him offering me the out. "I do, actually."

"So are you a Titans or Packers fan?"

I can't help but laugh. We talk about football and our predictions for when the season starts in a few months, then we move on to discussing other things. Bastion tells me a story about him and his sister attending a party in high school.

The story makes me curious how old he is, but again, I don't ask.

Before I'm ready, he collects our empty mugs to return to the counter, saying that he'd better be going. Something like panic grips my chest. It's been so nice spending time with him, talking and connecting over regular things, and the idea of not getting to do it again feels crippling.

"Will you be back in town next week?" I ask, standing as well. I try to keep my voice casual, but I'm pretty sure I don't succeed.

His smile makes his deep blue eyes sparkle with satisfaction. "I will."

Oh no, he's going to make me ask, isn't he? My face heats, and though I feel awkward as heck, I know I'll regret it if I let him leave here without asking.

"Would you like to meet up next week?" I hold my breath as I wait for his answer.

Holding both mugs in one hand, he steps forward and squeezes my elbow. "I'd really like that, Hattie. I'll see you then."

And with that, he heads over to the counter, leaving the empty mugs with the girl who works here, and walks out the door. Again, without a backward glance.

The spot where his skin briefly touched mine is still warm as I make my own exit a couple of minutes later.

8

BASTION

The following week, I don't arrive in Wisconsin until Monday night, just to prove to myself I have the self-discipline. I spoke to my lawyer, and things are moving along nicely with my plan. All that needs to happen is for me to bait the line and watch Hattie bite down on it.

I'm meeting her tonight, and today I plan to make another sweep of her apartment to see if anything I missed the first time can lend some more insight into her now that I know a little more about her.

I watch her leave her building, punctual as usual. Her hair is pulled up in a ponytail, and she has on a sheath dress in a floral pattern that looks as if it's at least a size too big for her.

As I did last time, I wait twenty minutes to make sure she isn't going to return, then I pull the baseball cap over my head and grab the clipboard from the passenger seat. I'm back in her apartment in under three minutes. Seriously, the rush is addicting. I can't do this many more times.

It looks much the same as it did the last time I was here. Everything is in its place, though there are different books on the coffee table. She must be an avid reader. Then again, she does nothing else.

A quick tour of the bedroom and the bathroom reveal nothing new, and I end my tour in the kitchen. I've just pushed the junk drawer closed when I hear a key in the lock.

Fuck.

A quick glance around tells me there's nowhere to hide, and trying to slip out of the sliding glass door in the living room will only announce my presence to who I assume is Hattie.

Goddammit, this whole thing is going to be over before it even starts. Why the hell did I insist on coming here again?

The door closes softly behind Hattie, and I hold my breath, praying that she just forgot something, grabs it, and goes. And that whatever it is, it isn't in the kitchen.

Heavy steps make their way from the door into the living room.

My stomach lodges in my throat. She's going to catch me, and there's not an excuse in the world she's going to buy for what the fuck I'm doing in her apartment.

"Still reading your smut." The deep chuckle of a man rings through the silent apartment.

My forehead creases. Did she lie to me when she said she didn't have a boyfriend?

Footsteps sound again, making their way away from the kitchen and down the hall. I slowly creep out of the kitchen without making a sound until I'm in the living room, where I stand looking between the escape of the sliding glass door and the entry to the hallway.

I should get the hell out of here before I'm caught. But I want to know who the fuck this guy is and what he's doing here. Why does he have a key to Hattie's apartment? I'll dig into my curiosity later.

Slowly enough not to make a sound, I head toward the hallway entrance, pausing when I hear something. It takes me a minute to figure out what it is—the sound of Hattie's dresser drawers opening and closing. Somehow, I think this guy has a different agenda than I do for being here.

Deciding not to press my luck, I turn and slowly make my way to the slider, careful not to make any noise as I open it before slipping outside and closing it. I return to my car and wait.

Fifteen minutes later, a beat-up old pickup truck pulls out of the parking lot with a man behind the wheel. I snap a picture of the license plate and text it to Mr. Smith, telling him I want to know everything there is to know about the man who owns the truck.

I have an idea, but I want to know for sure what the fuck is going on.

I purposely arrive ten minutes late to the café that night. Not so late that Hattie will have given up on my arriving, but late enough that she'll worry whether I'm going to show up at all. I want her to feel the disappointment of thinking I won't be there, then the relief when I walk through the door.

It's an old trick I learned from my younger days when I used to fuck rich married women for the financial benefits.

When I step through the café doors, Hattie is quick to spot me, raising a hand in greeting. Even from the distance between us, I can see the way her shoulders move away from her ears, how her forehead relaxes now that I've arrived.

I quicken my pace across the café to reach her. "I'm so sorry I'm late. I got caught up with something for work and I was going to text you to let you know I'd be late, but I realized that we haven't exchanged numbers."

"That's okay, I understand."

She doesn't immediately offer me her number, which irks me, but I don't let it get to me. Maybe I have more work to do here than I thought.

"Just give me a minute and let me grab a drink. You all set?" I glance at the steaming cup of hot chocolate sitting on the table beside her.

"Yes, sorry, I was going to get you something, but then I realized I don't know how you take your coffee." Her blush says she's embarrassed, as if she feels bad she didn't memorize my order as I did hers. But she's not a con artist. I am.

"That's okay, Hattie. I won't hold it against you." I wink and head over to the counter.

I return to the lounge area a few minutes later. Instead of

taking my usual seat across from her, this time I sit in the chair to her left.

"My apologies again for being late." I set my coffee on the table beside her hot chocolate.

Hattie waves away my concern. "It's really not a big deal." She gives a nervous chuckle. "Though I was starting to wonder whether you were coming."

"Why wouldn't I?"

She shrugs and glances at her lap.

"Anything exciting happening in your life?" I ask.

That question draws her gaze back to mine, and she gives me what I interpret as a "you know better than that" look.

I raise my hands. "It's possible."

"Just not probable." She rolls her eyes playfully.

"We can't all lead a life full of mystery and intrigue like me. Don't beat yourself up about it."

She laughs. "You are a little mysterious."

"Is that so?" I arch an eyebrow.

"Can I ask you something I've been wondering about?" She licks her lips, as if she wants to ask this question but is scared at the same time.

I pick up the mug and bring it to my lips. "You can ask me anything." *The real question is whether I'll tell you the truth.*

She presses her lips together before she voices what's on her mind. "How old are you?"

"Didn't your parents teach you not to ask a man his age?" I wink even though the subtle mention of Carla makes me want to hurl this coffee cup across the café.

"Sorry, it's rude of me to ask."

I chuckle. "Not at all. I'm thirty-seven."

"Oh."

Usually Hattie's thoughts are projected on her face like a film reel, but I can't actually tell what she's thinking in this moment.

"Not what you expected?" I hold her gaze.

"No. Yes." She's apparently flummoxed and shakes her head. "I mean, I didn't really know how old you were."

It's clear now that she's asking herself whether I'm too old for her to be spending time with, even though if I had to guess, she probably hasn't even admitted to herself that she likes me. She's probably thinking, *what would my parents think if I brought this man home?*

"Age is just a number as far as I'm concerned. Believe me, I don't feel any older than you inside." That might be the most truthful thing I've ever said to her.

"You really think that?"

Am I seeing hope in her eyes? She really is into me. Satisfaction fills me as I realize that maybe what she's worried about is whether I think she's too young for me. "I do. It's a stupid thing to get hung up on."

She smiles, and we spend the rest of the evening getting to know each other better.

Well—I get to know her better. She gets to know a version of Bastion Clarke who never really existed. Perhaps he would if he'd had a loving, nurturing mom to raise him.

9

BASTION

I arrive in Wisconsin the following week with a smile.

My lawyer called shortly after I landed to let me know that I'm the proud new owner of a manufacturing business in all things ventilation. It wouldn't be exciting except for the part that it's where Hattie works.

I'm almost giddy. It's finally time to put my plan into action. The trap has been set, today I'll lay the bait, and this time next week, I'll spring the trap.

But first, I have to deal with the man I found in Hattie's apartment last week. Mr. Smith sent me a dossier on him a few days ago. Turns out he's the landlord of a few buildings in town, including the one where Hattie rents her apartment.

He's also a registered sex offender. What are the chances that the piece of shit only sneaks into Hattie's apartment? Pretty slim.

He reminds me of the men who used to take advantage of my mother when I was young. I don't like men who prey on the weak. I was once the weak they preyed on too.

I think it's time for someone to teach this asshole a lesson. And I'm not doing this for Hattie. I'm doing it for the other women and children he's preying on.

After I check into my room at the hotel, I head out in search of Russell Balcom. The two of us need to come to an understanding.

Following the GPS directions, I drive past Russell's nondescript bungalow and park down the street. A quick assessment tells me that the best plan of attack is to make my way into his backyard through his neighbor's—I don't spot any cameras, and there are a couple newspapers on the front porch that make me think they're away. People are so fucking stupid sometimes. Why not just take out an ad in the local paper that says you're out of town?

I put the black mask on my face and pull down my ball cap as far as it will go, then exit my car. Moving quickly, I gain entry into the neighbor's yard. It's a two-story home with a walkout basement, and the deck off their kitchen allows me to look into Russell's yard. There's no sign of him, a dog, or anything concerning.

After identifying which window I want to use, I climb off the deck and hop the fence, dropping to my feet in the grass. Quickly, I approach the house, peeking through the window to make sure I don't see anyone.

The coast is clear. I came prepared today, and I pull out my lockpick. It's an old door, so it won't take me long.

Sure, I could bust the door down, but I don't know if he's inside, and I want to preserve the element of surprise.

Within minutes, I push open the door to the laundry room. I'm careful to be quiet as I move farther into the house. There's a TV on in what sounds like the living room I spotted in front of the house when I drove by, so I assume the lazy piece of shit is in there.

I move forward, stopping every couple of feet to listen. There's still just the sound of the TV. If there were a dog, he would have already sniffed and searched me out by now.

I'm in the kitchen, which has an opening that looks onto the dining room. Beside that is the living room.

When I peek around the wall, I'm ready to ambush him should he be facing me. But he's in a chair facing a TV in the corner with his back to me. I grin against the mask on my face. Too easy.

The curtains on the front window are closed, though they're only sheers, and they allow some light to filter through.

The floorboards under the carpet creak when I'm about three feet away from him, and I watch him straighten in his chair before his head whips around. His eyes widen in alarm when he finally realizes he's not alone.

I surge forward as he's straightening to get up from his chair, and when he's standing, I tackle him to the floor. He lands underneath me with an oomph, and I straddle his chest, pinning his arms with my legs.

"Who the fuck are you?" he shouts.

Thank fuck Mr. Smith's intel about this guy said he lives alone, otherwise, he'd definitely draw attention from someone else living here.

"You should worry more about why I'm here," I growl.

He tries to buck me off him, but I've got thirty pounds on him, and I'm twenty years younger.

"So you like sneaking into the apartments of the young girls you rent to, do you?"

I had Mr. Smith do some digging on the other properties Russell owns, and wouldn't you know it, most of them are rented to women in their twenties.

"I don't know what you're talking about."

I slam a fist into his face. "You'll get one of those each time you lie. Let's try this again. You sneak into the apartments of the pretty young women you rent to, don't you?"

"Go fuck yourself."

When I land a punch to his face this time, his nose squirts blood. It's broken.

The piece of shit whines and cries.

"Last chance, Russell."

His eyes widen a little when I use his name. Good, maybe he's finally figured out he might not know me, but I know him.

"Fine," he says between gritted teeth. "I do it. What do you care?"

"I care when I know someone is preying on the weak."

I ignore the voice in the back of my head telling me I'm doing the same thing to Hattie. Am I not the predator and she the prey?

But that's for an entirely different reason and circumstance. I'm not going to force Hattie to do anything she doesn't want to. She's going to be a willing participant the entire time.

"You're a sick fuck, aren't you?"

He shakes his head back and forth in a desperate attempt to convince me that he's harmless.

"Men like you make me sick." An image of Stan flashes through my mind, and I shake my head to clear it. "I want you to stay out of those apartments, Russell. If I find out you've been slipping in and going through any more underwear drawers, one of two things is going to happen. I'll either take care of the problem—you—myself, or I'll call the police and provide them with proof of what you're doing. Do you think they'll let you out of jail this time?"

I don't have proof of him going into the apartments, but he doesn't need to know that.

Tears glisten in his eyes. "Who are you?"

"Wrong answer." I hit him again, busting his lip. "Do we have an understanding?"

He's sniveling and crying now, but he gives me a shaky nod.

"Good." I lean my weight into my legs, pressing into his arms, and he cringes. "And don't even think about calling the cops to report this. If you do, I'll have my own report for them. You understand?"

He nods on a shaky exhale.

"I'm glad we see eye to eye on this. And don't think just because I haven't made my presence known that it means I'm not watching." I get up off the floor and give him a swift kick to the gut that should leave him breathless long enough for me to get out of here in case he has a gun hidden in the cushions or something.

After Russell's taken care of, I head back to the hotel to have a shower before I meet Hattie, who will be none the wiser that I just did her a favor. She should be thanking me really, but by the time I'm done with her, she'll be doing the opposite.

10

HATTIE

*L*ately, all I think of is Bastion.

I shouldn't. It's stupid. Maybe it's just a girlish crush on an older man. I don't know. He hasn't even given me any indication that he sees me as anything other than someone he enjoys conversing with when he's away from home.

But it's the first exciting thing that's happened to me in a long time, even if by most people's standards, it's just casual conversation.

Still, I can hardly sit still as I wait for his arrival at the coffee shop Tuesday evening.

Tuesday has become my favorite day because of our meetups. Every time, I have to remind myself that these rendezvous are finite. I try to tell myself that I'm fine knowing these meetings will eventually come to an end. I mean, Bastion has to finish his business in Wisconsin at some point, right? And then he'll have no other reason to come back to town.

I push that thought from my mind, determined to enjoy the time I do have with him. I haven't even told Taylor about him, and I'm not sure why.

Maybe because there's nothing to tell.

And there isn't really. I mean, we share one drink together, talk a little, and part ways. It's not as if we're having an illicit affair.

I feel guilty for even having the thought. I shouldn't think of Bastion like that.

I'm here at the café ten minutes early, and this time, I made sure to buy Bastion's drink. I felt awful last week when I realized I couldn't order his coffee because I didn't know how he took it, when he'd remembered my order after our brief meeting the time before.

He walks in five minutes early, sparing me from having to wonder whether he's going to show up or not. I smile and wave with my free hand, holding up his coffee with the other.

He grins and makes his way toward me. He looks as if he just got out of the shower—his hair is half damp and has more wave to it than usual. He's wearing a pair of dark gray jeans and a black T-shirt that fits him perfectly. As usual.

Bastion's never said outright that he has a lot of money, but I can tell by the way his clothes fit him that they're better than anything I could ever afford. Not to mention his expensive watch and just the way he carries himself.

"You remembered." His ocean blue eyes twinkle with mirth.

"I did."

He stands in front of me, and I pass him his coffee. Our fingers brush in the exchange, and I inhale a swift intake of air. It's an innocent touch, nothing more, but it still makes me feel... things.

We catch up on what we've both been up to this week. Me—work, spending time with my parents, attending church and a few of the groups I joined through church. Him—putting out some fires at work and dealing with some employee issues.

Whenever I ask exactly what business he's in, Bastion just says the entertainment industry. I've wondered if maybe he deals with celebrity clients or something, but I've never asked outright since it seems like he doesn't want to talk about it. I figure he must want to preserve their privacy.

Bastion's just finished telling me a story about how he once jumped off a roof into a pool when I shake my head. "I could never do that."

"Sure, you could." He sips his coffee.

I give him a look as if he's crazy. "No way. I'd be too afraid I'd get hurt."

He studies me for a moment. "I think if you did it, you'd probably love it. It's a rush taking risks once in a while."

"I'll have to take your word for it."

He takes another sip and sets the empty cup on the table. "I'll get you to break free from your chains at some point." He winks at me, and I smile. I'm really starting to love that wink. Bastion sets his hands on the armrests of his chair and pushes himself to his feet. "Unfortunately, I have to be going. I have an early flight out in the morning."

His abrupt departure takes me by surprise. He usually spends longer.

"Of course." I stand too, collecting our cups.

"I have some more news." His lips turn down to a frown, and I brace myself for whatever it is he's going to say, but I think I already know. "Next week will be the last time I can meet you. My business in Wisconsin will all be concluded the next day."

"Oh." A wave of nausea courses through me.

"It's been really wonderful getting to know you, Hattie. Should we meet up for one last time next week?" He rests his hand on my shoulder and squeezes.

My eyes almost drift closed to bask in the sensation, but I somehow manage to keep them open.

"Definitely." I nod, swallowing past the growing lump in my throat.

"Perfect." He removes his hand from my shoulder. "I'll see you then." Bastion gives me a small smile, then makes his way out of the café.

He said he's enjoyed getting to know me, but he didn't seem at all hesitant to leave. As usual, my difficulty in reading people gives me little insight into where his head is.

I set the two empty cups on the counter as I leave, then make my way to where I'm parked down the street.

Deciding I don't want to go home yet, I head over to my parents'. I'm welcome to stop by whenever I like, and right now, I don't want to be alone. I know I'll only think about how next week is the last time I'll probably ever enjoy Bastion's company.

It was nice having someone to connect with while it lasted, and who knows when the next person will come into my life? I really need a change, because if Bastion taught me anything, it's that I want to put myself out there more.

I knock on the door, which feels odd, but I didn't grow up in this house. It feels more like theirs than ours. My mom answers almost right away, as though she knew I was coming and was waiting at the door.

"Well, this is a nice surprise. Come on in, sweetie." She leads me toward the kitchen. "Would you like some hot chocolate?"

I don't want any, but I'm afraid if I turn her down by saying I just finished one, I'll have to lie about coming from seeing Bastion. So rather than having to explain all of that, I just say, "Sure."

She takes a couple of pumps of the moisturizer beside the sink and spreads it over her hands and forearms. "Your dad just ran out to grab a prescription from the drugstore." She takes the electric kettle over to the kitchen sink to fill it.

"Everything okay?" I sit at the kitchen table.

She waves off my concern. "He just had to refill his cholesterol pills."

I nod with relief, then glance at the papers littering the table in front of me. My mom looks over her shoulder at me while she sets the kettle on the base and turns it on. Something about her unsettled look has me picking up the piece of paper in front of me.

I blink in surprise at the big red lettering on the notice I hold. "You guys are behind on this medical bill?"

"We're a little behind, but it's not for you to worry about." She comes to sit across from me, gently plucking the piece of paper from my fingers before setting it back on the pile.

"What happened?"

She stacks the papers in a nice pile, then sets it to the side, out of my reach. "The repairs on your dad's vehicle were more than we expected, so we had to short our payment the last couple of months."

My stomach drops to my feet. "Why didn't you say something? I could have helped."

"It's not a big deal, sweetie. We'll be back on track soon enough."

My mom doesn't say it, but I know she's thinking of those few days she had to take off last month because she wasn't feeling well. If she'd worked, she might have had the money to make up the difference.

I hate that they didn't come to me for help. That there's not more I can do for them.

I've prayed on it so many times, asking God to show me the way I can make a bigger difference in their lives, but so far, no answers have presented themselves.

"I have a bit of money in savings. Let me use it to make up the difference."

She's already shaking her head before I've even finished. "Absolutely not. I already don't like that you contribute to the payment every month. You're doing more than you should."

I take her hand. "We're a family. That's what we do."

Tears fill her eyes, and guilt weighs heavy that I'm the one who put them there. "How did I get so lucky to get a daughter like you?"

Something like a haunted look crosses her face, but the kettle whistles and clicks off, so she gets up from the table.

My mom puts a few scoops of hot chocolate powder in a mug, then pours the water over top. "I appreciate the offer, but you let us worry about it, okay? I know your dad would feel the same."

I sigh, knowing I won't win this argument. Still, I have to find some way to help.

My mom stirs the hot chocolate, grabs some milk from the fridge, and adds it. Before she brings it to the table, she puts some more lotion on her hands and spreads it around.

"What's with all the moisturizing?" I chuckle.

"My hands and my arms have been so itchy lately. I'm wondering if something in the garden is irritating them."

"Do you have a rash or hives?"

She shakes her head. "Nope, but that's the only thing I can think of. I'm used to having dry skin during these Wisconsin winters, but it doesn't usually bother me going into summer." She laughs and sets my hot chocolate in front of me.

"Thanks, Mom."

We chat for a while, and I stick around until my dad returns so that I can say hello to him. Eventually I return to my apartment, and as predicted, the only thing I can think about is how next week will be the last time I'll see Bastion.

11

HATTIE

I woke up feeling sad this morning. It's Tuesday, which for a few weeks meant I would wake up excited and looking forward to that night. But now, knowing it means I'm losing the only person I've really felt connected to since we moved to Wisconsin, my mood is a one-eighty from where it was.

It's ridiculous, I know. I haven't known Bastion that long, but it feels as if I've known him forever. From the moment we met, it felt as though he knew me. I've grown comfortable already, and last week, I felt myself starting to shed the shy exterior I have with any new person I meet. The only other person I've really been able to do that with was Taylor—and to a lesser effect, Rich.

I'm going to miss that feeling of connection once it's gone.

I tell myself I can find it again with someone else, but will it really be that easy? Since I met Bastion, it's felt as though we have some kind of connection I can't explain even though it doesn't make sense, even to me. A wealthy businessman thirteen years my senior who has clearly lived a much less sheltered life than me? But somehow, the connection is there.

I walk into work, saying a quick hello to some of my coworkers before taking a seat at my desk. I go through my usual routine of putting my purse in my drawer, turning on the computer, and checking for any voicemails before I get started on my tasks for the day.

But before I can really get going, my coworker Marwa swings by my desk. "We're all supposed to meet in the conference room in ten minutes. The big boss has called a meeting."

I frown. "What's the meeting about?"

She shrugs, sending her long black hair behind her shoulder. "Not sure. I'm just spreading the word." She flits off to tell the next person.

By big boss, I know she means the owner, Mr. Fitzpatrick. He's not in here very often because he's essentially half-retired, so it seems odd that he's called a meeting.

The next ten minutes pass as though each second is an hour. I grow more anxious as I stand from my desk and make the trek across the office to the conference room. It's standing room only when I arrive and look around. Everyone is gathered in little circles, whispering about why we're having this meeting. Theories are thrown out from everyone.

A couple of minutes later, Mr. Fitzpatrick enters the room with his son Tim, who runs the day-to-day operations now that Mr. Fitzpatrick has taken a step back. Mr. Fitzpatrick is dressed as though he's stopped here on his way to the golf course, and I relax a little. If this were bad news, he probably would have dressed more professionally.

"Thanks for coming, everyone." Mr. Fitzpatrick's booming voice fills the room, and everyone quiets. "Sorry for the short notice and the impromptu meeting, but I need to speak with you all about something that has recently transpired. I'm going to cut right to the chase." He looks around the room and sets his hands on his hips. "I've sold the company."

It's as if he's lobbed a grenade in the middle of the room, and everyone is too in shock to say or do anything at first. It's quiet for a few seconds before rapid-fire questions are directed his way.

Mr. Fitzpatrick raises his hands. "I know you all have questions, but rest assured, it will be business as usual. The new owner isn't looking to change anything."

"Who's the new owner?" someone calls out, though I can't see who it is over Ned, the tallest guy in the office who never has the courtesy to stand in the back.

"The new owner wishes to remain anonymous and will not be involved in the day-to-day operations. Tim will continue on in his role, as will all of you."

Mr. Fitzpatrick's gaze snags on me. Did I imagine that? No, he definitely paused for a moment. Oh jeez, I can't lose this job.

"The truth is, I didn't have any plans to sell, but I was approached with a good offer. When I was assured there wouldn't be massive layoffs, I couldn't refuse. Now I can really go enjoy my retirement." He laughs, but no one joins in, all too scared of what this means.

Even though he's assuring us that no mass layoffs are coming, everyone knows that the sale of a company means change. Surely this new mystery owner plans to do something differently.

"Tim, do you want to say a few words?" his dad asks.

Tim glances around the room. "For the majority of you, nothing will change at all. You'll go about your business as you do now. Finance, obviously there will be some changes with new ownership at the helm, but once all the accounts are transferred over, we should be in the clear."

I mentally process what extra work might be coming my way. Maybe this will be a good change. At least it's not more of the same old thing, right?

Mr. Fitzpatrick says a few more words that I think are meant to make us feel more secure, then they tell us that we're free to go back to work.

As I'm walking behind Ned, Tim calls, "Hattie, can you stick around for a moment?"

My stomach slides down my leg like a child on a waterslide.

Why me? So it wasn't my imagination.

My coworkers file out, some of them giving me questioning glances and the others pitying ones.

Maybe he just wants me to handle something regarding the changeover for the finance team? At least that's what I'm hoping for.

"Come have a seat." Tim gestures to the chair at the conference table to the right of where he sits at the head.

I do as he asks, attempting to maintain my composure as though I'm not worried about what's coming.

"There's no easy way to say this, Hattie. I'm afraid we're going to have to let you go."

I'm sure my mouth falls open. I'm positive I'm staring at him. But he doesn't even let the words sink in before he continues.

"The new owner wants to cut our personnel expenses, and he insists that we're overstaffed in finance. It was decided that the person with the least amount of seniority would be the one to go."

Tears well in my eyes, and I open my mouth, but nothing comes out.

"It's not personal at all. If it were up to me, I'd offer Marjorie an early retirement package and keep you, but the new owner didn't want to do that."

"I... I..." Still nothing comes out of my mouth.

My mind is too busy considering all the implications of losing my job for me to form complete sentences. How long will it be until I find a new one? How long will the small savings account I have keep me afloat? How will I be able to help my parents with the medical bills if I don't have a job?

A cold sweat breaks out under my clothes as Tim carries on, though I don't hear the words.

I've just been fired.

Laid off technically, I suppose, though it doesn't hurt any less. Plus, the end result is the same—I'm unemployed. I haven't felt this low since everything went down with Rich at the end of college.

Tim stands from his chair and extends his hand, so I do the same, assuming I must have been dismissed. Though my hand connects with his, I feel numb, and I swear I can't even feel our palms pressed together.

"Thank you for all the hard work you've done for the company these past three years. Please feel free to use me as a reference on your resume, Hattie. You were a great employee."

A great employee who has just been laid off. A lot of good that did me.

"I'm not going to embarrass you by walking you out or anything, but if you could go collect your personal belongings from your desk and leave, that would be great. I know you'd never do anything to sabotage the company."

I nod numbly, unable to do anything else.

I feel as if I'm floating as I make my way out of the conference room. I can't even feel my legs. Diverting toward the copy room, I find a box of paper that only has a few reams left in it and empty it, carrying the box to my desk.

No one pays me any attention until I remove items from my desktop and place them in the box. There's not much to take —some pictures of me with my parents, a plant, and a plaque with a quote from one of my favorite books. It's sad, really, that this is what constitutes my life when other people's spaces are overflowing with personal effects.

Once I grab everything off my desk, I open the bottom drawer and pull out my purse, tossing it in the box as well. I hear the murmurs start around the office, and I can't decide whether I should go around and say goodbye to everyone or whether I should just leave.

Marwa saves me from having to make the decision when she approaches. "What happened? Why did Tim want to talk to you after?" Her dark eyes are filled with concern.

"I've been laid off." My voice comes out raspy.

She gasps, and her hand covers her mouth. "What?"

"Apparently the owner said one person had to go from finance, and I've been here the least amount of time, so..." I shrug, willing myself to keep the tears at bay.

"Oh my god, are they going to be laying off anyone else?"

I shake my head. "I don't think so."

"I'm so sorry, Hattie." She pulls me in for a quick hug, which surprises me. We get along, but we've never been close—mostly my doing.

"It's not your fault." I pull away, wanting to get out of here and away from all the attention. "I need to go, though."

She nods in understanding. "Of course. Hit me up on socials, okay? Don't be a stranger."

I nod. "Will do. Say bye to everyone for me."

And after one goodbye, I collect my box and somehow manage to keep the tears at bay until I seek refuge in my car.

12

HATTIE

his is the worst day ever.

First, I lose my job, and now the only new friend I've managed to make in years is leaving.

After I left work, I went back to my apartment and spent the majority of the day crying. Once I managed to get myself together, I began looking for a new job. I can't afford to be out of work for long if I want to help my parents with their medical bills, especially now that I know they're behind. Sure, there's unemployment income I could apply for—and will most likely have to—but that's only a portion of what I was making. I can't afford not to get my full salary and benefits.

But there's nothing around here in my area of expertise. Just a whole bunch of minimum wage service jobs, which I'll take if I have to, but doing so will barely let me scrape along and pay my own bills, let alone help my parents.

And then my attention shifted to getting ready to meet

Bastion. Our last meeting. If I weren't already in a terrible mood, that alone would do it.

After I park down the street from the café, I step out and lock the vehicle. Each step toward the café feels as if I'm on a death march, which is ridiculously dramatic, but true nonetheless. I reach the café and open the door, remaining on the threshold.

This time, Bastion has beaten me to the café and is waiting with a hot chocolate. He holds it up and smiles at me. Something about the image makes me want to burst into tears. After this morning, I'm feeling extra emotional. Instead of crying, I plaster on what I hope is a convincing smile and make my way to the rear of the café.

"Hey." I try to keep my voice breezy and light.

"Rough day?" Bastion's forehead creases in concern as I take my seat.

Am I that transparent? "Why do you say that?"

He slides the hot chocolate in my direction, and I thank him.

Bastion's head tilts. "Something is obviously wrong. You look like you've been crying."

"So you're saying I look terrible?"

He chuckles. Being able to make him laugh lifts something in my spirit. "Of course not. You could never look terrible."

My entire body heats from his words, and I force myself not to look away as I normally would.

"Thank you, but I don't want to spend our last night together crying on your shoulder." I bring the mug to my lips and blow on the steaming liquid.

"Why not? Isn't that what friends are for?" He holds my gaze, and I can't look away from his twin pools of deep blue.

I want to ask, is that what we are? Friends? But that's not me.

"I suppose." I take a tester sip of my drink, then run my tongue along my top lip, feeling some of the foam there.

I swear Bastion's eyes track the movement.

"Well, then, let's hear it. Maybe I can help or at least help you feel better."

I sigh. "You can't help, but you're right. Maybe I'll feel better if I talk about it." I shift to set my mug on the side table.

After I got home this morning, I didn't even call my parents or Taylor to tell them what happened. I was too embarrassed.

"I lost my job today." My shoulders slump.

Bastion takes my hands. "Oh, Hattie, I'm so sorry. What happened?" It feels so natural when he runs his thumbs up and down over my skin that I don't pull away.

"The company was sold, and the new owner decided there was one person too many in finance, so I was laid off." I cringe.

"That's no fault of your own. Why do you look ashamed?" He squeezes my hands.

I really didn't want to dump all this out on our last night, but it's occupying all my thoughts. "I'm embarrassed. I'm unemployed. I haven't been unemployed since I was fifteen."

"I'm sure you'll find something else. I don't know you that well, but it's clear to me that you're an honest, intelligent woman."

I look away and slip my hands from his. "I'm sure I can get *a* job. But I need one that pays well in my own field. I..." Tears well in my eyes, and I squeeze them shut, trying to stem the tide of anxiety and worry that threatens to overtake me.

Visions of my parents working themselves to the bone well into their seventies accost me. I picture them getting further and further behind on the payments and losing everything they've worked so hard for. It only takes one unexpected financial hit to pull people under sometimes. First, it was my dad's accident, but what if that was only the start of it? Anything could happen that would continue to make them never pay back the medical bills. What if—

"Breathe, Hattie."

My eyes snap open. That's when I realize my chest is tight and I'm breathing far too quickly.

He scrunches down in front of me, meeting my gaze and resting his large hands on my shoulders. "Calm down. Breathe."

He overexaggerates his breathing for me to follow. I start taking deeper, longer breaths until my chest doesn't feel as if a band is wrapped around it.

"I'm sorry, that's never happened before."

"You don't need to apologize." He squeezes my shoulders before he lets his hands drop and goes to sit back in his chair.

"I'm anxious about more than just losing my job. Yes, I need to be able to pay my rent and buy groceries and all that, but I'm more concerned about my parents."

Bastion's forehead wrinkles, and he tilts his head.

"I found out last night that they're behind on their medical bills. They had a large car repair bill, and if they don't fix my dad's car, he can't get to work, so they had no choice but to get it repaired, but now they're behind. I'm afraid it's going to snowball, and they'll just get further and further behind."

"You already help them out, right? I remember you mentioning that."

I nod. "But if I'm not employed, I won't be able to, and that will only make the situation worse. I just feel so helpless right now."

Bastion looks at me intently, studying my face.

I wipe under my eyes at the tears that are gathered there, poised to fall. "I'm sorry I'm dumping all of this on you. It's not your problem."

"Hattie, what can I do to help?"

Shaking my head, I say, "Nothing. There's nothing you can do."

He slumps back in his chair.

"Let's talk about something else. I don't want our last night to be me blubbering like a baby." I try to laugh, but it comes out strangled.

Bastion says nothing for a beat. I've really blown this. His last impression of me is a crying mess. "What if it's not our last night together?"

"Did your business in Wisconsin get extended?" I frown.

He straightens in his seat and leans forward, resting his elbows on his knees. "No, but I have an idea. You might think it's a little crazy, but it will solve a problem for both of us."

My mind whirls with what it could be, but I come up empty. "What is it?"

"Come work for me." His gaze doesn't leave mine.

It's a little bit before I realize he's serious. "In Seattle?"

Bastion nods. "I'm looking for someone who can be my right hand and take over some of the financials. I've always done most of it myself because I don't trust a lot of people, but I trust you. There'd be some other administrative functions you'd have to do—keep track of my schedule, act as a liaison between myself and my employees. Nothing you couldn't handle."

"You don't even know what kind of employee I am. Why would you offer it to me?"

"Like I said earlier, you're intelligent. I know you could do it, and I trust you. That alone is worth its weight in gold. At least where I'm concerned. Your last boss is a fool to let you go."

My hands fidget in my lap. "But it would mean moving to Seattle."

He nods. "But with the amount I'd pay you, it would be worth it. You could easily help your parents. Hell, you could even keep your apartment here if you wanted, just in case you don't like Seattle and want to come home."

I feel rude asking, but I have to know if I'm really considering uprooting my entire life. Am I considering it? "How much does it pay?"

Bastion tells me the amount, and my mouth drops open. He's right, that much money would make a huge difference. The idea of leaving my parents, though...

If I were back in Tennessee, my answer would be an easy no. But Wisconsin has never felt like home. I haven't formed any true friendships here, so the only people I'd miss are my parents.

Plus, I've felt a little confined here. And I really do want more adventure, to see the world and experience new things. I hate that it comes at the expense of moving away from my parents, but in the end, if I could give them the peace of mind that their bills are all paid, it's worth it.

"I don't know what to say." Excitement and relief war with reticence and worry in my head.

"Say yes. Maybe this is that taste of adventure you've alluded to wanting." He arches an eyebrow.

I realize that he's right. I have been craving something different in my life, and this is too good of an opportunity to pass up. With that salary, I could help my parents out even more. And as Bastion said, I could still afford to pay for my apartment if I wanted, at least for a few months until I know whether I want to stay or not.

"Are you sure? I don't want you offering me this job just because you feel bad about the situation I'm in."

He locks his eyes with mine. "Hattie, do you trust me?"

Slowly, I nod. "I do." I have no rational reason why, but I do.

"Then take this chance with me. I promise you won't regret it."

I quickly weigh the pros and cons in my head.

Pros: I get to spend more time with Bastion, I'd be able to help my parents with their medical bills, and I'd be making enough to keep my apartment so I could easily change my mind if I wanted. I'd be getting a little of that adventure I've been wanting. I wouldn't have to take weeks or months looking for another job only to be forced to take a job I hate out of necessity.

Cons: I wouldn't see my parents as often as I do now.

The one and only con is a big one. Still, I think taking the job is worth the risk, even if it doesn't end up working in the long run. The benefits outweigh the risks, and I can always return to Wisconsin. I'll just have a lot more money in my bank account when I do.

"What are you thinking?" Bastion asks when I've been quiet for a long while.

"I think... I think I'll take the job."

"Really?" His eyes sparkle with triumph, and I can't help the small chuckle that escapes.

"Really." I nod enthusiastically.

"Wonderful. Like I said, you won't regret it."

He smiles at me, and something clicks into place inside me. I think he might be right. I won't regret it.

13

───────

HATTIE

"You what?" Taylor screeches, her mouth dropping open on the phone screen.

It's been a couple of days since I agreed to move to Seattle to work for Bastion, and I'm still wrapping my head around it. "I got laid off from my job here, so I accepted a job in Seattle."

Taylor's stunned and frozen face stares back at me. "You're actually going to leave the roost. I thought I'd never see the day."

I narrow my eyes. "I don't live with my parents."

"No, but close enough. This is so exciting! But how the hell did you find a job out of state so quickly?"

I inwardly cringe at hearing her use the word hell. It's not like I've never heard people use it or the Lord's name in vain, but it's especially jarring coming from Taylor since we grew up in the church together. It still seems weird to me even though she left religion behind years ago.

I tell her all about Bastion—how we met and struck up a friendship and then met up for the next several weeks. The longer I go on, the more and more narrow her eyes get.

When I'm finished, she says, "I'm going to table the fact that over the past month, you've not once mentioned that you're off meeting with this handsome, older stranger every week. And I'm just going to ask if you've lost your goddamn mind?"

I ignore her using the Lord's name in vain because I'm so shocked by her reaction. "What do you mean?"

"You accepted a job across the country in a city where you know no one from a man you hardly know. How do you know his real name is even Bastion? What if he's a human sex trafficker or something?"

I roll my eyes. "He's not a sex trafficker."

"How do you know?" Taylor crosses her arms and looks at me pointedly.

"I don't know, I just do."

Taylor shakes her head at me. "Sometimes you can be so naïve, Hattie."

"You've never met him. He's not a trafficker. He's a successful businessman. I can't believe you of all people are reacting like this. You're the one always telling me to take more chances." I throw my hands in the air.

"Something about this doesn't sit right with me. This guy shows up out of nowhere, you share a few coffees, and suddenly he's offering you a job you can't refuse."

I actually thought this would be the conversation with my parents. I thought Taylor would be singing my praises and giving me an "atta girl." This, I didn't expect, and it makes me wonder if I am actually too naïve. Could Bastion not be who he said he is?

"If you met him, you'd know you have nothing to worry about."

"Hattie, I love you, but sometimes you're not the best judge of character."

She doesn't have to say Rich's name for me to know what she's referring to. Her comment stings more than it should after all these years.

"This isn't like Rich. I'm not romantically involved with Bastion."

"Maybe not, but I think perhaps you'd like to be."

I scowl at her through the screen. "What are you talking about?"

"I can tell by the way you talk about him that you're crushing pretty hard."

"You're wrong. He's a nice man, but there's nothing between us." I don't bother to say that's because there's no reason a successful, attractive man would ever go for me. And I leave out the little amount of sexual tension I've felt the last two times we met up. "It's a great opportunity for me, and at the first sign of trouble, I'll leave, okay?"

Taylor sighs. "Just be careful, okay?"

"Always."

"And text me every day. If I don't hear from you, I'll fly out to Seattle myself to track you down. And this Bastion is going to be in a world of hurt."

I laugh. "Agreed."

"What do your parents think of all this?"

I bite my bottom lip.

"Let me guess. You haven't told them yet."

The truth is that I'm nervous about telling my parents. Not because I think they'd try to stop me. They've always been supportive of whatever I wanted to do with my life. But I'm afraid to see the look of disappointment on their faces when I tell them I won't be living close to them anymore. It's been the three of us for as long as I can remember. But I'm twenty-four years old now. Maybe it's time to start building a life for myself.

"I'm going to tell them."

"When?" She gives me a look as though she thinks I'm full of it.

"Tomorrow night when I go over there for our Friday night dinner."

"Do you think they'll have a shit fit?"

I shake my head. "No. I think they'll have concerns, but in the end, they'll be supportive."

Taylor nods slowly. "How are you going to go about finding somewhere to live?"

"Bastion owns some rental properties, and one of his tenants just vacated, so he's going to let me move in there."

"How convenient," she says, making it sound the exact opposite.

"Taylor, stop. I'm lucky he's offering me this job. I could've ended up in fast food, barely able to pay my rent. It's not like this is a thriving metropolis and there are all kinds of jobs up for grabs."

She sighs. "I know. I'm sorry. I'm just worried, that's all, and I hate being so far away while you're going through all this."

I frown. "I hate it too."

"When are you leaving?"

"Bastion left it up to me, but I figured the sooner the better, right? For both of us. So I'm going to fly out on Monday. Use the weekend to pack up what I want to take. He said that works well because things are usually quieter on Mondays."

"And what exactly does he do?"

"He's in the entertainment industry. He gave me the name of his corporation, but Google isn't much help. I think maybe he deals with a lot of celebrities or something because he's pretty tight-lipped about it."

Taylor frowns. "I don't love the sound of that."

"Stop. Listen, I'll text you as soon as I'm in my new place on Monday, okay? You can interrogate me then."

"All right. But listen, be careful. I love that you're trying something different and taking some risks. Just keep your eyes open and trust your gut, okay?"

My chest warms because despite her misgivings, I know it's only because she cares. "I promise to be careful. At the first sign of trouble, I'll come home. There's nothing to worry about."

"If you say so."

We chat for a while longer, and Taylor brings me up to speed on what's going on in her life. After we finish the call, I grab the boxes I picked up at the moving depot a few towns over earlier today and pack a few of my things. My personal belongings will come with me in suitcases, but I'm going to ship some boxes to the address Bastion gave me to arrive after I do.

After I've packed the first box, I glance around my apartment and wonder if I'll miss it.

I don't think I will. I'm nervous, sure, but excited at the same time.

It's my first real adventure.

14

HATTIE

*T*elling my parents went pretty much how I thought it would—they were shocked, and after that wore off, they inundated me with questions, then they listed their concerns. After I had appeased their minds a bit, they were finally supportive.

It didn't make saying goodbye to them at the airport any easier, though. I was a blubbering mess, as was my mom. My dad tried to be stoic, but I saw the tears in his eyes. Being so far away from them will be the hardest part, but I have to remind myself that they're part of why I'm doing this— though they don't know that. I conveniently left that part out when I explained all my reasons for wanting to take this job. I knew they'd be adamant about not uprooting the little life I had in Wisconsin to pay their bills.

The flight was uneventful, and I was shocked when I checked in to find that Bastion had put me in first class. I've only been on a plane a handful of times, and never in first class.

By the time the plane lands, the sadness has worn off, but anxiety has taken its place.

What if this is a big mistake? What if I hate it here? What if I'm not good at the job? What if I'm homesick?

I push away all those thoughts as I wait for my luggage to be spit out onto the baggage carousel. I've made the decision already, and I'm here. There's no point in being negative about it unless I know for sure there's a reason. I need to take things as they come.

The first of my pieces of luggage approaches, and I step forward to grab it, but when I lean down to reach for it, another hand beats me to it. It takes me a second to react and look from the hand to the owner's face, and when I do, a jolt of... something rushes through me.

"Bastion. You're here?"

He grins and sets down the large bag. "You don't pack light, do you?" He winks.

Jeez, that wink makes my stomach all fuzzy and bubbly.

"I thought you were sending someone to pick me up?" I ask.

"I pushed aside my work for the day so that I could be here to help you get settled."

His words probably shouldn't make me all giddy since he's now my boss, but I can't help but smile. "Thank you."

He inclines his head toward the baggage carousel. "How many more?"

I cringe. "Two more bags." When he shakes his head, I add,

"I'm moving across the country. That's a lot of personal belongings to pack up."

"I'm just messing with you. Just point them out when they come by, and I'll grab them."

I do as he says, and within five minutes, he's rolling two suitcases to my one out of the airport.

"I grabbed us a driver since I wasn't sure how much luggage you'd have and couldn't be sure it would fit in my car." Bastion directs us down the concrete walkway toward a large black SUV with blacked-out windows. "You get in, and I'll help the driver with the luggage."

"Thank you." I slip into the back seat of the air-conditioned vehicle and relax into the buttery soft leather.

There aren't many jobs where your boss flies you out via first class, then personally picks you up at the airport and helps with your luggage. But it all fits with the person Bastion has shown me he is. Taylor's crazy. He's not a sex trafficker.

I'm excited to see my new apartment and thankful that I don't have to go through the process of searching for something affordable in a new city, where I don't know what area offers what.

Bastion joins me in the back seat, and a minute later, we're pulling away from the curb. We don't talk about anything in particular as we make our way toward downtown, but Bastion points out different landmarks and tells me about them.

"How long have you lived here?"

He gives my question some thought. I like the way he always takes a moment before answering. "Almost a decade. I bounced around a lot as a kid, so when I started my business, I knew I wanted a home base. I liked Seattle, so this became it." He shrugs.

"Why did you move around so much?"

Shadows darken his eyes. "That's a long story we don't have time for because we're almost there."

I thought maybe he was an Army brat, but something tells me it's more than that, so I let the topic drop. I'm not going to pester him when he's offered me so much with the job and the apartment. "That must be why you're so good at meeting new people. You must've had to do it a lot growing up."

"Is that your way of calling me charming?" He accepts my shift of subject and lightens the mood.

"I wasn't, but that doesn't mean that's not the case."

His eyes dance with mirth. "This is it."

Before he can say anything more, his phone vibrates, and he pulls it out of the holder in the door. After a quick glance at the screen, he answers.

"Hey, how are you?" There's a brief pause before he says, "Good. Ariana, can I call you back in a bit? I'm in the middle of something."

A female voice on the other end says something, and he laughs and ends the call.

Something about the way he laughs—in such a comfortable way, as though he's done it a thousand times before with this Ariana—twists my insides. There was a carefree and light note to it that I've never heard him use with me.

Who is she? A girlfriend? A wife? The idea makes bile race up my throat. I've never asked if he's married, though he doesn't wear a ring. Maybe it was someone who works for him. It is Monday afternoon after all. His business doesn't stop just because he's helping me.

The better question is, why do I even care? He's been a little flirty with me at times, but he never outright said anything to make me think he's interested in me. Do I even want him to be? Now that he's going to be my boss, it's an especially bad idea, never mind the age gap and how clearly different we are.

"Hattie."

I blink and look over at Bastion.

He tilts his head and studies me. "Where were you just now?"

I shake my head. "Nowhere. Sorry, this is all a little overwhelming. Did you say something?"

"I asked if you're ready to go inside." He motions to the window behind me.

It's then I realize that we've turned into a parking garage under a tall condo building.

"I'm confused. This isn't the place you showed me on your phone." I turn to look at Bastion as the driver parks the car near an elevator in the underground garage. The place that Bastion showed me was a triplex, and I was meant to be staying on the top floor.

He cringes. "Sorry, I forgot to tell you. There was an issue with the roof, and it leaked into your unit. I'm going to have it repaired, but the damage was extensive. I had to improvise."

"Oh no, that's too bad. I'm sorry you have to deal with that. Am I going to be able to afford this place?"

This building is way fancier than the other one he showed me. It was nice, but from what I saw on the outside, this one screams money. A quick glance out the window confirms it. There's barely any dust on the asphalt, and the brass elevator door gleams.

"Well, I think so. It's free." He grins.

I shake my head, confused. "How is that possible?"

With one hand on the door handle, he pushes open the door. "You'll be living with me."

Then he exits the back seat and slams the door closed.

I'm sorry. What?

I so wasn't prepared for this.

15

BASTION

"Bastion, I can't live with you!" Hattie rounds the back of the SUV where I'm talking to the driver, tipping him while instructing him to hand off the bags to the doorman in the lobby.

I have to suppress my grin. Hattie played into my plan so perfectly when I offered her the job. And when she agreed to live in my apartment? Even better.

There is an apartment, and it is currently vacant, but there's nothing wrong with it. She doesn't have to know that. Getting Hattie to live with me is just one step closer to the goal. The more time I spend with her, the more I can get her to like me and the faster I can get her into my bed, among other things I have planned.

I don't know what it was like to be excited for Santa to come on Christmas Eve—my childhood didn't allow for that—but I imagine it must be something close to what I'm feeling now.

I turn away from the driver and move Hattie toward the elevator door with my hand on her waist. It's not lost on me that even after I've sprung this on her, she doesn't pull away. My mother did her a disservice by making her so trusting.

"There's no other option. Rent in Seattle is ridiculously expensive, and the vacancy rate is low. I just found out about the apartment early this morning, and I'm certainly not going to put you out on the street. You can stay with me until the repairs to your unit are done." I press the elevator button.

"Are you sure? I don't want to intrude. You don't have to do this, Bastion." There's so much concern in her eyes, and I get the feeling that she's more worried about if this is okay with me than the fact that she's had this sprung on her.

How this woman got through life this far without being completely taken advantage of, I have no fucking clue.

"If it weren't fine, I wouldn't have brought you here." The elevator dings its arrival, and I hit the button for the penthouse.

"You live on the top floor?"

Her panicked voice spurs a chuckle from me. I almost find her naïveté endearing. Almost.

"Of course." The elevator doors open on the top floor, and I step out of the elevator first. There's only one other condo on this level, and I lead Hattie to the right and down the hall. After I push in the code to enter my place, I look over my shoulder at her. "I'll text you the code so you have it." Then I swing the door open and motion for her to enter first.

Her hazel eyes widen as she slowly steps past me, her eyes soaking in the space. I try to see the place I refer to as home through her eyes—the two-story windows overlooking part of the city and the water, the massive open kitchen that opens to the living and dining areas, the wet bar at the far end of the space, and the glass-front wine cellar filled with only the best bottles.

"Wow. I've never seen anything like this before."

I figured. "Shall I give you the tour?"

"Are you sure it's okay if I stay here with you? I don't want to cramp your style if you want to have Ariana over or something."

Shit, I didn't give her enough credit. She's fishing. And the only reason she'd do so is if she was the slightest bit jealous. That shouldn't make me as happy as it does.

"My sister lives thousands of miles from here, so no need to worry about that."

The tension in her shoulders relaxes. I thought she was worried about the prospect of sharing space with me, but maybe it was mostly her thinking my sister is my girlfriend.

"Oh, your sister?"

I nod.

"Even so, I'm sure you date, I mean..." She motions toward me. There's her indication she finds me attractive. It's so damn easy with her. She wouldn't play a mind game with someone unless they offered to pay her parents' medical bills.

I can't fight my smile. "Hattie, are you telling me you find me attractive?"

Her cheeks instantly pinken. "What? No. I mean, yes, but… not like that."

"Huh." I run my hand down my face, allowing my eyes to roam up and down her body. "Shame." Then I walk by, ignoring her lingering stare. "This is obviously the main living area. You're welcome to help yourself to anything in the fridge, bar, or wine cellar. Sadly, I do most of my eating at restaurants or by ordering in, but pick up anything you want and stock the cupboards if you'd like."

I motion for her to follow me down the hallway. "Down here you'll find the washroom, laundry, and this is my bedroom." I gesture to the right, where the door is open.

Hattie pauses beside me, but doesn't go in.

"You can go in and check it out if you want."

She whips her head in my direction. "No, that's okay."

I chuckle and continue down the hall. "This is the gym. I don't know if you work out or not, but you're welcome to use it. Down here is another bedroom, my office, and then your room." I step inside the last room on my left.

She follows, and I watch her take in the space with wide eyes. She's completely overwhelmed.

"There's a large walk-in closet, and this is your private en suite with a soaker tub. Do you enjoy soaking in a hot bath, Hattie?" A vision of her naked in the water with a few bubbles surrounding her runs through my brain, and my dick twitches in my pants. Shit.

She swallows and looks away from me when she answers. "Maybe."

I smile behind her back as she enters the bathroom to check out the space.

"All this furniture is yours to use, but if you find anything not to your liking, let me know and I'll replace it."

She turns around to look at me, and her forehead creases. "How long will I be here for?"

I shrug. "Not sure. Depends on what the roofer and contractor find when they look at the apartment."

Hattie nods a bit hesitantly. The chime for my condo goes off before I can say anything more.

"That's probably your bags. Come on. I want you to meet Jeffery." I leave the room.

Hattie follows. "Who's Jeffery?"

I look over my shoulder at her as I reach the end of the hall. "He's the daytime doorman. You can see him for almost anything you need, and if he can't help you, he'll find someone who can." I reach the door and swing it open. "Jeffery, thanks for bringing these up."

"No problem." He wheels in a luggage cart stacked with Hattie's bags.

"Jeffery, this is Hattie, the owner of all this luggage. Hattie, Jeffery." I gesture between the two.

"Pleasure to meet you." He extends his hand toward Hattie, and she takes it with a smile.

"Nice to meet you, Jeffery. Sorry you had to bring all of this up here."

He waves off her concern. "It's no trouble, miss."

"Jeffery, those can go in the bedroom at the end of the hallway on the left."

"Yes, sir." He pushes the luggage cart through the living room and disappears from view when he turns to go down the hallway.

Hattie walks over to me. "I feel bad," she whispers.

I lean in closer to her. "Don't. It's his job. I'm sure he's happy to be gainfully employed."

She presses her lips together and nods. "I guess…"

Jeffery reappears with an empty luggage cart.

"Hattie is going to be staying with me for the foreseeable future, Jeffery, so anything she asks for, please make sure she gets it."

He nods. "Of course, sir." Then he looks at Hattie. "It was great to meet you. Don't hesitate to reach out for anything."

"I will, thanks."

I get the door for Jeffery, and once he's gone, I turn to face Hattie. "I'll let you get settled. I have to go into the office for a while, so I might not be home until pretty late. You have my number, though, so reach out if you need anything."

"You're leaving me here by myself?" Her alarmed expression is comical.

Oh, Hattie, already so attached? Perfect.

I chuckle. "I'm sure it won't be the last time now that you live here. Make yourself at home. I'll see you later."

When the door shuts behind me, I take a minute to enjoy the moment. Ruining Hattie is going to be such sweet justice. Carla will regret ever making me an afterthought in her life by the time I'm done with her stepdaughter.

16

HATTIE

Bastion texted me last night around eight to tell me that he probably wouldn't be home before I went to bed, and he was right. With the time change, I ended up falling asleep around nine thirty, and I didn't wake up until after eight this morning.

Which was no problem, because he said we didn't have to head into work until around noon anyway. I'm not sure what type of office doesn't start until noon, but maybe he's being nice and trying to ease me into things by only making me work a half day.

Apparently, we're to head into the office together today, which I guess makes sense given that we're leaving from the same place. I don't want the other employees to think anything of me showing up with the boss, though.

I'm so nervous because I have no idea what to expect. Bastion has been very vague whenever I've asked for specifics. He keeps telling me not to worry about it, that I'll be fine. I'm trying to hold the same confidence that he has in me, but it's difficult when I know how I tend to struggle connecting with strangers. I have no doubt I'll be able to handle the responsibilities of the job itself. It's the social aspect of a new work environment that makes me anxious.

I haven't seen Bastion this morning. I left my bedroom around nine to make myself some breakfast, and there was no sign of him. His bedroom door was closed, so maybe he's sleeping. I have no idea what time he returned to the condo last night. And when I finished eating, I went to shower and get ready for work.

Unsure what to wear, I chose a blouse with short sleeves with a bow that ties around the collar and falls down the front of the shirt. I paired it with a long, flowing floral summer skirt and white flat sandals. Then I pulled my hair back into a bun and put on a little mascara and lip gloss.

As I stare at myself in the full-length mirror in the walk-in closet, I think I look professional. It should be fine for today. Once I get a sense for the work environment, I'll be better able to plan my outfits. When I asked Bastion what most of the other people wore to work, he told me, "Whatever they want," which I took to mean there isn't a dress code. But I always prefer to be overdressed than underdressed, so today it's a blouse and a skirt.

I step out of my bedroom at a quarter to twelve and make my way to the main living area. I spot Bastion in the kitchen, standing at the counter and finishing what looks like a smoothie. When he turns to face me, the air rushes out of my lungs.

I've never seen this version of him. He's dressed in a tailored suit that fits him to perfection. It's dark gray with a pale blue shirt underneath and a dark tie. Rather than his hair being a little mussed and flowing naturally away from his face, he's put more effort into it and has it styled back with product.

This is businessman Bastion, a man I haven't met before today. But he's just as appealing, maybe even more so, as the man I met in Wisconsin.

I swallow hard, pushing back my attraction. The last thing I need is to screw this up. He's offered me a great opportunity to help my parents get ahead and be able to retire without a mountain of debt. Making him know I'm attracted to him will only ruin things.

"Good morning," he says with a smile and sets his glass in the sink.

"Morning." I offer a smile, hoping it appears natural.

"Do you need to eat before we head in?"

I shake my head, finding it difficult to speak when his gaze roams me up and down. Suddenly, I'm self-conscious. Am I dressed okay? But he doesn't say anything.

"All right then. Let's get going." He motions for me to head to the door first.

I do, then we walk side by side to the elevator, where he extends his arm and presses the button.

"It's only a few blocks away. It's a nice day, so I figured we'd walk."

I blink in surprise. "Oh, I didn't realize it was that close. That's handy."

He chuckles. "It is."

The elevator dings, and the doors swing open in front of us. I step in first, and he follows.

Maybe I was too in my head yesterday, or maybe it's just seeing him look so different than I'm used to—more power-ful, more assertive, and more dominant—but the space in here feels stifling. I'm keenly aware of his every move, every breath, and the complete quiet as the elevator zooms toward the ground.

Needing to fill the silence, I ask him something that was on my mind last night while I was in the condo by myself. "What should I say about my living situation?"

He shifts to look at me, pushing his hands into his pants pockets in a casual stance. "What do you mean?"

"If someone asks, should I say I'm staying with you?"

He shrugs one shoulder. "You can say whatever you like. I have nothing to hide, but if you'd be more comfortable with no one knowing, I understand."

I gave it a lot of thought last night. "It's probably best. I don't think it would go over well if people knew the new girl lives with the boss. They might think I'm getting special treatment."

"You are," he deadpans.

The elevator comes to a stop, and the doors swing open, revealing the wide expanse of the white marble lobby.

"I know. But I mean..."

"What?" He stops and turns to face me, arching an eyebrow.

"We're not... you know..." Jeez, my face is so hot.

"Fucking?" he says with a grin.

My face is officially on fire. I swallow hard and try to collect myself because I've never heard someone say that so blatantly and unapologetically. "That, or dating, or... anything more than friends."

I don't know why I wait on bated breath to see what he'll say. Do I want him to dispute it? Tell me I'm wrong? What exactly was that between us back in Wisconsin?

"I don't fuck my employees. Everyone who works for me knows that." He doesn't elaborate before he makes his way toward the building exit, saying a quick hello to Jeffery.

I give Jeffery a wave before passing by Bastion as he holds the door open for me.

As soon as I step onto the sidewalk, I'm met with more sights and sounds and smells than I'm used to. City life is a little overwhelming, but taking in everything around me, I love it.

"We need to buy you some clothes," Bastion says. "Something more appropriate for the workplace."

I glance down at my dress. "You said there wasn't a dress code?"

"You look like you're headed to church, Hattie. That won't do."

"Oh, is it more formal than this? I can go change quickly." I thumb behind us toward the building as we approach an intersection and wait for the light to change.

"Not more formal," Bastion says before the light changes and he starts to cross.

I quickly walk to catch up with him. "If you tell me what I should be wearing, I'll make sure I dress properly tomorrow."

"I doubt you have what you'll need. No worries, I'll arrange for someone to come to the condo with some options this week." He leads me off the road and back onto the sidewalk with a hand on my lower back. The intimate touch that feels almost possessive sears my skin.

We walk for a minute before turning a corner. When I see the familiar red letters on a large sign at the end of the road, I don't even think. I just reach for Bastion's forearm and tug.

"Oh my gosh, I always wanted to come here. I've seen it in so many movies!"

Bastion chuckles and places his large hand over mine that's still gripping his forearm. "Then we'll have to check it out."

I take one last look at the PUBLIC MARKET CENTER sign before we turn the corner and it disappears from view. We walk for another minute before Bastion stops us in front of a black building with a marquee outside that says The Black Orchid in a gold script. Below that I see the words Gentleman's Club.

I'm a little confused, but when Bastion pulls a set of keys from his pocket and unlocks the door, holding it open for me, I realize with horror that this is our destination.

The Black Orchid is his club?

Bastion owns a strip club.

17

BASTION

This is the moment of truth.

I savor the moment the recognition hits her—that when I said I work in the entertainment industry, I meant that I own a strip club.

The entire time I've been planning this, I knew that this moment was pivotal. If she's going to scare easily and run, it'll be right now. She's not invested, hasn't seen her first paycheck and what it can do for her, and I haven't grown any closer to her or gotten her to act on her attraction to me.

"Come on in and I'll show you around." I gesture with my hand for her to go ahead of me.

"Do... do you own a strip club?" She glances back up at the marquee as if she didn't read it right the first time.

"Many actually." I smile at her, relaxed as if it's not a big deal even though my heart is pounding and I'm worried this will all go south before we get to the good part.

"I... I didn't realize..." She glances down the sidewalk, back the way we came.

Shit. I'm losing her.

"I'm sorry if you didn't realize, Hattie. It's a force of habit at this point when people ask what I do." I sigh and really play it up by looking away from her, pulling on those easy heartstrings of hers. "I've been judged so many times for what I do that I guess I just got used to being vague."

She places her hand on my shoulder. "I'm sorry, I wasn't judging you. I didn't mean to make you feel that way. I'm just surprised, that's all. Let's go in, and you can show me around."

Way too fucking easy.

I meet her gaze and smile. "Thank you. You have no idea what it means to me that you'll give this a chance."

She nods and steps inside.

When the door shuts behind us, I fight the feeling of being a predator who's cornered his prey. I tell myself that I'm not like Russell back in Wisconsin.

"The place is empty right now. The dancers won't come in for a couple of hours. I wanted to be able to show you around before you're bombarded with having to meet everyone else. When the lights are all on and the music is pumping, it can get a little intense."

Hattie stops and looks around, turning in place. "I've never been to a strip club before."

"That's okay, you don't have to be an expert in them to help me out day to day."

"Where will I be working?"

The way she says it makes me think she's afraid I'll plop a desk down in the middle of the stage and make her work naked.

"Follow me."

I lead her to the door beside the stage and down the hallway that passes the room where the dancers get ready, the employee kitchen, the stockroom, and finally to my office at the very end.

"You and I will be working in here." I unlock the door and push it open, waiting for her to walk in first.

My desk is where it always is, and I've set up a desk for her on the far wall. Coincidentally, my desk looks onto hers.

She looks around the space, not saying anything.

"I took the liberty of setting you up here and bought you a laptop, but if there's anything else you need, you just have to say the word."

When she still doesn't say anything, I take her hand. It's only now that I notice the scent of her perfume—a light floral scent with a trace of vanilla. It's... fuck... it's her. If I paid someone a shit ton of money to come up with a fragrance that would define Hattie, that would be it.

"Are you going to be able to do this job? Again, I'm sorry. I probably should have mentioned the working environment, given that your faith is such a strong part of your life. I just thought with what this job pays and the situation you're in..." I allow her to fill in the blanks.

"It's fine. It will take some... adjusting, I'm sure, but you're right. This job allows me to help my parents out significantly more than I could at my old job. I'm sorry if I'm coming off ungrateful. I just wasn't expecting this."

"I understand." I drop her hand and walk over to sit at my desk. "Shall we get started? I can walk you through where everything is in the cloud and what you can start with."

She nods. "Yes, of course."

After she grabs a pen and notebook from her desk, she brings them and her computer and sits on the other side of my desk. Damn, we're way too far away from one another.

"On second thought, why don't I come sit beside you so we can both look at the screen on your computer?" I stand and drag my chair closer to hers so that when I sit down, our legs are almost touching. In fact, I intentionally brush my leg against hers under the guise of stretching several times as I show her what she needs to know.

Hattie picks everything up quickly, asking intelligent questions. The one truthful thing I did tell her was I knew she was smart and could do this job efficiently.

I'm not sure how long we've been at it when there's a knock on the door. My office door is open, but no one would dare walk in without announcing themselves.

The two of us shift in our seats to see who it is, her leg bumping mine this time. Ray stands in the doorway, his hulking body almost filling up the space.

"Hey, boss." He glances at Hattie.

"Hattie, this is Ray. Ray, Hattie. She's the one I told you about who's going to make my life a whole lot easier, right?"

She gives me a shy smile and stands, walking across the room and extending her hand toward Ray. "Nice to meet you, Ray."

He looks a little taken aback by the gesture, as he should. It's not often that people are shaking hands around here. But he steps forward and takes her hand. "Good to meet you too. Whereabouts you from?"

"Is it that obvious I'm not from around here?" She cringes, glancing over her shoulder at me.

Ray's smile grows, and the beast inside me growls.

Ray lets out a big laugh. "Don't stress about it, it's not a bad thing."

But I can tell by the way her shoulders sag that she's self-conscious. "I'm from Wisconsin by way of Tennessee."

Ray smiles wide. "I have some family in Tennessee. Whereabouts?"

The two of them discuss the different areas of Tennessee for a few minutes, and I find myself growing more and more irritated as I watch Hattie become more comfortable with him. I don't know why, but the idea of her giving her attention to another man is riling me up. Her sole focus needs to be on me so that I can move my plan along.

Growing impatient, I finally interrupt them. "I'm assuming there's a reason you wanted to see me, Ray?"

He realizes his error and sheepishly looks away from Hattie. "I just wanted you to know that Sean showed up here after we closed last night. You'd already left, but I told him I would let you know he's looking for you."

My jaw clenches. I haven't heard from Sean since our little showdown, but it's not as if I didn't expect to have another conversation on the same topic.

I nod at Ray. "If he shows back up and I'm not here, text me. If I'm close, I'll come by."

"Yes, sir." He starts to make his way out of the room, then turns at the last second. "Good to meet you, Hattie. You ever have any problems while you're here, come find me or one of my guys, okay?" He winks and walks off.

What the fuck was that wink about? I've never seen Ray wink at anyone. Actually, he makes little conversation with anyone. Even the dancers sometimes complain about his broody attitude.

"He seems nice," Hattie says as though she's surprised. I'm not sure how many outwardly different types of people she's been around in her life.

"People aren't innately bad people just because they work at a strip club." I say it with more bite than I intend, given the mood Ray put me in.

"I didn't mean—"

"Let's just get back to work. I have a lot to catch you up on."

Looking chastised, Hattie tucks her skirt and sits back down, and we get back to it.

If only I could decipher who I'm more irritated with—her or me.

18

HATTIE

I don't know what I said wrong, but Bastion's mood soured after Ray left his office. Though I try not to let it get to me, the change puts me on edge, nonetheless.

The good news is that I catch on quickly to everything he goes over with me. In fact, I have some ideas on how to streamline a lot of his processes. I won't mention them now, but once I dig in and get the lay of the land, maybe he'll be receptive to hearing them.

The bad news is that I now work at a strip club.

I can't even believe the words when I say them in my head. My parents will definitely not approve. I'm not sure I do. But Bastion's right—the salary this job affords me can change a lot of things in all three of our lives, so it's worth giving it a chance, right? Plus, Bastion is nice. Ray is nice. If it's a nice work environment, then what's my problem?

Maybe I'll be sequestered in here all the time and never be exposed to what goes on outside of this office.

A few hours in, things must be up and running because the deep rumble of bass sounds through the walls of the office, and I can hear people—mostly females—talking farther up the hall from where we are.

Bastion claps his hands together and leans back in his seat. "Shall we take a break?"

"Whatever you want." I give him a tight smile, hoping his mood comes back around.

"I want to go make the rounds now that the club is open. Come on, I'll introduce you to everyone."

My throat constricts, and I can't squeeze out a word, but I nod in agreement, eyes wide.

He chuckles, which I've noticed he does when he sees my nervousness. "There's nothing to be nervous about. They won't bite." He takes my hand and pulls me up from the chair.

He leads me to the door but drops my hand as we enter the hall. We walk side by side, and he takes me into the room where all the dancers get ready before they perform.

My face is as hot as the surface of the sun as soon as we walk in. A handful of women are in various stages of undress, though none of them seem concerned at all that we've entered. I chance a glance at Bastion, and he doesn't appear fazed in the least by all the bare chests and butts.

"Hey, boss," one woman says as she pulls a triangle bikini top up over her breasts.

He gives her a wave and puts his fingers in his mouth, whistling. Everyone stops what they're doing, staring at him.

"Ladies, I want to introduce you to someone." Bastion gestures to me. "This is Hattie, and she's going to be my assistant from here on out. If she gives you a directive, consider it the same as if I were giving it to you. She's new in town, so please make her feel welcome."

All the women say hello, and I'm not sure where to keep my eyes. A couple of them are half naked, but no one else seems to think anything of it. I try to make it seem as if I'm unfazed, but I'm sure I'm failing miserably.

I raise my hand and smile, looking around the room. "Hi, nice to meet you."

"Where'd you find her, Bastion, the cornfields in the Midwest?" one of the ladies at the back calls out.

"Don't start, Ashley," Bastion says in an authoritative voice. "Hattie is very good at what she does, and I expect you to treat her with the same respect you treat me. Everyone understand?" His eyes scan the room.

The women nod and all say yes, except for Ashley. She just rolls her dark eyes and turns to face her locker, pulling out a change of clothes.

"All right, ladies, have a good shift." Bastion turns to leave.

A few of the women look me over, and I rush behind him to keep up. I realize now what Bastion meant about my wardrobe. I stick out in a major way, but it's what I'm used to. I'm certainly not going to wear what the women in there were wearing. Don't they worry about what other people are thinking, how they're gawking at their bodies, and thinking about having sex with them?

Seriously, Hattie? Of course they don't. They dance naked for money.

Bastion leads me farther down the hall, and we enter the main room he led me through when we first arrived. It's like a completely different place now.

A few men have taken up residence at some of the tables, and the lights are now dim with various shades of neon backlighting casting down on the stage where a woman is currently spinning around the pole. Music pumps through the space, and a couple of bartenders are serving customers behind the backlit bar.

Bastion leans in close to me so I can hear him over the music. Again, I feel his breath on my neck, and it makes me want to close my eyes. "This is the main room where all the action happens. I'll introduce you to the bartenders and the DJ some other time."

"What's back there?" I point toward where a security guard stands at the entrance to a hallway.

I'm not sure I trust Bastion's grin. "C'mon, I'll show you." He leads me over to the man and says over the music, "Dmitri, this is Hattie. She's my new assistant."

Dmitri doesn't say anything, just gives me a terse nod, which I return with a smile, not sure if I should say anything more. But then Bastion continues on and leads me down the hallway where there are a bunch of doors with numbers above them.

"These are the VIP rooms." He opens the second one we come to and goes inside.

The room isn't exactly small, but it's not huge. Glittery silver curtains that meet in the center of the ceiling go to the top of the wall and are draped down behind the leather banquette that lines the walls. Music from the main room filters in through speakers mounted in the corners, and there's a low circular table in the middle of the space.

I'm not so sheltered that I've never heard of a VIP room or what is rumored to go on in them, but I am curious about the truth, so I ask Bastion, "What happens in here?"

He turns and meets my gaze. "Whatever the girls and their customer agree on."

It's apparent what he's not saying—that anything and everything goes. I look around the space again. It's weird to think that people have sex and do other stuff in here. I have a hard time wrapping my head around the idea. I was taught that sex was something to be saved for marriage and that it was something special you share with someone you love and want to spend your life with. That giving your body to a man meant something. But here, it's a commodity to be bought and sold. I can't... I just can't.

"I think I've seen enough."

Before Bastion can say anything, I rush from the room. He calls my name, but I don't stop. Instead, I rush through the club, back down the hallway behind the stage, and push into the women's bathroom with tears in my eyes.

I don't think I can do this. I owe it to my parents to try, but if they knew where I was working, they'd be mortified. They'd be embarrassed to tell all the people at church. Our precious Hattie? Oh yeah, we disowned her. She works at a strip club.

"You okay, sweetie?"

One of the dancers comes out of a stall. I don't remember her name from the quick introduction a short time ago. She's wearing a pink wig, sparkly black booty shorts, and a white stretchy crop top that has a bunch of holes in it.

"Just a little overwhelmed." I feel like an idiot. She's probably looking at me, judging me as some goody two shoes. That I think I'm too good for this place.

Her lips tip down, and she squeezes my shoulder. "It's a lot if you're not used to this kind of thing. I'm Renee, by the way."

Her genuine niceness allows me to relax a little bit.

"I remember my first time onstage, I thought I was going to pass out. My legs felt like Jell-O." She laughs, obviously remembering it. "I was sure I was going to fall flat on my face and make a fool out of myself. I almost didn't step out on stage."

"What made you do it?"

She smiles, and her eyes sparkle. "I remembered who I was doing it for. I just pictured my little baby boy at home. If I wasn't going to provide for him, who was?"

It's obvious from the look on her face that she loves her son very much.

"How old is he now?"

"Elijah? He's four now. Best thing I've ever done. I'll show you some pictures next time I have my phone with me."

I give her a smile. "I'd like that."

She sets her hands on her hips and sighs, looking me up and down. "Listen, I mean no disrespect, but looking at you, it's clear you're not used to this kind of life, so I'm gonna assume that if you took this job, there's a reason. You just gotta remember your why. Any time you're questioning it, remember your why."

"Remember my why," I repeat, picturing my parents in my head and that stack of bills with red print.

"Exactly. I have to go finish getting ready, but I'll see you around, okay? Hang in there." She squeezes my shoulder again and walks toward the exit. When her hand is on the door handle, she turns and looks at me over her shoulder. "Oh, and don't worry about what Ashley said in the changing room. She's just a bitch." She winks at me, then leaves the restroom. "Oh, hey, boss."

Does everyone in Seattle wink?

I feel a little better now. Maybe Renee is right—I just need to remember my why.

I'll give it the week and see how I feel. If the why doesn't outweigh how uncomfortable I am, I can always go home.

Decision made, I turn and leave the restroom.

Bastion leans against the wall opposite the door with his arms crossed. "Feel better?"

"Yes, actually, I do."

He nods. "Good, let's go back to my office. We can order something to eat while I go through the rest of the stuff with you."

"Sounds good." I follow him, feeling a little guilty for not telling him that I'm giving this job a week before I make a decision about it. But I have a feeling he could convince me to do almost anything, as evidenced by the fact that I've moved to a new city, I'm living with him, and working at his strip club.

No, I need to figure out whether I can stay in Seattle for myself.

19

———

HATTIE

*S*ince Bastion told me I can set my own hours, on Tuesday and Wednesday, I make sure I'm at the club by nine in the morning. At least this way I can get work done uninterrupted, and I'm not forced to face the debauchery of the environment I'm in. No one else is here except for the cleaners, who arrive mid-morning. Bastion arrives around lunchtime.

I make sure to stay in the office once everyone else arrives mid-afternoon, and when I leave, I keep my head down until I'm back out on the street.

As far as the tasks I have to do for my job, that portion of things is going well. That's one thing I've always liked about numbers—they're constant. And while the software I'm using might be different, as are the processes that each business uses, math is math, and it doesn't change.

I haven't seen Bastion around the condo since I've been going in to work early and he stays late at the club, so it's like I have the entire place to myself. Though it sounds good, I've been lonely. It reminds me a lot of when I first moved to Wisconsin. I decided last night that I would see if there's a church nearby that I can attend. Not only will it help me center myself, but it might lead to me making some friends. Lord knows there's no one at work I have anything in common with.

On Thursday evening, I'm about to shut everything down for the day when my phone buzzes on my desk. I pick it up to see a message from Taylor.

Checking in that you're still alive and well.

I smile, my chest aching, and wish we were in the same city.

I keep telling you I'm fine.

I haven't told Taylor or my parents what happened with the apartment I was supposed to move into and that I'm living with Bastion. Nor do they know about the strip club—obviously. Every time Taylor insists that we video chat so I can show her the place, I make an excuse, but that will only last so long. Thank goodness my parents aren't tech savvy, so they haven't insisted on trying a video chat.

I just have to make sure mystery man hasn't kidnapped you and sold you into sex slavery or something.

I roll my eyes. No matter how many times I tell her Bastion is a good person, she doesn't seem to believe me. And I still believe it. We may have very different lifestyles and beliefs, but at his core, I know he's a good person.

"What's with the eye roll?"

Bastion's voice surprises me, and I straighten in my chair, setting the phone face down on the desk.

"Nothing. Just my best friend being overprotective."

He's just come in the office door, and instead of going to sit down at his desk as he normally would, he leans against the edge of his desk and crosses his arms, studying me.

"Overprotective about what?" His gaze is steady, and I shift in my seat.

"Nothing serious. She's just concerned about me moving across the country on my own and not having anyone here."

"You have me," he says matter-of-factly, but we're never together.

"I've barely seen you." I don't know where the words come from when they slip out of my mouth or why they sound so sharp.

He tilts his head, a small smile on his face. "I came in here to

tell you to pack your things up. We're due at the condo in"—
he glances at his expensive watch—"twenty minutes."

"What for?" My pulse picks up as a mix of excitement and
trepidation courses through my body.

"A surprise. C'mon, grab your stuff and we can walk back
together." He pushes off the desk and walks back to the
office door.

I sign out of the computer and shut it down, make sure
everything is arranged neatly on my desk, slide my phone
into my purse, and join him. Bastion locks the office door
behind me, and we walk down the hallway together.

We step out of the doorway beside the stage, and as
always, it takes a moment for my eyes to get used to the
dimness of the bar and the neon lights reflecting off all
the shiny surfaces. Music pumps through the packed
space.

I avoid looking at whatever is going on onstage, concen-
trating my efforts on looking ahead so I can get out of here,
but Bastion pulls me to a stop when we're about halfway
through the space. When I turn to look at him, he holds up
his finger in a one-minute gesture and walks over to talk to
the bartender.

Great. Now what am I supposed to do? If I rush out of here,
I'll look like a child, but my muscles grow more and more
tense as I stand here.

A quick glance at the stage, and I spot Renee. She's still
dressed, thank God. I think she must have just started her
set. Though I want to look away, it's difficult. She's a great
dancer, mesmerizing, and I can't take my eyes off her.

I'm not sure what I thought the women did on stage, but I didn't realize they were so talented. In my head, they just took off their clothes.

Renee moves over to the pole and swings around it once, coming to a stop and arching her hips out while facing the audience, looking around the room. She catches my eye and winks before hooking her leg around the pole and twirling around again.

"You ready?"

I startle at Bastion's voice—as though I've been caught doing something I shouldn't by watching Renee. I spin around to face him.

"Yep!" Then I head toward the exit as if I'm on the Olympic speed walking team.

Bastion chuckles as he exits behind me. "You know there's nothing wrong with watching. It doesn't make you a bad person."

I ignore his taunt and change the subject. "Everything okay?"

He catches my meaning and says, "Yeah, I just heard from one of our liquor suppliers that we're going to be short-shipped this week and wanted to let him know."

"So, what's this surprise?" I ask as we turn the corner to head up the street.

"You'll see."

I sigh as we cross the street, dodging the other pedestrians.

"What's wrong, don't you like surprises, Hattie?"

"I used to, but this last surprise kind of threw me for a loop, so I'm reconsidering my stance on them."

"God, you kill me sometimes," he murmurs to himself.

We reach the sidewalk, and Bastion sets his hand on my lower back to steer me around a large group of teens headed our way. The urge to pull away rises, if only because it feels too good having his hand there.

"Again, I'm sorry I wasn't more upfront with you, but has it really been that bad?"

I don't bother responding. I don't know how I feel yet. Logic and my feelings are at war with my conscience, and everything is muddled in my head.

"How long do you think this surprise will take? I was going to head back out after I ate dinner."

"Where were you planning to go?" Bastion asks.

"Shopping. Like you said, I need to grab a few things to wear to work. I feel like a child when I'm at The Black Orchid."

Bastion hums his approval.

A few minutes later, we're entering the lobby of Bastion's building, saying a quick hello to Jeffery, and heading up in the elevator. When the doors close, I'm keenly aware of Bastion's proximity and the scent of his expensive cologne. I didn't know that cologne could be sexy until I met Bastion. His cologne always makes me aware of his presence.

I squeeze my eyes shut. *Stop it.*

My thoughts are completely inappropriate. This man is my boss and my friend and he's giving me a great opportunity, whether I choose to stick with it or not. Thinking like that can only lead to trouble.

The elevator dings, and we step off in tandem. I let Bastion lead the way down the hall and open up his condo, then I follow him inside.

"Why don't you go change into a robe?" he says.

My feet stop as if they're encased in concrete. "Excuse me?"

"There should be one in your closet. I hung it in there this morning."

I don't move. "Why... why would I need a robe?"

He tucks his hands into the pockets of his expensive dress pants. "I have a stylist meeting us here. She's going to outfit you with some things to wear to work."

My mouth drops open, and it takes me a beat to recover. I ignore my teenage self getting giddy about getting a makeover. "What if I can't afford the stuff she brings?"

I'm pretty sure a stylist isn't going to show up here with pieces from Kohl's or JCPenney.

"You're not buying any of it. I am."

My heart hammers. "I can't let you do that... why would you do that?"

He steps forward and takes my hand, holding it lightly in his fingertips and running his thumb over the top. "Because I know how uncomfortable you are while you're there, and I think if you were dressed differently, it would help you relax a bit, fit in more."

"I'm not going to be half naked." There's no way I could pull off something like the dancers wear when they're hanging around.

"Noted. Now go get changed, and she'll go through everything with you when she gets here shortly. You don't have to take anything you're not comfortable in."

"You're not going to leave me, are you?" I'm not sure why the idea freaks me out so much except for the fact that I'm uncomfortable around new people, and I never know what to say.

Bastion smiles, twin pools of blue twinkling. "I'll be right here the whole time."

It sounds like a promise and a declaration.

20

BASTION

*H*attie is in her room, putting on her robe, when Jeffery calls up to let me know that the stylist and her team are here.

I had to think of something to bring Hattie back onside. It's been clear all week that she's uncomfortable as hell when she's in the club, and if I want her to stay, I need her to feel more at home. A new wardrobe will go a long way toward that, and this weekend, I intend to show her around Seattle.

I let Ivy and her team into the condo and direct them to set up in the living room. Ivy is probably in her early thirties, with chin-length black hair that's parted in the middle. She's dressed in a pair of cream pants and a silk blouse.

I've consulted with her a few times in the past when I was looking to update my own wardrobe. I'd rather suffer through a few hours of trying on clothes in my own home than go to actual stores and deal with salespeople. The two of us say our hellos and catch up for a minute before Hattie walks into the room.

Hattie stands at the edge of the living area with her mouth agape as Ivy's team organizes the racks and racks of clothing and accessories.

"Hattie, I'd like you to meet Ivy and her team. They're going to help you find some items you like."

Ivy inspects Hattie, sizing her up, calculating her size, her curves, her coloring, and hopefully she has an idea forming of what would work best. "Pleasure to meet you, Hattie." She stretches out her hand between them, and Hattie accepts the handshake.

"Nice to meet you."

"Bastion tells me you need some outfits to wear into the office. Classy with a side of sensual is the directive I was given. Does that sound about right?"

Hattie's gaze darts over to meet mine. "Um... I guess we can see how that looks."

Ivy nods and claps her hands together once. "Perfect. Let's get started then. I'm going to have you try on some things to start just so I can see how different cuts and fabrics look on you. From there, we'll refine, okay?"

Hattie bites her bottom lip, but she nods.

"Okay, Clarissa, why don't you pull the Armani so we can..."

Ivy's voice fades as she heads across the room to deal with her team, and I walk over to Hattie.

"Relax, this is supposed to be fun." I squeeze her shoulder.

"What if I don't like anything?" she whispers. "I don't want to offend Ivy."

"Your only job here is to be honest. You don't have to like everything she suggests, and she's not expecting you to, okay?" I dip my face down so it's level with hers and wait until she nods. "If you don't like something, tell her. She's hard to offend. Trust me."

The corners of her lips tip slightly, but she cringes before I can pull a full-on smile from her. "I'm going to feel bad if I tell her I don't like something."

"Hey, there's no reason to. The only reason you should feel bad is if she leaves here and you have a bunch of clothes you don't like and never want to wear. If you're not honest, she can't do her job properly. Think of it like that."

My words seem to relax her a little.

"Now, I'm going to go work in my office while you guys get down to business, but if you want my opinion on anything, just come find me, okay?"

She nods. "Yeah, okay."

I squeeze her shoulder and head off down the hallway to my home office, where I close the door behind me. I have a call to make, and I need privacy to do it.

I sit at my desk and pull the burner phone from the desk drawer. Most of the time Sean and I meet in person, but the odd time that we have to speak on the phone, I always use a burner so that it can't be traced back to me.

The phone rings several times, but Sean picks up right before I'm about to hang up.

"I heard you've been looking for me. I hope it's not to try to continue the last conversation we had." I lean back in my chair and pick up a pen off my desk, rolling it up and down my knuckles.

"The higher-ups weren't happy when I went back to them with your answer."

"Too fucking bad."

"They're not just going to drop it."

"You're all lucky I haven't kicked you to the curb already. I don't appreciate business partners who try to change the terms of the agreement midway through." I squeeze the phone so hard I'm surprised it doesn't come apart.

"You gotta work with us—"

"See, that's the thing. I don't. And you'd all do well to remember that. Accept my terms or don't, I really don't care. I'm certainly able to find someone who will."

It's like these assholes think they're the only game in town.

I hang up before Sean can respond.

Maybe I should tread more carefully, but these assholes are pissing me off, trying to push me around and act as if they own me. I've never been good when people underestimate me.

The phone in my suit pocket vibrates, so I return the burner to my desk drawer and pull out my regular cell phone to see my sister's name on the screen.

Impeccable timing as always.

"Hey, Ari. How's it going?"

"You sound tense. What's wrong?"

I blow out a breath and push my hand through my hair. "Nothing's wrong. And how can you tell I sound tense? We've been on the phone for less than five seconds."

"I know you, Bast."

She says it as if that's answer enough. I swear, since my sister became a mother, it's like she's got a radar for these things. Which I don't hate, actually.

"I'm fine. It's just work bullshit."

"Ah, gotcha." She says nothing more, nor do I expect her to.

Ariana has never judged me for the business I'm involved in. After the way we were raised, that's not really a surprise, but I think it helps that one of her sisters-in-law by marriage used to be a stripper. In fact, she's the one I got the idea from to open my first club. I was visiting Midnight Manor to spend some time with my sister's family, and Cinder and I got to talking about how lucrative stripping was and the issues she saw with most of the clubs. I felt as though I could do better, so I did.

"How're the twins?" I rest my feet up on the desk and lean back in my chair.

"Keeping me busy as always. Sable thinks she should still be able to sleep in the bed with Obsidian and me, and Donovan wants a dog. Insists he'll look after it."

"I'm sure Sid finds both those things thoroughly amusing."

She laughs, and as it always does, it spurs a warm feeling inside. There was a time in our lives when Ariana didn't laugh much. Now the sound fills me with happiness. She's found peace in her life.

"You know him, he puts up a good front, but those two have him wrapped around their fingers. I have to be the heavy all the time."

I laugh, knowing she's right. I love those kids as though they're my own. "Well, good luck with that. I'm pretty busy with work this summer, but I'll see if I can get out there while the kids are out of school so I can spend some time with them."

"That would be wonderful. I know they'd love to see their Uncle Bast. Speaking of visits, Dad and Eleanor just left."

"Oh?" I don't speak to my dad nearly as much as I used to now that he's settled down a bit and I have a business to run. "How're things with them?"

"Good, good, I just wanted to let you know that Eleanor mentioned to me that Dad had to go on some pills for his blood pressure and his cholesterol."

I frown. "Okay, isn't that kind of thing normal for his age?"

"I guess, it's just... it's weird. He's getting older, you know? I guess I just sort of realized it when they were here."

I think back to the last time I saw my dad during the holidays. She's right. Even I noticed how much older and frailer he looked.

"It's all a part of getting older, and he's obviously on top of his health if he's on medication for it. Try not to worry too much. Besides, if he needs anything serious like surgery or something, you and Daddy Warbucks can afford it."

"Fuck off," she says, and we both laugh.

Satisfaction rolls through me that I was able to make her laugh and get her out of her funk. There's nothing she hates more than when I bust her chops about marrying a billionaire. Trent raised us to think they were the scum of the earth.

A knock on the door has me looking in that direction. "Come in."

The door opens, and Hattie walks in.

"Ari, I have to go." I hang up before she can argue because standing in front of me is an entirely different version of the woman living in my house.

I was already finding it hard to resist Hattie, but this version will be impossible. Thankfully, it only makes me hate her more.

21

HATTIE

The way Bastion's looking at me makes me feel a certain type of way I've never felt before. Beautiful, sexy, desirable.

But as soon as that thought floats through my mind, I shut it down. I shouldn't be thinking things like this. Shouldn't be feeling them. It's not right.

"I wanted to see what you thought of this," I say.

His eyes practically devour me, sending goose bumps cascading down my arms and legs.

The clothes aren't sexy if you're looking at them on the hanger, but the black pencil skirt fits me like a second skin, and the white blouse dips down further than anything I've ever worn in my life. And I've never worn heels this high. I hope I don't break my ankle before getting used to them. It took all my nerve to come in here and get Bastion's approval.

"I think you look phenomenal."

His words caress my self-consciousness, and a smile blooms on my face. "Thank you."

His eyes continue to roam over me, and his gaze turns heated. Have I... have I turned Bastion on? The idea is both frightening and exhilarating.

"We'll go figure out another outfit, and I'll come show you."

He nods in approval, and when I turn to leave the room, I swear he groans.

Outfit after outfit, his reaction is the same. He expresses only his approval, and with each one, his looks grow more tense and passionate.

Or maybe I'm seeing what I want to see. Maybe I'm seeing things I subconsciously wish were happening and aren't. But by the time a few hours pass and we're saying goodbye to Ivy and her team in the foyer, I feel as if I might come out of my skin. It's not a sensation I'm used to. Not a sensation I've really had before.

After he closes and locks the condo door, Bastion turns to face me. "Happy with your new outfits?"

"Very, but I can't let you pay for them." I mean it, but truthfully, I know I can't afford any of the new items lining my closet. It was apparent from the designer tags and the fabrics that they're way above my pay grade.

"You can and will, Hattie. It's nonnegotiable." He steps past me and heads toward the kitchen.

"That must have cost you a small fortune. I'm sure I can find something on my own that can work. Why would you go to so much trouble for me?"

He grabs a bottle of sparkling water from the fridge and faces me. "Why wouldn't I?"

He says it as though it's a perfectly reasonable question.

"You don't owe me anything. We're only just getting to know each other."

Bastion shrugs and removes the cap from his drink. "That's reason enough, don't you think?"

"No." There's no other way for me to put it. No niceness I can add in. It's all so much, and the friendship I thought was blooming before I got here has changed.

Taking a sip of his drink, he steps closer. "I see something in you, Hattie. You're a good person, and I just want to help. Will you let me help you?"

With his free hand, he tucks a stray piece of hair behind my ear. My breath comes hard and fast as our eyes meet. Our gazes lock and hold, and I should look away, the tension building between us feels like a volcano set to erupt, but I can't bring myself to do it.

To my surprise, Bastion is the first to look away. "If you want to return the favor, you can come with me to an event next month. It's boring as fuck, but I have to go every year and would love the company of someone I enjoy spending time with."

Heat races up my neck and settles in my cheeks. I want to ask if it's a date or just a friend helping a friend. "Okay, you have yourself a deal."

He nods, and I return it before heading over to one of the cupboards to see if I can find something to drink. This cupboard has a bunch of powders and drink mixes. I tried a watermelon one the other day and thought it was pretty good, so that's probably what I'll have again. I peruse for a moment, but I don't see the watermelon one I was hoping for. Maybe Bastion finished it.

"Here." He steps up behind me and reaches over my head, grabbing something from the top shelf.

My breath catches when his pelvis brushes against me, and the scent of his cologne wraps around me like a warm hug. The heat from his body radiates into my back, and it's all so much.

Though I shouldn't want to, the urge to move back, just a little, is so great that I have to lock my muscles into place so I don't do anything stupid. I won't ruin this opportunity for my parents and me.

"I grabbed you some hot chocolate since I know you don't like coffee." His warm breath tickles my neck as he sets a canister of hot chocolate mix on the counter in front of me. It's even the one with marshmallows like I prefer.

I turn around to thank him but draw back from his closeness. The words die on my lips.

There can't be more than a few inches between us, but Bastion doesn't step back. I'm already against the counter, so he pretty much has me caged in. Not that I'm complaining.

"Thanks," I say in a hushed tone.

Once again, the tension between us pulls tighter and tighter, feeling in danger of snapping.

Bastion clears his throat and steps back. "I'm going to retire for the evening, but I was hoping I could steal some of your time this weekend. I'd like to show you around the city."

"That's nice of you, thank you. Saturday would work for me."

"It's a date then." He nods, turns, and leaves the kitchen.

I stare after him, knowing he didn't really mean the word date, but wishing he did.

Stupid, stupid Hattie.

The next day, I wear one of the outfits Bastion bought me to work, and he's right—I do feel much more comfortable walking through the doors of the club.

There's nothing super sexy about the white shorts and black blouse I'm wearing, besides the fact that the shorts are about six inches shorter than I've ever worn outside of bed, but it does come off as classy and sensual somehow, just like Ivy said.

I notice that some of the dancers I haven't met yet take the time to introduce themselves when I come across them in the kitchen or the bathroom that day, and they don't give me the once-over like everyone else did earlier in the week. It feels silly to think it's because of the clothes—I've never really given my wardrobe much thought before—but the outfit does change my attitude and makes me feel more confident than I would feel otherwise.

Feeling braver than normal, I decide to work a little later than I have been. I'm trying to finish up something before the weekend. But I need a little boost, so I go make myself a hot chocolate in the break room and decide that rather than drinking it alone in my office like I have been all week, I'll take a break in the main part of the club.

Maybe if I spend more time there, I'll realize it's not as big a deal as I'm making it in my head. Besides, I gave myself until the end of the week to decide whether I could hack this environment or not, so I have to know what I'm really getting into. I can't just hide from it and pretend it isn't happening.

I take my mug and find an empty table near the back of the club where I'm out of the way and hopefully no one will notice me. Destiny is up on stage. I met her earlier. When she told me her name, I didn't have the guts to ask whether it was her stage name or her real name.

All the men are watching her with rapt attention. There's even what appears to be a couple here, based on the fact that the man and woman are holding hands as they watch with delight.

Destiny gyrates to the music and slowly pulls off her shirt before dropping it on the stage. Her full breasts sway as she dances and makes her way to a set of stairs she uses to make her way into the crowd.

I sip on my hot chocolate, feeling uncomfortable watching this in a room full of strangers, but I force myself to remain where I am.

Several men holler at Destiny to come their way, holding up cash to make it more enticing. The first few slide the bills into her G-string, and she gives them a sultry smile in return. As I watch her, I can't help but wonder what it must feel like to be secure enough in yourself to command a room like this while half naked. What must it feel like to have that type of power, to know that all admiring eyes are on you?

Destiny moves to the other side of the room and has a short conversation with a man sitting at a table by himself. There's an exchange of money, and she lowers herself onto his lap, her back to his front.

So, that's a lap dance.

I've never seen one before, and my gaze is glued to them as she rocks her pelvis back and forth. He's lounged back in his chair, legs spread wide with a lazy grin on his face, clearly enjoying himself.

About halfway through the song, she straightens and turns around, straddling him so they're face-to-face. His hands are tucked into fists as if it's taking all his control not to touch her.

Destiny sets her hands on his shoulders and rocks her pelvis against his. My skin grows tight, and I hold my breath as I watch her simulate sex with him. Then she reaches for his face and brings it down between her breasts. She arches and flings her head back as though she's in the throes of ecstasy as she moves his face back and forth over her naked flesh.

I'm horrified, but worse than that, I'm turned on and unable to stand from my seat.

The space between my legs thrums, and I feel the distinct urge to shift and press my thighs together. As the notes in the song climb and climb, thrumming closer toward a crescendo, so do her movements. I, as well as the others, watch with rapt attention.

It's only when someone walks through my line of sight that I snap out of my daze. I blink slowly as if coming out of a stupor.

"What am I doing?" I bolt up from the table with my mug in hand and hurry across the expanse of the club to the relative safety of the door leading backstage.

My breaths come fast and quick as I hustle down the hallway to the office, rushing inside and closing the door behind me. Thankfully, Bastion isn't here.

What is happening to me? I was watching that man and that woman, and I was enjoying it. The thought of what my parents would say, what the people at my church would think, has bile racing up my throat. I swallow it back and collapse into my seat.

I was more than enjoying it. I craved more of the feeling watching them gave me. My body physically responded. I... I've never had that happen before. I may not be a virgin— something I hate to think about—but I've never felt arousal like that before.

This is exactly why my parents and the church warned me away from places like this. They're constantly testing you, and not everyone passes the test.

"I can't work here anymore."

I swivel my chair to face my computer. If I send Bastion an email with my resignation and thanking him for giving me a chance, maybe I can be out of here and packed and on a plane back to Wisconsin tonight.

I pull up my email to begin my resignation, but my gaze snags on the first email in my inbox—NOTICE OF DIRECT DEPOSIT. I open it to see that I've been paid for my first week of work, and my mouth falls open.

It's not that I didn't know how much this job paid, but seeing it in black and white hits different. This is practically what I made in a month at my old job.

My eyes close, and I slump back in my seat. This money could help my parents so much. And me—I could establish a real nest egg. Then in the future, if anything else happens with my parents, I'd be able to help them.

I don't know what to do. Will I become morally corrupt if I remain in this job? Is it selfish to quit when doing so won't let me help my parents? If they knew where I was really working, they'd tell me to be on the first flight home regardless of the fact that it would hurt them.

Then there's the idea of leaving Bastion... something about that doesn't sit well with me even though we're nothing more than colleagues and friends. And roommates for the time being.

When I think about him showing me around Seattle tomorrow, that bubble of excitement enlarges. Wasn't this what I wanted? To have a new adventure because I felt like something was missing in my life?

Maybe that's exactly why I've been led here. Perhaps it doesn't have to mean anything that I was aroused watching the show out there. Isn't that the whole point? I just won't expose myself to it again, and it will be fine.

I can still remain the Hattie I've always been, regardless of the temptation surrounding me.

There's a brisk knock on the door, then it whips open to reveal an attractive woman at least a decade my senior. She scowls at me. "Who the hell are you?"

22

BASTION

When I walk through the threshold to my office, I find Steph with her arms crossed and standing over Hattie, scowling at her. Hattie seems as though she's in the middle of explaining her role here.

"She's my assistant, Steph. Sorry, I'm late. I had to clear something up with our liquor distributor. Hattie, this is Steph. She's my eyes and ears at all the other locations. Steph, this is Hattie. She's helping me with the finances and whatever else I need."

Steph arches one of her manicured eyebrows at me, probably wondering if Hattie helps me in the same way that she does. Not yet, unfortunately. Especially after that fashion show the other day. Her new outfit is actually killing me today.

"Nice to meet you." It's clear from Hattie's voice that she's intimidated by Steph, and for some reason, that irks me.

"Hattie, why don't you take off for the day? You were here early."

She looks between Steph and me, then nods, grabbing her purse and phone before darting from the office. Once she's gone, I close the door and turn to give Steph an unimpressed look.

"What?"

"There's no reason to go around pissing on your territory, Steph, because it's not actually your territory—it's mine, remember?" I walk over and sit at my desk.

She rolls her eyes and sits in the chair on the other side. "If you'd given me a heads-up that you hired her, I wouldn't have been interrogating her when you walked in."

I steeple my hands on my desk. "Let's not pretend you wouldn't have."

She shrugs, lips pressed together. "My point still stands. You should have told me."

I lean back in my seat, arms crossed. "You work for me. You're only entitled to know what I choose to tell you. Now, I want to hear how it went this week. Any issues I need to deal with?"

She looks appropriately chastised before she launches into telling me what I need to know, and I relax a bit, hoping she won't cause Hattie any more grief.

When we finish our meeting, it's apparent to me that she's hoping I'll go lock the office door so we can have some fun, but I'm not interested. My mind is on only one thing right now—advancing my plan with Hattie. And with the way she ran out of here, I suspect I may have to do some damage control.

"Where are you planning to be next week?" I ask, getting up from my chair and making my way to the door.

"Los Angeles."

My hand closes around the door handle, and I pull it open, motioning that she can head out. "Great. Let me know how it goes."

She stands from her chair, looking as though maybe she's going to say something, but she must realize that her words will fall on deaf ears, because she simply nods and leaves.

I pass Steph in the hallway as she's talking to one of the dancers, and I can feel her watch me until I disappear from view. Steph better not be getting territorial on me now, or the two of us are going to have an unpleasant conversation.

I quickly make my way to my condo, then I confirm with Jeffery that Hattie arrived about twenty-five minutes ago.

When I enter the condo, Hattie isn't in the main area, so I head down the hall to her room. Her bedroom door is open, and several boxes are piled beside her dresser. She's sitting on the end of the bed with her shoulders sagging, staring down between her legs. Something is wrong. Something besides Steph's attitude toward her.

"I almost quit today." Her words come out soft and forlorn as I enter the room.

Fear spears me, sharp and swift. "Why?"

She raises her head and meets my gaze. There are tears in her eyes, which I should relish, but somehow they make me feel... protective. I push back that this whole thing is getting a little twisted and recenter myself on the plan.

"I don't want to tell you." Hattie looks away from me. "I'm ashamed."

I sit on the edge of the bed beside her. "What would you have to be ashamed about?"

"When I took a break today, I went out to the main room, and I was watching Destiny give a lap dance to one of the customers and it…" Her face crumples, and she squeezes her eyes shut. "It turned me on," she whispers.

Jesus. She's more innocent than I thought if being turned on causes her this much guilt. I have to wonder if this woman has ever even had an orgasm. Is she a virgin?

"That's nothing to be ashamed of." When she tries to look away from me, I place a finger under her chin and turn her head in my direction. "Hattie, that's what's supposed to happen. It's a biological response. A normal human response. You don't have to be ashamed of it." I keep my voice gentle, hoping she'll hear the truth in my words. Because I won't get anywhere with her if she thinks every time she's turned on, it's bad.

As much as I resent this woman, I hate that she was raised to think there's something wrong with her because of her sexuality and what she desires.

"You don't understand. My whole life I was taught that things like that, places like that are wrong. And now I work in one, and not only am I lying to everyone back home about it, but I'm starting not to hate it, not to think it's so terrible. I was *enjoying* it."

"Have you considered that a bigger issue might be if you hadn't?"

Her forehead wrinkles. "What do you mean?"

Here goes nothing. "I know that you were raised with certain beliefs, and I'm not here to tell you they're wrong. Not at all. But sexuality is a part of being human. Sometimes it's just for fun or pleasure, sure, and if that's not your thing, okay. But it's also a big part of expressing your feelings for someone you care about. It's not just about procreation." Taking a gamble, I place her hand over my heart. Her hazel eyes widen. "It's about connection and intimacy, knowing a person the way very few other people ever will. It's about giving and receiving pleasure. There's a reason it's called making love." I shake my head. "No one should ever feel guilty about that, so stop beating yourself up about it."

She lets out a shaky exhale, and I drop her hand from my chest. "I hear what you're saying, and on some level, I know you're right. I do. It's just so hard to push against the voice in my head because it's been there for a long time."

"You said you were going to quit. What changed your mind?"

"Originally, it was when I saw my pay stub in my inbox. But what really solidified it was those boxes." She motions to the small pile at the corner of the bed. "Those arrived today, and I was thinking back to when I was packing them. I was so excited to experience something new. Still nervous about how it would turn out, but I was open to new experiences, and it felt right. Coming here to discover a little bit of who I might be away from everything I know somehow seemed important, and I decided that I don't want to give that up just because I'm scared or ashamed or am having difficulty adjusting."

"So you're staying then?" Even I hear the hopeful thread to my voice. I tell myself it's just because I want to be able to carry out my plan, but I can't entirely push away the thought that I may be lying to myself.

She nods. "After my mom died, all I remember is how sad my dad was. I was young, but all I wanted was for him to be happy again, and it seemed like that was never going to happen. I worked so hard to make sure I was never a problem and never gave him anything to be upset about. Then Carla came into our lives, and I saw him start to come around. Then finally, he was like his old self. I didn't want to rock that balance, so I kept striving to be everything they wanted me to be, but I'm just now realizing that I never stopped to ask myself who *I* wanted to be."

The mention of my mother's name feels like shards of glass in my throat, and it takes me a moment to respond.

"You're a good person, Hattie." Despite myself, I mean the words. "But you can't live your life to please everyone else. You'll never really be happy that way. You need to be whoever is going to make you happy. And the only way to do that is to jump in and try new things and see how you feel."

She thinks over my words and nods slowly. "I think maybe you're right."

I squeeze her hand, rubbing my thumb back and forth. I don't miss the way she sucks in a breath.

"I look forward to seeing who you become." I'm unable to stop the grin that spreads on my face. I just hope it doesn't look too feral.

"Thank you for listening. You're really good at that."

"I'm here for you whenever you need me. In whatever capacity you need me." I keep rubbing my thumb over her knuckles and maintain our eye contact.

It would be so easy to kiss her. As our gazes hold, we both inch forward a bit. Her gaze dips to my mouth, and she licks her lips. We drift another inch closer, the rope between us taut with sexual tension.

Our lips are an inch apart when I wait for her to take the leap, then a buzzing sound rips through the sexual haze like cymbals crashing in an orchestra.

Hattie bolts up from the mattress, appearing a little frantic as she searches for her phone.

It's on the other side of me on the mattress, so I reach for it to pass it to her. The name Mom flashes on the screen.

She takes the phone from me and glances at it. "That's my mom. I'd better take it."

I stand stiffly, annoyed that Carla is fucking with my plan. Then again, maybe she did me a favor. When I was leaning in for that kiss, I wasn't at all thinking of the game I was playing with Hattie. I was motivated by pure animal instinct.

"I'll leave you be." I smooth my tie down my chest before I turn and leave the room.

Next week, it's time to move forward with my plans for Hattie, helping her discover who she can be out from under the confines of her never-ending morals.

23

HATTIE

By the time I fall into bed on Saturday night, I'm exhausted.

Bastion made good on his promise to show me around the city today. We went up to the top of the Space Needle, he took me to the Pike Place Market, and we had a private tour through the Museum of Pop Culture, which was really cool. It was a jam-packed day full of new and interesting things.

But the whole time, I couldn't stop thinking about our almost-kiss the day before. At least, that's what I think it was. I'm not the most skilled or experienced person when it comes to that sort of thing, but I swear if my mom's phone call hadn't interrupted us, we would have kissed.

What I'm still trying to sort out is how I feel about that.

In the moment, I only felt disappointed by the interruption. But that's horrible because he's my boss and much older and more experienced than I am. But then I think about what he said about discovering who I am without the confines of all the barriers I've grown accustomed to, and I feel disappointment again. My head is in a vicious cycle of wanting one thing, feeling bad about it, and then wanting it again.

Was Bastion right that sexuality is just a part of life and I owe it to myself to discover what role it plays in my own life without feeling ashamed?

I still hadn't figured it out by the time I went to bed, and what made it even more confusing was that Bastion had been completely platonic with me all day. Not that I want him to maul me in front of other people, but there was no sign of any attraction to me at all. Maybe he regretted what had almost happened, and for him, the phone call interruption was a good thing.

When my eyes snap open and the room is dark, it takes me a moment to realize what woke me. Then I hear it again— hoarse screams coming from down the hall.

Heart racing, I whip the covers off me and rush down the hallway. It sounds as if it's coming from Bastion's bedroom. I whip the door open.

Bastion's curtains are open, allowing some of the light from the city to filter into his room. It's dim, but I can make him out on the bed, thrashing around, the bed sheets twisted. His eyes are closed, and he's screaming, "No, no, no."

"Bastion!" I rush to the side of the bed and stand for a beat, unsure what to do.

Are you supposed to wake people up when they're having a nightmare? Will that make it worse?

But then he screams again, his face contorted as though he's being tortured, and I can't take seeing him in agony anymore.

I crawl over to him and place one hand on his shoulder to try to get him to stop moving and one on his cheek. "Bastion, wake up. You're having a nightmare." He fights me a bit, so I apply more pressure. "Bastion, wake up!"

His eyes pop open. At first there's a look of horror in his eyes, then he blinks and comes back to himself. His chest heaves up and down as he sucks in air and stares at me.

"You were having a bad dream."

"What... what are you doing in here?" His voice is hoarse as he slides up his bed to rest his back against the headboard.

Suddenly, I realize that I'm in bed with him and he's shirtless, wearing only his boxers. I can't help but admire the lean muscles of his body. When his eyes drag over me, I remember that I only wore an oversized T-shirt and a pair of underwear to bed.

"I'm sorry I barged in, but you were screaming. You were having a nightmare."

He scrubs a hand over his face. "Right, yeah. I remember now."

"Do you want to talk about it?" I run my hand down his cheek the same way my mom always does to me. I've always found the gesture comforting, and I'm hoping he might too.

He goes rigid, then closes his eyes and leans into the touch. "No, it's enough to relive it. I don't want to talk about it."

I frown, wondering what part of his past was traumatizing enough to cause that kind of nightmare. Pulling my hand away, I shift to move off the bed, but Bastion reaches for my wrist.

"Stay with me?"

My mouth goes dry. On one hand, I want to stick around to offer him comfort and make sure he's okay. On the other hand, I've never slept in the same bed as a man. But the lingering fear in his eyes has me nodding and moving closer to him.

I lie back on a pillow, and when he pulls the blankets back up from where they ended up at the end of the bed, I can't help but admire the muscles in his back. My nipples pebble under the cotton T-shirt, and I shift onto my side so that my back will be to him. I'm not here to ogle him.

I feel Bastion shifting into place behind me, getting comfortable, and his arm slides around my waist, pulling my back to his front. All the air in my lungs remains trapped there for a minute.

He moves his face into the crook of my neck. "Is this okay?"

I should tell him no, tell him I'm going back to my room. But I can't. It feels too good—both physically and emotionally—so I nod and relax into his hold.

Darkness sets in minutes later.

I wake up in almost the same position, except now I can feel the rigid length of Bastion's erection pushing against my underwear. I don't know what makes me do it, but I arch my hips.

He groans from behind me, and I still. "No, don't stop." His voice is rough with sleep.

When I realize I want to do it again, the familiar shame that comes with a realization like that pushes into my thoughts, but I force myself to ignore it. This is exactly what Bastion meant when he said I should feel comfortable exploring my sexuality and figuring out what it means to me.

And I want to. In this moment, I want to so badly.

I arch my pelvis again, and this time, he arches his hips into me. A low moan leaves my throat, and I slap a hand over my mouth.

Bastion's arm comes around me and pulls my hand away. "I want to hear every sound you make. Don't you dare censor yourself."

His words hit their mark when I realize that's exactly what I've been doing. For years, I've been censoring myself, rather than figuring out who I am.

I arch my hips again as Bastion trails his nose through my hair and the side of my neck. His hand comes to rest on my hip, and he squeezes, pulling me back into him. My heart is a bass drum, and my breathing comes out in fast pants.

"Will you let me make you feel good, Hattie?"

"I... I'm not going to have sex with you." After my experience with Rich, I'm far from ready for that.

"Who said anything about sex? I'm going to make you come without even putting anything in your pussy."

The vulgar words coming off his lips should disgust me,

have me running from his bed. But they have the opposite effect.

"Has a man ever made you come before?"

I shake my head. I may have had sex before, but I've never had an orgasm. Not even by my own hand. Every time I was brave enough to try, shame would arise, and I would stop.

"Let's see if we can remedy that, shall we?" Bastion's hand appears in front of my face. "Suck on my fingers."

Before I register his intent, he's pushing his index and middle fingers into my mouth. It takes a moment, but I do what he says, sucking gently on the two digits.

Bastion lets out a moan and bites gently on the curve of my neck while thrusting his hips into me. My breasts grow heavy, and the space between my legs aches. I arch into him some more, sucking on his fingers. He growls and pulls them from my mouth.

His hand comes to rest at the edge of my panties, and I hold my breath as the anticipation builds. Slowly, so slowly, he slides his hand under the waistband until it rests on my mound. He strokes the hair there. Every muscle in my body goes taut as I wait to see what he's going to do next, desperate for him to take me where he promised.

Finally, his fingers continue their journey, but instead of giving attention where I really need him, they slide further.

"Spread your legs, babe. Hook your top leg around the back of mine."

I do what he says, opening myself to him fully.

Bastion's fingers dip to my entrance, but he doesn't push them in. Instead, he rims the entrance with the tips of his fingers, applying just enough pressure to drive me wild but providing me no real relief.

"Bastion..."

"Yeah, babe? What do you want?" He nips my neck again.

"More..."

He speeds up his pace, and my hips gyrate with a will of their own. It's too much and not enough all at once. I feel as if I'm going to crawl out of my skin.

Bastion must know it too, because his deep chuckle rings in my ear, and he moves his fingers to exactly where I need them. He delivers the most primal pleasure with a circular motion of his fingers, and I'm unable to stop myself from moving against them.

"That's it. Take your pleasure, Hattie. Take what you want."

His words spur me on to do just that. I grind my pelvis against him, and my base need ratchets higher and higher. The feeling becomes so intense that I instinctively back away from it, stilling my movements.

"I don't think so," Bastion rumbles in my ear.

Then his fingers switch up their movement, applying more pressure, catapulting me toward the precipice. My hands instinctively grip his wrist, but he won't be deterred.

Every muscle in my body tenses, and my back bows. Fear grips me as a feeling I don't recognize takes over my body. I'm completely out of control, and it's terrifying and exhilarating.

Then Bastion hurtles me over the cliff, and the most intense feeling of bliss showers my entire body. I'm crying out, jerking in his arms as I spiral out of control.

I don't know what I do, what I say from there on, but when I come back to myself, I'm breathing heavily and Bastion is nuzzling my neck.

"Fuck, babe. That was something else."

The fog from my orgasm clears, and I take note of where I am, what I just did, and who I did it with. Despite my earlier success at pushing back the shame, it now coats me like a bucket of paint thrown over my head.

I don't know what to do, what to say, so I blurt out, "I should get up. I probably have to leave soon."

After untangling myself from Bastion's arms, I don't turn around to look at him before I bolt from the room.

Despite my panic, I'm pretty sure I don't regret what happened. How can something that feels that good be bad?

24

BASTION

Sensing that Hattie needs some space, I don't fight her when she leaves my bed. I blow out a breath and push my hand through my hair, staring at the ceiling.

That was... fuck.

It's not like I expected any of that to happen, though I've been planning to get us there since she arrived. The only reason I backed off yesterday was because after our almost-kiss on Friday night, I wanted her to feel what it was like not to have my attention. I wanted her to miss my affection so that when I again bestowed it on her, she'd be receptive.

I'd say that plan worked. Just as it always has with my conquests.

Maybe a little too well, because now I'm sitting here with a raging hard-on that I'm going to have to take care of myself.

No. I refuse to beat off with Hattie on my mind. That is not part of the plan.

I'm supposed to be seducing her, not the other way around.

But Jesus Christ, that was the hottest thing I've ever witnessed.

I've been with a lot of women, but none who gave themselves over to me like she did. It makes me want more—my face between her legs, my cock in her mouth, her cunt.

No, dammit, think of something else.

The remembrance of why she was in my bed floats through my mind then—the nightmare that was really more of a memory. I was nine and found my mom passed out in her own vomit, and I thought she was dead.

"Fuck that." I refuse to take a trip down memory lane.

I twist out of bed and stalk into my en suite, turning the cold water on in the shower. It's not until I'm exiting the shower five minutes later that I remember that Hattie brushed me off today.

She's new in this city. What the hell could she be up to?

Only one way to find out.

An hour later, my question is answered as I watch her disappear through the doors of a church a few blocks away from my condo building. I can't help but wonder if she already had plans to be here today or if this is a result of what happened this morning. Maybe she feels the need to confess her sins. God forbid she had an orgasm.

Since I have no desire to walk through those doors, I wait until the service is over for her to leave. It's clear the service is finished when groups of people make their way through the door and down the stairs, but Hattie doesn't come out. In fact, it's not until most people have left that she walks through the doors, making conversation with a man I'm guessing might be a couple years older than her.

She laughs at something he says, and my hands fist, my jaw setting. I'm even more annoyed when I realize that she appears relaxed with him. I only see that side of her sometimes. Lately, she's always on edge when she's around me.

They make their way down the steps together before saying their goodbyes and heading in opposite directions. I wait until she's far enough ahead that I won't be seen before I follow her.

She's definitely not headed back to the condo based on the direction she's going, unless she's forgotten her way back. But within a few minutes, it's clear she has a destination in mind when she pulls out her phone a few times to glance at it, as if checking her current location against the directions on the screen.

As I follow her, I tell myself that it's only because I need to know where her head is.

After a ten-minute walk, she looks at the sign over the door of an old brick building before entering. I don't slow my pace. I'm unable to see what this place is from this far, and I didn't walk all this way not to find out where she's going.

I draw closer and realize it's a soup kitchen for the homeless. She must be looking to volunteer here. Once I've passed the building, I continue walking, telling myself I've seen what I needed to see.

Still, for some reason, it's hard to walk away, to not wait outside until she reappears and see where she might go next. So instead, I'll do the next best thing—I'll go through her room at the condo and see what I might find.

A half an hour later, I'm going through the things she's unpacked, and the only interesting thing I've managed to find thus far is the book on her nightstand. This one is way smuttier than the one she was reading in Wisconsin, and when I see the price sticker from the airport bookstore, I figure she must've bought it on her way here.

I open the nightstand on one side of the bed and find spools of yarn and what I think are crochet needles. In the other drawer I find socks and... her underwear.

The sight makes my dick twitch. I'd forgotten that she doesn't wear plain cotton panties.

I think back to this morning. Though I didn't get to see them, they definitely weren't lace. I reach into the drawer and pull out a pair of silky maroon ones. They must've been like these because they were smooth.

My dick grows to a half chub, and I drop the underwear back in the drawer.

I need to maintain control here. I can't afford to let myself actually be attracted to Hattie. It would jeopardize my entire plan.

I slam the drawer shut, annoyed with myself for even having a reaction.

"I need to get out of here," I grumble.

I start for the door, but as I reach the threshold, I plant my hands on either side of the doorjamb. My head drops forward as I try to will myself out of the room, but my feet won't move.

Not until they spin around and hurry over to her closet. Yanking the hamper open, I grab the panties at the top of the pile—silk and lace hot pink panties—then I'm charging out of the room, heading straight to my own, and slamming the door behind me.

Before I consider my actions, I unfasten my jeans, shove them down my legs with my boxer briefs, and sit on the edge of my bed with my dick in one hand, Hattie's panties in the other. I bring the fabric up to my nose and inhale. My eyes practically roll back in my head. Fuck, I can't wait to taste her. God, I'm no better than her sleazy landlord back in Wisconsin.

My bottle of lube rests on the mattress beside me, and I squirt some down the length of my cock with my free hand, then fist the base. I stroke it, imagining Hattie's small hands doing the work, inhaling her scent once again.

I can imagine all I want, but it's not like it would be if Hattie were doing the work. Visions of the two of us and all the things I want to do to her swarm my head. She'd pack up and leave so fast if she had any idea the kinds of things running through my head.

Fuck, I wish she were here right now, touching me, torturing me with her wide-eyed innocence.

I wrap her panties around the base of my cock and use them to stroke my shaft. Looking down, I watch the bright pink lace and silk slide against my slick cock, and I grow even harder. My shaft twitches as my hand moves up and down the length, and I cup my balls and squeeze lightly.

My low groan rings out into the empty room, and I increase my rhythm. I imagine the panties currently stretched around my girth on Hattie's body, pressed up against her cunt, and the tingling starts in the base of my spine.

I grip my cock harder, imagining Hattie wearing them and only them, bending over in front of me so I can get a peek of what I know will be her pretty pink pussy through the lace, and my dick gets impossibly hard before I bring the fabric up to the head and come on a roar. My orgasm just keeps coming, feeling almost never-ending.

Once I've spilled everything I have onto the pink silk and lace, I unwrap them from around my length, pull open the top drawer of my nightstand, and toss them in. Hattie won't be getting them back. It's not as though she'd ever ask me if I knew where they were anyway, so she'll be left to wonder.

Then I go into my en suite and have my second cold shower of the day.

25

HATTIE

Around dinner on Sunday evening, I finally work up the nerve to return to the condo. I did have plans to check out a church service before anything happened between Bastion and me this morning, but I may have prolonged my time away on purpose.

After service, I got to talking with some of the church members, and they mentioned a soup kitchen nearby where a lot of the members volunteer. I've always enjoyed volunteering, and I've noticed in my short time here that Seattle seems to have a lot of homeless people who could use some help, so I figured I'd check it out and see if I could be of service.

When I was done there, it was a beautiful summer day, so I decided to walk around and explore the areas I haven't been to yet. That left me a lot of time to think, and the only conclusion I've come to is that I don't regret what happened between us, but I also don't know if anything like that should happen again.

Fooling around with Bastion has the potential to mess up my job and my living situation if things go sideways. At the same time, that orgasm this morning awakened something inside me. Some part of me was slumbering, just waiting to come out.

All afternoon, all I could think about was what happened. I must have replayed what we did in my mind about a hundred times. And then I imagined other things we might do together. Other things Bastion might help me explore.

He's not the ideal candidate—what with him being my boss—but the thought of doing anything like what we did with someone else doesn't have the same appeal. Which leaves me in a predicament—do I ignore how I feel and keep Bastion at arm's length, or do I opt for more with him and risk losing the job and salary that my family needs?

I press the code into the keypad beside the condo door and step inside. Though I hoped I'd be able to make it to my room without seeing Bastion, he's in the main living area and watching a baseball game on TV. I'm not sure why I find it so unusual. Maybe because we're rarely on the same schedule, and I never witness him casually doing something he enjoys.

"I got you some food when I ordered. It's on the counter," he says, his eyes never straying from the television.

"Thanks." I make my way into the kitchen and see that he got takeout from the Italian place I like down the street.

My pasta dish is lukewarm, so I spoon it into a bowl and put it in the microwave. When it beeps to signal it's ready, I take out my food and walk around the large island, then stop, looking between the table on the opposite side and the living area where Bastion is.

"I won't bite," Bastion says, still looking at the TV but somehow knowing what's happening in my head behind him.

With a sigh, I walk over and sit on the couch with him.

"Not like I did this morning." He turns his head and meets my gaze.

It takes me a beat to catch his meaning, then visions of him biting the curve of my neck this morning come to the forefront of my mind. My cheeks heat, and I bury my head into my pasta.

"I take it from the way you've avoided this place that you regret this morning?" There's no bite to his tone, but I still worry I've offended him in some way.

My head whips back in his direction. "No."

He arches an eyebrow in challenge.

"I don't regret it, it was... I'm just not sure it's wise for anything like that to happen again."

"Because you're ashamed?" Bastion's tone turns to almost hurt.

I shake my head, moving my plate from my lap onto the coffee table. "Because you're my boss, and I'm staying here right now, and you're so much older than me, and you're so much more experienced than me, and..." I trail off before the truth of what scares me the most leaks out.

Bastion leans closer. "And what, Hattie?"

"Nothing." I will my face to remain neutral.

"Bullshit. What were you going to say?"

My legs bounce as I consider whether I should share with him my biggest source of shame.

He places his hand on my knee, preventing it from moving, and squeezes. "I won't judge you. I hope you know that." The truth rings through his words, clear as a bell.

If I tell him, maybe he'll understand where I'm coming from. "I went to a religious college, and I met a guy there named Rich. We dated for a few years, and he was raised within the church like I was, so we held similar values, so we never... you know."

"Fucked?" Bastion deadpans.

I nod. "Right, that. But in our last year, he pressured me to sleep with him. He said he loved me and that we were going to be together forever anyway, so what was the big deal? I loved him, and I wanted to make him happy, so over time his demands wore me down, and I agreed as long as he promised to never tell anyone else. I was swept up in what I thought we had, what I thought he felt for me."

Bastion squeezes my knee, somehow sensing that this next part is the most painful to say out loud.

"After we slept together the first time, that's all he wanted to do. We barely went out on dates after that, and it began to feel like that's all I was to him—a vessel for his sexual release. About six weeks after we first slept together, I caught him talking to a friend of his about me." My chest squeezes painfully even after all these years. "He was telling him all about how we'd slept together, all the details, bragging almost. But the worst part was when his friend asked him if we'd still get married, Rich said that there was no way. The kind of woman he wanted to marry wouldn't give it up before marriage. He wanted someone pure of heart *and* body."

I squeeze my eyes shut as the familiar shame and pain lance through my body. "It felt like that was my punishment for sleeping with him before we were married. I went against what I knew was right, and I suffered the consequences. Maybe if I hadn't let him talk me into it, I would've passed the test and we'd be married now."

When Bastion doesn't say anything, I open my eyes to look at him. His face is burning with pure disdain, enough so that I shrink back from him.

"Hattie, it wasn't God punishing you. You were just dating a piece of shit. Nothing more, nothing less. Did you ever stop to think that if God was involved, maybe he was saving you, showing you what kind of man this Rich guy really was so that you didn't end up married to him for the rest of your life?"

I blink several times. Not once had that thought occurred to me. Not once. I was so quick to soak in the shame and blame that I didn't even stop to think it could be anything else. What if Bastion's right and everything that went down wasn't about punishing me for sinning, but to lead me toward the right path?

"I've never thought of it that way." My voice is a whisper, and I look down at my lap, trying to make sense of my thoughts.

"I believed in Rich, and he turned out to be a liar and a manipulator. I don't trust myself to make the right call. That's why I haven't dated anyone since we broke up. I didn't want to make the same mistake again and be hurt like that. Feel like that."

Something flashes across Bastion's face, some emotion I can't quite grasp before it's gone. "I'm not Rich. I'm not going to use you for my own pleasure and then judge you for it." He looks as though there's something else on the tip of his tongue, but he doesn't say it.

I meet his gaze. "I believe you."

"Anything that happens between us will be your decision. I'm not going to pressure you into something you don't want to do. It *needs* to be your choice."

"I don't know what I want right now. I think I need a day or two in order to clear my head."

There's no irritation on Bastion's face. He merely squeezes my knee again before letting go and shifting away from me. "Then that's what you'll get." He turns his attention toward the TV again. "Do you like baseball?"

"I don't not like it."

He chuckles. "All right then, stick around and let's see if I can make a fan out of you."

I pick my plate back up and set it on my lap, the pasta likely lukewarm again. "Okay, let's see what you can do."

"Is that a challenge?" He glances at me, his blue eyes glittering with amusement.

I shrug. "Maybe."

"Careful, Hattie. There's nothing I like more than a challenge. You should know I always play to win."

26

———

HATTIE

$\mathcal{B}$y the end of the following week, I'm strung tighter than a bow. It's not a feeling I'm used to. Not at all. I've never craved physical intimacy with anyone before, but with every day that passes, the feeling gets worse. Memories of Bastion's fingers and the way they worked expertly run like a loop through my head. I can almost understand why Rich's attitude changed so much after the first time we had sex. I've been completely preoccupied, and I haven't even had sex with Bastion.

It doesn't help that I can feel his gaze on me throughout the day while I work. Sometimes I push my thighs together in an attempt to ease the ache. The looks he gives me are enough to make me want to flick the lock on his office door and beg him to give me another orgasm.

I could put an end to my suffering by just telling Bastion that I want to explore some more with him, but I need to be sure. I can't compromise my parents' future for sexual satisfaction. It wouldn't be worth it in the long run.

We haven't talked in depth about it, but Bastion isn't offering me a long-term relationship full of love and romance, that much is clear. There will be an expiration date, of that I have no doubt. The question is, can I handle sex with no strings? That's something I'm still trying to figure out.

I shut down my computer and stand from my desk, smoothing the front of my dress, aware that Bastion is watching me with a heated stare.

"I'm done for the day. I'll see you back at the condo?" I pull the strap of my purse over my head to lay crosswise over my chest.

"I'll see you there."

True to his word, Bastion hasn't pressured me at all. It's clear that if I want more to happen, I have to be the one who initiates it. Though he makes it obvious enough what he wants with the way he looks at me. Something that is secretly thrilling me.

I leave the office without another word and make my way down the hall. Renee walks out of the changing room with Paige, who I've only talked to once before, but she seemed nice.

"Hattie, are you done for the day?" Renee asks, and I stop walking.

"Yup, what about you guys?"

"Nah, we're just going to grab something to eat before it gets really busy out there. Do you want to join us?" Renee's expression is open as she waits for me to respond.

When I look between her and Paige to see what she thinks of this, Paige is smiling too. "Come with us. We're just going to a poke bowl place down the street."

I can just imagine what Taylor would say if she knew I was going to go out for dinner with a pair of strippers. But I don't have any friends in Seattle, and these women have been nothing but kind to me.

"Okay, sure. I'd love to."

I'm mostly quiet on the walk over to the poke bowl place, my sudden bravery failing me when I realize I'm going to have to sit through an entire meal and hold a conversation. I'm always so nervous that I won't know what to say or that I'll say something stupid that I tend to just sit there and say nothing. But I can't do that this time, so I tell myself I must make an effort no matter how uncomfortable it makes me.

I figured it would be a takeout place, but it's actually an all-you-can-eat restaurant. You just tell the waitress what you want in your bowl.

When the waitress asks what we'd like to drink, Renee and Paige order a lime cooler. I was going to ask for a fruit drink, but now I feel like I'll look like a child. I've never had alcohol except for half a glass of wine during holiday dinners. But I don't want to stick out. It's already apparent how different I am from everyone else at The Black Orchid. I don't need something else to make it even more obvious.

"I'll have the same as them," I tell the waitress and let her know what I'd like in my bowl.

"How are you liking Seattle?" Renee asks once the waitress leaves to grab our drinks.

"I really like it so far. At first it was a little overwhelming because I'm not used to being in a city this big, but I went exploring over the weekend, and I'm liking it more and more."

"Did you come from a small town?" Paige asks.

Nodding, I say, "I moved here from Wisconsin."

Luckily, neither of them asks why I moved here. I'm not sure what I would've said. Hopefully they just assume I'm another small-town girl looking for adventure in the big city.

"Are you both from Seattle?"

Paige nods. "I grew up in the suburbs."

The waitress arrives with our drinks and sets one in front of each of us.

"I'm originally from Oregon. I moved up here after my baby daddy decided he wasn't into the whole parent thing," Renee says. "Figured there were better job prospects here than where I'm from."

I frown. "He just left you and your son?"

"Yup. Went to work one day and never came back. Piece of shit."

I pick up my drink and take a small sip, prepared to have to school my expression at how bad the cooler tastes, but it's actually really yummy.

"I'm sorry that happened to you." I don't know Renee well, but I feel terrible for her. She must have been so scared.

She shrugs in an "it is what it is" way.

I take another sip of my cooler as Paige says, "I started when I was in college. My family couldn't afford to help me financially, and it seemed like a good option. I didn't want to leave school saddled with debt. After I graduated, the money was better at the club than it would have been in the field I studied in, so I decided to stick around." She brings her drink to her lips. "I can't do it forever, obviously, but I have my degree now. I can always fall back on that."

"What did you take in school?"

"English and creative writing. I wanted to be a reporter."

When the waitress arrives to deliver our bowls and asks if anyone would like another drink, I realize that I've finished mine. That's probably why I feel so light and happy right now.

Renee holds up her hand. "One-drink limit when we're on the clock, but you go ahead, Hattie."

The waitress turns to look at me. I should probably say no, but... "Yes, another one please."

She nods and goes to check on another table.

"Is the one-drink limit your rule?" I ask.

Paige shakes her head. "Bastion's. There's a strict no drinking or drugs policy while you're working, which I understand. Before I landed at The Black Orchid, I worked with some girls who could only get out on stage if they were fucked up."

My head tilts. "Do you guys ever feel self-conscious when you're out there?"

"I used to," Renee says. "Then you realize pretty quickly that women are their own biggest critics, and most men are just happy to see a naked woman—doesn't matter the size or shape."

"I could never do it. I don't have the same level of self-confidence that you guys do." I laugh, and I think it might be a little too loud because a few of the guests at surrounding tables turn to look.

The waitress returns with my drink and our meal. We thank her and dig into our food.

"You could totally do it. You've got that doe-eyed innocent thing going on. Men love that." Renee spoons the contents of her bowl.

"Agreed. You'd clean up out there," Paige says with a smile.

"No way." I shake my head and pick up my drink for another sip.

"How do you like working for Bastion?" Renee asks.

Is she asking because she knows something? My eyes widen, and I look at my bowl, shoving some food into my mouth to buy myself some time.

When I'm done chewing, I look back at them. "He's easy to work for." I pick up my drink and down a couple of gulps as more nerves set in.

"He's easy to look at," Paige says, and she and Renee devolve into a fit of giggles.

"C'mon, Hattie, don't tell us you haven't noticed," Renee says.

I shrug. "I mean, I guess."

"He's totally hot," Paige says.

Renee sighs dramatically. "Too bad he doesn't shit where he eats."

"Except with Steph." Paige rolls her eyes before taking another forkful from her bowl.

I stiffen in my seat. "What do you guys mean?" Though I try to keep my voice light, I don't know if I succeed. I'm starting to think that maybe I'm a little tipsy from these drinks.

Renee leans over the table a bit. "Bastion has this rule about not sleeping with any of his employees. But we all think he and Steph have hooked up."

I bring the cooler to my lips again, trying to wash down the bad taste left in my mouth by her words. "Why do you think that?"

Paige shrugs. "Just a vibe we get. She always acts territorial about him. It's annoying as fuck, actually."

"Totally," Renee says before taking another mouthful of her poke bowl.

"Have you met her yet?" Paige sips her own drink.

"Yeah. Just briefly, though." I push the contents of my bowl around with my fork.

"And how was she?" Paige arches a perfectly plucked brow.

"Kind of how you said." I frown.

"See? They're totally fucking." Paige shakes her head.

Renee changes the topic, and though I relax as the conversation flows naturally from one topic to another, at the back of my mind, all I can think about is Bastion and Steph.

Are the girls right? Is he sleeping with her? If he is, what does what we did mean? Does he mess around with multiple girls at once? Maybe that's what most people do. How would I know?

By the time we're done eating, I'm fired up and maybe a bit jealous of Steph. I finish the last of my second cooler and slam the bottle on the table harder than necessary based on the way Renee and Paige startle in their seats.

Who does this Steph think she is? It all makes sense now why she was so snippy and clearly trying to make me feel like an idiot the night I met her. Well, too bad for her. She can't have him. And I'm going to tell Bastion exactly that.

Why am I so worried about messing around with Bastion because he's my boss when apparently he's already messing around with another one of his employees?

"You guys ready to head back?" Renee asks.

"Yup." I jolt up out of my seat, eager to get back to the club so I can confront Bastion. Once I'm standing, I wobble a bit and have to grip the edge of the table.

"Whoa, girl. I think those drinks might have gone right to your head." Paige comes around the table and grips my elbow.

"I've never really drank before." I grin at them, then devolve into a fit of giggles.

I think they share a look before Renee says, "You've never had alcohol before?"

"Nope." I pop the "p" on the word.

"Oh boy. If I'd known that, I would've slowed you down." Renee leads the way out of the restaurant.

Paige and I follow, her supporting me by my elbow.

Once we're outside, Paige says to me, "Are you okay to walk on your own?"

"Of course." I pull my elbow from her grip and head in the direction of the club.

"Do you want us to take you home?" Renee asks.

"No!" The two of them look at me from my panicked reply, but I can't let them know I live with Bastion. "I'm going back to the club. There's something I have to do there." I start walking again.

Renee comes up alongside me. "I'm not sure you're in the best shape to work right now. Bastion might have a fit if he sees you."

"This won't take long. He won't be the wiser." The more I walk, the easier it gets. I can totally do this.

"Hattie, I—" Paige starts, but I cut her off when I raise my hand.

"It's fine, really. You guys worry too much." Then I laugh, though I'm not even sure why.

It doesn't take us long to reach the club, and when we enter, I see that it's busier than when we left. I say a quick goodbye to the girls as they peel off to enter the changing room, and I continue down the hall to Bastion's—*our* office.

The door is open, and he's in there, leaning against the side of his desk, looking at his phone in his hand. He looks up when he hears me close the door, and I waste no time walking straight over to him.

"I want you to show me what I've been missing."

He says nothing, setting his phone on the desk beside him. "Is that so?"

"Are you fucking Steph?" I put my hand over my mouth, surprised about the swear word that came out of it.

Bastion's eyes widen. "Not presently. Right now, I'm here with you."

My hands fist at my sides. "But you have."

He doesn't skirt his gaze away when he answers. "Many times."

A sound akin to a growl escapes my throat.

"Are you jealous?"

I ignore his question. "I thought that you didn't sleep with the women who work for you?"

He shrugs, and something about the casual rebuff makes my blood burn. "I don't sleep with the dancers. Steph is different."

I step closer to him. "Because you care about her?"

He straightens up from the desk, and I arch my head back to

look up at him. "Because I don't, and she understands that I never will."

I'm not sure whether to like or dislike his statement. "Is that how it would be with us?" I move even closer to him, my chest brushing his with each intake of breath.

"You tell me." His eyes devour me, and I love that they do.

"It would be safest."

"Is that what you want? Safe?" Bastion brings his hand up to rest on the curve of my waist, and my nipples pebble in my bra.

"It used to be what I wanted." I'd do anything to avoid the pain I felt after Rich. But do I really think I can mess around with Bastion and not develop feelings for him? I'm still unsure.

"And now?"

"Now I just want you." I wrap my arms around Bastion's neck, and he brings his lips down to mine.

He slips his tongue along the seam of my lips, and I open to him, wanting more than anything to taste him. I melt into him and experience a kiss I never have before. I'm lost in the bliss of him. His scent, his moans, his strength—until two strong hands grip my upper arms and push me away.

It takes a moment for my alcohol-soaked brain to catch up. "What?"

"You've been drinking." Disapproval shines in his formerly lust-filled eyes.

A scowl forms on my face. "So what? You're judging me?"

"Not at all. But I'm not going to take this any further with you inebriated. I need to know that this is really what you want. You *need* to know it's what you want."

"Yes, so you've said a few times. Do you want me to beg?" I drop to my knees harder than intended, clasping my hands in front of me. "There, are you happy? I'm on my knees, begging you."

He blows out a breath and pushes a hand through his hair. "In all the times I pictured you on your knees in front of me, Hattie, it was never like this. Jesus." He hauls me up under the arms. "Come on, I'm taking you home to sleep this off. We can talk about this tomorrow night."

I pout and intend to argue, but my head feels a little fuzzy as he leads me toward the door.

"Where were you drinking anyway?" He pulls the door open and leads me down the hall with one hand on my upper arm.

"At dinner with Renee and Paige," I say cheerily.

"I'll be sure to thank them." I can just make out the note of disapproval in his tone over the music as we make our way out to the main part of the club.

"Please don't get them in trouble. They're my only friends here. They didn't know that I've never drank before." I stop and spin around, reaching for the lapel of Bastion's suit. "Please, promise me."

He studies me for a moment, and in the dim light, his face bathed in the glow of the neon lights, he looks like a god. Not my God, but one that promises damnation rather than salvation.

Bastion holds my stare for a minute, then gives me a curt nod. I drop my hands from his suit jacket, and he spins me around to continue toward the door. The entire walk back to the condo, he doesn't say a word to me. I can't tell if it's because he's angry with me or what.

But once we're inside the condo, he says, "Go get changed for bed."

I don't know why I don't argue with him, but the thought doesn't even occur to me. I'm not in my bed more than a minute before I'm out.

27

BASTION

I sit on the edge of Hattie's bed, staring at her sleeping form. I could've had her tonight. She was primed and ready. But I refuse to take her for the first time when she's drunk. When she realizes who I really am, when Carla knows what I've done with her daughter and the path I've led her down, they both need to know that she chose it willingly.

It's a shame Hattie is who she is. Otherwise, I could really enjoy our time together. That's not to say I'm not going to enjoy fucking her, but there's always that nagging reminder at the back of my head that she got everything I was supposed to have.

The dichotomy of the two ways of thinking is fucking with my head. I find myself forgetting what she's really doing here, obsessing about her when she's not around. Jesus Christ, I even jerked off with her underwear.

I blow out a breath and shake my head, forcing myself to walk out of the room. There's no way I can afford to let

Hattie become anything other than what she is—a means to an end.

The following evening, I arrive home earlier than I normally would on a Friday night so that Hattie and I can have a conversation about the previous night. She mostly ignored me at work today, only speaking to me when spoken to, and I don't plan on letting her pretend nothing happened. Not when it puts me that much closer to my goal.

Alcohol might have been the mechanism that got her to open up, but I don't doubt for one moment that she meant every word.

As I make my way toward the kitchen, the distinct scent of garlic reaches me. There's music playing in the background —some kind of indie stuff, I think.

When I turn the corner, I find Hattie at the island, sprinkling cheese on what looks to be a lasagna. She startles when she sees me.

Now this is the kind of reaction to me she would have had when we met if she'd had any kind of self-preservation.

"You scared me." The hand on her chest moves up and down with her breaths.

"What are you doing?" I walk over to where she is, admiring her ass in the tight-fitting cream skirt. She hasn't changed since she returned from work, and I, for one, am thankful.

She looks away from me, her tell that she's embarrassed. "I didn't realize you'd be home so early. It's not ready." She rips some foil from the package on the counter beside her and places it over the lasagna pan, then turns and places the pan in the center of the wall oven.

"Why are you making lasagna? You could have ordered in."

She turns and goes back to the island, beginning to clean up her meal prep. "I wanted to apologize for last night." She still hasn't looked at me.

"Why would you need to apologize?" I step closer to her.

"I practically ambushed you because I was tipsy."

"I think you may have been drunk." Another step moves me right behind her with only an inch to spare.

She laughs low, but it's a nervous laugh. "Maybe. I always thought alcohol must taste terrible, but those coolers were like candy."

"Don't try to change the subject, Hattie. We were talking about you wanting me to fuck you last night." I place my hand on her waist and tug her back, forcing her to feel the turgid length of my cock pressing against my dress pants.

She sucks in a breath but doesn't say a word.

"Did you mean what you said?"

She nods.

"Words, Hattie."

"Yes, I meant it. But I shouldn't have forced myself onto you."

I grind my hips into her, and she leans her head back into my chest. "Babe, if you hadn't been drinking, I would've had you bent over my desk with your pussy wrapped around my cock so fast your head would spin."

Hattie arches his hips into me, and I groan at the press of her against my hard length.

"Is that what you still want?"

She nods. "Yes." Her answer feels like triumph through my veins.

"Then you'll get it. But not tonight."

"What?" She tries to turn around, but I keep her where she is by pressing my hips forward so she's pinned between the counter and me.

"I appreciate the lasagna, but what I really want is to taste you." Reaching down, I gently pull up her pencil skirt until it sits around her waist, then I step back. With one hand on either side of her hips, I slide down her blue silk panties. My hand moves to my groin, and I squeeze the head of my erection while I admire her bare ass. "Don't move."

Fuck, it's so perfect I want to take a bite out of it.

"Are you sure you want to go down this road with me?"

I watch from behind as her head moves up and down. "Yes." Her hands grip the edge of the counter.

"Put your arms in front of you across the counter."

She does as I say, and I groan, squeezing my cock again. Then I step up to her. With one hand on either side of her hips, I lift her so that her hips are at the edge of the counter, her feet dangling below.

"Is that comfortable enough?"

Her cheek lies against the counter when she nods, and I see the slight tremor in her hands.

"Try to relax. You're going to enjoy this." I don't even have to ask to know that she's never been eaten out before.

My hand trails a path down her back and over the curve of her ass as I lower to my knees. Then with one hand on each of her ass cheeks, I spread her. She's already glistening with arousal, and my mouth waters for a taste.

As I lean in and take the first swipe with my tongue, some part of me celebrates the fact that I'm the first one to ever do so. I'm the only one on this earth who knows how this woman tastes. Hattie's body jolts under my tongue, and I press her against the counter to keep her in place.

"Such a pretty pussy. How long do you think it will take me to make you come? Should I draw it out, or take it easy on you?"

"Please, Bastion…"

"Please what?" I use my tongue to play with her clit.

She moans. "Please, please make me come."

The desperation in her words undoes some of my control, and I lean in, devouring her, unable to get enough of her sweet taste. I fuck her entrance with my tongue for a bit, then return to her swollen bud. Her breaths grow heavier, her moans louder.

I make a few swipes with my tongue through the whole of her sex, stopping the last time to pay extra attention to her puckered hole. Hattie's hand slaps the counter in response, but she doesn't tell me to stop.

"You like that, do you?" I murmur against her skin. "Maybe if you're lucky, I'll fuck this ass one day."

She presses her swollen sex farther back into my face, and my deep chuckle sounds against her wet flesh. I tongue her slit before I trace her entrance, then I slowly, so slowly, push my finger in an inch, then another.

She's tight. God, she's so fucking tight I can't stand it. All I can think about is how she'd feel wrapped around my cock.

As I rock in and out of her, my tongue flicks her clit again and again and again. Hattie cries out, almost there. When I suck hard on her clit, she shouts my name, her pussy clamping down and contracting around my finger.

As much as I don't want to, I pull myself from her and use both hands on her ass to keep her in place as I continue to suck on her clit while she rides out her orgasm. When I pull away, Hattie doesn't move, remaining splayed in front of me, her cunt glistening. I commit the vision to memory, knowing I'll revisit it shortly when I jerk off.

"Did you enjoy that as much as I did?" I wipe my mouth and chin with the back of my hand.

She starts moving, so I help her off the counter, letting her find her footing before I let go of her waist. Her eyes are glazed when she turns to face me, and there's a lazy smile on her face. Gone is the tight-laced, friendly, yet professional veneer she usually displays.

"Yes, that was..." She shakes her head, almost as though she's in disbelief. "I didn't know it could be like that."

I tug her into my chest by the waist. "I have so much more to show you."

Then I bend and bring my lips to hers for our first real kiss since I'm not counting the one last night. She comes willingly and opens to me when my tongue runs across the seam of her mouth. Then she stills, likely tasting herself on my tongue. I don't let her retreat, pulling her body in closer to mine and devouring her mouth like I just did her pussy.

When I pull away, her eyes are even more glazed. She runs her hand down my chest, but before she can reach my belt, I grasp her wrist.

"I think that's enough for one night."

I'd give anything to plunge into her right now, but patience is key. I'm still afraid that if I press her too hard, she'll pull away. I need her craving more.

She frowns. "Why?"

"Because I don't think we should do any more tonight. Let you process what's already happened."

"But don't you..." She nods toward the raging hard-on that looks as if it's about to rip a seam in my pants.

"I'll take care of myself." Without thinking, I kiss her forehead as a token of affection.

It's not the act itself that makes me step away from her. It's the fact that it *wasn't* part of an act to get her to trust me. I just did it because it felt right.

"I'm gonna go shower." Before she can say anything, I back away and turn toward the hall.

It's an effort to slow my pace so it doesn't appear as if I'm running away.

28

HATTIE

On shaky legs, I slide my panties back on and pull down my skirt.

I'm glad Bastion pushed me away last night because I would not have wanted to experience that without being completely sober.

I thought the other morning in his bed was life-changing, but this... this was something else entirely. Between the sensation of his tongue, the sounds slipping out of him, and the ownership he took, I was breathless. I didn't even know it could be like that, feel that primal, as though I might die if he stopped before granting me my release.

But why did he want to stop there? I understand his reasoning, but I don't like the idea of him walking away unsatisfied. I'm not sure what kind of a job I would do with my mouth on him, but I'd like to try so he can feel what I just did.

He's the one who told me to own my sexual desires and explore them, and here he is walking away.

Harnessing my courage, I head down the hall.

When I knock on his bedroom door, there's no answer. I slowly open the door and take a few steps inside. "Bastion?"

He's nowhere to be found, so he must already be in the shower. A quick glance at the light casting into his room from under the partially closed en suite door tells me I'm right.

I turn to leave, to grant him his privacy, but I stop. His words —*take what you want*—ring through me again. What if I joined him in the shower? Would he really turn me down if I did?

My chest tightens at the thought of going in there and being rejected, but before I can talk myself out of it, I unzip my skirt, dropping it to the floor with my underwear. Next to go is my shirt, then my bra. Before I can think better of my decision, I'm padding across the floor toward the en suite.

This is what I wanted, isn't it? To explore who I am, what I want, what I like? If that's the case, then I need to be brave and take risks I normally wouldn't.

Drawing in a deep breath, I slowly push open the bathroom door. But I never prepared myself for what I'd see.

Bastion is inside the massive walk-in shower, and though the glass is fogged, his silhouette is visible. I can still make out the rhythmic movement of his hand and what he's holding. It's not that he didn't warn me he would do exactly this, but seeing the effect of what we did, how desperate it made him, gives me a powerful feeling I've never felt before.

When I make it halfway across the room, Bastion's head whips in my direction. His palm wipes across the glass, removing most of the condensation. His eyes widen the closer I draw.

I force my legs to keep moving. Force my mind not to ponder what he might be thinking at seeing me completely nude for the first time.

"What are you doing?" His voice is as rough as the water in the bay last week during the thunderstorm.

"I want you to show me." I step through the opening into the shower. It's so large that I remain outside of the spray.

My gaze dips down. I've never seen a naked man like this before, but I know that no other man can be as beautiful as Bastion. The lean muscles covering his body, the trail of dark hair that leads from his belly button down to where his hand holds his thick erection.

"Show you what?" His forehead creases.

"How to do what you're doing." I walk toward him, staying just out of the spray of the water. "How to please you."

When Rich and I had sex, we never tried anything else. I never touched his penis. I laid there underneath him while he took his pleasure, and when he was done, he'd kiss me before rolling off of me. I thought that was what sex was, something you got through for him, that women didn't get the same pleasure a man did.

Now that I know that's not the case, I realize there's mutual pleasure to be shared, and so far, the balance between the two of us has been weighted in my favor. I want to know that I can deliver as much pleasure to Bastion as he does to me.

His hand slips from his length, and he crooks his finger. "Come here."

I do as he says, stepping under the spray, and the hot water runs down my back.

Bastion's eyes track down to my breasts, and his chest heaves slightly with his breaths. My nipples tighten into hard peaks and my breasts grow heavy because I love his reaction when he looks at me. God, I want him to touch my breasts, but this isn't about me right now. He swallows hard and brings his gaze back up to meet mine.

He takes two steps back so that he's completely out of the spray of water and points in front of him. "Get on your knees."

I walk forward and do what he says, lifting my chin to look up at him.

"Now wrap your hand around the base." He lovingly pets the top of my hair and down the side of my face, tilting my head as he studies me. "I knew I'd enjoy the sight of you on your knees, wrapping your hand around my cock." He groans when I grip him harder. "That's it, a little harder, then stroke me."

I look away from his intense gaze, fascinated by how soft his shaft feels, yet at the same time, how hard it is. He's thick— my fingers can't touch when I grip him, but it doesn't seem to lessen his satisfaction. He groans again and slides his fingers into my hair.

"Now go all the way up, and when you get to the head, twist your hand a bit." I do as he instructs and his head rocks back for a second. "That's it, just like that."

His eyes are closed, his mouth open. I have a vague memory of thinking he looked like a god last night in the club with the neon lights on his face, but now, like this, he looks like a god made into mortal flesh.

I keep pumping him, and I try not to react when he grows even harder in my hand. I wouldn't have thought it was possible. His fingers tighten in my hair, then his hips pump forward. Even though I just had an orgasm of epic proportions, the space between my legs tingles as I watch him piston his hips in and out of my fist.

"Fuck, Hattie. I'm gonna come."

My eyes widen at the awe and desperation in his voice. That powerful feeling overcomes me again, from taking this man who always seems so in control and turning him out of control. Just watching him and his reaction from my hand is mesmerizing. His thick length pulses in my hand, and he jerks forward and groans as white cum sprays all over my chest.

Somehow, I instinctively know to keep pumping him for a moment, but with a gentler pace and grip.

Bastion brings his hands to either side of my face and bends down to kiss me. There's so much reverence in the kiss that I don't want to let go when he pulls away. He holds out a hand to help me up off my knees.

When I'm standing again, he glances at my breasts with a satisfied grin. I could get used to that look in his eyes. "Let's get you cleaned up."

There's no conversation as we shower together, but it's not awkward. It's a comfortable silence as we reflect on everything that's gone down. He helps me rinse off, and though I hope he might take the task of soaping me down, I'm disappointed when he simply hands me the bar of soap. This isn't how I thought it would go. There are times Bastion is so hot and cold with me, and I wonder if it has something to do with that nightmare.

When we're done, he holds open a large bath towel, wrapping it around me. It's not until we step out of the en suite into his bedroom that the acrid scent of something burning makes my eyes widen.

"Shoot! The lasagna!" I run out of the room, Bastion's laugh trailing me the whole way.

I may have ruined the lasagna, but it was totally worth it.

The day after I spread Hattie out on my counter and devoured her as though she was my last meal, I tell her that I'll be really late returning home. It's not inconceivable that I'll spend all night at the club on a Friday, since it's one of the busiest nights, but that's not why I'm sticking around.

It's because I need some separation from Hattie in order to get my head on straight. I need to remember why she's here in the first place and reset my plan in my head.

After I made her come on my tongue, all I felt was victory over the fact that my plan was moving forward. But when she joined me in the shower, knelt before me with those big doe eyes and that look of awe on her face as she jerked me off, as though it made her so genuinely happy to bring me pleasure... something shifted inside me that didn't sit well.

It doesn't matter how sweet, how innocent, how hot she is or how much fun I'm having showing her a new side to herself —she's the girl my mother chose to give all the nurturing and care and love and attention that I was supposed to have. And I cannot forget that.

So I'm at the club, pretending to work when really I've been staring at my computer screen, or if I'm out talking to some patrons, I'm barely hearing a word because I'm reliving everything that happened last night.

I blow out a breath and straighten in my chair, determined to get some work done. Before I can get started, there's a knock at the door. "Come in."

Steph waltzes through the door wearing one of her more daring dresses. The front dips low, and the hem might only extend a couple of inches past her ass. When she closes the door behind her, I know that she's not just here to talk business.

"Hey, Steph." I motion to the chair across from my desk, and she sits.

"Surprised to see you here." She takes her time crossing her legs, but a small pout crosses her lips when she sees I'm not watching.

"I do own the place."

She smirks. "From what I hear, you haven't been staying late for the past few weeks."

I arch an eyebrow and relax back into my chair. "Checking up on me?"

Steph shrugs. "You could say that. Just want to make sure everything's okay. You've seemed... different lately."

"Nothing for you to concern yourself with. I'm assuming you have business to discuss?"

Steph accepts my change of subject and fills me in on what I need to know as far as the business goes. But as soon as we've discussed the final matter, she gets back to why she's really here. She peels herself out of her seat and saunters around my desk until she's to my left, leaning her ass against the edge of my desk. I shift my chair to face her.

"You seem like you need to take the edge off." She leans in, resting a hand on my shoulder. The perfume that I used to like now smells cloying to me.

"Is that so?" She's probably right. I've felt on edge since I stepped out of the shower with Hattie last night and the burned lasagna turned into an omen.

"Why don't you let me take care of you? We can have a little fun." Her hand trails down my arm and over to my stomach.

This is usually when I take control and tell her what I want, but for some reason, this time her hands are unwanted. Wrong. The mental picture of her hand wrapped around my cock the same way Hattie's was last night turns me off.

She keeps descending, gripping me between the legs, and frowns when she finds me flaccid.

I bat away her hand. "I'm not in the mood."

Steph frowns and pulls away. "You haven't been in the mood in a while."

"Maybe this little tryst has run its course."

She straightens off the desk, and I ignore the terrifying expression she tries to school. "What does that mean?"

"It means I don't want to do this anymore. Shouldn't have done it in the first place."

She scoffs and glares. "You're serious?"

"Yes. You used to know the score, but lately it seems like you think you have some claim over me. A year ago, if I had put you off, you'd have thought nothing of it. Now you seem to take it personally."

She crosses her arms and cocks out her hip. "Who is she?"

I motion to her. "This is exactly the kind of shit I'm talking about. It's none of your business. And if there were someone, what would be the difference? I was clear about what this was the first time we hooked up, and you happily hopped on board."

"So you're just tossing me aside?"

"I'm telling you that it seems like things are getting complicated, and I don't have time for complications in my life. Moving forward, our relationship will be strictly professional."

Her eyes narrow. "You're fucking the new girl, aren't you?"

I roll my eyes. "I'm not, but if I were, it's none of your business. You seem to forget that you work for me, Steph, not the other way around. If you don't like it, leave."

Steph leaving would be a loss that would be hard to replace, but if she's going to cause me problems, it's not worth keeping her.

Her arms drop to her sides, and she presses her lips together. Though she looks as if she wants to say something, she draws in a deep breath and stops herself. "Fine. Your loss."

Without another word, she stalks from my office and slams the door.

Things will be touchy with her for a while I'm sure, but she'll get over it. I never promised her anything, and I was clear from the start—and we both agreed—that us messing around was fun and nothing more.

My attempt to get back to work fails when three minutes later, I'm thinking about Hattie again. Things are progressing nicely. We've messed around, and she was actually desperate for me and what I'd give her. She's gotten drunk, and I didn't even have to facilitate that one myself. Imagine what I can do with a few more weeks under my belt.

I smirk and force myself to work for the remainder of the night.

On Sunday, I once again find myself following Hattie around Seattle.

Sure, recon isn't anything new for me, but I've never been a guy who stalks women. From what I've read between the lines from my sister, her brother-in-law Nero might have stalked his now-wife at one time, and I remember thinking, "Why the fuck would anyone bother?"

I get it now, Nero.

When I heard Hattie leave the condo, I told myself not to bother, but the next thing I knew, there I was, putting on my shoes and racing to catch the elevator so that I could find her on the street before she was too far from view.

I'm not some fucking creep—at least I never used to be— but something about this woman gets under my skin. I don't know what it is, but a part of me wonders if I get my fill of her, will this sensation in my chest ease?

As she did last week, Hattie attends service at church, then walks to the soup kitchen to volunteer. I enjoy watching her move throughout the world and interact with others without her knowing that I'm standing sentinel.

I've given a lot of thought to how I want this to play out, when the best time to bed her will be, and I've decided that I want her begging for it. The two of us can screw around until then, but when I finally take her, and when she looks back on that moment for years to come, I want her to know that it was because she had to have it. That her *un*doing was her own doing.

And part of that won't just be the physical satisfaction I can give her. Part of it will be the emotional connection she thinks we share. I need Hattie to fall in love with me so that when I finally expose the truth to her and Carla, it will be all that much more devastating. Maybe they'll understand a shred of how I felt growing up with a mother who didn't give two shits about me.

With a smirk, I walk away from the soup kitchen. I'll put the next phase of my plan into motion tonight. I'm sure inno- cent Hattie will walk right into it.

When Hattie returns late afternoon, I make sure I'm in the living room, waiting.

"Hey, you're home." She sets her purse on the table near the front door.

I haven't seen much of her this weekend, by my own design. Thankfully, after the distance, I have my head on straight, and I'm ready to move forward.

"I am. What did you do today?"

She joins me in the living area, taking a seat a few feet away from me on the large sectional. "I went to church and then did some volunteering at the soup kitchen."

I nod and turn off the TV. "I was going to call you if you didn't show up soon."

"How come?" There's anticipation in her gaze.

"I made plans for us tonight. I hope you're free."

"You did? What are we doing?"

"I'm taking you to dinner." When her mouth opens to argue, I raise my hand. "No one we work with will be there."

She frowns. "How do you know?"

"Because they're not going to pay a couple hundred dollars a plate, and that's what this place charges."

Her eyes widen. "Oh. What should I wear?"

"Something dressy, maybe a little sexy."

A shy smile tilts her lips as she stands from the couch. "How much time do I have to get ready?"

I glance at my watch. "An hour."

"I'll make sure I'm ready." She heads out of the living room but swings around at the last minute to face me. "Thank you for planning this, Bastion."

I nod, thankful when she disappears from view.

An hour later, on the dot, I'm waiting in my suit at the door when she glides around the corner looking like a fucking goddess. She's wearing a one-shoulder electric-blue dress with a ruched waist that goes to her knees and has a slit up her left thigh. She paired it with a set of silver sandals that have a heel higher than any I've seen her wear before. Her hair is pulled up into a tight, high ponytail, showing off the curve of her neck, and it makes me want to tug her into me and bite down on it.

Hattie is gorgeous in the limited makeup she wears on a daily basis, but tonight she's wearing eyeliner and lipstick, and it makes her look more her age.

"You look phenomenal." I rest my hands on her waist.

"Thank you." She bats her eyelashes, and I don't think she does it on purpose, but it makes her look like a minx.

"You realize how hard it's going to be to get through dinner with you looking like this and not spread you out on the table and eat you for dinner, don't you? Or maybe that's what you want." I lean in and run my tongue up the column of her neck, and she shivers under my touch.

"Not at the restaurant, but after."

I groan at the thought of her taste on my tongue again. "I'm going to hold you to that."

I pull away and take her hand, leading her out of the condo. We make our way to the parking garage and my SL-Class Mercedes-Benz. I open the door for Hattie, and once she's seated inside, I close the door and make my way around the front of the car.

"I'll be a gentleman and keep the top up so the wind doesn't ruin your hair." I start the car and put on my seat belt before pulling out of the parking spot.

"This is so much nicer than my car back in Wisconsin." Hattie laughs as she looks around the interior, almost in awe.

"Nothing but the best for you." I pull out of the parking garage onto the street.

"Are you going to tell me where we're going?" she asks.

"It's a surprise, but even if I told you, you probably wouldn't know it. I'll tell you this—the food is spectacular, and the view is great. It overlooks Lake Union."

"I'm pretty sure I've never been to a restaurant this fancy before. I'm afraid I'm going to mess up and make it obvious I don't belong there."

I glance at her when I stop at a traffic light, hating the expression of defeat on her face. I remember the first time one of my marks took me to a fancy restaurant. The pressure, the eyes I felt, the judgment as if they could see who I really was underneath the expensive suit. It took me a while to not feel that way, and I would never want anyone else to feel the same.

"Hattie, you belong there as much as anyone else. All you have to do is eat and relax, okay?" My hand drifts through the slit of the dress on her left thigh, touching her soft, silky skin. Fuck, I hope I can control myself tonight.

She nods and bites her lip. "Okay."

I run my hand up and down her thigh, and the tension builds between us. The temptation to inch my fingers closer to her pussy is so great, I'm not sure I trust myself.

There's a honk behind us, and when I look forward, I see that the light has changed. I retract my hand and put it on the steering wheel for the rest of the ride.

When we arrive, we're taken right to our table. Usually this place requires reservations at least a month in advance, but the owner used to frequent my club until he got married, so I called him up, and he made it happen for me. He's obviously given us the best view in the house. The sun is still up, but by the time we leave here, it will have set, making for a glittering view of the city and boats below.

"I'm Fredrick, and I'll be your server tonight. Can I start you off with something to drink?" He looks at me.

I motion for Hattie to answer. I'm curious to see if she'll choose alcohol tonight or if it was a one-time thing. She looks between the waiter and me, a deer in headlights, so I save her.

"I think we'll share a bottle of wine." I take a quick glance down the wine list, make my choice, and the waiter leaves.

Hattie cringes. "Thank you. I wanted wine, but I didn't know what to order."

"It's not a big deal. I only deferred to you because I wasn't sure whether you'd want alcohol or not. I know you said you'd never really drank before the evening you were out with Renee and Paige."

"I wasn't sure either, but this place is so beautiful, it seems like the kind of place where you drink wine with your meal, you know?"

I chuckle and nod. "I do, yes." I remember the first time a woman asked me to pick the bottle and the cool sweat that beaded along the back of my neck.

"Don't worry. I won't get tipsy and embarrass you. I'll make sure I don't drink too much."

"You could never embarrass me. Hattie, I thought I made it clear by now that you don't have to act a certain way around me. Just be yourself."

She sighs. "I know, it's just a hard concept to get used to. It's something I've done my whole life."

"Were you that terrified that your parents wouldn't love you if you didn't act a certain way?"

She shakes her head before I've even finished asking the question. "My parents are amazing, and I know they'd love me no matter what I ever did. I just hate the idea of disappointing them."

"Well, you don't have to worry about me judging you, Hattie. More than anything, I want you to figure out who you are. The only way you're going to do that is to try out different things and see how they suit you."

"You say that now, but if you're carrying me out of here over your shoulder, you won't be thinking that."

I laugh again. "Fair enough."

Every day that she lives with me, Hattie emerges a little more out of her shell. I almost hate myself for the corruption because it really is an admirable thing to see someone trying to take a hold of her life and find herself.

The waiter returns with our wine, and we go through the motions of me approving the wine before he pours us each a glass and leaves the rest of the bottle in the ice bucket beside the table.

"Shall we do a toast?" I raise my glass, and Hattie follows suit. "To new horizons and bold steps forward. Here's to you discovering the truth of who you really are."

Hattie smiles and clinks her glass with mine, and we each take a sip.

"The waiter didn't ask for our order," she says.

"We're on the prix fixe menu, so they'll serve us seven different courses."

She leans forward and whispers, "What if I don't like what they serve us?"

I do the same. "You don't have to eat it if you don't like it."

"Then I'll feel bad." She frowns.

I can't help but chuckle. "Hattie, you need to stop feeling bad about everything. Just own your feelings. It's okay not to be agreeable all the time."

Hattie groans. "I know, I know, you're right." She reaches for her wineglass. "In the spirit of everything you just said, there's been something I want to ask you, but I thought I might be overstepping."

I motion across the table to her. "Go ahead. I'm an open book."

"Are you close with your parents? Sometimes when I talk about mine, I get this feeling it makes you unhappy to hear about them. I thought maybe that was because you don't get along with yours."

Fucking hell, maybe I'm making her too comfortable in my presence.

30

HATTIE

$\mathcal{B}$astion's countenance changes as soon as the question leaves my mouth, and I know without him answering that I'm right. He's never said anything specific, but when I talk about how wonderful my parents are, his beautiful blue eyes grow cloudy, his lips press together, and his jaw flexes. It just seems like parents are not a topic he's comfortable talking about.

He takes a sip of his wine. "I didn't know my father. He was never in my life, and my mother..." His jaw flexes and his nostrils flare. "She was into drugs and alcohol, so I ran away when I was eleven."

My mouth slips open, and tears prick my eyes. Of all the answers I thought he'd give me, that was not it. I thought he'd say his parents didn't agree with his business in strip clubs or there was some falling out. Maybe a nasty divorce when he was young. But his mom was a drug addict?

"Oh, Bastion, I'm so sorry." I reach out to touch his arm, and he shifts it away. My hand falls to the side of the table.

"Don't look at me like that," he snaps.

It's the first time I've ever heard a hint of anger in his voice directed at me, and I still, surprised by the venom lacing his words.

He twirls the stem of his wineglass, his eyes transfixed on the sloshing liquid. "I'm sorry, I shouldn't have spoken to you like that. It's just a difficult subject for me. As you can imagine, it still hurts even after all these years."

I reach across the table for his hand, taking my chances again. "Of course it is. I can only imagine how bad the situation was for you to run away at such a young age."

He nods, not meeting my eyes and looking at my hand on his forearm. "I got lucky, though. The man I consider to be my father took me in and raised me even though he was already raising a child of his own. Ariana, she's not my sister by blood, but she is in every way that counts."

I give him a small smile. "That's like me with my mom. I'm her stepdaughter, but she's always treated me like I was her own."

Bastion's gaze meets mine, but there's no smile. There's something else I'm struggling to decipher because I can never read people very well. "You should be thankful that she came into your life and chose to raise you as her own. You don't know how lucky you are, believe me."

"I know. When I was little, I'd thank God every night for sending her to my dad and me."

Bastion's jaw clenches and his nostrils flare again, but before I can ask more questions, the waiter arrives to serve the first course.

He sets down a plate in front of each of us while explaining what it is. I'm thankful to see that the plate isn't filled to the brim, given that there are seven courses. In fact, it's just a small amount of food, but it's so pretty.

"It looks like art on a plate," I say to Bastion after the waiter leaves, in an attempt to shift the mood from our serious conversation a moment ago.

"Wait until you taste it. I've never had a dish I haven't liked here." He picks up his cutlery, and I follow suit.

I take a small piece of the dish and bring it to my mouth, moaning when the flavors mix on my tongue.

"Careful, Hattie, if you make noises like that all through dinner, I'm likely to spread you open on this table in front of everyone and make you my meal."

His words should send me running, leave me appalled, something other than pressing my thighs together under the table because I'm turned on.

I don't know what to say, so I go back to eating my meal, my face heated.

I'm careful to only sip my wine through the rest of the meal so that I don't end up drinking too much. Bastion and I chat about everything and nothing, and it's not until we're eating the dessert course that I realize how he's become someone important in my life. How he's shown the patience to allow me to be my complete self with him.

I was certainly more comfortable with him when we just met than I am with most people, but now when I'm around him, it's the same as if I'm talking to Taylor. I don't dissect every thought through my head before I say it, I don't worry about what he might think of me. I get to just exist in this place where I feel like I can completely be myself.

"I haven't asked you, probably because I've been afraid to, but how are you enjoying your life here in Seattle now that you've settled in some more?" Bastion brings his wineglass to his lips and finishes it off.

I think back to the night I was determined to leave town as quickly as possible. It feels as if it was a million years ago. So much has changed for me so quickly, but it doesn't feel like a bad thing anymore.

Yes, I've questioned what God and my parents would think of me because of all of this, but it's hard to feel like what I'm doing is a sin when I'm still the same person I always was at heart. Does enjoying sexual pleasure with a man I care about negate all that? I'm not sure, but one thing I know is that the Lord is a forgiving and benevolent God. In the end, if I decide all of it was a mistake and I was wrong for doing it, I will be forgiven. For now, I'm trying to follow my heart and go with my gut on what feels right.

"Do you really have to ask?" I smile.

He chuckles. "Well, I know you like *that*, but what about the rest of it?"

"Well, I enjoy the job a lot. And I think I've found a good fit in the church I've been attending. I've found somewhere to volunteer, which is always rewarding. And I think I'm starting to develop some friendships. I really like Renee and Paige. They're doing a wine and painting night next week, and they asked me to join them."

Bastion's grin says he's happy with my answer. "That's great. I'm glad you're settling in. I'd be crushed if you told me again that you intend to leave."

"You would?" My chest warms.

"Very much so." Bastion takes the cloth napkin off his lap and sets it beside his plate, glancing at my empty plate. "Are you ready to head home?"

"Don't you have to pay the waiter for our meal?"

He rises up off his chair and comes around to pull mine out for me. "They have my card on file." He drags his hand over my bare shoulder, and I suppress a shiver at the electric current that runs down my spine.

I stand and turn to face him. "Thank you for dinner."

"My pleasure." He kisses the corner of my lips, then slides his fingers between mine and leads me toward the exit.

I take one last look at the view of glittering lights below before we head out.

Once the valet has brought Bastion's car around and we're both seated inside, I turn to him. "Do you think we can ride with the top down this time?"

He looks at me with a grin, then presses a button, and the roof recedes over our heads. "Your wish is my command."

Once the roof has retreated entirely, he steps hard on the gas, and we race off into the night. I yelp and close my eyes, raising my hands as the air rushes over me. I can't help but let out a gleeful shout, and Bastion chuckles next to me. I've never felt so free and unencumbered.

The drive home is exhilarating. I'm sure I look a hot mess by the time Bastion brings the convertible to a stop in the condo's parking garage, but I don't care. That was so much fun.

Bastion looks at me with amused affection as he opens the passenger door and extends a hand to help me out. He rubs his thumb against mine on the elevator ride up, and by the time we're walking through the condo's door, I'm breathing heavily in anticipation of what will come next.

The moment the door closes, Bastion places his hands on either side of my face and backs me up against it, pressing his lips to mine. I sink into the heat of our kiss until he slides one hand to the top of my head and fists my ponytail, using the leverage to angle my head to the side. His lips trail a path down my jawline to my neck.

My nipples pebble in my dress, and I press my thighs together to stem the tide of need that rolls over me.

"We can each go our separate ways, to our separate bedrooms, or you can join me in mine." He bites gently on my earlobe, and I shiver. "The choice is yours."

I delve my hand into his hair, pulling him back so that we lock eyes. "Take me to your bedroom."

31

HATTIE

I thought I would be more nervous as Bastion leads me by the hand to his bedroom. But it's only excitement and anticipation swirling inside me. When we're inside the room, he turns the lights on, but only enough that we can see each other.

The look he gives me as he slips off his suit jacket and tie, laying them across the long, padded bench at the end of the bed, makes my knees wobble. It's full of promise and all the wicked things he plans to do to me.

There may have been a time when that would have intimidated or even frightened me, but now I look forward to discovering this side of me—with him.

"Your turn." He nods at me as he slips out of his shoes and socks.

"I could use some help with my zipper."

He chuckles as he pads toward me, as though he knows I

need no help at all. It's true, I can undo the side zipper myself, but I want his hands on me.

Bastion stands in front of me, and I move my arm away from my side so that he can slide his hand underneath and slowly slide down the zipper. When the zipper is at the bottom, he leans in and kisses my collarbone as his hand strokes my shoulder, sliding the strap down my arm until the dress rests at my waist.

I didn't wear a bra, so my breasts are bare to him, nipples peaked, begging for his attention. I'm desperate for him to touch them tonight.

He takes half a step back, his eyes glazed with lust, then runs the backs of his index and middle fingers down the curve at the side of my breast. "You're like a fucking goddess, so perfect."

He bends down and lifts my breast to his mouth, enveloping the nipple and swirling his tongue around the rigid peak. I gasp, and my hands fly to the back of his head, lacing my fingers through his thick hair to hold him there. The sensation runs straight from my nipple down between my legs, and it's almost as though he has me spread on the kitchen island again with his mouth on my clit. Each pull against my nipple is a pull between my legs.

His free hand takes the weight of my breast in his hand, and he thumbs my nipple. I arch into him, wanting more, and when he pinches the taut bud, I gasp and grip his hair harder. He bites down on my nipple, and the lash of pain melts into a warm sensation as his tongue swipes over it.

Bastion pulls back and takes me in, his eyes darker than normal, more like a stormy sky. Then he grips my dress at the end of the zipper and rips it apart by the seam until the fabric is discarded on the floor. The act of aggression heightens some primal instinct in me, and when he bends at the waist and hoists me up over his shoulder, I don't fight him.

One hand holds my legs, and the other is splayed across my ass since I wore a thong to avoid panty lines. He sets me on my feet near the floor-to-ceiling window that overlooks the city and the water. With his fingers on my cheek and his thumb on my chin, he brings me in for a kiss. It's slow and languid, the opposite of how I feel right now—charged up and ready to go—but I follow his lead.

"If we're going to do this, I need to get you ready, Hattie. I don't want to hurt you." He trails his nose over my shoulder and up my neck.

I think back to the size of him in my palm and how long it's been since I had sex. God, he's right.

"How are you going to do that?" I ask, feeling a little foolish, as though I should already know the answer.

In response, he spins me around so I face the glass. I'm aware that though I can't see anyone specifically, there are other buildings around that can likely see in here. Old me would have shirked away from being bare to the world, but the idea that someone might be watching, that someone could possibly see us but I would never know, only sends a triple shot of lust through my veins.

Bastion slowly lowers my thong to the floor, bending down onto his haunches behind me. I'm still wearing my shoes, but he doesn't remove them.

As he stands, his palms glide up either side of my legs, then my hips, and last my ribs. With my back to his chest, he nudges against me, forcing me to walk forward until I'm flush against the glass, pressing my breasts against the cool surface. I shudder when Bastion's hard length pierces me from behind and he clasps my wrists, drawing my hands up over my head.

"Do you think anyone's watching?" he whispers in my ear. Goose bumps scatter along my neck.

"I... I don't know."

"What do you think they see?"

I close my eyes, and my forehead drops to the glass, picturing what we might look like with me naked and him pressed against me from behind, still clothed. I stifle a groan.

"Do you think they're jealous of me?" He chuckles, and the vibration from deep in his chest hits my back. "I know they are, because I'm the lucky son of a bitch who knows what you taste like. Who knows how glorious you look when you come. And soon, it will be my fat cock shoved inside you, making you see stars."

"Please, Bastion." My knees give out, and I slide an inch down the glass. I'm losing all strength and willpower, soon to sink into a puddle of lust, but Bastion holds me flush to the glass. "Don't make me wait any longer."

His hand slips between my legs, and he groans, finding me wet and ready for him. "Arch your hips for me, babe."

I do as he asks, and he rims my entrance with his finger before inching it inside me. It's not like last time, though, when he barely entered me. This time, he doesn't stop until he's all the way in, and I clench around his finger, gasping.

"Fuck." He bites my shoulder. "You're so tight."

Bastion's finger slips out, and he gently pushes it back inside over and over until I'm panting and begging for more. Somehow, he knows, because he adds another finger inside me, slowly pushing in and out, in and out again until I grow used to it and the resistance decreases.

His forehead falls to my upper back, and he groans, holding his fingers still for a moment. "Fuck, babe, you're so tight, so fucking wet. I can't wait to be inside you and claim you as mine."

The word "mine" does something to me. It's as though a wild animal comes alive in my chest, clawing to get free, and I say things I could never have imagined coming out of my mouth a month ago.

"Fuck me, Bastion. Please don't make me wait any longer. Make me yours."

He growls against my heated skin and moves his fingers again, rougher this time. His rhythm causes me to move up and down the glass, my nipples dragging back and forth. The friction feels so good that I don't ever want him to stop. I want to stay here all night and have him show me what my body desires.

I lower my hands from over my head to down beside my shoulders, and I fist them against the glass, looking at the night sky and sparkling lights below. Picturing what others see, what we might look like, makes me clench, and he must feel it because he groans again behind me.

Bastion's other hand circles around my waist and dips down until he's circling my clit. When he scissors his fingers inside me, I cry out, all the pent-up pleasure fighting to be released.

I push back into his hands, needing more, never wanting it to end, and he adds a third finger. "Oh my god!"

The sound of him moving in and out of me fills the room along with our panting, and it only brings me closer to the brink.

"Fuck, woman. What are you doing to me?" There's pain laced in his voice.

I can't give him an answer. No way I could form a coherent sentence right now. I'm rocketing toward my orgasm, and it's going to be more powerful than all of them.

"Are you ready for me, Hattie? You ready for me to ruin you?"

Finally. "Yes, please, yes."

"You want me to fill you up?"

"Yes!"

"You want to see yourself stretch around my thick cock?"

"Oh, god." I moan, envisioning what we're about to do.

Bastion pinches my clit, and it's like the trigger for an atomic bomb—I explode.

There's no awareness of what I do or what I say, just a spiraling pleasure until I'm ricocheted back into my body, sweating and panting and leaning against the glass.

Bastion spins me around, and his mouth is on mine, owning me, and all I can do is follow his lead. I realize with a startling clarity that I'll follow this man to the edge of the world.

He dips down and lifts me with his hands on both thighs until I'm straddling his waist and he's walking me toward the bed. Then I'm on the mattress, crawling backward toward the middle, while he removes his shirt and slacks.

Once he's naked, he strokes himself as he stares at me, and I'm so greedy for him that all I can think is that I want my hand on his cock.

He must be able to read my mind because he says, "You'll get your turn later."

Bastion crawls across the mattress until he hovers over me, letting some of his weight drop onto me, but not all. Our eyes meet as he dips his head to kiss me. There's so much in his kiss that I don't know what to make of it. It feels like a confession of sorts, but of what, I don't know.

I open my legs to make room for him, and his hips slip between my thighs as he kisses down the side of my neck.

"Show me what this can be, Bast, please."

He straightens to lock his gaze with mine. "You called me Bast."

I draw back, unsure why, but it just came out. "I'm sorry, I—"

He crashes his lips to mine again, but he ends it too soon. When he draws back, he says, "Only those closest to me call me Bast. Never call me Bastion again. Promise?"

I nod, my heart swelling.

Bast takes my lips again. Within minutes, I'm writhing underneath him, desperate for more, for all of him. The hard length of him pressing against me is a constant reminder of what I'm missing.

"Please don't make me wait any longer," I say against his lips.

"Let me get a condom," he says.

I want to cry out when he rolls off of me to go to the top drawer of his nightstand. His hand darts around inside it for a moment, then he pulls out an open box of condoms, and my brain makes note.

But I can't think about other women right now. Can't think about what number I am to him. Tonight, it's only us.

He reaches for something else, but I only see a flash of hot pink. Then Bastion takes a condom from the box and tosses the box back in the drawer, bringing the package to his mouth and ripping it open. I'm not sure why, but watching him roll the condom down his length is so hot, my heart beats even faster.

He comes back over me, and I spread my thighs, inviting him in. "You ready for me, Hattie?"

I bite my lip and nod.

Holding the base, he notches the head at my entrance, pushing in slowly.

He's big. Definitely bigger than Rich was, though it wasn't as if I didn't already know that.

He's a couple inches in when he groans, his forehead dropping to meet mine. "Fuck, babe, I need a minute."

Pleasure spreads through my body like a spiderweb. I'm doing this to him. Not some super-experienced sex kitten, but me, innocent Hattie, who has only been with one other man.

My hands clutch his shoulders before I bring them around to his back, digging my nails up. I bring my mouth to his ear and whisper, "Fuck me, Bast."

And my words do the trick. He loses control and pushes all the way in, claiming me as his, and I've never been happier.

32

BASTION

This must be what heaven feels like, I think, as pleasure flows through my body like honey. Hattie's pussy is a vise around my cock, and all I want is to ride her so hard she doesn't know up from down. But this needs to be good for her too, so I have to go slow—at least, at first.

I force myself to still, to allow her to get used to my size. I kiss her brow. "You okay?"

She nods, and I slowly pull myself out, then slide back in. After a few pumps, her body relaxes, and I speed up the pace. Hattie's legs tighten around me as I drive into her. The ponytail she wore to dinner is splayed across the bedding. When I first saw her tonight, all I could think of was what it would feel like to wrap it around my wrist while she's giving me head, but that's for another day.

Hattie's eyelids droop with lust, and her mouth is parted as she stares up at me in awe. Having a woman like her look at a man like me with that expression could get addicting if I let it. I'm getting pulled into her. I can't deny she's sucking my soul out of my body and into her own.

Staring at her isn't going to help if I want my plan to work.

With pain lacing through me, I pull out of her without warning and sit back on my knees, pushing a hand through my hair. "Get on your hands and knees."

She flips without argument. At least this way I won't have to look her in the eyes.

My palm runs down the globe of her ass. I have no control, so I give it a swift smack that echoes through the room. Hattie yelps, but the yelp turns into a moan, and she arches her back as if she wants more.

"You like that?" I fist the base of my cock and run it through the wetness at the center of her.

She groans my name and pushes against it.

"Look at your greedy cunt, Hattie. Just waiting to be filled by me. Is that what you want? You want me riding you from behind like I own you?"

Her fingers squeeze the bedding. "Yes. God, Bast, yes."

The sound of her using the shortened version of my name makes me slam into her. Hattie cries out but pushes back into me, meeting me thrust for thrust. Both our breathing is heavy, and I watch as I fill her again and again. The condom glistens with her arousal, and for the first time in my life, I want to feel what it would be like to fuck a woman with nothing between us.

I continue to pound into her, and she takes me. She takes every inch of me without complaint, reveling in it. I lean over her so that my sweat-slicked chest is flush with her back and reach around to grip her neck, then I pull her up so that she's raised on her knees before me.

She leans her head back into me so that her throat is even more exposed, and I tuck my face in there as I bring my other hand around to her mound and her swollen bud. With my hand gently squeezing her neck, I push up into her, showing no mercy. My other hand circles her clit, and the faster I go, the more she tightens around me.

I lift my head to watch our reflection in the window, like a transparent version of us overlaid on glass. My balls tighten at the sight, and I'm already ready to throw in the towel.

"Are you gonna milk my cock when you finish, Hattie? Is your cunt hungry for my cum?"

"Yes, Bast. Please," she pleads. "Please, Bast, please."

Her begging only draws my orgasm closer.

She's come undone, and knowing I'm the one who's gotten her here makes me feel like a fucking god. *Her* god.

I pinch her clit, and Hattie's cunt clamps down on me while she bucks in my arms, moaning my name. Her orgasm is too much, and my balls tighten up. I spill into the condom, holding myself inside her as my dick twitches.

Releasing my hold on her neck, I nudge her forward and we lie down, me behind her with my softening dick still inside her.

"Are you okay?" I ask in a rough voice.

"Yeah." She nods against the pillow and shifts her legs to get in a more comfortable position. I pull out of her.

When something scratches my shin, I look down between us. "You still have your shoes on."

She looks down, then looks over her shoulder at me, and we both laugh.

"I'll be right back." I go to the bathroom and dispose of the condom, then wet a washcloth to help clean Hattie.

But when I return to the bed, she's fast asleep. The thought that I should bring her back to her own bed occurs to me, but that seems like a dick move, even for me, and I'm trying to get this woman to fall for me. So I pull the covers over her instead, then join her.

I tell myself that the reason it's so easy for me to fall asleep is because I just had an epic lay.

I wake up to the feeling of soft fingers tracing a path on my left shoulder blade, and before I open my eyes, I know what Hattie is looking at.

"Morning." My voice is rough with sleep as I slowly open my eyes.

"Were you born with this?" Her finger continues to trace my heart-shaped birthmark.

"Yeah, I used to tell the girls in high school that it meant I was born to be a lover."

"Oh, boy." She chuckles, and I push away the warmth that blooms in my chest at the sound. "Did it actually work?"

"Sometimes." I roll over to face her. "Would it work on you?"

She bites her bottom lip. "Well, I already know you're a good lover, so that's not a fair question."

I raise an eyebrow. "Good?"

She flutters her eyelashes and shrugs. "How about fantastic, amazing, the best ever? That better?"

"Much."

I study her and how she looks having just woken up. Her makeup is still on from last night, smudged under her eyes, and her hair is mussed. Regardless, she has this innate childlike innocence. Suddenly, I feel every one of the thirteen years between us.

"How are you feeling after last night?" I'm not sure why I'm asking, nor why I care that it even came to my mind in the first place.

"Amazing. You're amazing." She presses a chaste kiss to my shoulder.

Something comes to life in my chest, but I push down the feeling and change the subject. "I have to go into the club early today to meet someone, but you stay here and go back to sleep for a while."

I arranged to meet with Sean later this morning. Sure, I could have done it later in the day, but I liked the idea of forcing that asshole to get out of bed, and I don't really want Hattie around when he's around. She knows nothing of the arrangement he and I have, nor do I want her to. I'm not sure how she'd feel about it and subsequently me, so it has the potential to derail all my plans.

But Sean needs to know that I've put out feelers to some other organizations in the area if he doesn't back down about decreasing my cut.

"I am tired. Someone kept me up late last night." Hattie runs a finger down my chest, and my dick twitches under the sheet.

I need to get the hell out of here before I'm balls deep in her again and miss my meeting.

"Mmm, well, be prepared for me to do it again tonight." I give her a chaste kiss. "If you want."

She rolls her eyes. "Like I'd turn you down. All I can think of since we started fooling around is what else we might do and when we'll get to do it again. Watch out, you might have turned me into a sex addict."

My head tips back, and I roar with laughter. "You're not a sex addict. If I had to guess, you're just now going through what a lot of people do when they're teenagers first discovering sex."

"All right, that makes me feel a little better."

I roll out of bed, tugging the sheet back. "I'll see you later then?"

She nods before rolling over and pulling the blanket up over her shoulder.

I allow myself one last look at the outline of her gorgeous curves under the sheet before I go to the en suite and pretend that I didn't like seeing her in my bed.

33

HATTIE

few days have passed since I had sex with Bast, and I've slept in his bed every single night.

Lately, I'm a giddy schoolgirl who wants to doodle Bast's initials in my notebook all day. I'm not sure if it's the sex or him or a combination of both, but I've never felt like this before. Even with Rich.

I want to shake my head when I think back to my relationship with Rich. Comparing what I feel when I'm with Bast versus what I felt when I was with Rich, they're not even close. I must have been fooling myself to think that Rich and I had what it would take to go the distance.

Not that that's what I'm thinking about Bast. I have no idea what we are. Nothing, I suppose. I'm not sure I'd call him my boyfriend even though he did take me out on a date. Lover sounds ridiculous. I keep telling myself not to worry about the label because it doesn't matter. I'm figuring out who I am, and when being with him stops feeling like the right thing to do, I'll end it.

"Earth to Hattie."

I blink a few times, and the canvas I'm working on comes into view. I turn my head to see Renee and Paige looking at me with amusement.

"Sorry, I must have zoned out."

"No shit," Renee says with a laugh. "What has you so distracted?"

"Nothing. Just daydreaming." I pick up the wineglass that's on the table with all the paints and brushes the instructor provided for the activity tonight.

"It's a guy. I can tell," Paige says.

I shake my head. "You cannot."

She narrows her eyes and points her paintbrush at me. "You've got it bad for someone."

I sigh, wishing I could talk to them about what's going on between Bast and me, but I can't. Which is horrible because they could probably offer me the advice I need. Then again, maybe I can tell them something. I like these women, and I want to get closer to them. I realize how lonely I really was in Wisconsin now that I have some female companionship in my life.

"There is someone I'm interested in, and we're sort of seeing each other, but we haven't put a label on it, you know? Which is fine. It's a bit of an unusual circumstance." I dip my paintbrush in the pale-yellow paint and bring it to my canvas.

"What's unusual about it?" Renee asks, voice filled with concern.

"We're not really dating, I don't think, but we're..." My face heats at just thinking about saying the words.

"You're banging?" Renee asks, and I nod. "Nothing wrong with that." She shrugs and looks at Paige, who nods her approval.

"I know that there's nothing technically wrong with it. I'm an adult and can make my own choices, but I was raised in the church, so it feels complicated for me."

Renee gets up off her stool to stretch side to side. "What was that like?"

To my surprise, there's no judgment from either woman when I explain my upbringing. In the past, anyone who wasn't a Christian or had spent a lot of time at church would look at me as though I were a member of some cult or something. Their judgment was always clear in their eyes. But Renee and Paige listen intently and ask some questions when they want me to elaborate.

"So you feel like you're doing something wrong." Paige's words don't really come out like a question.

"Basically, yeah, a little. Even though I'm enjoying the heck out of it."

All three of us laugh, and when we're done, Renee takes her seat again. "To each their own. I wasn't raised religious at all, but I think the only person's opinion that should matter to you is your own. You're a good person, Hattie. Someone only has to be around you for a few minutes to see that much. I think that's what matters most, not whether some guy you are or are not officially seeing is giving you good orgasms."

I laugh again. Renee has a way of putting things that is always so amusing to me.

"Do you guys have anyone in your lives?" They've never mentioned anyone, but we haven't spent that much time together.

Renee shakes her head. "I have no time. It would mean getting a babysitter for my son, and there's hardly anyone I'd trust with him. Plus, my experience with my ex kind of turned me off the idea for now."

I hope that she's able to find someone special at some point. She deserves happiness.

"What about you, Paige?" I ask.

She studies her canvas for a beat, fixing something with her paintbrush before turning to look at me. "I have a boyfriend. We've been together for almost a year now."

I don't know why that surprises me. I mean, I'm sure both of these women have no lack of men propositioning them at the club. "Where did you guys meet?"

"Oh, I love this story." Renee giggles, leaning back from her canvas and picking up her wineglass.

Paige rolls her eyes good-naturedly. "I was marching in a protest, and things got a bit heated when there was a confrontation with the police. Someone pushed me, and I fell and sprained my ankle. Grady was on duty and helped me up, made sure I was okay, and got me out of the ruckus. Then he asked me for my name and number and I refused to give it to him because I thought he was going to get me in trouble or something for being at the protest. Turns out he just wanted it so he could ask me out."

"I love that." I place my hand over my heart. "Can I ask you something?"

I add some orange to my sunset to make the transition a little better.

"Of course." Paige picks up her wineglass and turns her stool away from the easel so she's facing me.

"Does he have a problem with what you do for a living? Isn't he jealous?"

She shakes her head. "I told him straight up before we even went on a date that I'm a stripper and that I wouldn't be quitting for any man. He knew that if he couldn't handle it, then he could fuck all the way off."

I can't help but grin. "I love your confidence."

"That said, he would never come in while I'm working. There's no point in causing problems for myself." Paige winks.

"That makes sense." I study my painting for a beat and decide to add pale pink into the sunset at the bottom. "What's it like out there on stage?"

"Are you thinking about giving it a try?" Renee asks as if she's scandalized.

I shake my head rapidly. "No, I could never. I'm just wondering if you feel the way you appear out there."

"And how do we appear?" Paige asks.

"Powerful. In control. Like you're in charge."

Before I ever stepped foot in a strip club, I assumed that the women would feel degraded and worthless, and maybe that's true in some instances, but it certainly isn't the case at The Black Orchid. Or it doesn't seem to be.

"I can't speak for everyone, but that's how I feel," Renee says. "There's power in knowing I'm providing a life for myself and not relying on anyone else to do it."

We both look over at Paige.

"Agreed. I feel sexy when I'm onstage and looking out into that crowd. Turning on a man always makes you feel powerful, even if it's not *your* man."

"When I started, I used to worry more about how I looked and whether I had a dimple on my ass or if my boobs looked good in a certain outfit. But you realize very quickly that the men literally do not care. At all."

I think about what they're saying, and I can see it. I can see how turning any man on feels good even if you have no desire to be intimate with him.

The instructor comes over. "Ladies, how are we doing? Do any of you need any help?"

We abandon the topic at hand, and I watch as the instructor answers a question Renee and Paige have. A few months ago, I would have thought I had nothing in common with a stripper, *any* stripper. I never would have thought we could ever be friends.

My life had always been black and white, right and wrong, moral and immoral. I'm starting to realize that there are shades of gray to everything. Maybe everything isn't as rigid as I always thought it was.

I smile as I bring the paintbrush back to the canvas. I'm glad I made this move. Not only am I learning so much about life, but I'm learning so much about myself too.

Sharing a little with the girls earlier tonight made me want to open up to Taylor about everything going on between Bast and me, so when I arrived home, I told him I had to make a phone call and disappeared into my room.

"Oh, you are alive," Taylor answers my video call. She's in her apartment.

"I'm sorry, I've been busy, that's all."

"Are you sure you're not avoiding me?" She gives me a stern look.

"Why would you say that?" I lean back on the headboard.

She gives me a "duh" look. "Because I know you, Hattie. And you're the worst liar. It's obvious when you're trying to keep something from me. Is everything okay?" Her voice is filled with concern.

Now I feel guilty for keeping everything from her for so long. "Everything is fine. Great, actually, but you're right, I do have something to tell you."

"Hang on, let me turn my TV off. I feel like this is going to require my full attention." She sets the phone down, and I'm staring at the ceiling of her apartment for a minute before she returns, lying on the couch and holding the phone overhead. "All right, let's hear it."

I tell her everything. From living with Bast to where I really work and what's been going on between the two of us. She's silent the entire time, only interrupting me here and there to ask pertinent questions.

When I finally finish, she bolts up into a sitting position and grins at me. "Hattie Sinclair, you sneaky, sneaky woman. I didn't think you had it in you."

I'm shocked. I thought for sure she'd lecture me and tell me that I had to be careful like she did when I first told her I was coming out here. "I thought you'd be upset or tell me I'm being an idiot and that I need to be careful."

"Well, I still think you need to be careful, but it sounds like this guy only has your best interests at heart. He doesn't judge you, and he makes sure you're okay with everything before you guys do anything. I'm glad you have someone out there who's looking out for you. Now for the real question, does your boyfriend have a brother?"

We both laugh, but I can't let her think I was saying this is something it's not. "He's not my boyfriend."

"He's not *not* your boyfriend, though."

"Is this what people do? Sleep with people before they've figured out what's going on between them?"

Taylor shrugs. "All the time. But it doesn't mean you have to. If you want to know what's going on, ask him."

I sigh and stare at the ceiling. "I guess." I'm afraid I'll come off clingy or needy—or even worse, like a child. Bast is probably used to dating women older than me, women who know the score.

There's a knock on the bedroom door.

"Hang on a second," I tell Taylor, then call out for Bast to come in.

He opens the door and strides into the room. "Oh, sorry, you're still on the phone. I was wondering if you'd fallen asleep." He thumbs over his shoulder. "I'm going to make myself a hot chocolate float before I head to bed. Wanted to see if you want one."

Bast made me one a couple of nights ago, and it was so good. It's like a combination of dessert and a drink.

I smile at his thoughtfulness. "Yes, please."

"I'll have one too," Taylor calls.

I know exactly what she's doing, and I might be annoyed with her if I hadn't been keeping so much from her since I arrived.

"Who's that?" Bast makes his way over to the bed, and I turn the phone so that he can see the screen.

"This is my best friend, Taylor. Taylor, this is Bast."

He smiles at her. "Good to meet you, Taylor. I promise that if you come to visit Hattie, I'll make you one."

"Deal!" I can hear the elation in her voice at having her plan work and to have gotten a glimpse of the man I was just going on and on about.

I look at Bast. "Just let me say goodbye and I'll be right out."

He winks at me. "All right."

I turn the phone back around and look down at it.

"Oh my god," she mouths.

One glance at the door tells me that Bast is out of the room. "Okay, he's gone."

"Holy shit, Hattie. He is fucking hot!"

"Shh!" I glance back at the doorway to make sure Bast is still gone.

"I can see why you're doing what you're doing. No judgment from me." She laughs. "I'm happy for you, girl. You're the best person I know, and you deserve to be able to explore this side of yourself."

"Thanks, Tay. I feel better now that you know everything."

"I understand why you were hesitant to tell me, but you know you can tell me anything. I'm never going to think less of you."

"You're the best."

"I know. You're one lucky girl to have me as a bestie."

I laugh, then glance at the doorway again. "Well, I'd better go. I'll catch up with you later this week, though."

"Yes, do not keep that man waiting."

I shake my head. "Goodbye, Taylor."

After I click end on the call, I set my phone on the nightstand and get off the bed, already feeling lighter as I make my way out to the kitchen.

34

———

BASTION

A few weeks have passed since I first fucked Hattie, and I loathe to admit that I'm enjoying having her in my bed every night. And not just for the sex. Her company is a breath of fresh air, and she's funny—mostly when she's not trying to be.

We have plans today after she's done volunteering at the soup kitchen. I'm taking her to Von's 1000 Spirits for an early dinner. It's not about the food, though—when I asked her what she wanted to do, she said she wanted to do something she's never done before. Since I know she didn't drink until she arrived here in Seattle, I thought she might enjoy trying some different drinks.

I wait outside of the soup kitchen for her. She gave me directions, and I pretended I needed them. The deceit is lingering a little longer inside me lately, though.

She pushes the door open, but she's looking down into her bag. When she raises her head, looking for me, I instantly see that something is wrong.

My body goes on alert. "What's going on?" I approach her.

She shakes her head. "Nothing, let's get out of here." She attempts to walk past me, but I take her hand, pulling her to a stop.

"What happened?" I brush my thumb over her hand, and her bottom lip shakes.

I don't know who made her this upset, but whoever did is about to be very sorry when I'm done with them.

"I thought I was making friends in there with some of the people I attend service with who volunteer too. Today, a new girl joined us. She asked where I work, and for the first time, I didn't avoid the question or just say I'm an administrator or something." She shakes her head, and her hazel eyes grow glossy. "I told them where I work, and you should have seen the looks on their faces. It was like I was disgusting to them, even though two minutes earlier they were so nice and treating me like I was one of them."

I frown, seeing how much this is affecting her, and I pull her in for a hug. "I'm sorry, babe. People can be judgmental fucks."

She nods into my chest and wraps her arms around me, her body relaxing. My chest squeezes at how good it feels to be the one to give her comfort.

"At first, I thought that maybe they thought I was a stripper, but I made it clear what I did, and they still looked at me with such judgment. They didn't talk to me the rest of the afternoon." She pulls away and looks up at me, her sadness morphing into anger. "And even if I was a dancer, who cares? I still attend church with them, still have morals and values, and am volunteering my time alongside them."

"Damn straight." I like this fight I'm seeing in her. Probably a little too much. I tuck a piece of her hair behind her ear and take her hand, leading her in the direction we need to head.

"I swear, Bast, sometimes I feel like everything is upside down from what I thought it was. When I told Renee and Paige about how I was raised in the church and what that meant for me, they didn't bat an eye. They asked me some questions because they were curious, but they didn't judge me... at all. And when I think back on it, I'm pretty sure I've been judged more by my fellow churchgoers than anyone else in my life. That's why I tried so hard for so long to keep my desire for adventure and new things under wraps."

I squeeze her hand as we cross the street. "No one has any right to judge you, Hattie. Not if they know you. You're the best of what this world has to offer, that's for damn sure."

The words pour out of my mouth before I consider them. They're not part of some scheme to make Hattie fall for me. I realize they're how I actually feel. I'm ignoring what that means right now.

The knowledge rocks me to my core. Where is all the animosity and bitterness I felt for this woman? Do I need to unearth it like a corpse so I can keep my head on straight?

"Thank you, Bast. That means a lot coming from you. You always know how to make me feel better."

Damn, that Superman complex is a real thing, huh?

We approach our destination, and I tug her to a stop, pulling her in by the waist, needing my lips on hers. When I place my hands on either side of her face, I notice the sun brings out the gold flecks in her hazel eyes. I bend down and bring my lips to hers, but she pulls away.

"What if someone sees us?"

I shrug. "I don't care. Do you?"

Her head rocks back and forth. "I don't love the idea of people at work thinking I only have my job because we're sleeping together or something, but beyond that, no, I don't care."

Guilt snakes through my veins. She doesn't have her job because she was sleeping with me when I offered it to her, but she does have it for another reason that doesn't have much to do with her skill, although she's shocked even me with how good at her job she is.

"If anyone at the club has something to say, send them my way." I pull her back into me and kiss her, not caring who sees.

Three hours later, we leave Von's, and both of us are pretty tipsy. Well, I'm tipsy. Hattie seems like she's moving into the steadily drunk area. Tonight was her first night drinking hard liquor. She was game to try almost anything, so we picked a bunch of things off the menu and had a liquid dinner. We ordered food, but it sat mostly untouched in favor of the alcohol.

I'm getting a glimpse of what Hattie is like when her walls are down and she's had a few drinks, and I understand better why she acted the way she did the night she burst into my office, demanding to know the nature of my relationship with Steph.

We hold hands as we walk down the sidewalk, and she swings our arms between us like a child might do to their parent if they were holding hands.

"That was so much fun! I want to do it again!"

I give her an amused grin. "Let's see how you feel in the morning when you have to get up for work."

She guffaws. "Easy peasy, lemon squeezy."

"You say that now."

"I'll be fine. You'll see."

I laugh and keep walking, but she pulls me to a stop. When I turn to look at her, she's staring across the street.

"What?" I ask, unsure what she's staring at wide-eyed.

"It's a country bar! Oh my god, Bast, I haven't been to one like that since I was in college. Can we go?" She puts her hands in a prayer pose. "Please? Can we?"

"What the lady wants, the lady gets." I lead her by the hand over to the curb. "Let's go."

We enter the bar, and it's pretty much what I would expect from a country western bar—lots of wood, a decent-sized dance floor though there doesn't appear to be any line dancing going on, and a live band on stage.

I notice an empty table for two at the edge of the dance floor, and I point it out to Hattie before guiding her over there. It's clear as soon as we sit down that she's ecstatic. The server comes over to take our drink order, and though I suggest maybe she sit this one out, Hattie insists on ordering a beer—her first apparently—and I do the same.

Once the server walks away, she leans in over the table and speaks loudly enough so I can hear her. "I feel like I'm back in college. I never drank when I went, but there was a place just off campus that had a really great live band and played all my favorites. I haven't been to a place like this since I lived in Tennessee."

"When was that, six months ago?" I chuckle.

She rolls her eyes at me. "We can't all be your age, Grandpa."

The laugh that barks out of me is a surprise.

The band starts a new song, and Hattie claps excitedly. She sings along at the top of her lungs, loudly enough that I can hear her clearly.

Earlier tonight she told me that she was never a part of the church choir because she can't sing worth shit (her words, not mine). Turns out she's right. But it's still cute as fuck to see her not have a care in the world as she sings along, having the time of her life.

The server returns with our drinks, and we clink the necks of the bottles, each taking a sip. Hattie's face contorts in disgust, and after she swallows, she does a whole body shake.

"I think I found the first kind of alcohol I don't like." She stares at the bottle as though it's personally offended her, and I can't help but smile.

"Just set it on the table and don't drink it then." I'm going to have to carry her home if she has much more anyway.

Hattie looks at me like "as if" and takes another swig. I can only shake my head and laugh.

"So do you think you'll go back to that church again after today, or will you try to find another one?"

She considers it for a moment. "I think maybe I'm done with church for a bit. I feel like I need to develop my own relationship with God separate from organized religion." She shrugs. "I don't know. I'm sure I'll go back at some point and find a community again, but for now, this is what feels right."

I'd be lying if I said I wasn't surprised. I open my mouth to tell her just that, but before I can, the band changes the song, and Hattie bolts up out of her seat. "We have to dance!"

I raise my hands and shake my head. "No way."

She pouts, and if it were anything but dancing, I might give in. But as bad as Hattie is at singing, I am the equivalent at dancing. Hattie comes around the table and reaches for my hand, trying to drag me out of the chair, but I remain where I am.

"I'm gonna sit this one out. You go, have fun. I'll watch."

She pouts some more but does just that. "Your loss."

Watching her from our table turns out to be the better end of the deal by far. She's out there laughing and dancing around, having fun. At one point, she's welcomed into a group of other women when they notice that she's by herself. The joy I see on her face does something to me. I get this weird feeling in the pit of my stomach that I've never felt. The hell if I'm going to examine it too closely.

Then I see a man who's probably closer to Hattie's age than my own come up behind her and set his hand on her hip. I know exactly what to name this emotion—blind jealousy.

35

HATTIE

A large hand lands on my waist, and I smile. Bast decided to join me after all. I'm so glad. I'm having the best time out here. He was really missing out.

I raise my hands and lean back. The women dancing around me encourage me on. No doubt. Bast is so hot, and if the roles were reversed, I'd be egging them on too.

I close my eyes and wrap my arms around Bast's neck behind me, moving to the music and gyrating my hips. His other hand falls to my waist so both his hands are rubbing up and down my sides.

When I open my eyes, I glance over at our table, wondering if Bast left my bag there and whether it will be okay, but instead of finding it empty, Bast is there, staring at me. He's risen from the chair with his hands fisted at his sides, and I freeze in place from the look of rage on his face.

"C'mon, baby, don't stop now."

It takes my brain a second to catch up to the fact that the voice that just sounded in my ear is not Bast's.

I unwrap my hands from around his neck and whirl around, stepping back. "Oh my god!" My hand flies up to my mouth. "I thought you were someone else. I'm sorry."

The sandy-haired man grins and wraps a hand around my waist and tugs me to him again. "I can be whoever you want me to be, baby."

I push against his chest, but he doesn't release me, only pulling me in tighter. The smell of the alcohol on his breath is clear, as are his glazed eyes.

"You have one second to get your hands off her."

My head whips to the side, where Bast stands looking as though he's about a millisecond away from murdering this man. I push again at the man's chest, but he doesn't let go.

"Back off, asshole. Get your own girl. This one's coming home with me." He smiles at me. "Aren't you, sweetheart?"

I almost gag at the waft of alcohol coming off his breath. "Let me go."

"Don't make me ask you again. If you don't get your hands off her, I'll do it for you." Bast steps closer.

The guy holding me pushes me away without a second glance. He's too busy staring down Bast, the new target of his interest. "I'd like to see you try, old man."

Bast chuckles, but his nostrils flare and his jaw clenches. It's clear to me that it's taking everything in him to hold back.

"Bast, let's just go."

He raises a hand but doesn't look away from the drunk man. "He had his dirty paws all over what's mine and needs to be taught a lesson."

The guy shakes his head at Bast as if he finds this comical.

"Tell you what, this old man will let you get the first hit in. Then I'll finish it." Bast waves his hands toward his chest in a "come and get it" gesture.

Drunk guy laughs, then, without warning, he cranks his hand back and punches Bast in the face.

"Oh my god!" My hands fly up and cover my face as I stare in horror as Bast's face whips to the side. When he turns around, blood is spurting from his nose and dripping down his face.

I want to rush over, but some of the girls I was dancing with hold me by my arms. I need to make sure he's okay.

But Bast gives the guy a feral grin, blood staining the edges of his teeth. He has two good punches in before the guy even reacts, then they're toppling to the floor. Bast has the advantage on top and rains punches down on the guy, who tries to buck him off to no avail.

Everyone around us is screaming and shouting, forming a circle around the duo until two massive security guards push through the crowd and separate them.

Bast pays them no mind. "Next time, keep your hands off my woman. And if she tells you to let her go, you do!" His face is red and angry and covered in blood that's now smeared everywhere, but all I can focus on are the words that have come out of his mouth.

My woman.

The bouncers push the drunk guy toward the back door and Bast toward the front. I follow, stopping quickly to grab my bag from the table. The bouncer pushes Bast out the front door, and he immediately whirls around to make sure I'm there.

"Are you okay?" I raise my hand to his face but don't actually touch him in case it will hurt.

"I'm fine." He pulls his phone from his pocket and taps on the screen. "Uber will be here in two minutes. Are you okay?"

"I'm fine. I'm not the one who just got in a fight."

His brows drop low "He had his hands all over you."

Is he mad at me? "I thought it was you behind me. As soon as I knew, I tried to get him to let go."

He runs his hand down my back. "I know."

The Uber pulls up along the curb, and Bast opens the door for me. When he slides in the back seat beside me, the driver looks as though he's about to protest, but Bast slides him a hundred-dollar bill. The driver takes it without a word and turns back around.

Bast's quiet the entire drive back to the condo, so I follow his lead and say nothing. When he doesn't say anything on the elevator ride up, I worry that maybe he's angry with me.

As soon as the condo door closes behind us, he heads for his room. I stand for a moment, debating what I should do.

"Forget this." I'm not going to let him sulk or whatever he's doing and shut me out.

I slide off my shoes, then stomp down the hall until I reach his bedroom. He's just exiting the en suite, having washed the blood off his face.

"If you're mad at me, just come out and say it."

He looks at me, eyes narrowed. "I'm not mad at you." He reaches behind his head and pulls his shirt forward and off his body.

"Then why aren't you speaking to me?"

His jaw clenches, and a rush of air leaves his lungs. "Because I'm trying to calm myself down. I'm worked up, and I don't want to take it out on you. I need to purge this adrenaline from my system somehow." He walks into his closet. "I'm going to change and go work out."

Relief swamps me that he doesn't think I was doing anything intentionally to upset him. My mind flashes back to how angry he was and how affected he was by another man paying me attention, and I get an idea of what Renee and Paige were talking about when they said they feel powerful on stage. I brought out that reaction in him, which is a turn-on, and suddenly I get an idea.

I follow Bast into the massive walk-in closet to find him pulling his workout clothes out of a drawer in the center island. "I can think of other ways for you to work it out of your system." I bite my bottom lip.

Bast glances at me, then does a double-take. "If I fucked you right now, I'd probably split you in two, Hattie."

I saunter over to him, exaggerating the sway of my hips the same way I've seen the dancers at the club do. "What if you didn't fuck me?"

The curse word feels foreign on my tongue, but Bast's eyes light with pleasure at hearing me use it.

He swallows audibly. "What did you have in mind?"

Not answering him, I drop to my knees when I'm only a few feet away.

A hum of approval leaks out from low in his throat. "Have you ever done this before?"

I slowly shake my head, my eyes locked with his. Bast closes his eyes as though he's savoring my response.

"Can I?"

Wordlessly, he undoes his pants, shedding them and his boxer briefs until he stands naked in front of me, stroking himself.

My nipples pebble in my bra, and my breasts grow heavy.

Bast steps up to me and runs the tip of his length over the seam of my lips. "Do you know what it did to me to see another man's hands on you?"

I take his length in my palm, staring up at him through my eyelashes as I stroke.

"I could have killed him for touching what's mine without permission, Hattie."

Opening my mouth, I draw him in—just enough to encase the mushroom tip—and I suck lightly. Bast shudders, and his fingers thread through the hair on the side of my head. I pull back, then suck him in again, a little deeper this time, doing it again and again until he's as far back in my throat as I can take.

"Look at you taking me like this. You look so pretty with my thick cock between your plump lips, Hattie. Like a fucking angel."

The space between my thighs tingles from his words of praise. When I pull away, I circle my tongue around the tip before driving back down as far as I can. I gag a bit, but Bast must like it because he groans, and the fingers in my hair tighten.

"Hard to believe you've never taken a cock like this before, babe. You're so fucking good at this."

His words light me up inside, and I double my efforts.

Bast chuckles low in his throat. "I think someone has a bit of a praise kink."

Maybe I do. I love it when he tells me I'm pleasing him.

"Suck on my balls while you stroke me." He uses the hand in my hair to pull me away from his length, directing me lower.

I do as he says, gently pulling one into my mouth and sucking while I guide my hand up and down his shaft.

"Oh fuck." Bastion flexes the hand in my hair. "Jesus Christ, you are so fucking good."

His words light me up. I move to his other testicle, tonguing it for a moment before I draw it into my mouth.

"I need to fuck your face, Hattie." He pulls me back by the hair and stares at me with such burning desire in his eyes that it takes my breath away. "Can I?"

I nod, knowing I'd do almost anything to please him. He sets his hands on either side of my face and slides himself into my mouth. Bast starts slow at first, but as his breathing picks up, so does his pace. Soon he's thrusting in and out of my mouth, hitting the back of my throat.

When I gag, he says, "Try to relax your throat."

I do as he says, breathing through my nose. He pistons in and out of me as I watch from below, his head thrown back in ecstasy. Then he tilts his head down and meets my gaze, and he swells in my mouth, becoming even harder to take all of him, until he cries out and pulls away.

He holds his shaft a few inches or so from my face, and I close my eyes as his release rains down on me. Bast strokes the side of my face in a loving gesture. The way I want to lean into his touch and bask in his admiration tells me it's over, I've fallen for this man.

It wasn't my plan, it isn't anything he and I have discussed. I'm afraid to bring it up for fear that he'll think I'm a naïve little girl. He's thirteen years older than me and is probably used to having sexual relationships that don't involve getting serious or any real feelings. I'm not sure how he'd react to the feelings I've developed for him.

Just because he was jealous when another man touched me tonight doesn't mean he sees us going the distance. I think I'll keep this little revelation to myself, for now at least.

Bast holds his hand out to help me up off the floor. "Let's go take a shower."

After leading me to the en suite, Bast starts the shower and draws me in under the water. When we've both rinsed off, he pulls me in for a kiss, and I taste the faint trace of blood on his tongue from his fight.

"I think you're going to have a bruise and some swelling," I say, looking at his face.

He shrugs. "It was worth it to put that asshole in his place. And believe me, I've had worse." Bast laughs as though he's reliving some memory, and I'm afraid to ask.

Instead, we finish cleaning up. Afterward, I head back to my room to get into some pajamas.

Once I've dressed and brushed my hair, I pull out my phone to plug it in on my nightstand and realize I've missed a text from my parents in our group chat. My heart drops out when I see they want to come visit.

My stomach clenches—not because I don't want to see my parents, but because if they come to visit, they're going to see where I live and where I work. It's a reality I have to face at some point, but I'm not ready yet. Especially when I don't even know what Bast and I are.

So I text them back and tell them that I'll let them know when a good weekend is, but that I'm planning on returning home for a visit soon and we'll figure it out. It's the better of the two options. If I return to Wisconsin for a visit, I can push them off longer.

I plug my phone into the charger and return to Bast's room.

He's already in bed, leaning against the headboard and watching sports updates on the television.

"Have you heard when the apartment will finish being repaired?" I climb into my side of the bed. It's a given now that I'll be sleeping here.

He glances away from the screen at me. "Contractor said that there was more water damage than he thought once he started pulling everything apart. It's going to be at least another month."

"It sure is taking him a long time." I snuggle into Bast's side.

"You eager to get away from me?" He holds my gaze, and there's something in his I can't figure out.

I frown. "Of course not."

"Good." His arm comes around me and squeezes me into his side.

I try not to read into his words tonight—mine, my woman, good—but my hopeful heart finds it impossible.

36

BASTION

I need to get my head straight. Ever since Sunday night, my mind has been a fucking vortex. Seeing that prick with his hands on Hattie, I swear to God, it's lucky we were in public because I wanted to murder him.

And the words that were coming out of my mouth—mine, my woman—what the fuck was that about? The worst part is that they weren't even part of the act to get Hattie to fall in love with me. Though I think she is. At least that much is going my way.

Until she asked about the condo.

But I have to remember why I'm doing this. Who I'm punishing. And even if I realize that maybe Hattie doesn't deserve my punishment, Carla does. And Hattie is the most effective way to deliver the killing blow. She's just collateral damage, nothing more.

Trent always said going to war meant innocent casualties, and Hattie is going to become one. I need to not give a shit.

I've been pondering all morning how to ensure that the blow I deal Carla is as painful as possible, and the idea of getting Hattie to try heroin came to mind. I'm waiting for Sean to show up, and it would be easy enough to ask him for some. I'd never let him sling that shit in my club, but I'm sure he has sold it elsewhere.

Imagine if Mommy Dearest found her daughter going down the same self-destructive path she had. That would be the ultimate revenge. Then she'd know what I'd had to deal with all those years she was hooked.

But I can't do it. I know I can't.

I'm intimately familiar with the hell that path leads to, and while I don't have any sympathy for people who willingly embark down that road, I can't manipulate Hattie into it. Why? Because I'm fucking soft where Hattie is concerned, which has to change. Trent would have been so disappointed in me for falling for my mark back in the day. I have to figure out some way to further ruin her and make Carla pay.

The door to the VIP room opens, and Ray takes up almost all the space. "Sean is here."

"Send him in." I lean back in my seat and cross my legs, resting my right ankle on my left knee with an unaffected air.

This will not be a pleasant meeting. Sean is getting fired today. He just doesn't know it.

The door opens again, and Sean steps inside. I gesture to the area with the wrap-around couch to my right, so we'll be facing each other.

He takes a seat and starts right in on his bullshit. "I hope you asked me here because you decided to be smart and take our offer."

I chuckle and smooth my tie down my chest. "Sorry to disappoint you, but no. I asked you here to tell you that I don't take kindly to business partners who try to stab me in the back. We had a good thing going here—we were both making money, there were no problems, no drama—and then you had to go and change that because you got greedy. Do you know what the most important thing in business is to me, Sean?"

"I'm not gonna sit here and listen to a lecture."

"It's trust and loyalty. It seems I made a mistake when I thought you possessed the same mindset. Consider this your official notice that we are done doing business together. Effective immediately, you, your goons, and any of your assets are not welcome in any of my clubs."

He shoots up off the couch, anger coating his features, fists clenched at his sides. "You can't do that!"

I remain where I am, stone-faced with zero emotion. "I can do whatever I want. This is my club. You want to sell your shit through a strip club, start your own."

"My bosses won't be happy."

"Then maybe your bosses should have taken the answer no when I told them the first time. And it's a done deal. I already have a new partner."

"You're gonna regret this, asshole."

I shrug. "I think you mean *you're* going to regret this. My business is just fine." I hold his stare as it filters through a range of emotions—anger, disbelief, anxiety, and fear.

Oh yes, I bet he's afraid to report up the chain how he's handled this and how he fucked it all up. But that's not my problem. He created this problem for himself.

Sean stabs his finger in my direction. "You're going pay, asshole, big time."

I stand unhurriedly, buttoning my suit jacket closed. Then I grin at him. "I don't think so." I saunter toward the door and leave, passing by Ray stationed at the end of the hall. "Make sure Sean leaves without causing any problems."

He nods and heads back to the room I just left. I've already instructed Ray to tell his staff that Sean and his goons are no longer welcome here.

Sean might try to cause me some trouble, but I won't accept working with someone who tries to change the rules of the game just because they think they can take advantage of me.

When I return to my office, Hattie is already gone. I figured she would be, but for whatever reason, I feel more on edge that she's not here with me. I collapse back into my chair, annoyed with myself, and undo my suit jacket, then I slide my phone from the pocket. I felt it vibrate with a text when I was talking to Sean.

There's a text from my sister asking me to call her and another from Steph asking when I want to schedule our meeting this week to go over what we need to.

I ignore Steph's message and pull up Ari's contact.

"Hey, thanks for calling me back."

"Don't mention it."

I hear her cover the phone and murmur something to someone.

Gross. She's probably in bed with her husband, doing who knows what.

"What's wrong?" she asks.

"You've been on the phone with me for a total of three seconds. Why would you possibly think anything is wrong?"

"Because I know you, Bast. Now what's going on?"

"Work bullshit. Don't worry about it. Tell me why you're calling." I don't like being short with my sister, but I can't help it. I just want to get this phone call over with and get back to the condo so I can bury myself in Hattie.

"Okay... well, I was talking to Dad and Eleanor earlier, and I think something is up. I asked about his last doctor's appointment and how it was going with his medication and stuff, and they seemed cagey."

Hmm. That does seem odd.

"I haven't talked to Dad in a couple of weeks, so I don't know anything. Sorry."

"Would you be able to fly down there and check on him? I'd do it except the kids are back to school soon and I have a lot to do to prepare."

I blow out a breath. My dad and his wife live in Northern California, so it is much faster and easier for me to get there. Maybe a couple of days away from Hattie would do me some good. Help me clear my head and get me out from under Hattie's thrall.

"Sure. I'll head there tomorrow, stay the night, and see what's up."

"Thank you, Bast. I really appreciate it. Let me know what you find."

"You owe me though, Ari."

"Yeah, yeah." I can almost see my sister rolling her eyes. She giggles, then I'm the one rolling my eyes.

"Go finish whatever you were doing. I'll talk to you after I get back to Seattle." I hang up and stand from my chair, immediately leaving my office to head home.

I know exactly how I'm going to work out these emotions rolling through me, then tomorrow will be a fresh start. When I return, I won't be obsessing over Hattie anymore. But for tonight, I'll allow myself to indulge.

On my way to the condo, I book the first flight out of Seattle in the morning and a rental car, texting my dad to tell him I'm coming tomorrow for an impromptu visit. It's overdue anyway, something I should have made time for in the past several months.

When the elevator doors open on my floor, I slide my phone back in my pocket and stalk down the hallway, my dick already half hard. I unlock the condo and walk into the main area to find Hattie snuggled into the corner of the large sectional couch, reading. I head straight for her, having one goal, and that's to get inside her.

"Hey, how was—" She must see something on my face that causes her to abruptly stop.

Hattie sets her book aside, her eyes transfixed on me. When I reach her, I bend at the waist and hoist her over my shoulder.

"Bast, what are you doing?" She sounds more amused than afraid.

She's wearing a tank top and a pair of cotton shorts that give me easy access to her pussy, so I place my hand between her legs on the walk down the hall and play with her. Hattie moans, and the scent of her arousal hits me, making my dick push against the zipper of my slacks, demanding to be sated.

We reach my bedroom, and I deposit her onto the mattress. Her eyes go wide, and I admire her hair sprawled out on my bed.

"I need you" is all I say, pulling my shirt out of my pants and toeing out of my shoes. "Take your clothes off."

She peels off her tank top. Of course she doesn't argue, she's perfect. She'll take what I dish out with no complaints, and the best part is that she'll reap the rewards.

Once I'm naked, I cup my balls and stroke myself, fixated by this perfect creature.

"I want to film us." Fuck, the idea of being able to watch us together long after I've destroyed everything between us would be a gift. A little something to torture myself with. Panic cuts across Hattie's face, and I put my hands up in defense. "I would never show anyone. It would be for us only."

For me.

The panic subsides, and I already know she's going to agree before she says, "Okay." I block out the trust in her eyes because it spurs nausea in my stomach.

I grab my phone and head across the room to the area where the TV is mounted on my wall above my dresser. I don't have a tripod or anything, have never needed one, but I'll improvise.

After I start the recording, I flip the camera so it's facing me and prop it up against some decorative figurine the designer said my bedroom would look cold without. I should send her a thank you note after this.

Once I've angled the phone so it faces the bed, I walk over to Hattie. She's propped up on her elbows, biting her lower lip.

"Don't be nervous, it's still just us." I slide open the drawer of the nightstand and retrieve a condom, spotting the panties I stole from Hattie's room. Another idea takes shape.

"I want you bare." I turn and look at her over my shoulder.

"I'm on birth control." When my eyes narrow, she adds, "For my periods."

I need to cool it with the jealousy shit. I remind myself it's exactly why I'm heading out tomorrow morning.

"I've been tested recently, and I don't have any STIs," I say.

"I was tested a long time ago after... and you know I haven't..."

I step forward with the underwear clenched in my fist, then

use my free hand to thread through the hair in the back of her head. "I know you've only spread those thighs for me."

"Are those mine?" She eyes her pink panties in my hand.

"Yes."

"Where... what..."

I slide my hand down from her head to her breast and pinch her nipple, watching the way her eyes dilate and her mouth drops open.

She nods, her lids heavy with lust, forgetting her question about why I have a pair of her panties in my drawer.

"I need to take you hard and fast, Hattie. Is that okay?"

"Take me however you want me."

Fuck, this is why I need to get the hell out of Seattle tomorrow.

"Crawl to the edge of the bed and spread your legs." I back up to give her room, and she does exactly as instructed.

When I see her glistening cunt, I lean down and take a swipe, coating my tongue with her essence. Hattie moans, trying to shove her pussy in my mouth. Gripping the base, I run the head of my cock back and forth through her folds. Hattie's breathing picks up, and she arches off the bed like a beautiful offering. Then I line myself at her entrance and slam home.

She cries out, and I shove the panties in her mouth. Her eyes open to meet my gaze, questioning, but as I pump into her, she bites down on them, moaning into the fabric.

My hands press on her inner thighs, keeping her open for me. Fucking her without a condom was a mistake because I'll never forget this feeling and will never be able to recreate it after she's gone.

"Fuck!" I pound into her mercilessly, and with stroke after stroke, my pleasure builds, but I don't want to come yet. I don't want this to end.

Bringing one hand to her clit, I thumb the swollen bud until Hattie's head thrashes back and forth on the mattress, and she screams into the pink lace and silk as her pussy bears down on me, and she comes. Still, I don't let up. I continue stroking her until she's bucking off the bed, tears streaming out of her eyes, and she's coming again.

This time, I rip the underwear from her mouth and bend down, capturing her lips. Our kiss is sloppy and desperate, and she claws at my back with her short nails.

As soon as she comes down from her orgasm, I flip her over and drive back into her. Her greedy cunt welcomes my cock, stretching around my length, and I feel the odd pulse of her orgasm squeezing me.

I take her like a rutting animal staking his claim, the slapping sound of our skin meeting filling the room. With a hand on each ass cheek, I spread her for my viewing and press my thumb against her puckered hole, not pressing it inside, but applying pressure.

She moans and drops her head to the mattress, arms splayed out over her head and gripping the sheets in tight fists.

My balls contract, and the buzzing starts at the base of my thighs. I'm not going to last much longer. With a roar, I pull all the way out of her and jerk myself as the orgasm overcomes me and I paint her ass with my cum.

I catch my breath, admiring my handiwork on her amazing ass, rubbing it all over her sweat-streaked skin, as though I want a part of me to become entwined with a part of her.

Hattie slumps forward on the bed, heaving for breath, and I study her, taking one last moment to see her like this. Because when I return from my father's, I'll no longer be looking at her through this rose-colored lens.

37

BASTION

I arrived at my father and Eleanor's earlier today, and Ariana is right, something is wrong. I haven't questioned him directly, but I've caught him and Eleanor sharing a few glances that lead me to believe they're hiding something.

Hattie seemed disappointed that I was leaving, but she didn't complain. She never complains. Sadly, no matter how many miles I've put between us, she's still at the forefront of my mind.

I haven't wanted to talk to anyone about what's going on until now, and maybe my dad is the perfect candidate. God knows he's run enough of his own scams over the years that he's not going to judge me. Hell, I was a willing participant for most of them. Together we've conned people, lied, ripped them off, and stolen from them. He knows my past and where I came from, and he'll understand why I'm doing what I am.

So once we're settled on his back porch, each of us with a beer in hand, looking out over his property, I decide it's time to fill him in—after I figure out what's going on with him.

We're both silent for a few minutes. Eleanor is in the house, cleaning up after dinner, and the two of us seem content to listen to the chirping insects surrounding us.

"Your sister sent you, didn't she?"

I look over at the man who took me in when he didn't have to. The man who's showing his age. It's a stark reminder of how quickly time passes. "I used to be a better grifter. Skills must be rusty."

The corners of his lips tip up. "You've still got it, kid, don't worry. But you haven't been for a visit in a long time, then suddenly you text and tell me you're coming the next day. Add on the fact that it just happens to be the day after Ari and I get into it on the phone because she thinks I'm hiding something?" He arches a graying eyebrow. "Don't need a PhD to figure it out."

I blow out a breath. "She's just worried. As am I since I arrived. You and Eleanor do a shit job of trying to pretend nothing's wrong."

He shakes his head. "It's nothing to concern yourself with."

"Perfect, then you can fill me in." I take a pull of my beer.

His finger taps the end of the armrest while the finger on his other hand taps the beer bottle. "I have prostate cancer." I open my mouth to say something, but his hand goes up to stop me. "Before you say anything, they caught it early, and my doc thinks I'll be fine. I have to have surgery in a couple of weeks, some radiation, and then I should be good to go."

"Jesus. I'm sorry, Dad. Let me know what you need me to do. I'm here to help."

He scowls, shaking his head. "I don't want you kids making a big deal of it, all right? That's why I haven't told your sister. She'll be down here in a heartbeat, hovering over me, acting like I'm dying and driving me crazy. Or worse, make me move into that damn mansion. Her heart is in the right place, but you know what she's like."

He's not wrong. Ariana can be overbearing, but I think that's what you get when your mother leaves. You cherish your family. So, I don't blame her.

"I can't keep this from her."

His jaw flexes and he keeps his gaze on the forest beyond. "Fine, but make sure you tell her the part about me being fine."

"Right, I'm sure that will ease her mind." I take a pull from my beer, knowing she'll be on the first plane out.

"I'm serious, Bast. Make sure she knows that she doesn't have to go all mother hen on me."

I nod, though we both know it doesn't matter how I spin it. Ari's going to freak out.

"I swear ever since she had those kids, she worries about everything. What happened to the little girl who used to pull one over on people with me?"

My dad wasn't happy when Ariana told us she was leaving the family con business more than a decade ago. I know he loves my sister, but I think he still sees it as her turning her back on us. On him.

"Ariana's happy with her life, and that's what matters. Let her fuss over you a little bit. Otherwise, you two will be at each other's throats."

He grunts and takes another sip of his beer. "Now what's going on with you?"

"What makes you think something is going on with me?"

He turns and looks at me with that dad expression he perfected at some point. "Call it fatherly intuition."

I push my hand through my hair. "I've been dealing with something for a few months. Thought I had the situation under control, but... things have shifted."

"Is it business?"

"Nah. It's personal."

"Well, don't act like a mopey teenager I have to pull the information out of. Tell me what's going on."

I stand, leaving my beer on the table beside the chair, and go up to the porch railing. With my hands on the railing, I stare at the lush trees at the end of the yard. "I hired someone to track down information on my mom."

He says nothing.

"Figured he'd come back and tell me she'd ODed, but the joke is on me. She's alive and well, living in Wisconsin."

Only silence continues behind me.

It's only dawning on me now that maybe my dad won't take well to the news that I was looking for my birth mother. He was the one who brought me up. Sure, at first it might have been for me to help him with cons, but our relationship shifted to father and son.

When a minute passes and he still doesn't say anything, I turn around, leaning against the railing. All the color has drained from his face, and his eyes are wide.

"I didn't do it because I want a relationship with her or anything. I was just... curious. I wanted to know what had happened to her."

He clears his throat. "And what did happen to her?"

I cross my arms. "She lives in Wisconsin with her husband that she's been married to for a long time. He had a daughter before they married, and she's raised her as her own."

"Have you talked to her? Your mother, I mean?" His voice sounds wary.

I shake my head. "I told you, I didn't track her down so I could strike up a relationship with her. In fact, after I read the whole report, all I was interested in was revenge."

"What did you do, Bast?"

He knows me better than I do most times.

I tell him all about Hattie and how she was raised, me hiring her and wanting to corrupt her. I tell him everything.

He blows out a breath. "And now you care about this girl."

"I don't know."

He stares blankly at me again.

"I need to get my shit together where she's concerned so that I can finish this. I can't wait to see the look on Carla's face when she realizes what her perfect little daughter has been up to in Seattle and exactly who's been doing it to her."

My dad goes quiet again, his color still not returning.

"Are you feeling okay? Do you want me to get Eleanor or something?"

He's staring at his lap, but he holds up his hand, then doesn't say anything for at least another minute before he slowly raises his gaze to mine. "I agree. I figured your mother would be dead by now too."

"Not sure what her reason was for getting clean, but I obviously wasn't a good enough one for her." That familiar ache in my chest, the one I always carry to some degree, intensifies.

"Bast, I have to tell you something. And I need you to hear me out."

I stiffen, knowing from the tone of his voice that I won't like whatever he's about to tell me. "What?"

"Your mother showed up at our door about a year after I took you in."

I'm not sure I understand what he's saying as hard as I'm trying to register his words. It feels as though someone punched me in the gut and knocked the wind out of me.

"My mother came looking for me?" My voice is hoarse. He nods solemnly. "Was she fucked up or was she clean?"

A pained look crosses his face. "She was clean. At least she said she was, looked like maybe she was, although she was frail and thin. But after everything you'd told me about her, I didn't believe her, didn't trust that she'd stay that way."

"What did she want?" Though I think I already know.

His gaze doesn't veer from mine. "She wanted to take you with her. And I refused."

"She what?" I roar, stepping toward him. If he wasn't sick, I'd rip him up out of that chair and toss him off the porch.

My mother came for me?

My mother came for me.

"What did you tell her? Why didn't I go with her?"

He shifts in his seat, guilt lining all his wrinkles. "I told her that you wanted nothing to do with her, that you ran away for a reason and that you hated her. Said that you told me you'd run away from her again if you ever had to go back there. Threatened her if she ever tried to come back again."

Tears prick the backs of my eyes, but I do what I always do and swallow them back down. "But I didn't say any of that."

He frowns. "Maybe it was the wrong thing to do, but I wasn't about to send you back there to be neglected and abused on her word alone."

"You sure it's not just because I was bringing in money for you and helping you with your grifts?" Venom coats my words. My anger's too big to hide.

He glares at me. "I did what I thought was right at the time."

I push my hand through my hair and turn away from him, then pace the length of the porch.

My mother came for me.

My mother cared for me—to some degree at least.

My head is a swirl of thoughts, my heart a mess of emotions. I don't know how to feel about this confession.

I turn to face him. "How come you never told me?"

He blows out a breath. "Didn't think it would do you any good. Thought it would just mess you up more. You had come such a long way in that year. Your nightmares were subsiding, you were healing, and I really didn't think she'd stay clean, Bast."

"How did she find me?"

He frowns and shakes his head. "No idea. Never asked."

I think back to around the time he's talking about and realize something. "Let me guess. Right around then was when we moved, wasn't it? You moved us because of her?"

Shame crosses his features. "Yeah, it was. I didn't want her showing back up, fucked up or something. You didn't need that."

I'd like to believe him, but Trent has always looked out for number one. I'm under no illusion that if I hadn't been useful to him, I would have stayed in his care. Regardless, the man did raise me—put a roof over my head, clothed me, and fed me. That's no small thing.

Anger burns like a hot coal in the pit of my stomach. I don't know how to feel about any of this—Trent, Carla... Hattie.

"I can't believe you never fucking told me." My tone is almost a growl.

Would anything have been different if I had known? Maybe. Quite possibly.

My eyes squeeze shut, and my chest tightens.

"What are you going to do about the girl?" he asks after a moment, completely disregarding what he did all those years ago. That I'm in this mess partly because of him.

I turn and stare at the forest. "I have no idea."

38

———

HATTIE

It was only one night alone in Bast's bed, but I barely slept. Each minute lying there awake in the dark felt like an eternity. I'm not sure when I grew so completely attached to the man, but I have.

It probably didn't help that yesterday morning before he left, he seemed pensive, as though something was on his mind, but when I asked him if he was okay, he said he was fine. And he was open with me that the impromptu trip was because his sister was worried about their father. It would make sense for him to be concerned too.

Still, he didn't text me yesterday—or today so far. I must have checked my phone a hundred times. Sure, I could text him, but I don't want to come off like a needy girl who can't go a day without talking to her... whatever Bast is to me. That's still the burning question I keep trying to put on the back burner, but it's becoming more and more pressing. I need some kind of definition for our relationship. If only to keep my own expectations in check.

Pushing away from my desk, I go to make myself a hot chocolate. I'm not sure whether Bast is coming here or to the condo when he arrives in town, but I assume he'll let me know at some point. So, I'm going to work until I hear from him.

Renee's in the break room. She must just be coming in for her shift because she's in street clothes. She's leaning against the counter and scrolling through her phone.

"Hey, how are things?"

She glances up from her phone and smiles. "Good. I'm glad I ran into you."

"Oh yeah? What's up?" I grab a mug from the cupboard, setting it on the counter.

"I'm taking the little man to the Children's Museum next week. We've never been, but I think he'll love it. Wanted to see if maybe you'd like to come along?"

Warmth spreads through my chest. Renee is selective about who she allows around her son, and if she's inviting me, it's because she trusts me. I haven't met him yet, but I've been hoping to. I love kids. They're so sweet and innocent and look at the world through a lens that's so much simpler than adults.

"I would love to. Just text me the details." I want to swarm her in a big hug and thank her, but that would probably be too much.

"Awesome!" Her face lights up with a smile. "I've been telling him about my new friend at work. He's excited to meet you."

The clicking of heels on the tile behind me alerts me to someone else's presence. I see a momentary flash of irritation on Renee's face before she schools her features, so I turn around to see who it is.

Steph stands a few steps into the doorway, looking the two of us up and down as though we don't deserve to breathe the same air as her. She wears a skintight red bodycon dress with a plunging neckline. It seems like a little much for a summer afternoon, but I guess this is a strip club. Even if she isn't a dancer.

"Bastion isn't in his office. Do either of you know where he is?" She looks between the two of us with a bored expression.

"Was he expecting you?" I surprise myself with the challenge in my tone.

One quick glance at Renee tells me she finds this interaction amusing.

"Yes, in fact he was. We have a meeting." She crosses her arms.

"He must have forgotten. He's out of town." I smile nicely, trying to mask the annoyance swirling in my chest.

She stiffens. "Where did he go?"

My head tilts. "I'm not at liberty to say. I assume if he wanted you to know, he'd have told you." I use my sweetest voice, but her eyes narrow.

All I can picture when I look at her is her with Bast, and it makes me feel sick to my stomach. I keep telling myself it was before I came here, but that doesn't seem to matter. It's then I realize that I haven't asked Bast whether he's been with her since I started living with him, since we... no. He wouldn't do that. Sure, he told me that one night I drank a little too much that he hadn't, but what about since?

Even if you don't have any agreement to keep things monogamous between you two?

The thought hits me before I can stop the train, and I have to force the smile to stay on my face in front of Steph.

"Is there something I can help you with?" I ask before Steph can respond to my last statement.

She gives me the once-over again. "Not with the business we take care of in our meetings."

Her meaning is clear, and my short fingernails push into my palms when I clench my fists. Steph glances down at my hands, then meets my gaze with a soft giggle and an amused grin.

"I'll be sure to tell him you came by." I turn back around and open the other cupboard to grab the hot chocolate packet.

"No need, I'll just call him. Maybe he'll want to meet up after hours at his place."

I clench my jaw and take the plastic lid off the hot chocolate container.

"Bye, ladies."

Neither Renee nor I say goodbye back.

"God, she's such a bitch," Renee says.

Rather than respond, I make my hot chocolate.

After a few moments, Renee leans in closer to me. "Hey, you all right?"

My chest is tight, and I'm so angry, I fear fire could come out of my mouth if I open it right now. I don't know why I let her get under my skin. I'm the one sleeping in Bast's bed every night.

That's a lie, I do know. Because she's everything I'm not. She fits in here. She's glamorous and beautiful and dresses sexy. I'm sure Steph is confident and seductive and knows exactly what she's doing in bed.

"I'm fine. She just annoys me."

Renee barks out a laugh. "You and everyone else. Okay, I have to go get ready to be on stage. I'll text you the details, okay?"

I nod. "Sounds good."

The reminder that Renee wants me to meet her son lifts my mood a little, and I decide to focus on that rather than whatever Bast and Steph had going on. But that only lasts as long as it takes me to walk back to the office, because as soon as I get inside, I see a hot pink sticky note in the middle of Bast's desk. It wasn't there when I left.

I know exactly who wrote it before I even pick it up.

Sorry I missed you.
We have so much to cover.
Call me when you're back.
xo - S

. . .

I roll my eyes and toss the note in the garbage. I'm sure it's more for my benefit than Bast's anyway. I don't think Steph knows anything is going on between us, but I do think she's afraid I'm going to veer into her territory and wants to make it clear that I'm not welcome.

The temper I didn't even know I had rears up again. Though I try to take a few deep breaths and let it pass, it remains.

Not wanting to have to deal with anyone else this afternoon, I shut the office door. Maybe they'll think no one is in here and leave me alone. As I walk back to my desk, my eyes snag on the noise-canceling headphones sitting on the corner. I use them when I'm working and want to listen to music so that I don't disturb Bast.

Once I sit down, I slip them on and find my Christian rock playlist. I may not be going to church right now, but focusing on God always makes me feel more centered and like everything will be okay.

I'm not sure when Bast is expected, but I know I don't want to be in this mood when he arrives.

A couple of hours later, I'm still working at my desk when I take a break to roll my neck and stretch my arms. Sometimes I can get in the zone and it's like there's nothing else around me.

I'm rolling my neck side to side when I stop.

What is that smell?

I sniff a bit and still.

Is that smoke?

I turn my chair to look at the closed door and see the smoke coming from under the door like a spirit creeping into the room. I simultaneously bolt up out of my chair and toss my headphones onto the desk.

My stomach turns to lead and drops to the floor when I hear screams coming from outside the door. Panicked, I race for the door and yank it open to be met with a wall of smoke.

I cough and look down either side of the hallway. Flames roll up the opening leading to the main room and the front entrance, so I bolt to the back door. I can barely see through the thick smoke, sucking in some of it and coughing, but when I push on the door to get out, it doesn't open. I try again to no avail, so I keep pushing, trying to get a cleansing breath.

I look over my shoulder. Having no choice but to find another way out since the door won't budge, I rush back to the office and slam the door closed. My eyes burn and water from the smoke. I concentrate on the steady stream of smoke filling the room from under the door.

I grow nauseated and panic. What am I going to do? Grabbing my phone off my desk, I huddle in the corner, my forehead against my knees, arms wrapped around my legs as I rock back and forth.

My phone is still gripped in my hand. I should use it to call 9-1-1 and tell someone I'm here, but I'm too frozen in terror to do anything but sit.

39

BASTION

*A*ll last night, after my conversation with my dad, all I thought of was Hattie. I can't continue to lie to myself that she means nothing to me. How much I missed her. That's when it occurred to me that she's no longer a pawn in this game. She's embedded herself in me, and I want her to be mine. Shit, it's going to be tricky, and I'm not sure she's even going to want me if she ever finds out about the scheming I did.

"What is taking so long?" I ask, wanting to see her, to touch her, to hold her.

"Don't think I can get much closer. Something must be going on up there."

I look up from my phone to see where we are. We're just down the street from the club. Smoke is rising into the air from the side of the street the club is on.

"What the fuck?"

I'm out of the car in seconds and running down the street toward the commotion. My panic rises as I get closer and see that my fucking club is on fire. A bunch of the staff are standing on the other side of the street in shock, looking at the building.

By the looks of it, the fire department has just arrived. They're hooking up their hoses to the fire hydrants.

I quickly survey the crowd and don't spot Hattie. Fear grips me so tight you'd think I have a noose around my neck.

Maybe she's already at the condo. It's a little later than she normally stays. I was going to call her to see where she is, but I had to stop by the club first to check on things. I figured if she were here, I'd see her, and if not, I'd see her when I got home.

"Bastion!" Renee shouts when she sees me.

I run over to her. "Where's Hattie?"

Her eyes are filled with tears. "I don't know. I think she might still be inside. I heard someone say the back door wouldn't open, so they had to go out the front."

Not wasting time, I pull my phone from my pocket and pull up Hattie's contact. It rings once, and there's no answer.

"C'mon, answer." My hand fists my hair.

It rings again, and again there's no answer.

A sensation I've never felt, not even growing up with Carla, fills me—absolute dread. What if she's...

"Hello?"

Her small, scared voice comes on the line, and I momentarily breathe with relief.

"Hattie! Where are you?"

She sobs and sniffles. "I'm in the office. There's nowhere to go. The front is all flames, and the back door won't open."

Her tears turn into a cough that seems more like choking, and the sound absolutely guts me.

"I'm coming for you." I race to the corner so I can go down the alley that runs along the back of the buildings on this block.

"No! Bast, you'll—"

I hang up before she can say anything else. She needs to preserve her strength, and like hell am I going to leave her in there to burn to death.

Running as fast as I can, I rush down the alley until I reach the club's back entrance, and it becomes obvious why Hattie couldn't open the door. A bunch of large, and I assume heavy, crates are stacked in front of the door. It looks innocent enough, as though a delivery guy set them there by accident and walked away. But they're not from any supplier we use. This fire... this back door being blocked... it's intentional.

I set my rage aside for the time being as I move the crates away from the door. Another set of hands helps me, and I turn to see Ray picking up the boxes and tossing them aside, letting them crash behind us. He must have followed me when I ran from the group.

I'm the only person who has a key to the back door from the outside, so I fish my keys out of my pocket and unlock it before whipping it open. I immediately choke on the smoke.

I turn to face Ray as I pull my T-shirt up over my face. It's not much, but it's something. "You stay out here and tell the fire department that I'm going to my office to get Hattie out. If I don't come back, send them in to find us."

"You got it," Ray says, though he looks as if he wants to say more.

I rush into the darkness of the smoke to save the woman I love.

My eyes immediately sting. It's impossible to see, and the smoke is disorienting as fuck, so I push aside the need to rush in and scramble to find Hattie. I need to be smart about this or we're both going to die.

I rest my hand on the hallway wall as I take measured steps forward, feeling a small amount of relief when my hand crests over a doorjamb. That has to be the office. I keep going and feel that the door is closed, so I lower my hand and search around for the handle.

The metal is warm to the touch but not hot since the fire is still farther up the hall. Twisting it, I call Hattie's name as I enter and close the door behind me.

"Hattie, are you in here?"

"Bast?"

A rush of relief floods me, but her voice sounds so small and meek that it's almost my undoing.

"I'm here, babe. I'm here." I head in the direction of her voice.

It's a little easier to see in here than it was in the hallway, and when I get a couple of feet away from her, I can make out her figure rocking in the corner. I swear I almost burst into tears—whether in relief or sorrow, I don't even know.

"Hattie, can you stand?"

She looks up, slowly blinking as if maybe I'm not really here.

I pull off the T-shirt covering my face and pull it down over her head, then I bend and pick her up. Her hands wrap around my neck. I say a silent thank you that I found her and she's safe.

When I spin around, I can still make out the door, and I head that way.

"I'm gonna open this door in a second, but I want you to take a deep breath and try to hold it until we're out of the building, okay?"

She tucks her face into my neck.

"All right, one, two, three." I suck in as much air as I can, then whip open the door.

The fire on the right side is only a few feet away from the door now, and when I step out into the hallway, we're met with a wall of heat. Hattie jolts in my arms. I squeeze her tighter, hoping it conveys that everything is okay and I'm going to get her the hell out of here.

We don't have time for me to be careful about our exit, so I turn left and barrel down the hallway even though I can't see shit. When we're a couple of feet away from the exit, the outline of the door and the light in the doorway come into view. I burst outside, letting fresh air fill my lungs, and slam the door shut with my foot.

I cough, tears streaking down my cheeks from the smoke, but I don't let Hattie go.

I'm never letting her go. That's what I figured out at my dad's. This woman in my arms wasn't supposed to come to mean so much to me, but she does. If there was any doubt left in me about whether or not I love Hattie, thinking I may have lost her has shredded it to pieces. I love this woman, and I'm going to have her as mine.

Once, I couldn't wait to reveal the truth of who and what I was to her. And now I have to make sure she never finds out.

40

BASTION

The paramedics gave Hattie and me oxygen and looked us over, declaring us both fit enough to leave, though they'd prefer that we go to the hospital. Neither Hattie nor I was interested, though I wouldn't mind Hattie being looked over. But all I wanted to do was hold her, have her in my arms so that I know she's real and she's here with me, so I immediately took her back to the condo.

We took a shower to get the smoke scent off our bodies. It took two rounds of shampoo and two deep scrubs to achieve. I'm pretty sure I'll still be smelling smoke for weeks.

Once we're dried off and Hattie has dried her hair, I lead her to bed, where I wrap my arms around her and tuck her into my chest. "Are you okay?"

She's been quiet since we arrived. I keep waiting for her to break down, but it's as though she's trying to hold back for some reason.

Hattie nods into my chest, and I squeeze my arms around

her, kissing the top of her head before pulling away to see her face.

"Talk to me. What are you thinking?"

Her gaze lifts to meet mine, and I see tears in her eyes. My chest squeezes painfully.

"I was so scared." Her voice is still rough from breathing in the smoke.

"I was too." I drop my forehead to hers. "When I knew you were in there, I felt like I couldn't breathe. I was so afraid of losing you."

"I kept praying to God to save me, but when you called and said you were coming to get me, I didn't want you to because I was scared you'd be hurt... or worse."

I kiss her forehead. "I'm here. We're both here."

There's so much more I want to tell her, but now is not the time. She's had a traumatizing experience, and the best thing for her right now is rest.

"Are you hungry?"

She shakes her head. "No, I don't think I can eat right now."

"All right. What do you say we put on a funny movie or something, cuddle up here?"

A little glimmer of the usual sparkle that's in her eyes rises. "Okay," she says in a soft voice, then clears her throat.

The paramedic said we can expect to have irritated throats and that a cough might develop too.

I get everything set up on the TV and pull her back into me. We both drift off at some point and stay in that position for the rest of the night.

The next morning, I'm making Hattie breakfast—one of the few meals I can make—when Jeffery calls up.

"Sir, I have your sister here to see you."

I squeeze my eyes shut. What is Ariana doing here? I said I'd call her last night with an update about Dad, but she couldn't wait for me to touch base with her? She had to fly out here? What the hell?

"That's fine, send her up."

Now I'm going to have to explain Hattie's presence here, which isn't a huge deal given that I plan on Hattie being by my side forever, though I haven't told her that. Nor have I told her about my past and how I grew up. Let's hope Ariana still understands my nonverbal signs for don't fuck this up.

I walk to the couch where Hattie's cuddled up, reading a book. She seems more herself this morning. Some of the haunted look has disappeared from her eyes, but I'd be an idiot to think it doesn't still linger there.

"My sister is here."

Hattie's gaze snaps up from her book, eyes wide. "What?"

I shrug. "I'm not sure why, but Jeffery just called. She's on her way up."

"Oh my god, Bast, look at me. I can't meet your sister." She looks down at her oversized T-shirt and pajama shorts.

I lean forward, bracing my hands on the back of the couch and caging her in. "You always look exceptional, plus you were trapped in a fire last night. I think Ari will forgive you for not having a cocktail dress and full-face makeup on." I kiss her lips.

Before I can really get into the kiss I want to have with her, there's a knock at the door. With a sigh, I straighten and walk across the expansive living area to the foyer and open the door.

I don't even have a chance to greet her before Ari's arms are wrapped around my waist and she's squeezing me tightly. "Thank God, you're all right."

I return the hug and run a hand down her back over her long red hair. I'm not sure how, but she obviously knows about the fire. This must be the reason for her visit.

"I'm fine."

She pulls away and smacks my upper arm, glaring at me. "I called you a million times last night, and when you didn't answer, I thought the worst."

I cringe. "Sorry, I ditched the phone when I got home, and I haven't looked at it since." My full attention has been on the woman behind me.

My sister pushes past me, stomping in through the foyer. "Do you have any idea of the things that were running through my head? I made Obsidian call the pilot in the middle of the night and drag him out of bed to fly me out here." She comes to an abrupt stop, obviously just having clocked Hattie sitting on the couch. "Oh." She glances over her shoulder at me. "I didn't realize you had company."

Walking past her, I gesture toward Hattie. "Ari, this is Hattie. Hattie, this is my overbearing sister, Ariana."

Ariana glares and sticks her tongue out at me before walking over to the couch.

Hattie stands with her hand extended. "It's a pleasure to meet you."

"You as well." Ari takes her hand and gives Hattie the once-over.

I know it for what it is—just sibling curiosity because I've never had any other woman here when my sister's around—but Hattie must take it differently.

She tugs on the hem of her T-shirt. "Sorry, I didn't know you were coming or I would have dressed differently."

"No one did, hence the overbearing part." I walk over to Hattie and place a kiss on her temple. "You look beautiful as always." When I turn my gaze to my sister, her perfectly shaped eyebrows are bunched up and she's staring at us quizzically, but her face quickly morphs to delight. "I'm just getting breakfast started. Do you want some?"

She waves me off, not taking her eyes off Hattie. "No, I ate on the plane."

"Of course you did. You got a private chef on that private plane of yours?" I chuckle and dart out of the way when she goes to smack me again. "My sister married a billionaire, babe."

Ari scowls at me for mocking her. "All right, that's enough." She shakes her head at me and turns back to Hattie. "It's true, but that's not why I married him."

Ariana takes Hattie's hand and gestures for her to sit again, obviously using the opportunity to grill Hattie while I'm cooking. She better not make Hattie uncomfortable.

When I glance over a couple of minutes later, I know that Hattie told Ari about her experience in the fire yesterday because she's hugging Hattie. I hear Ari say, "You poor thing. That must have been so frightening."

I crack another egg into the bowl and return the shell to the carton. "You never mentioned how you knew about the fire," I call out to her.

Ari's head snaps in my direction. At least she looks guilty. "You own the club, of course I heard."

"Hmm." I leave it there, but we both know that I now realize she's keeping tabs on me—courtesy of her billionaire husband and his connections, I'm sure.

Though I can't complain too much about his connections. I have a feeling I'm going to need to use one myself. I'm waiting for the official word that the fire was caused by arson before I act. Because if it was set intentionally, I don't need to be a psychic to know that Sean is involved.

I finish making breakfast while the women chat, and Ari joins us at the breakfast bar while Hattie and I eat. She pretty much carries the conversation, telling Hattie about her twins and Sid and his brothers and the mansion they live in. How I need to bring Hattie there to visit because she'd love it.

When we're done, Hattie sets her napkin down beside the plate and shuffles out of her chair. "I'm going to go shower. It was really great meeting you, Ariana."

I'm not surprised Hattie uses an excuse to give Ari and me time to chat by ourselves.

My sister smiles at her. "You too. I hope I can convince you to join Bast out at Midnight Manor sometime soon."

Hattie glances at me as though she's not sure how she should answer. How I want her to answer.

"That sounds wonderful. I want her to meet the twins," I say.

The corners of Hattie's lips lift before she turns and leaves the room.

Ari watches her go before her head whips around and she narrows her eyes at me. "You've been holding out on me, brother."

She has no idea.

I take Hattie's and my plates over to the sink. "I don't know what you're talking about."

She rolls her eyes at me. "Yeah right. She's a little young for you, though, isn't she?"

"Are you, of all people, serious?" She and Obsidian have a ten-year age gap. Ours is thirteen, barely any different. Ari grins, and I can see now that she was baiting me. "Fuck off."

"She's really lovely, Bast. I like her."

"Wonderful, now that she has your seal of approval, my life is officially full."

She joins me at the sink and places her hand on my back. "I'm serious, I'm happy for you. I've always wanted you to have someone special to share your life with."

I sigh and turn off the faucet, then open the dishwasher. "It's complicated."

"What's complicated?" Her tone suggests she might know that I probably, most likely, have fucked up this whole thing. "You clearly care about each other. The way Hattie tells it, you risked your life and ran into a burning building to save her."

"There's a lot you don't know." I glance toward the hallway to make sure Hattie's not around.

"Then fill me in."

Blowing out a breath, I load the dirty dishes into the dishwasher and close the door, then lean against the counter. "Let's head into the living area."

Ari follows me, and once we're comfortable, I tell her all of it, including the part about how our dad kept the fact that Carla came looking for me a secret. By the time I'm done, her eyes are sad, her smile is gone, and she looks as if she's six and woke up to see her tooth still under her pillow.

"You must be angry with him."

"Fuck yeah, but... he raised me. It's hard to stay angry when he's the one who gave me shelter, food, and..." I can't say it, but in his own way, Trent showed me love. Sure, he taught me his lifestyle, his career, and it wasn't on the up and up, but he could have left me to fend for myself.

She takes my hand. "I'm sure he only did it because he thought he was protecting you."

I nod, knowing she's right. "Yeah, but it's hard not to play the what-if game, you know?"

She does know. Her mom took off when she was young, and I'm sure at some point over the years, she's imagined what it would be like if her mom had come back.

"So, what are you going to do? You have to tell her, Bast. You can't keep this kind of thing a secret. It's going to come out eventually."

She's speaking from past experience with her husband, I know. There were a lot of secrets between them when they first got together, but they came out together in the end. Hattie and I can too.

"I'm not going to tell her, but I am going to keep her. She can't ever know who I am to Carla."

"Aren't you worried that Carla will recognize you if you and Hattie go the distance?"

I shake my head. "I haven't used my birth name in more than two decades, and it's been that long since she saw me." I shrug. "She's never going to recognize me."

Ari frowns. "Bast, this isn't the way to start something with someone. I don't agree with you keeping this secret."

"You don't have to. It's my life. Just trust that I know best how to handle it."

She presses her lips together to stop herself from saying whatever she's thinking.

"I do need to fill you in on what Dad told me while I was there."

Her eyes flare with alarm. "I almost forgot, what with all the fire stuff. Is everything okay with him?"

As hard as it is to be the bearer of bad news, I tell her everything Dad told me about his illness. When I'm done, the unshed tears in her eyes have fully released.

"I knew something was going on. I can't believe he lied to me." She gets up off the couch, pacing.

"He just doesn't want us to fawn all over him. You have to promise that you won't be all over him about it and checking in all day every day. It sounded like he and Eleanor had things handled, and the prognosis is excellent."

She chews her bottom lip for a minute. "God, that's gonna be so hard, Bast. I want to know what's happening on a daily basis."

"I mean it, Ari. He won't tell us anything if you don't get it in check."

She rolls her eyes. "Fine. Whatever. I'll act like I don't give two shits. Happy?"

"Ecstatic," I deadpan, knowing this will be a hard road for all of us. "Would it improve your mood to know that I need your help with something? Two things, actually."

My sister loves to help anyone. It's like her own little treat to herself.

"Duh." She comes to sit back down on the couch.

"Can you drop Hattie and me off in Michigan when you leave here?"

Her forehead wrinkles. "Not exactly on my way, but why?"

"I don't want anyone to be able to track where I'm headed. That's impossible unless you're flying private."

She gives me a wary look. "Why? Who are you hiding out from?"

"I don't think the fire at the club was an accident. I'm waiting on the official word, but I don't want Hattie around here just in case she's in danger."

"Bast." Her eyes widen. "You're scaring me."

I huff out a breath. "I just want us out of town until all of this settles."

"All of what, Bast?"

I ignore her question. "I also need you to tell Obsidian that I need one of his contacts in the Vitale family."

She stills and looks around, as if saying their name will somehow summon the northwest's most notorious crime family. "What have you gotten yourself into?"

"Nothing. I just need their help with something."

She knows enough not to ask any questions. So she nods. "I'll pass the message along."

"Thanks, sis." I stand from the couch. "Now, I'm going to go get packed and tell Hattie that we're going on a little getaway. Make yourself at home. We'll be out and ready to go in a bit."

I'm almost out of the room when my sister says my name. "I hope you know what you're doing."

I give her a small smile to calm her nerves, but I'm not sure I do when it comes to Hattie. "Uncharted territory for me, but I'm keeping my head above water." I wink and turn back around.

If Sean started that fire, as I highly suspect he did, he'll get what's coming to him, as well as anyone who helped him.

I don't give a shit about the building—that's what insurance is for. But he almost took the life of the woman I love, and that can't go unpunished.

41

HATTIE

"**W**hen are you going to tell me why we're here?" I turn away from the railing of the ferry off Lake Michigan and face Bastion sitting behind me.

After I gave him and his sister some time to catch up on their own, he came into the bedroom, telling me to pack because we were going to his home in Lake Michigan on some island. When I asked why, he insisted he'd explain later.

The fire had definitely shaken both of us, and at first, I thought that maybe he just wanted to get away from it all, but I get the sense there's more than that.

Bastion rises off the bench and cages me, his hands resting on the railing on either side of me. "Can't a man whisk his woman away on a romantic rendezvous?"

I place my hand on his chest. "He can, but you and I both know it's more than that."

He kisses my temple. "We'll discuss it when we're alone."

I frown but nod, seeing I'm going to get nowhere with him right now.

"We're almost there." He points back behind me. "Welcome to Avalon Pointe."

When I spin in his arms, the dock comes into view. Farther off in the distance is a huge, regal-looking building that sits at the top of a hill.

"That's the main building." He bends, resting his cheek along mine, pointing at the building that demands to stand out. "It houses the rec center, a restaurant and bar, among other things. You won't see much of it, though, because I'll be keeping you in my bed all day, every day." He pinches my side, and I yelp and laugh.

Once the ferry docks, Bastion links our fingers together, and we walk off. When I question why we're not getting our bags, he says, "The staff will deliver them."

He leads me to a deep blue convertible sports car in the parking lot. I have no idea what kind of car it is, but it's clearly expensive.

"I called to say that I was coming, so the staff brought the car down for me." He opens the passenger door, and I slip inside.

He pulls out of the parking lot and drives down a single-lane road. It's hard to focus on one thing because this place has everything—tennis courts, basketball, volleyball, water-slides, pools, and shopping.

"What is this place?"

Bastion glances at me. "Think of it like a resort, only everyone on the island owns their own home on the water. The only way you can set foot on this island is if you live here or work here."

"So, it's like a playground for the rich."

Bast shrugs. "Essentially."

The fresh air whips through my hair as we drive to wherever Bast's house is. After a few minutes, he slows and pulls into a long driveway. When the house comes into view, I have to hold back my gasp because it's gorgeous.

It's a two-story home with dormers on top and grayed cedar shake for the exterior, reminding me of something you might see on the East Coast. The gardens are immaculately kept, and the sprawling lawn leads down to the water. I'm not sure why we're on this island, but I'm suddenly happy that we are.

Bast parks the car and comes around to let me out, taking my hand and leading me inside. "Let me give you the grand tour?"

"You don't have to. I'm sure I'll figure my way around." I let go of his hand and walk farther into the house.

This space has a different feel than his condo in Seattle— homier and more relaxed, though I'm sure everything in this space is just as expensive.

Bastion walks past me toward the back of the house. "The fridge should be stocked." I hear him open the fridge. "Yup, we're good."

I follow the sound of his voice.

He turns when he hears me enter the kitchen. "Do you want to go out on the boat?"

"There's a boat?"

He motions to the large windows that line the breakfast area. Sure enough, at the end of the rolling lawn is a dock with a fast-looking boat. I can't help but notice the jet ski. I've never been on a jet ski, but it's something I've always wanted to try.

I whip around to face Bast. "Can we go out on the jet ski instead?"

He chuckles at my excitement. "Jet ski it is. Do you have a swimsuit?"

My shoulders sag. I don't. I left mine in Wisconsin when I moved west, not thinking I would need one in Seattle. "I don't, but maybe I can just go in my shorts and a T-shirt?"

Bast slides his phone from his pocket. "No worries. I'll tell the staff to bring one with them when they bring our bags."

A half an hour later, I step out onto the back patio wearing a yellow bikini with little blue flowers. It's one of those triangle-styled ones I've always thought showed way too much. I do love the small ruffle along the bottom portion, though. I think it looks cute on me, but it has way less fabric than the one-piece or tankinis I usually wear. I feel practically naked, which shouldn't matter given that Bast has seen me actually naked, but what about anyone else? I take a deep breath and push open the door.

Bast turns and whistles. "Fuck, babe, let's ditch the jet ski idea." His eyes soak me in, and I love watching the change in his eyes as he enjoys my body. "You look hot."

I preen under his attention while admiring him as well. He's wearing a pair of navy board shorts, and his tan skin glistens under the sun's rays.

"You look pretty good yourself."

He chuckles. "Do you want some sunscreen?" He motions to the bottle on the table beside him.

"Yes, that'd be great." I hold out my hand for him to pass it to me.

"You think I'm not going to take this opportunity to rub it all over your body?" He shakes his head playfully, and I laugh.

"All right. Do your worst." I turn my back to him and hear him squirt some of the lotion out of the bottle, then set it back down on the table.

His large palm comes down on the center of my back. I close my eyes when he reaches my shoulders and neck, squeezing. When he's done the rest of my back, he gets down on his haunches and slides his hands along the backs of my legs.

His fingers are so close to the center of my thighs, and my breath hitches when he drags his hands all the way up. But he doesn't give me the relief I need, chuckling as though he knows exactly what I'm thinking before he stands and turns me around by the shoulders. I face him, and when his gaze drags down my body, my nipples pebble in my bathing suit, something he doesn't fail to notice.

He squirts more lotion onto his hands and begins with my stomach, spreading it around and coming mere millimeters from the bottom of my breasts. I suck in a breath and arch toward him.

Bast chuckles low in his throat, and I smack his arm. "You know exactly what you're doing."

His eyes twinkle and his lips curve into a smile, but he doesn't say anything, continuing until my skin is glistening and smells like coconuts.

We head down to the dock, and Bast grabs two life jackets out of the small outbuilding. I slide mine on, and when we're standing beside the jet ski, he looks at me. "You want to drive?"

My eyes widen. "Absolutely not." I chuckle. "I'll just hold on."

He shrugs. "All right, well, let me know if you change your mind."

Ten minutes later, I'm screaming and holding on for dear life as we whip over the waves. I feel as though I might be gripping Bast too hard, but he doesn't say anything or ask me to loosen my hold.

The sun heats my skin, but the spray from the water cools it down immediately. I feel a world away from the events of yesterday. Beyond my raspy throat and the cough I still have, you wouldn't know, looking at us right now, how traumatic yesterday was.

I've been trying to push it from my mind, but I keep getting flashes of the flames, the smoke, the feeling that it would soon all be over, and no one was coming to help me. But Bast did come, risked his life to get me out, and that's something I can never repay.

By the time we finish up on the jet ski, I'm famished, so rather than take the time to make something, Bast orders for us from one of the restaurants on the island. We shower while we wait for it to arrive. Afterward, we relax and watch a movie until we can barely keep our eyes open.

Bast still hasn't brought up why we're here, but I get the impression that it's more than just wanting to get away from it all. Shouldn't he be handling things with insurance and stuff?

It isn't until we're lying in bed and I'm looking at the stars glistening in the night sky out the window that I work up the courage to ask him, hoping he'll be straight with me.

"Will you tell me now why we're really here?" I ask in a quiet voice. I roll onto my side and tuck my hands under my cheek.

I watch Bast's profile. He closes his eyes in the dim light before he turns his head and looks at me.

"Because I want to keep you safe."

The breath rushes from my lungs. "Safe from what?"

A pained expression crosses his face, but he tells me who Sean is and what he and his organization do in Bast's clubs. It takes me a moment to wrap my brain around it all, and I'm silent for a long while after he finishes speaking.

Bast rolls over me and places a hand on my cheek. "Hattie, I'm so sorry you got caught up in my bullshit. If anything had happened to you..." Tears glisten in his eyes before he lowers his forehead to mine.

I don't blame him for the fire, if it was indeed set intentionally. That was someone else's action, not his own. But allowing drugs to be sold in his club and taking a portion of the profits...

It doesn't match up with the man I know. I don't understand his motivation. At all.

"I know that you're going to look at me differently now, but you deserve to know. Believe me, if I had ever thought he was a threat to you, even indirectly, I would have told you sooner."

"Why did you let him do that in the first place?"

He stares at me, studying my face in the dark. From the way he runs his fingers through my hair and the low huff, he's hesitant to tell me. "Honestly? Money."

But it's more than that. I can tell by the stricken look on his face. "Tell me the truth. If you really want me to understand, you have to tell me all of it."

He rolls off of me and pushes himself up so that his back rests against the headboard. I can see that he's retreating, but I won't let him. I'm going to fight for us even if he can't in this moment. So I get up too and straddle him, laying a hand on each of his cheeks, forcing him to meet my gaze.

"I just want to understand. Help me understand."

He holds my gaze for a beat before a ragged breath shudders out of him. "When I was eleven years old, I ran away from home because, as you know, my mother was an addict and couldn't or wouldn't protect me."

A horrified gasp slips from my lips. "Bast... that's..."

His eyes harden a bit. "You have no idea. No. Idea."

I nod. "I know, I know. I'm so sorry. Where did you go? How did you survive?"

He goes on to tell me more detail about the man who isn't his birth father. How he took Bast under his wing.

"Thank goodness he found you." I run my hand down his cheek the way my mom always did to offer me comfort, and he stills before taking my wrist gently and pulling my hand away from his face.

"You may not think that when you hear how I was raised."

I frown. "What do you mean?"

"He taught my sister and me how to run cons on people. Some big, some small, but we fleeced people out of money the entire time I was growing up. It wasn't until about a decade ago that I stopped, started my business, and left it all behind."

I try to wrap my brain around everything he's told me, but it's hard to imagine Bast as a child, going from one horrible situation to another. And to be raised that way... no wonder he thought nothing of letting drug pushers sell their wares inside his business. It probably seemed like nothing compared to what he was used to. This man didn't stand a chance of being a well-adjusted adult with good morals and values.

But I've seen the man at the heart of him. That's who I fell in love with, and I'm not going to give up on him.

There's one thing I still don't understand, though. "What does all that have to do with why you let Sean into your club?"

He presses his lips together and looks at me with remorse. "You don't know what it's like to be hungry because your mom's been on a bender for a week and you haven't eaten in days. You don't know what it's like to sit in a dingy, cold, dark apartment because she didn't pay the bills or even get you a winter coat to keep you warm. To be so envious of the kids on the street who would walk by with a pop. A pop. It's nothing, yet some days, it felt like everything." His voice cracks, and I grip his hand. "I used to steal to survive—food, wallets. That's what put me on Trent's radar to begin with, why he took me in if I'm being honest. I was a grifter because it seemed like an easy way to make money, but eventually it got old, and I wanted to earn money for myself. I never wanted to feel like that little boy in those cold apartments again. Ever. So when Sean showed up and propositioned me, I accepted because it would put more money in my pocket. It was greed, plain and simple."

I disagree, I think it was trauma, but I don't say that. "Didn't you ever feel guilty, though, given that your mom was an addict?"

He shrugs. "Sometimes. But I'd convince myself that if someone decided to partake, that was their own decision. I wasn't shoving drugs up their noses."

A part of me knows I should be angry or look down on him for what he did, but I can't find it in myself to do so. I just keep picturing him as a child, hungry and alone with no one to turn to. Manipulated by the man who ended up taking care of him—at least physically.

Bast's eyes are glossy with unshed tears and full of the pain he's been carrying around for his thirty-seven years.

"I know this probably changes how you see me, and I don't blame you, but I needed you to know the truth. I needed you to know who I am before this goes any further. So, I guess the question is... do you still want me now that you know how fucked up I am?"

42

BASTION

I can barely breathe as I wait for Hattie to respond. She studies my face, and I half wonder if she thinks I'm making up the whole thing. My hands are on her hips, so I squeeze them, trying to draw a response out of her. This waiting will be the end of me.

How did this woman take me from wanting to ruin her to making her my entire world?

A part of me thought I should make up some bullshit excuse about why we're here and hide the truth from her. But I'm already hiding so many truths. If we stand any chance of moving forward, I have to give her honesty.

If she decides to reject me, I won't take no for an answer. I won't allow her to wreck me, and I'll do everything to win her back, no matter how long it takes. She is mine whether she knows it or not.

"Say something, please." I beg her to get rid of the crushing weight on my chest.

"Bast, I..." She shakes her head and opens her mouth, closing it right away.

Time to lay out all the emotions wreaking havoc on me because I can't stand this clawing feeling in my chest any longer. The words still make that small boy inside me fear the reaction. Fear the power I'm giving to someone else to ruin me. But I know this emotion. I remember it from all those years ago. Sure, it's on a different level with Hattie, but I'm still terrified to speak the words, even if it won't change how much I'll be shattered if she breaks me.

I bring a hand to her face, stroking her cheek. I open my mouth to say them, but the devil on my right says stop. Pushing through the doubt and trusting Hattie, I finally tell her. "Hattie, I love you."

Her eyes widen, glistening with tears almost immediately.

"I tried not to, but god, you make it impossible. The person you are, the kindness and affection you offer with no conditions, no strings. It's just the core of who you are. I'm in awe of you."

Her eyes soften, and I really hope that means she's going to forgive me for what I've told her so far. "Bast, I love you too."

That's all I need.

I bring my lips to hers, sinking into the kiss. She tastes like joy and mercy and freedom from the chains that have banded me all these years. As I cup her face, I'm overcome by how much this woman has absolutely wrecked me when I was the one out to wreck her.

I harden underneath her, which comes as no surprise. This

woman never fails to turn me on with her mind, her body, and her spirit.

I grab the hem of her oversized T-shirt. We break our kiss only long enough to pull the fabric from between our bodies, then her hands are in my hair and she arches her back, offering herself to me. Her nipples are hard against my flesh, and I drag a hand over to one, gently stroking it with my thumb. She gasps, and I tear my lips from hers, kissing my way down her jawline, her neck, then her collarbone until I worship her with my mouth.

She holds my head to her breasts, fingers delved into my hair. "Bast, I need you." Her voice is breathy and filled with desire.

Hattie reaches for the waistband of my sleep pants, and I help her guide them down enough that my dick springs free. Her small hand wraps around my length, and my eyes close when she strokes me, my head falling back against the headboard, enjoying the sensation. When I can't take it any longer, I reach for her hips. With both hands, I rip her underwear apart, pull the ruined scrap of clothing out from between her legs, and toss it aside.

My fingers fit themselves between her legs. She's soaked. She moans as I slowly stroke her clit. I bring my other hand to the back of her head, forcing her to look at me as I push two fingers into her warm pussy.

"You mean everything to me, Hattie. Never doubt that." There's a desperate note to my words.

I can't ever let her find out the truth about who Carla is to me. I haven't figured out how I'm going to handle that situation yet, but I'll do what I need to in order to take the truth to my grave. She can never know because she'll never forgive me.

"I love you, Bast." She kisses me.

Hearing her say the words, knowing she means them, fills me with more joy than I ever thought I'd be afforded in this world.

I pull my fingers from her and fist the base of my dick. I don't have to tell Hattie what to do. We're a synchronized act by this point. She moves up then sinks down on me until I'm fully seated inside her. We gasp.

I tuck my face into her neck. "You're mine, Hattie."

She pulls back and cups my face. "And you're mine."

Then she rocks, and fuck, it feels so good. It's not like our usual frantic pace. This is slow and steady, and our eyes brim with emotion as the love between us manifests into physical pleasure. Our gazes don't divert, not once, and in hers, all I see is my future.

Our breathing picks up as we near our peak, and still we don't look away. The moment feels intimate and somehow life-changing, as though I'll be a different man after tonight.

Her hands are still on my face. She brushes one down my cheek, and for the first time, the gesture doesn't send me into a spiral.

I turn my face to kiss her palm. "I want to do this with you forever."

She moans and speeds up a little more. She's close. I feel the first tugs of her orgasm around my swollen cock.

I thrust up into her gently, and we come together in a kiss as we climax at the same time. Groaning into each other's mouths, I release into her while she milks me for every last drop. Her body falls into mine as if all her muscles are limp, and I run my hand down her back, both of our breathing labored as we come down from our orgasms. She threads a hand through my hair and presses her lips to my neck.

A few minutes go by, and I turn soft inside her. She draws back and stares into my eyes. "Thank you for loving me." She places a chaste kiss on my lips. "Thank you for helping me discover who I really am."

"Hattie, you've brought out a side of me I didn't even know existed. I may not have been a good person for the majority of my life, but I swear to you that from here on out, I'm going to be a man you can be proud to call yours."

"You already are." She kisses me again.

I harden inside her again. Of course, once isn't enough when it comes to her.

A couple of days pass as we spend a lot of the time out on the water, either on the boat or the jet ski. Turns out Hattie is a fan of water sports. She even managed to get up on a set of water skis.

We've been to the rec center a couple of times, but seeing the other rich assholes check her out makes me want to hurt someone, so I've convinced her that it's in everyone's best interests if we spend most of our time at my place.

Our evenings are spent in the hot tub or around the fire pit, looking at the stars, and our late nights are spent exploring one another's bodies. It's bliss until the real world intrudes.

On the third day, I receive a phone call informing me that it's highly likely the fire was set intentionally. It's no big surprise. It just means I have to deal with Sean, which normally wouldn't bother me much, but I swore to Hattie a few nights ago when we made love that I was going to be a better person. But there's zero chance I'm going to let him continue to be a risk. Who knows what he'll do next?

We're eating lunch on the back patio, looking out over the blue, glistening water under the sun, when Hattie's cell phone vibrates on the table.

She swipes it off the table, sliding her thumb over. "Hey, Dad, sorry I didn't get back to you when you texted the other day. Things have been crazy." She gives me a coy smile.

I try to act as if my heart isn't pounding against my chest. I get up from the table and go back inside, feigning getting a drink.

I'm committed to getting past who her mother is, but I haven't quite figured out how. It helps now that I know Carla tried to come after me, but it's difficult to wipe away decades of rage in an instant. She would have tried more than one fucking time if I meant anything. The fact is that she *was* a drug addict who neglected me and put me in harm's way. That may not be who she is to Hattie, but that's who she is to me.

I tidy up the kitchen, washing and drying the cutting board we used to prepare lunch. I'm just closing the cupboard when Hattie walks in, all the color leached from her face.

"What's wrong?" Panic causes my heart to skip a few beats.

"I don't know. My dad said I need to come home, that there's something he and my mom need to talk to me about."

I draw her into my arms. "Maybe it's not a big deal."

She shakes her head and pulls away from me, tears swimming in her eyes. "No, I can tell by his voice that something is very wrong. I need to get there right away." Hattie turns, heading for the stairs.

"Hattie, I got word this morning that the fire was set intentionally. It's still not safe."

She whips around on the stairs to look at me over her shoulder. "My family needs me, Bast. I'm going home." Turning, she bolts up the stairs.

I watch her retreating back for a beat with my hands pushed into my hair.

Fuck. Fuck.

I'd hoped to avoid "meeting the parents" for as long as possible, but that's clearly not happening. Because I'm not letting her out of my damn sight until I get this thing with Sean handled. Racing up the stairs, I join her in the master bedroom.

"I'm going with you."

"Bast, you don't have to—"

I meet her gaze. "I'm going with you." My tone leaves no room for argument.

She nods and turns to grab her things from the dresser.

"Do your parents know about me?"

There's a guilty expression on her face when she turns around. If she only knew. I'm the one who should be looking guilty.

"No. It wasn't that I wanted to keep you a secret. I just didn't know exactly what we were, and if things were going to end with us, I figured..." She piles her T-shirts into the suitcase.

"Do you want them to know about me? Do you want me to stay away from your parents while we're in town?" I really hope not. Although it would make it all easier, if she doesn't want me to meet her parents, it would be because she's embarrassed of me or what we have. I'm not sure I could handle that right now.

She shakes her head. "I want you there. I want your support for whatever this is about."

"All right then. I'll be there." I still her hands from packing, taking them in mine. "Whatever this is, we'll get through it —together." I kiss her joined hands, and her body sinks into mine.

I close my eyes and relish the feeling of having her in my arms, because the fear underneath all this says it might be one of the last times if this parent thing goes very wrong.

43

BASTION

We take a ferry to Milwaukee, rent a car, and arrive at Hattie's parents' house shortly after dinner.

I pull the car into the driveway and kill the engine. No matter how many times I've tried to convince myself Carla won't recognize me, my heartbeat still drowns out everything else. It's been twenty-six years since she saw me last. There's no way she'll see the little boy inside the grown man I am now. Still... what if she does? It will ruin everything I've built with Hattie. If she recognizes me and I lose Hattie, it will be yet another thing Carla has taken from me.

I push all those thoughts aside, though, because Hattie is clearly nervous as hell about whatever her parents have to tell her. I need to be here to support her.

"You ready?" I open her door and hold out a hand to help her out of the car.

She nods and takes my hand.

When she's standing outside of the car, I kiss her temple. "Whatever it is, we'll figure it out, okay?"

Hattie sucks in a deep breath and nods again, but she must find some comfort in my words because her shoulders relax, if just slightly.

Hand in hand, we approach the stairs at the front of the house. There's so much shit going on inside my head, it's difficult to separate one thought from the other. How will I feel when I see Carla up close or hear her voice? How will Hattie's parents feel about me being here? Will they have a problem that I'm thirteen years older than her?

Hattie knocks on the door before she opens it, leading us inside.

"Hey, I'm here," she calls.

I use the time before anyone appears to look around the house. The living-slash-dining room combination we stand in is well-kept, though clearly outdated. Family photos are scattered on a couple of the walls, and a large cross is hung on the one in the dining room. It has a lived-in, homey feel, a family feel, a loved feel, and my heart squeezes.

Her dad comes around the corner, walking with a cane. His hair is gray and a little longer on the top, though the sides brush his ears. He has a mustache and a big smile until he sees me. He freezes briefly before continuing toward us.

"Who do we have here?" he asks Hattie.

She shakes her head and places her hand on my forearm. "This is Bastion, my boyfriend. Bast, this is my father, Robert."

I like that word—boyfriend. For the first time in my life, I love belonging to someone. Though based on the way I feel about her, the title feels somehow trivial.

Robert blinks from being taken by surprise. I wonder if she's ever brought a man home to meet her parents. I would have assumed that her asshole ex met her parents at some point.

"It's a pleasure to meet you, sir." I step forward, cursing myself for the hope that he'll think I'm good enough for his daughter. Since when do I give a fuck what people think of me?

"You too, Bastion." His eyes fall down my body, but I can't tell if he finds me lacking. "I apologize if I appear surprised. It's just that Hattie didn't tell us she'd have someone with her. Nor did she see fit to tell us she was seeing anyone." He eyes her over my shoulder.

When I glance at Hattie, her cheeks are red, and she's staring at the floor.

"I'm afraid I insisted on coming with her. She was upset after your phone call, and I wanted to make sure she got here okay and be by her side to support her. As for me being a mystery, we only recently made things official. I'm sure she planned to tell you the first opportunity she had."

Hattie steps to my side and wraps her arms around my bicep, squeezing, and Robert's gaze clocks the gesture.

"Yes, well, I'm sorry to drag you away from Seattle, but we wanted to have this conversation in person," he says. "You two made good time."

"We weren't in Seattle. We were at my home on Avalon

Pointe, so we took a ferry to Milwaukee and drove in from there," I answer.

Robert's head rocks back. He's clearly heard of the island and understands the meaning of me having a home there—I'm rich. I'm not a nobody.

"Well, let me go get your mother. She's just lying down. Sweet pea, why don't you offer your friend here a drink?" He heads down the hall, leaving us alone.

Robert's slight dig—referring to me as Hattie's friend and not her boyfriend—doesn't get missed. It might take some time to win Robert over. More importantly, the time I've dreamed and dreaded for more than two decades is about to come. My body is about to go into fight-or-flight mode, so I anchor myself to Hattie.

Her face is lined with tension, so I grab her hand, tugging her toward me and wrapping my other hand around her waist. She melts into my embrace.

"How are you?" I ask.

She shakes her head in the crook of my neck. "I just want to know what they have to tell me."

I nod, understanding. She and I both. I'm about to come face-to-face with the woman I've despised my entire life.

"Let's go out on the patio. It's a nice evening."

I follow her through the small kitchen with cluttered countertops and out a set of sliding doors, much like the ones I used to break into her apartment not far from here. The backyard is well kept, with flowerbeds lining the fencing, and an above-ground pool sits in the center of the yard.

Hattie and I make mundane conversation while we wait for her parents to appear. The reality of seeing Carla feels like an oppressive weight on my shoulders that's getting heavier with every second that passes.

The screen door opens behind me. Hattie stands, so I follow suit, turning and seeing my mother face-to-face for the first time in more than twenty-five years.

My breathing becomes shallow, and all I hear is my heart thudding. The noise of their voices greeting each other sounds as if they're underwater and I can't make out what they're saying. A cold sweat breaks out across my neck, and my knees weaken as if they're about to give out. All the memories from my childhood rush to the surface. All the shitty things I intentionally blocked out. Things I never want to remember again.

Bile rushes up my throat, and nausea swirls in my stomach.

All three of them turn in my direction. My eyes go to Hattie first, to calm me, or at least, I hope. She's smiling at me. That sweet, sweet smile centers me slightly. I'm not sure what was said, but I assume it was an introduction, so I step forward on shaky legs, hand extended.

"Good to meet you."

Carla slides her hand in mine, smiling. I meet her gaze, and when her eyes don't waver, I tip my head down. How stupid am I? We share the same eye color, a detail I'd forgotten over the years.

Panic flares inside me that it's over. She recognizes me. "Good to meet you, Bastion. I'm glad you're here."

She squeezes my hand, and I glance down at our joined hands. Hers are the same ones that held me as a baby and changed my diapers. They're also the same hands that held the needle she'd put in her arm or the bottle of booze she'd bring to her lips.

I drop her hand and give her a tight smile.

"Why don't we all go take a seat?" She gestures to the table behind us.

I turn to sit down and catch Hattie giving me a questioning glance. I'm sucking at hiding my reaction. I'm not sure how I thought I could. I should have had Hattie come alone, but at some point, if she's my future, we'd be here.

We all sit, and I use the moment to study Carla. Her gray bob swings as she sits, Robert helping her. She's got bags under her eyes, and the walk over to the table seems to have winded her. Something in my gut says whatever they have to tell Hattie, it has to do with Carla.

"I'm sorry we had to call you home like this, Hattie." Her mom gives her a weak smile.

Hattie takes her mom's hand between both of hers. "Mom, what's going on?"

Carla draws in a big breath and gives her a sad smile. Her eyes veer to Robert, and he scooches forward in the chair as if he'll take the responsibility to tell Hattie whatever it is, but Carla shakes her head and stares into Hattie's eyes. "I have kidney disease."

Hattie's face drains of all color. "What?" The pain in her voice makes me want to wrap her in a hug. I hate it when she hurts.

Carla looks at Robert again, who has a brave face, then back at Hattie. "We only just found out this week. It's been a bit of a whirlwind."

Tears gather in Hattie's eyes, but she sucks them back. "What does this mean?"

My chest squeezes as I watch her trying to be strong.

"We don't know yet. I have a doctor's appointment in a few days, and we'll get more information then and get the results of some more testing they've done. The doctors said I most certainly will have to start dialysis."

Despite my disdain for her, I feel a tug of sympathy.

Hattie bursts into tears and bolts off the chair. Carla wraps her arms around Hattie and rubs her back. When Hattie pulls back, Carla places her palm on her cheek and runs it down.

My hands wrap around the armrests, white knuckles emerging immediately. I have to look away, sucking in a big breath. When I return my attention to the table, I find Robert watching me.

"Are you going to be okay?" Hattie asks in a small voice that reminds me of a child. That's when I remember that if Carla doesn't make it, this will be the second mother she'll bury.

"I don't know, sweetie, it depends on what the good Lord's plan is. But we're going to do everything in our power to make sure I am. I'm praying, your dad and I both, every night. As soon as we know more, we'll put me on the church prayer list. The Lord has a plan. We just have to see what it is." Carla's voice is soft and gentle, consoling as though she's not the one with the shit end of the stick.

If I had grown up with this version of Carla, I wonder what kind of man I'd be. Definitely not the one I am today.

"I'll pray for you too," Hattie says, and the three of them take comfort in their faith.

I can't imagine what it's like to believe that some being greater than you is up there looking out for you. Sure as shit, there was no higher power looking out for me when I was homeless, dirty, and starving.

We sit around the table, and I don't say much for fear that I may burst and tell Carla who I am and how she ruined my life.

Eventually, Carla says she's tired, so Hattie and I make our exit, promising to come by the house tomorrow. Hattie dooon't say anything on the drive over to her apartment while I feign ignorance and ask for directions.

It's not until we're through the door of her apartment and I lock it behind us that she bursts into tears.

I pull her in and wrap my arms around her, squeezing her tightly. "I've got you. Let it all out."

And she does. For ten minutes, we hold each other while every tear, every emotion, and every fear pours out.

When she pulls away, she wipes her cheeks, now red and raw. "I can't go back to Seattle until I know what's going on with my mom. And even then..."

I smooth the hair on the top of her head and kiss her forehead. "We'll figure it out. Don't worry about your job right now, that's not what's important."

No part of me wants her back in Seattle right now anyway. With everything going on, I haven't had time to reach out to my brother-in-law to get the contacts I need for the Vitale crime family so I can take care of Sean. I'll worry about it once I know she'll be back in his vicinity.

"I know you have a business to run, but will you stay in Wisconsin for a bit? At least until my mom has her appointment and we know better what her prognosis is?"

I tuck a strand of her dark hair behind her ear. "I'll call Steph in the morning and tell her she needs to handle things in my absence."

"Thank you, Bast. I don't know what I'd do without you."

I'm not a religious man, but God willing, she'll never have to find out.

I pull her in and wrap my arms around her, squeezing her tightly.

44

BASTION

Out of respect for Hattie, when her father inquired where I was staying while I was in town, I lied and told him the same hotel I had stayed in all the other times I visited. I knew without Hattie having to tell me that he wouldn't approve of me staying with her. He doesn't even know that she lives with me in Seattle.

Robert and Carla know I'm her boss, but they don't know the nature of the business I'm in. Hattie looked remorseful when she asked me to lie about it, insisting that while she has no problem with it, her parents just wouldn't understand.

As I suspected, Hattie spends all our time over at her parents' house. Robert is at work during the day, but because Carla isn't well, she's no longer working at the salon. Which has made for a long couple of days.

It's given me time to see Carla and Hattie's dynamic. Seeing how close they are isn't easy, but I cannot reconcile the woman in front of me with the one I used to try to wake as a child, worried that she was dead. Seeing her well and the mother she is to Hattie only spurs my anger because now I see what I missed out on, the kind of mother Carla could have been to me.

Hattie says my name, and I blink, coming back to the present. I turn my attention her way, and she's frowning.

"Sorry, my mind drifted off. What did you say?"

She glances over my shoulder at the sliding glass door that leads inside. Carla went in a few minutes ago to get ready for her doctor's appointment. Robert should be here any minute to pick her up. Hattie and I are going to wait here until they return to let us know how it went.

"Are you okay?" Her head tilts.

"Of course, my mind just wandered to work. My apologies." I reach across the table and take her hand, stroking her knuckles with my thumb.

"I know you probably need to get home, but I really appreciate you staying to support me."

"You are my number one priority, Hattie. I'm sorry I drifted off."

"And that's all it is?" She's worried. All the shit is showing on my face now, and it's transparent to her.

I once thought this woman was naïve, but now that she knows me, she's too perceptive. "That's all."

"Because you seem really tense whenever my mother is around. It's almost like you're uncomfortable or something."

Shit. I need to do a better job than I'm doing.

Thankfully, before I have to come up with an answer, the slider opens, and Robert and Carla walk out.

"Well, we're off." Carla's voice shakes, revealing she's nervous about the appointment.

Hattie rushes over and gives her a hug, then moves over to her dad to give him one.

Carla's eyes veer toward me. "Why don't you kids go swimming or something? Don't just be waiting around here on pins and needles. We don't want Bastion to think this place isn't any fun. He'll never want to come back here."

Hattie pulls away from her dad and nods. "We brought our swimsuits today like you said."

"Good." Carla gives Hattie a kiss on her forehead. "I don't want you sitting around stressing the whole time."

She gives her mom a wan smile, and they leave. I walk over to Hattie and pull her into an embrace, wishing I could do something more, anything to make this better for her.

We separate, and she heaves a big sigh. "Okay, my mom is right. Let's try to enjoy our afternoon. What do you want to do? I want to say a quick prayer, then I'm all yours."

"In that case, you're gonna get on your knees, but you won't be praying, babe."

She laughs and smacks my arm playfully. It's good to see her smile, a laugh on her lips. It's been days since they've made an appearance.

"Should I get changed into my swim trunks while you do that, or do you feel like doing something other than hanging by the pool?"

"I brought a book with me, and some relaxation sounds good. It's hot out, so taking a dip might be good in a bit."

"Okay, I'll go change and meet you back out here."

I give her credit—in my experience, religious people are intent on converting everyone to their cause, but not once has Hattie tried to push her religion on me. Never tried to get me to church, never asked me to pray with her, none of it. The thought that maybe that's a bad thing, that perhaps she doesn't see me as a permanent fixture in her life, crosses my mind, but I push away the insecurity.

I join Hattie back outside and see that she's already changed into her swimsuit. It's a noticeably different style than the one she wore at my house in Avalon Pointe. This is a one-piece, and though she looks fabulous in anything, it certainly isn't close to as sexy as the bikini. I'm assuming this one feels more parent-approved to her.

Another side of Hattie has emerged since we've been around her parents, and I wonder if that will ever change.

She's seated on one of the loungers around the pool, her book and bottle of water on the table beside her. When she sees me approach, she holds up a bottle of sunscreen. "Can you put some on me?"

My dick twitches. I haven't been inside her since we left the island. I understand why, and I'm not going to be an asshole and pressure her to sleep with me when she's dealing with so much, but I still miss her, miss her body, miss our connection during sex. I only ever thought of the act of sex as physical, but with Hattie, it has a way of centering me, making me feel so much closer and loved.

"You know how much I love to do that." I grin, trying to keep the mood light. I take the bottle from her and sit at the end of the lounger. "Sit up and give me your back."

She does as I say, and I enjoy every second of rubbing my hands over her body. It's the most action I'm getting for a while.

I'm concerned about how Hattie will react if Carla doesn't get good news today. I continue to lie to myself that all I'm concerned with is Hattie's feelings, not the welfare of the mother who abandoned me.

We relax in the sun, and Hattie reads her book while I catch up on some work stuff on my phone. Eventually I lean my head back and enjoy the feel of the sun's heat.

"Do you want to go for a dip?"

I turn my head in Hattie's direction. She's shielding her eyes from the sun, looking at me. Her sunglasses lay discarded on the table beside her.

"Sure." I bolt off the chair and take a couple large steps toward the pool, then jump in cannonball style.

When I resurface, Hattie is at the edge of the pool, giggling.

Mission accomplished. I know she's stressed and worried right now. I just want to do what I can to lift her spirits.

"Let's see what you got, babe."

"Okay, prepare to be amazed. You might want to hold on to the side of the pool so you don't drown from this crazy wave I'm going to make."

I chuckle. "Let's see it."

She steps back, then runs toward the pool, leaping and dropping into the water in a cannonball that makes about half the waves my jump did.

Her head pops out of the water, and she's grinning. "Well?"

"Sorry, babe, I've got you beat." I tug her to me by the waist. It's not the easiest while you're treading water, but I manage to kiss her quickly.

The sun's rays reflecting off the water bring out the gold flecks in her eyes, and for the first time all day, there's something other than fear in them. I want to keep it like that for as long as I can.

"You want to play Marco Polo?" I ask.

"Sure! You try to find me first." She wiggles out of my arms and swims away.

"All right, I'll count to ten. Better hurry." I close my eyes and start the countdown out loud.

I'm not sure how long it takes me to catch her, maybe five minutes, then our roles reverse.

She comes after me with no luck. A few minutes in, I decide to play a trick on her. I swim to the pool's edge and oh so slowly pull myself out of the water. My sister and I used to do this to each other the few times our dad took us to the public pool growing up. I always found it hilarious to see Ari frustrated and searching around in the water, knowing she was never going to find me.

"Marco," Hattie calls.

"Polo," I say right before I completely pull myself from the water.

She swims in the direction of my voice, feeling around with her hands. When she comes up empty, she calls out Marco again.

I quietly slip to the end of the pool and say, "Polo," leaning over and dipping my hand in the water to make a splashing sound for good measure.

She swims that way with her eyes closed, and I move to the other side of the pool so I'm facing away from the house. Hattie lets out a growl of frustration when she makes it to the area I was just standing beside, and it's all I can do to not laugh.

"Marco," she shouts into the warm summer air, louder than the previous times and clearly annoyed.

This time I can't stifle my chuckle, but before I can give up the game I'm playing, something crashes behind me, and the sound of shattering glass rings through the warm air. Hattie's eyes pop open, and I whip around.

Robert and Carla are on the deck, the remnants of a serving tray, a jug, and several glasses spread on the concrete.

"Carla, are you okay?" Robert rubs her back.

Carla doesn't respond, her eyes on me with a mix of horror and disbelief. "Tyler?"

So she does remember at least one thing about me. I'd laugh in her face if my heart didn't wrench because I might lose Hattie.

45

HATTIE

"Mom, what's wrong?" I rush out of the pool, water sluicing down my body, but she pays me no mind, her entire focus on Bast.

I glance in his direction and see that he's staring at her too, rage etched into every line of his face.

"Tyler?" my mom asks again, her tone more urgent, more demanding.

My vision shifts to my dad, wanting him to explain why she's calling Bastion Tyler and what happened at the doctor's appointment, but all the color has drained from his face as he looks between my mom and Bast.

"What's going on? Who's Tyler?" Panic flares like a living, breathing being inside me, suffocating me. When no one answers me, I tug on Bast's arm. "What's going on?"

He doesn't turn to me, not removing his eyes from my mom. "Why don't you ask Mother Dearest?"

I turn imploring eyes in my mom's direction. "Will someone please tell me what's going on?" It's obvious I'm the only one who doesn't have a clue what's happening here and who Tyler is.

Bast's back straightens, and he slides his arm out of my grip, crossing his arms and widening his stance as if he's preparing for a fight. "Carla is my mother."

His voice doesn't waver or shake. It's cool and smooth and devoid of emotion. This isn't the Bast I know.

I understand each of the four words that came out of Bast's mouth, but they make no sense the way they were strung together. My mom is Bast's mom? How is that even possible?

My head whips in my mom's direction. "I don't understand."

Tears slip down her face, and she does nothing to wipe them away, her eyes still on Bast.

"Carla," my dad says, wrapping his arm around her shoulders, "maybe we go inside to talk. Or I'll take Hattie..."

She shakes her head. "Before I met your father, I had a child. Tyler." She sobs at his name before taking a few breaths to compose herself. "He ran away, and I never saw him again. Until right now."

I turn to look at Bast, and his eyes are locked with my mom's. "Is that true?"

He finally turns his gaze from my mom to me, giving me a single nod.

Oh my god. My mom is his mom. The drug-addicted horrible mom who neglected him as a child? My hands fly up, covering my mouth as tears prick the corners of my eyes.

Wait. Then the thought occurs to me. How he wasn't surprised when Mom said his name.

Has Bast known this whole time?

I tug at his arm. "Did you... did you know already?" My voice is a whisper.

Regret fills his eyes, and he doesn't have to answer. He did. My heart cracks.

"I hired a private investigator to track down what happened to Carla," he says. "I figured she'd be long dead of her addiction, but it turns out she wasn't. In fact, she had a pretty cushy life after I was gone. She even replaced me with another child."

My stomach bottoms out, and the tightness in my chest causes me to struggle for a breath.

"No, Tyler, I—"

Bast's hands fist at his sides, and he gives my mom a murderous look. "Do not call me that. My name isn't Tyler." His voice is cold. I've never seen or heard him like this.

Was this all a game? Is he even the Bast I've fallen in love with?

"So this... us..." I motion between us. "It was all just..." I can't even say the words as my heart splinters further.

His eyes soften the smallest amount when he looks at me. "At first you were a means to an end. I came to Wisconsin to see her, and when I saw the relationship she had with you, I wanted her to feel the pain she caused me. I ruin you, which ruins dear old Mom. I purposely met you at the coffee shop, I bought the company you work for, and I'm the one who

laid you off. All to get you to Seattle so I could... but then..."
He swallows hard, and his deep blue eyes gloss over. "My
feelings for you are real, Hattie. I fell in love with you."

I shake my head.

No. No. This is Rich all over again.

He lied.

Pretended.

None of this was real.

He wanted to ruin me.

Nausea overtakes me, and I race over to the grass, collapsing
on all fours, and throw up. My tears mix with the vomit in
the green grass as they drip from my cheeks.

A large hand rubs my back, and I flinch away from the touch
until I glance to my right to see my dad. He helps me up. I
fall into the safety of his arms, sobbing against his shirt.

"None of this changes how I feel about you," Bastion says
from behind me.

I let go of my dad and whip around to face the man who has
succeeded in ruining me, just as he planned. "It changes
everything! You lied to me. Over and over again. Did you
ever plan to tell me?"

He doesn't answer. It's not as if I would have believed him
had he said yes anyway.

I glance at my mom. She's still staring at Bastion in disbelief.

"You need to go." My voice is hollow, as though all the
emotion has been scooped out of me.

"No, Hattie." Bastion takes a few steps toward me with his hands up, but my dad puts himself between the two of us.

"I believe my daughter asked you to leave, young man."

I shouldn't let my dad fight my battles for me, but he feels like the only safe place at the moment. The man I loved has deceived me in the worst way, and the woman who raised me is not the woman I thought she was. My head spins. I can't make sense of anything that's happening right now.

"Just leave, Bastion." The words are full of desperation and pleading.

"Bastion?" he clarifies, hurt lining his eyes from me using his full name. His shoulders sag, and he walks toward the pool, gathering his things. Once he's done, he comes to stand before my dad and me. "This might have started as one thing, but it ended as another."

He makes his way through the shattered glass sprawled across the deck-slash-patio, crunching it under the soles of his shoes, until he stops right in front of my mother. "You deserve to suffer for what I had to endure. My only regret is that Hattie now will as well."

Bastion disappears into the house and out of my life, forever.

46

HATTIE

Once Bastion is gone, I race into the house, tiptoeing over the broken glass, and upstairs into the guest room. I dive into the bed, pulling up the covers over my head as if I'm a child and still believe it will shut out the world.

But nothing keeps the utter devastation from taking hold of my thoughts and emotions. There's so much to take in that I can't settle on one thought or feeling for long—heartbreak at Bastion's betrayal, shock at a version of my mother I had no idea existed, or trying to reconcile that the pain in Bastion's eyes when he told me about his childhood was caused by the woman who has loved and provided for me.

I sob into the pillow until my eyes sting. I haven't felt this much pain since my mom's death. Everything that went down with Rich was a fraction of the despair seeping into my body right now.

Sometime later, my bedroom door opens, but I don't come out from under the covers. It's a childish response, I know, but I can't bear to set eyes on either of my parents when I know that one or both of them have been keeping this from me.

"Hattie, honey, come out from under the covers." My mom's hand lands on the comforter over my shoulder.

I wonder if my father is in the room too. When I pull the covers from over my head, it's only her.

Tears swim in my mom's eyes as she looks at me. "I'm sorry."

That's it? That's all she has to say? I'm not even sure what she's apologizing for exactly. Does she know what she's apologizing for?

I clear the hoarseness from my throat from crying so long. "I don't understand how this can be true."

My mom sits on the edge of the bed and runs her palm down my cheek like she's done so many times in my life. She sighs and swallows. "I'm not sure what Tyler... er... Bastion told you, but whatever awful things he told you are probably true. The truth is that there's a lot I don't remember from those days. I suppose I'm lucky that way, unlike him."

Her face is filled with such unbearable pain that I sit up and draw her into a hug. She's tense at first but relaxes into my hold, shuddering out a breath, gripping me harder, and squeezing me as if she didn't know if I would forgive her.

When I pull away, I meet her gaze. "How did you know he was your son?" The word son tastes bitter on my tongue.

My mom's bottom lip shakes. "The heart-shaped birthmark on his back. I've never forgotten it. Because you didn't know about my past, you probably assume I didn't give any thought to Tyl... Bastion, but I've thought about him every day. Every prayer I say at night, he's included. I failed him once, but I've never stopped thinking about him, wondering about where he was, if he was happy, praying that he found happiness somewhere, even if it wasn't with me in his life."

Tears topple one another on her cheeks, and she buries her head in her hands. It's so hard to reconcile what she's admitting to me and what Bastion told me about his mother with the version of the woman sitting in front of me. I question whether I'll ever be able to because she was the perfect mother to me, even though she didn't give birth to me.

I don't say anything as I try to work it out in my head.

"I realize this must have come as a big shock to you. Is there anything you want to know?"

I guffaw. "Why were you like that? I mean, I can't even picture it. All the things Bastion told me about his mom and growing up..."

She cringes, shame coating her features. Then she tells me about her childhood and how she grew up. The first time she tried drugs and found her escape. The things she used to do to support her drug habit. From the reality she describes, I don't think she holds back, and as I picture a young Bastion living through the unstable upbringing of his mother being an addict, my heart breaks a little more. By the time she's done, my heart is left in shards, draining me from the inside out.

I'm quiet again, taking in everything she said. The thing I hate the most is that I can almost understand why Bastion would be out for revenge. To be exposed to and suffer through what he did... it's unthinkable.

God, he must have hated me when he found out about his mother adopting me as her own. The perfect daughter who seemingly grew up with the perfect life when all he'd ever known was misery...

I squeeze my eyes shut, and a lone tear escapes. I'm surprised. I didn't think I had any more left.

"When did you get clean? What happened?" I open my eyes, and a part of me wants to tell my mom not to bother telling me. I can see how painful it is for her to talk about her past, but I need to know everything. So much was kept from me. Now I want the truth.

"After Bastion left, I hit rock bottom. He was the only thing keeping me afloat, and I know how that sounds, I do, given what he was exposed to. But I knew that if I continued down the path I was on, I would die. And the thought of not getting a chance to make it up to him... I couldn't live with it. So I found a program through a local church to help me."

Realization hits me, and I blink. "That's where you met Dad."

I remember him talking about an outreach program in Chicago that he was a part of before we moved to Tennessee, where I was raised.

She nods solemnly. "It is. At first there was nothing between us. Your mother was still alive then. But he was a steady presence in my life as I fought my demons and tried desperately not to go back to that dark place. After your mother passed, we grew closer. We bonded over the pain of losing someone. I believe that God brought us together for a purpose. There's no way I would have ever been able to stay healthy if it weren't for your father. He means everything to me."

I know she means it. And I know she loves me. But they both lied for so long.

"Why didn't you ever tell me?"

She winces at the hurt and accusation in my voice. Her lips tremble as she reaches for my hand. "Because I didn't ever want you to look at me the way you are right now."

I feel guilty that I can't just tell her it's okay, no big deal, and move on, but I know it's going to take some time to come to terms with everything.

"I'm sorry that you got mixed up in this, that Tyl... Bastion... hurt you because I hurt him."

I give her a small nod. I'm not ready to talk about him yet.

"When your dad and I returned from my appointment and I saw the birthmark, I thought it was some unlikely coincidence. But when you first introduced me to him, I had this uneasiness in my gut. His eyes..."

I nod. "Yours."

She nods. "But what were the chances? I kept telling myself I wasn't feeling well, my mind was all over the place with being sick. But the birthmark was so unique." She shakes her head and grows quiet as if she's lost in her head.

It's not until she says that that I remember the reason Bastion and I were here in the first place. I take in the dark grooves under her eyes and the sick color to her skin.

"What happened at your appointment?"

She shakes her head. "That's not important now."

Fear grips me in icy hands. "What did the doctor say? Please, I don't want to be kept in the dark anymore."

She looks at me with sorrow, as if she's sad she has to deliver worse news after everything that's already happened today. I brace myself for what comes next.

"I have to start dialysis immediately while they look for a kidney donor."

"I'll give you one of mine!" I grip her hands.

She offers me a small smile. "Oh, sweetie, we'll talk about this later. It's been a long day."

"And if you can't find a donor?" I ask.

Her small smile fades, and she inhales. The truth is outlined in her deep wrinkles, and her eyes don't have a lot of hope. Without words, I know exactly what the doctor told her.

I gasp as my world crumbles for the second time today.

47

BASTION

My phone rings on my nightstand. I've been holed up in my condo in Seattle since I returned from Wisconsin.

After I heard Carla refer to me by my birth name, it took me a moment to figure out how she could have possibly known it was me. Then it dawned on me—my birthmark. It's not something I give much thought since it's on my back, but of course it would draw her attention.

There was no way I could deny it, and I prepared myself then to lose Hattie. I knew my entire plan was about to blow up in my face. While I'd once envisioned the look on Hattie's face when she found out, thinking I'd revel in it, the truth is that it nearly destroyed me.

The devastation on her face as if I was a stranger was almost my undoing. The only reason I left is because I thought it would do her more harm than good if I stuck around. But she's certifiable if she thinks this is the end of us. I still have a fight inside me, and I will get her to forgive me.

How I'm going to fight remains to be seen, though. Right now, Hattie needs space, but she better not get used to living without me.

I roll over to pick up my phone, and my head pounds, as if my brain is crashing against my skull with every movement.

I haven't gotten blackout drunk in a long time. After dealing with insurance all day, having to talk to the fire investigator, answering questions to prove that I didn't start the fire, and figuring out what to do for my staff that are now out of a job until the place can be rebuilt or I find another location, all I craved was the dark oblivion where the sharp edges of my problems dulled to a tolerable level.

With the phone in hand, I hold it up. Through bleary eyes, I see my brother-in-law's name and bolt up into a sitting position.

Fuck, I grab my head. That was a mistake.

Cringing against the pain, I press on the screen to accept the call. "Obsidian."

His deep chuckle echoes through the phone, sounding like a pair of cymbals smashing together right next to my ear. I pull the phone away from my ear and put him on speaker, tossing the phone on the bed beside me.

"You certainly sound like shit."

"Thanks. Kick a guy while he's down, why don't you?"

He sighs. "Ariana told me everything that's been going on with you. I can empathize with having a shit parent. It's a mind fuck, I know."

I don't know the details, but from all that my sister has said, his father was a nightmare to him and his three brothers growing up.

"She may feel differently, but I don't blame you for wanting revenge on the bitch who bore you," he says.

"Yeah, well, revenge is starting to feel like it's not as important as it once was." I glance at Hattie's empty side of the bed. "Though I'll admit it was satisfying to see the look of shock on Carla's face when she realized I was her son. Even better when I saw the shame. But the look on Hattie's face…"

"So, what are you going to do to fix it?"

"I don't know yet." The pain in my chest intensifies, and I rub at it with the heel of my hand.

"Well, figure it out and then do it."

I roll my eyes. I wish it were that easy. Maybe when you're a billionaire it is, and that's why he sounds so sure.

"Yeah, yeah. Anyway, I know you're not calling to console my heartbreak." I yank the covers off me and slide out of bed to trudge to the kitchen to get some water, cringing every time my head jostles.

"No, it's not. Ari mentioned that you want me to put you in contact with a certain family. I wanted to make sure you knew what you were getting into before I did that. My influence only goes so far, and if you fuck them over, I won't be able to help you."

"I have no intention of fucking anyone over. I just need some talented people who can keep their mouths shut, that's all."

I plan on delivering vengeance to Sean's doorstep and whoever else helped him burn down my club.

"All right then, I'll text it over to you. Tell them I referred you."

I reach the fridge and open it, taking out a cold bottle of water. "Will do. I appreciate it, Obsidian. I owe you one."

"Just figure your shit out. Your sister is miserable when you're miserable, and that in turn makes my life miserable."

I chuckle as I twist the cap off the bottle of water. "Deal."

"All right, talk soon." He ends the call.

I guzzle back as much water as I can stomach.

Obsidian's right, though—I need to figure out my shit and put a plan in place. First thing I need to deal with is Sean and eliminate that threat. Then I can focus on what I need to do to win Hattie back and get her back here. Unfortunately, it'll take more than an apology. She's going to need to accept that the woman who raised her in the perfect home is the same woman who neglected and damaged me. Right now, that feels like an impossible feat.

My phone dings with a text, and I see it's the contact information for the Vitale family from Obsidian.

With a resigned sigh, I make the call.

***

A couple of days later, I had my meeting with the representative from the Vitale family. I told them what I needed, we negotiated a price, and then I handed over the information they'd need to make it happen.

I had the Uber drop me off outside the scorched remains of the club, though I don't know why. To torture myself a little more maybe. Looking at the charred black structure—or what's left of it anyway—feels like a visual representation of my insides.

I was so sure of myself when I set off on this course, but Hattie wasn't who I thought she was, wasn't *what* I thought she was—the representation of a child my mother could love. As a little boy, I always questioned why I wasn't enough for my mom. Why she couldn't leave the drugs and alcohol behind and be the mother I needed, the kind of mother everyone else got to have.

Now I'm knee-deep in shit, and I'm not sure how to get out of it. How to make Hattie see that my feelings for her are real and have been for some time. I didn't tell her all of this because I wanted to protect her. Even if she believes me, I question whether the truth will be enough. A part of me thinks that the only way I can ever be with Hattie is if I can make amends with my mother.

But the idea of forgiving her... telling her that it's okay what happened to me...

I shove my hands in my pockets and squeeze my eyes shut before turning and walking back to my condo. Now that things with the Vitale family are in motion, I need to figure out how to win Hattie back.

I've faced many obstacles in my life, but something tells me this one will be the most difficult.

48

HATTIE

To say the past week has been hell is an understatement. I've leaned into my faith, trying to keep in mind that God has a plan, but it doesn't help with the anxiety. Everything is made worse by the fact that Bastion isn't by my side. It wasn't until he was gone that I realized how much I relied on him for support.

Taylor has been there, we've talked on the phone almost every day, but it's not the same.

The pain of Bastion's betrayal still stings—like flesh that's been burned and is healing. But at the same time, I can understand why he was so vengeful. When I think back to what he told me about his time with his mother... my mother... I can't imagine the kind of scars that leaves on a person. Of course he hates her. Of course he wants to make her pay. And of course when he saw me and my relationship with my mom, it must have been like salt in a reopened wound.

The fact remains that I can't see her as the woman Bastion described, and that makes it clear to me how hard it will be for him to see her differently. To see her how I do. And I don't know if there's any getting over that fact for us, which means there isn't a future.

Regardless, I'm back in Seattle because I have to beg for my mother's life. Her health has deteriorated rapidly, and she's in the hospital. If she doesn't get a transplant soon, I'm going to lose her. I need Bastion to find it in his heart to be tested to see if he's a match for a kidney.

I'm so nervous to see him again. Both because I'm afraid I'm going to see the cold, vindictive man who walked out of my parents' house that day and because I'm fearful I'll see the charming, caring man I fell in love with. Right now, I don't know which one is really him.

My leg bounces as the Uber gets closer to his condo. I didn't give him a heads-up that I'm coming because I wasn't sure he'd want to see me. My hope is that he hasn't told Jeffery I'm off his list of allowed visitors and I'll be able to walk through the lobby to the elevator with no problems.

When the Uber pulls up in front of the building, I say a quick prayer that things go well before I exit. I have just a carry-on with me because I only plan to be here one night, though I still have to book a hotel room.

I thank the driver and pull out my phone to tip him before sliding it into my purse. I'm approaching the building when I hear my name.

"Hattie, there you are."

I turn to my right to see Steph approaching me with a wide smile. I'm not sure I've ever seen her happy to see me, let alone this happy.

Oh god, what if she's here because as soon as I was out of the picture, Bastion jumped back into bed with her? The thought makes me feel sick.

"Um... hey, Steph. What are you doing here?" I try to keep my voice even.

"Looking for you, of course. Bastion wanted me to bring you to him."

I frown, my forehead wrinkling. "What do you mean?"

"He asked me to keep an eye out for you, and if you showed up here to take you to him. C'mon, I have a car right here." She gestures down the sidewalk where a navy blue sedan with tinted windows is parked.

"But he didn't know I was coming. How could he have known I might show up here?"

She waves me off. "How am I to know? You know him. He has his ways." Steph shrugs.

I guess she's right. It's not hard to believe that he's been keeping tabs on me, considering how easily he pulled off his plan to get close to me and "ruin me," as he put it. I could have a tracker on my belongings somewhere and not even know it.

"All right." I head in her direction. "Where is he?"

"At the temporary offices he's working from. He leased a place. A short-term until he figures out what to do until the club is rebuilt."

That makes sense. He may never have really cared about me, but he cares about the people who work for him, that's for certain. I'm sure he's trying to either help them find employment or find somewhere else to run the club in the short term to keep them all gainfully employed.

Steph walks beside me as I approach the vehicle. "I heard you were trapped in the fire. That must have been terrifying."

"It was, yes."

"Here, give me your bag and I'll put it in the trunk for you." She holds out her hand when we're mere feet from the car.

I don't know why she's being so nice to me. Maybe Bastion told her she has to be or maybe she's finally accepted that the two of them are done. Regardless, I give her a small smile and hand her the carry-on bag because if she's working for Bastion and if I'm ever to remain in his life, we have to learn to get along.

She steps forward and opens the door for me, gesturing for me to get in. I bend to get into the back seat and still. Sitting on the far side is a man pointing a gun at me. He has a buzzed head of dark hair and brown eyes, but he's not familiar to me. I turn to flee, but Steph pushes me inside, sending me sprawling over the man's lap. I scramble to get off him while he lets out a sadistic chuckle.

"Take her purse. I don't need him tracking her with her phone."

My purse is ripped off my shoulder by Steph, and I turn to look at her as the door closes and the car speeds away from the curb.

"What's going on?" I hate the way my voice shakes.

"You, my dear, are just a means to an end. Sorry about this. It's not personal. If you do everything I tell you, there's a chance you'll walk out of this alive."

But I know that's not true. It doesn't take a genius to figure out the fact that he's let me see his face means that he doesn't plan for me to be breathing at the end of whatever this is.

My body shakes even though I will it to stop. I think this man, whoever he is, will only enjoy seeing the fear he causes.

"Let's hope you can keep up the scared act for a while. I think it will prove to be an incentive for Bastion." He laughs and shares a look with the driver in the rearview mirror.

My eyes widen. This has to do with Bastion. My stomach sinks, finally realizing who this might be. "Are you... Sean?"

His eyes narrow. "I see Bastion's spoken about me to you. What did he have to say?"

I shake my head. "Nothing. I swear."

He gives me a sadistic grin. "Lying bitch."

The hand holding the gun barrels toward me, and everything goes black.

49

BASTION

I walk into the lobby, giving Jeffery a quick wave on my way to the elevator bank. He rushes around the desk.

"Sir." There's an urgent note to his voice that I've never heard from him before.

I frown and stop. "Jeffery?"

"I'm glad you're here. I was going to call you, but one of the residents called me." Sweat beads along his hairline, and the panicked look on his face alerts me that something is very wrong.

"What's the matter?" Unease settles in my stomach, and it's not from the booze I imbibed last night.

"I haven't seen Miss Sinclair around lately, so when I saw her exit a car and step up to the sidewalk, I was pleased to see her."

My chest expands with hope. "Hattie is here?"

He shakes his head, concern filling his eyes. "Before she came in the building, something must have caught her attention because she looked to her right and headed that way."

My eyebrows draw down. "Who was she talking to?" Hattie doesn't know many people in Seattle, and not anyone who lives by me.

"I don't know, sir. I couldn't see from behind my desk."

"And she didn't return?"

He shakes his head. "No. I thought maybe it was you she'd seen and you'd gone off together, but... I don't know. Something about the interaction just seemed off. She didn't look entirely comfortable with whoever she was talking to."

Fear punches me in the gut, and panic presses at my sternum, but I can't let my emotions override my thinking right now. "I need the footage from the security cameras outside."

"Yes, sir, though I don't know what angles they cover. It's all monitored remotely."

I clamp Jeffery on the shoulder. "I need you to get the video from the front of the building. How long ago did this happen?"

He thinks about it for a moment. "Maybe half an hour ago."

So much could have happened between then and now.

No. Don't go there.

"Get me that footage. I don't care what it takes. I don't care if you have to bribe people. Get it and send it to my email." I walk over to the desk, grab a piece of paper, and jot down the email address.

"Yes, sir. I'm on it."

I stalk toward the elevator and stab the button, trying to keep my shit together. I'm certain it was Sean who's taken Hattie. But I need to see for sure before I act.

When I arrive at my apartment, I pace around with my hands in my hair, picturing my poor, innocent Hattie and how scared she must be.

If she's still alive.

She's alive. He'd only take her to get to me, there'd be no other purpose, and if I had to guess, he's going to use her to draw me out.

Twenty minutes pass before my phone dings, and when I pull it out, I see a text from the admin account for the front desk, telling me that the email has been forwarded to me.

With shaking hands, I open my email and refresh it. There are a few videos, all from different angles outside. When I hit Play on the first one, my phone slips from my grasp, but I catch it before it shatters on the floor.

Steph.

What the hell?

She and Hattie have a brief conversation, and although I know Hattie has never felt comfortable around Steph, her body language says it's much more than an argument over my attention. Whatever Steph says, Hattie follows her to the waiting car. When she peers in, she draws back, but Steph shoves her in the back seat. The car speeds off into traffic.

My eyes veer to the time stamp. Fucking hell. An hour has passed already.

"Fuck!" I almost toss my phone, but all that would ensure is that Sean can't contact me.

After shoving my phone in my back pocket, I slide both hands through my hair, pulling hard at the strands. Wanting to be prepared, I rush to my office and open the safe, where I remove two of my guns and tuck the holsters into my waistband.

Then I stand and wait because there's nothing else I can do.

Maybe a minute passes before the rage takes control. Sean has taken something precious from me, and if he hurts one hair on her head, I will draw out his death until he wishes he'd never been born.

In need of an outlet for my fury, I swipe everything off my desk until it crashes to the floor. Then I rip the paintings off the walls and destroy them until they're in shreds. My desk chair bounces off the wall, leaving a dent, and I clear my bookcases. When there isn't one item left standing in my office, I stop and stare at the destruction, my chest heaving.

I need to be smart about this. I need to prepare for when Sean calls, so I fish my phone out of my back pocket and dial up my contact in the Vitale family.

"Change of plans."

***

The call comes from Gabriele Vitale that evening to let me know that his people found Steph while she was attempting to run. Apparently she was pissed about me setting her aside for Hattie, so when Sean approached her and offered to pay her to lead Hattie to him, she was more than happy to take his offer and get the hell out of Dodge.

Gabriele also tells me that she didn't know where Sean was keeping Hattie. I didn't bother to ask how he knew for sure she wasn't lying. I'm sure the Mafia has their ways, and the less I know, the better.

Gabriele is the head of the Vitale crime family, and when I questioned why he himself was involved, he told me that he doesn't take kindly to men who use the women in their enemy's lives as leverage. Apparently, someone once took his now-wife from him, so he knows how I feel.

Before we hang up, he tells me to keep him in the loop when I hear from Sean.

There's no sense asking what became of Steph. I can guess at the answer. Some sick part of me takes pleasure in the fact that she has paid for her part in kidnapping Hattie.

I don't let my phone leave my sight for the rest of the evening and into the morning as I sit on my couch and wait. All I can picture is how scared Hattie must be and how they might be mistreating her.

I'll never forgive myself if something happens to her.

I'm pacing in front of the floor-to-ceiling windows in the living area when the phone rings in my hand. When I look at the screen, I see a number I don't recognize, and I know it's him.

"You must not value your life."

Sean's sadistic chuckle rings through my ear, and he tsks. "Careful now, I'm the one holding all the cards now."

"What do you want?"

"Well, I told you what I wanted months ago, but you refused to give it to me. And then you had the nerve to sever ties altogether. If I had any feelings, they'd be hurt."

I made a grave mistake underestimating Sean. I'd thought he was some lackey or someone who could at least see the big picture. I can't imagine what he thinks he stands to gain once this is all said and done, besides revenge.

The irony isn't lost on me when I think of my own situation with Hattie.

"I'll ask again, what do you want?" It's a struggle to maintain my cool, but I have to for Hattie's sake.

"The same thing I've always wanted. You see, my bosses didn't like it when I came back to them and told them what happened. It's my ass on the line, which makes me a very desperate man, Bastion."

"That can't be all." I push my hand through my hair and pace again, just to relieve some of the anxious energy running through me.

Sean chuckles again, and the sound makes me want to reach through the phone and rip out his vocal cords with my bare hands. "Now you're a smart man. Too bad you weren't smart before. We could have avoided all this unpleasantness."

"Just spit it out."

"I want a lump sum payment for my troubles. Bring two million in cash to the address I text you at noon. Do that and let me run the drugs through your club at the newly negotiated rate I spoke about, and you can have your princess back."

"Done." I don't even have to think about it. I'd pay anything to ensure Hattie's safety.

"Come by yourself. If I see even a hint of someone with you, the girl is dead."

"How do I know Hattie is still alive?" The words feel like shards of glass coming up my throat.

"C'mon, say something, sweetheart."

I stop breathing while I wait to hear her, so I know she's okay. And then her small, frightened voice comes over the line. "Bastion?"

"There, you know she's alive. See you at noon."

He ends the call. I practically roar into the vastness of my apartment, then punch the glass. I split my knuckles, but I'm lucky enough not to break my hand. Then I spring into action, checking my safe for how much cash I have on hand. I get on the phone with my banker before calling Gabriele Vitale.

I will gut Sean like a fish if there's one hair out of place on Hattie's head.

50

HATTIE

I've never been as terrified in my life as I have been in the past twenty-four hours. While a large part of me feels like Sean won't hurt me because he needs me to draw Bast here, this man is clearly unhinged. I'm not sure if that's a result of the drugs he's been doing throughout the day and night, or just his usual self, but every time he comes over to me or looks in my direction, it takes me real effort not to fall apart.

My parents are probably wondering why I haven't called. I told them I was coming to Seattle, though not the why. My mom would never have let me come here if she thought it was to beg Bast to be tested as a match. But when I told her I was ready to talk to him to discuss what happened between us, she gave me her blessing.

God, I hope she's okay and that nothing drastic has happened with her health while I've been tied up—literally.

They're keeping me in what I think is a chop shop. Day and

night, people have brought cars in here, then immediately guys strip them down into parts.

My skin is crawling, and I want out of here so badly. But the thought that if and when I get freed, it will be because Bast is here makes me sick. The idea of him in harm's way panics me. Will Sean really let us both walk away if Bast comes through on his promises?

Somehow, I doubt we both make it out safely.

But Bast has to know that too, right? He'll come with a plan.

"Less than five minutes, sweetheart. Think your man will come through for you?"

Sean's standing behind the chair I'm tied to, on my right side and bent down so he's speaking into my ear. His warm breath on the side of my face sends a shudder up my spine.

"Aw, don't worry. I'm sure he will."

I say nothing. Though I've barely said two words the entire time I've been his victim, this time it angers him. He grabs the hair at the back of my head and wrenches back my head.

"You think you're too good for me or something? Can't bother responding?"

I whimper when his hand tightens in my hair, pulling hard.

"Get your fucking hands off her."

The sound of Bast's voice eases some of my anxiety, but at the same time ratchets it up. This is when all my fears could come true.

Sean does that annoying, awful laugh of his. "Glad you

could join us. You have the money?" He extends an arm past me, and he's holding a gun. My gut twists.

Bast's gaze is solely on me, running over me once, then again and again, making sure I'm in one piece before his eyes flick to Sean. I've never been more sure than now that what he said about his feelings for me being real is true, though I suppose the fact that he showed up here at all should have proven that. Still, his eyes show a mixture of panic, regret, and relief.

"It's all here." Bast tosses a duffel bag a couple of feet in front of him. It lands with a loud thud on the concrete floor.

Most of Sean's goons cleared out of here an hour ago—in anticipation of this meeting, I suppose—but there are a few I can still see and likely more hiding in the shadows.

Sean nods at one of his guys to check out the bag. He walks over, picks up the bag, and brings it closer to Sean, where he unzips it. My eyes bulge out at the stacks of money inside. The guy pulls out one and lifts it to his nose, then takes out a few to feel them and examine them closer.

"It's good," he says to Sean with a nod.

"You've been so helpful, Bast, really. It's a shame it has to end this way." Sean shifts the gun, holding it to my head, and an anguished cry leaves my lips.

The warehouse lights shut off, and I scream as we're plunged into darkness. There are shouts of men all around, trying to figure out what's going on.

When a set of hands lands on my shoulders, I yelp.

He runs his palm down the side of my face.

Bast.

Then I feel his hands undoing the rope binding my wrists behind me. They loosen and I tug, but it's not enough to free me.

The loud sound of a gunshot echoes through the dark.

Tears sting my eyes as I wait for Bast to free me, and I try to be patient and not move so it's easier for him. But more gunshots ring out, and I wait for the searing pain of one ripping through my skin.

It's chaotic and loud, and the flashes of light throughout the space make it impossible for my eyes to adjust to the dark.

The rope goes slack, and Bast yanks me up out of the chair, lifting me under the armpits.

"We have to get out of here. Can you run?" he whispers in my ear before a gun goes off again.

"Yeah."

"Don't let go of me." He takes my hand, squeezing, and leads me through the darkness.

I can only trust that Bast knows what he's doing and where he's going.

The yells from the fighting grow quieter as we move away. Bast opens a metal door in the back corner, and the sunlight scorches my eyes. It takes my eyes a minute to see anything, but I blink past watery eyes as Bast leads me down the side of the building.

Once I can see clearly, I realize that he has a gun in his right hand and goggle-looking things on top of his head. They must be night vision goggles.

"C'mon," he says, picking up our pace.

We round the corner of the building, and Bast comes to an abrupt stop, causing me to run right into his back.

"Bast, what…" I step up beside him and see why he's stopped.

Sean has a gun pointed at us. He must have left through another exit. The duffle bag Bast brought is in his hand.

"Just take the money and go," Bast seethes, squeezing my hand to give me some reassurance.

Sean cocks his head, and one corner of his lips pulls up in a grin. "After all the trouble you caused me, I think I'm due more than just a bag full of dough, don't you?" His eyes narrow.

Before Bast can respond, Sean pulls the trigger. The gunshot rings through the beautiful sunny afternoon, and I watch in horror as the bullet collides with Bastion's chest. His hand slips from mine, and he falls limp to the ground. I scream, dropping to my knees beside him.

"Bast, no, no, no!"

He lies on his side, facing away from me, and the pain of loss rips through me.

"You bastard!" I shout at Sean, who's laughing again. That horrible, jarring laugh.

I move to stand and bolt at him just to feel the satisfaction of my fingernails ripping through his skin when movement at my side makes me look down at Bastion. In one swift movement, he rolls over with his arm outstretched, gun in hand, and presses the trigger.

Sean sinks to the ground, blood pouring out of his head. Relief floods my veins.

"Oh my god, we need to get a doctor." I give Bast the once-over, but I don't see blood. "Where did you get shot?"

He rips his shirt open to reveal a bulletproof vest.

I plunge forward and wrap my arms around his neck, tumbling him onto his back. "Thank God you're okay."

His arms wrap around me, and for the first time since he left Wisconsin, I feel safe. I feel as if everything will be okay.

"Careful, I might think you still care about me."

I back up to meet his gaze as my own fills with tears. "You came to save me."

Bast places a hand on each cheek. "I told you, I love you. I may not have started out loving you, and I should have told you everything sooner, but my feelings for you were very real. *Are* very real."

I kiss him with everything I have, pouring every ounce of love and acceptance and gratitude into the kiss.

When we pull away, he rests his forehead against mine. "We should probably get going. The crew that was here to help me will clean everything up."

I nod and hug him again.

It doesn't matter to me who those people were or how Bast knows them. I'm just grateful they were here.

We stand and Bast grabs the duffle bag, leading me down the side of the building and through a series of streets to his car.

Once we're in the car and far enough away, he turns to me. "Hattie, we need to talk about—"

I shake my head, effectively cutting him off. "Tomorrow. Today, I just want to go home and shower, then make love to you, okay?"

He takes my hand and squeezes it. "Sounds perfect."

51

BASTION

*E*arly the next morning, I watch Hattie lying next to me, her chest rising and falling, just to assure myself that she's still breathing. I was so fucking scared yesterday. The vision of her tied to that chair with Sean beside her, holding a gun to her head, will be burned in my brain forever.

I gently trail a knuckle down her cheek. This woman means everything to me.

As a child, all I longed for was a roof over my head and food in my belly. As a teen and early adult, all I wanted was financial stability and to make money any way I could to ensure I'd never again feel like I had when I was younger. Now, at thirty-seven, I know that all I've ever needed was a love like this in my life. I could lose all the money and the prestige. I don't need this fancy condo and all my clubs. As long as Hattie is by my side with her innate goodness and gentle spirit, supporting me and loving me, I'll be okay.

But I'm afraid to hope for the future with her. She didn't want to talk about anything serious last night. Instead, we made love over and over, enjoying each other's bodies, connecting on an intimate level that left me wrecked.

Hattie's dark eyelashes flicker, and she slowly opens her eyes, then she gives me a warm smile. "Hey." Her voice is still rough with sleep.

"Good morning." I press a kiss to her forehead.

"How long have you been awake?" She yawns and stretches her arms over her head.

"Not too long."

"Why are you watching me sleep?" She chuckles.

"Because I'm afraid it will be the last time I'm able to." The raw, unfiltered truth leaves my lips.

It's by design. Gone are the days where I'm going to hide anything I'm feeling or thinking from this woman. If we're going to make this work, I have to be completely honest with her. It's our only path forward.

Hattie's amusement drops like stone, and she positions herself so that she's sitting against the headboard, so I do the same.

"I know we need to talk, it's just... after everything yesterday, I just wanted to be with you."

I nod. "I understand. I was so relieved when we made it back here alive. It just feels like I'm waiting for the other shoe to drop, that's all. Why did you come out here to see me?"

She sighs, and a flash of sadness crosses her features. "For two reasons. The first has to do with us." Hattie reaches out a hand to me, and I take hers. "Obviously, I was shocked when it came out who you are to my mom... our mom. Oh god, this is so weird." She drops her head and presses a hand to her forehead.

"It's fine, go on." I squeeze her hand.

"The fact that you lied to me for so long, that I was just a part of a plan—" When I open my mouth to interject, she holds up her hand, so I shut it and nod for her to go on. "I believe that your feelings for me are real now, Bast, I do. It took me a bit to realize that, but I know what we share, and I know you couldn't have faked that. Still, you lied, and it brought me back to when Rich lied, and I felt like the stupidest person in the world. Like this idiotic, naïve little girl who couldn't see what was right in front of her."

She pauses as though she's collecting her thoughts and tucks a strand of her hair behind her ear.

"I talked to my mom, and she told me what she was like while you were growing up—at least, what she could remember of it. She was upfront about the fact that she failed you in every way possible, and though it's still hard for me to imagine her like that..." She scoffs and shakes her head. "Almost impossible, really, I know you suffered greatly. I can understand why you would want to make her pay and why you might look at me as your enemy or the one who took your mom away or something."

My chest constricts, and it's a struggle to keep breathing. "Hattie, I am so sorry for what I put you through. If I could do it all over, I would have just marched up to Carla's door, given her a piece of my mind, and been done with it. I wouldn't have plotted to ruin you. God, that's the last thing I want now that I know you. But at the same time..."

"What?"

I contemplate keeping the last part to myself, but if I want an honest future with her, she has to know. "Had I not made that plan, I never would have found you. I never would have fallen in love with you. So, I'm sorry you got hurt, and I'm sure I went about this in a conniving, shitty way, but we came out of that. It's hard for me to completely regret the decision to ruin you." I stop rambling and wait for her reaction.

She nods, lips pressed together. "I know. I've had the same thought." She bends down and kisses me, but it's way briefer than I'd prefer. "But if we're going to be together, then I need you to set aside your resentment for... Mom. She's an important part of my life. I understand and respect that you had a very different experience with her, but if we can never be in her presence together, if I feel like I can never mention her in a conversation with you, it's going to drive a wedge between us. Us not working out would be inevitable."

I push a hand through my hair and blow out a breath toward the ceiling. "I don't know that I can forgive her, Hattie."

It's not the truth she wants, but I'm going to push through this honesty thing.

She squeezes my hand, and I turn my attention back to her. "I'm not asking you to forgive her. I can't imagine how complicated your feelings are where she's concerned. Only so I'm not walking on eggshells any time her name comes up and that I won't be met with resistance any time she's the topic of conversation."

I consider what she's saying and whether I can actually do what she's asking. For Hattie, I think I can.

I give her a firm nod. "I can do that. I *will* do that. It might take some practice and time, though."

She gives me a sad sort of smile. I'm sure she'd love for me to mend my relationship with her mom. "All right, good. But, Bast, I think you should try to forgive her in whatever way you can. Not for her, but for yourself." Hattie lays her palm on my cheek, sliding it down the way Carla does. "So you can stop carrying the weight of your hatred around."

I bring her palm to my mouth, kissing the center. "She used to do that to me too, you know."

Her head cocks to the side. "Do what?"

"Run her palm down my face." Pain seeps through my words as I remember a better version of Carla than I prefer to.

Hattie gives me a sad smile, obviously now understanding my reaction the few times she did it to me.

We look at each other wordlessly for a beat until I realize she hasn't finished telling me why she's here.

"You said there were two reasons why you came to see me. What was the other one?"

Tears spring to her eyes. "My mom is in the hospital. She needs a kidney transplant if she's going to survive." Her face crumples.

I wrap an arm around her, drawing her into my side. My heart aches for her having to go through this as well as everything with us. So, Carla didn't get good news that day at the doctor's.

"I'm so sorry." And I am. I may have no love for the woman, but the situation is clearly devastating to the woman I do love.

Hattie pulls away and meets my gaze. I realize that she looks sorry for whatever she's about to say, and unease trickles up my spine. The first tear falls from her eye. "I came to beg you to see if you would agree to be tested to see if you were a match. My dad and I have, but you're related biologically, and the doctor said the best chance of a match is you."

The air leaves my lungs.

Donate a kidney? Risk my life to save the woman who ruined mine? She's got to be mad.

52

BASTION

I should have seen it coming the moment Hattie mentioned the transplant, but I was too concerned with consoling her. She threw me for a loop, and it took me damn near a full minute to respond.

My first instinct was a hell no. Why would I risk my life with surgery to save someone who clearly never gave a shit about me? But I know if I said no, there would be no Hattie and me. Not because she was forcing me in any way, but because every time she looked at me, all she would see is the person who could have possibly saved her mother and didn't.

No, Hattie told me that my answer had no bearing on our relationship and that she understood what she was asking. That it's a personal decision and one only I could make. She promised that she wouldn't hold it against me if I wasn't willing. But I don't see how that could be true.

I've thought a lot about it, whether I could actually do it or not if it came down to it, and the truth is, I don't know. There's still so much rage deep inside me for Carla. But then

I look over my life, at some of the things I did with Trent, and it dawns on me that maybe I hold that same status in other people's eyes. That I'm the one who ruined them by interfering in their marriage after manipulating myself into a rich woman's bed and blackmailing her, or working with Trent to clean out a couple's life savings with one scam or another.

Maybe I shouldn't be the one to throw stones. I have no right to be righteous.

And so, I'm back in Wisconsin and at the hospital to see my mother and have a conversation with her. A real conversation about everything that went down, for the first time ever.

I told Hattie it was what I needed to make my decision. She didn't pressure me, just said she would be there to support me through it.

My palms are sweaty, and the collar of my shirt feels too tight as I step off the elevator with Hattie. As we make our way down the hall, she rubs my back, obviously picking up how difficult this is for me.

When we reach the room, Hattie stops and turns to me. "No matter what you decide, I'll respect it. But please go in there with an open heart." She places her palm on my chest. "So that *you* can heal."

I say nothing, unconvinced my voice would work even if I wanted it to. My vocal cords feel as if they're being squeezed in someone's fist. Leaning in, I kiss her forehead, then I walk into the room.

Carla's prone figure rests in the middle of the hospital bed, and Robert is at her side in a chair. She looks sicklier than the last time I saw her. They turn toward the doorway when we enter.

"Sweetie, you're back," Carla says to her daughter in a weak voice, then looks at me. "Bastion." She gives me a tight-lipped, nervous smile.

I have no idea if she knows why I'm here. I didn't bother asking Hattie. It doesn't matter. This is a conversation that's been needed since the moment I discovered Carla was alive.

Robert gets up out of his chair and hugs his daughter. When she goes to give her mom a hug in bed, his attention turns to me. I'm sure there's lots he'd like to say to me, but instead he nods before turning his attention to the two women in his life.

I do the same and see that they're both looking at me. Once again, the collar of my shirt feels like a noose around my neck.

Hattie turns to her father. "Dad, why don't we get something to eat so that Mom and Bast can talk?"

Robert hesitates, looking at Carla. Hattie hooks her arm through his, and he starts out of the room, but not before giving me a look that reads, "Upset her, and you'll have to deal with me."

I can respect that. If roles were reversed, I'd do the same for Hattie.

The door closes behind me with a click that reverberates through my bones.

"Thank you for coming."

I nod and shove my hands in my pockets, not moving any closer to the bed. Neither of us says anything for a long while. It's as if there's too much to say and neither of us is sure where to start.

"You can say whatever you want, Bastion. You don't have to hold back just because I'm dying." There's grief in her eyes that I imagine matches my own. "Scream, shout, tell me how worthless I am to you, say it all. You deserve that at the very least."

With a sigh, I approach her bedside and sit in the chair Robert vacated. "I don't want to scream and yell at you. I did. For a long while, I did. But it won't change anything, and I doubt it will make me feel better anyway. Not when it would hurt Hattie."

"You love her." There's reverence in her voice.

I nod.

"She's easy to love, isn't she?" Carla gives me a watery smile.

"When did it start?" I clear my throat. "When did you start using? I only ever remember you like that."

She cringes and closes her eyes for a moment. "A couple years after you were born. I won't make excuses, but it started with me wanting to forget what it had been like for me growing up. My..." Carla draws in a deep breath as though the next part is hard for her to say. "My father sexually abused me as a child. He was abusive toward my mother too. The memories would creep up, and I just wanted them to go away. I thought if they did, I could be a better mother to you. Obviously that plan didn't work out the way I hoped."

The corner of my mouth lifts.

"I grew addicted pretty much right away and deteriorated from there. I'd drink when I couldn't get my hands on drugs. A lot of that time I don't even remember. I think of what you probably had to witness, and I just—" A sob unleashes from her chest. It's filled with so much pain and despair that it's difficult to listen to.

Despite myself, I squeeze her shoulder while she cries, feeling once again like that little boy who wants his mom to be happy.

After a minute, Carla wipes her face that's blotchy now from all her crying. "I know that words are not enough, and I can never take back what I did to you, but I am sorry, Bastion. I am so sorry for the pain I caused you."

I didn't think her words would do anything to heal me, but to my surprise, they ease some of the ache in my chest.

"When Robert and Hattie came into my life, I saw it as a second chance to do right. But don't think for a moment that there was ever a day, an hour, that I didn't think of you or wonder if you were okay. I did." Her voice is a hoarse whisper.

A part of the rip in my soul stitches together. The thread is fragile, the stitch loose, but it's more than I've ever had.

I sit with her words for a moment, my elbows resting on my knees, staring at the floor. She lets me. Not pressuring me to say anything, allowing me to work at my own pace.

Eventually, I lift my head and meet her watery gaze. "I didn't know until very recently that you ever came after me. I thought I'd left and you didn't think twice about me."

She appears heartbroken, the lines in her face deepening.

"Why did you leave me with him? Why didn't you try harder?"

She heaves out a sigh. "I considered it. But the things he said... he was right. I didn't deserve you. All I'd done was cause you pain, and I believed him when he said you didn't want to see me. A couple of days after I first confronted him, I went back there and I watched you leave with a little girl who I suspect must be his daughter. You two walked down to the park, and you were having so much fun. Laughing and smiling. I couldn't remember the last time I saw you that happy. I figured you were better off with him than with me because back then, even I wasn't one hundred percent convinced I wouldn't relapse. I'd done so much wrong by you that I figured it was the one thing I could do right."

"Guess we'll never know."

She shakes her head. "No, we won't."

I remember that first year and how much I missed her even as I resented her for making me leave. But I also remember the laughs and fun I had with Ariana.

"How did you find me then?" It's something I've wondered since Trent told me.

She gives me a small smile. "Do you remember that waitress who took a liking to you at the diner down the street? When you first went missing, I went in there looking for you. I was in there weeks later, and she told me that she'd seen you come in with Trent. Guess she knew him."

"Yeah, she was always nice to me. Sometimes she'd give me free food when I went in there."

Carla looks stricken by my words.

"I don't say that to hurt you."

"I know, just the truth hurts."

I sigh. "If we're going to try to have any kind of relationship for Hattie's sake, we're going to need to be able to talk about this stuff without worrying what the other one might think."

"Bastion, you can say whatever you need to say to me. I mean that. It will hurt, but you don't need to protect me. Lord knows I didn't protect you when I should have."

I look at the floor for a moment. There's not much to say to that, is there? When I straighten, I sigh and push both hands through my hair, unsure where we go from here.

"What was it like being with Trent? I asked Hattie, but she would only say that it was your story to tell if you wanted to."

I can't help the small smile that forms on my face. That's my girl, always looking out for me.

"That's a story for another time." I'm not about to spill my life's secrets to this practical stranger.

She looks a little disappointed, but I can't find it in myself to care.

I have a decision to make. Can I walk away from this woman knowing that I might be able to save her life? What kind of person would that make me?

Hattie's right in that I have to find some way to let go of the past. Carla and I will never have a mother-son relationship, but I don't want to hold on to the anger and the resentment any longer. If only so that I can be the best version of myself for Hattie.

I stand, suddenly needing to get out of here. I've had all the heart-to-hearts with Carla that I can take for one day. "I'm going to take off."

She nods, looking disappointed again.

"Before I go, you should know that I'm going to be tested to see if I'm a match." I swallow past the lump in my throat.

Her eyes widen, and tears build. "You don't have to do that. That's not why I wanted to speak with you."

I shove my hands in my pockets and rock back on my heels. "I know. That's why I'm doing it. I don't know what the future holds for the two of us, but I know it would eat away at me if I knew I could have helped and I didn't do it. Mostly because it would hurt Hattie."

The first tear drips down her face. "You're a good man, Bastion. Despite me, you're a good man."

Having no idea what to say to that, I nod and leave the room. Robert and Hattie are leaning against a wall halfway down the hall. He gives me a nod as he passes by to rejoin his wife.

Hattie approaches me hesitantly. "How did it go?"

I pull her in for a hug, dipping my head down and inhaling the scent of her hair. "It was difficult, but necessary. You were right about that."

She squeezes me tighter, and we stand there holding each other while life goes on around us. Hattie doesn't ask if I've decided, and I love her all the more for it.

"I've decided something."

"Oh?" I can tell she's trying to keep the hope from her voice, likely for my benefit.

When I pull away, she's staring up at me with wide eyes.

"I'm going to get tested. If I'm a match, I'll donate my kidney to her."

Her face crumples, and she wraps her arms around my neck, squeezing tightly. "Thank you, Bast. Thank you. I would have understood if you didn't want to, but thank you."

The news comes a few weeks later—I'm a match.

EPILOGUE
HATTIE

The wind whips snow in my face as I make my way down the sidewalk toward the café. One thing I don't miss about Wisconsin is the winters, that's for sure.

Both Bast's and my mom's operations went well, although Bast's recovery is harder than my mom's, she has a longer stay in the hospital. My dad still needs to work, and having me around lets me help her during the week. She's doing much better, though, and I don't anticipate having to be with her for longer than another couple of weeks.

I've made a few weekend trips back to Seattle to see Bast, and he's come out here as much as he can to see me. This weekend is another one of his trips out here, and I'm eager to see him. Though I'm unsure why he asked me to meet him at the café where we used to see each other rather than coming straight to my place.

The bell dings when I rush through the door, looking down to stomp the snow off my boots on the mat. When I look up,

I still. The café is empty. The lights are all on, but no one is here. No customers, no employees, nothing.

"Hello?" I call and take a few tentative steps forward. "Is anyone here?"

No one answers, and I take another look around. This is so confusing.

"Hello?" I step farther in, and movement to my left behind the counter draws my attention.

Bast saunters out of the staff door, looking for all the world as though he owns the place.

"Hi..." I'm excited to see him but still so confused as to what he's doing behind the counter. "What's going on?" I motion toward the empty café. "What are you doing back there?"

He grins and hops over the counter with one hand on it with seemingly little trouble. "Don't I get a kiss hello?"

He draws me in with his hands around my waist and presses his lips to mine. It's a good thing no one is in here because the kiss turns heated quickly.

I'm always like this when I've gone through a spell without seeing him—desperate and needy for both his company and his body.

When he pulls away, he rests his forehead against mine.

"How was your flight?" I ask.

"Fine. How's Carla?" He nuzzles into my neck and places a chaste kiss there that makes goose bumps break out on my arms.

"Still making strides every day."

The relationship between him and my mom is still a little strained, but they've come a long way. They're not close by any means, but he can be in her presence, and no one feels as though they're walking on eggshells around them anymore.

Maybe they'll develop a mother-son relationship in the future, or maybe they won't, but either way, it's okay. I think just knowing each other has healed a little something in each of them.

"Does that mean I get you home with me soon?" he says against the sensitive flesh under my ear.

I hum low in my throat. "Very soon, I think."

He straightens and gives me a wide smile. "Good."

"Are you going to explain what's going on here? Why is this place empty?" I motion to the empty seats.

"Because I kicked everyone out."

I lean back, and my forehead wrinkles. "I don't understand."

Bast chuckles. "Come with me back to our section."

There's no denying that I get a thrill in my belly when he refers to it as our section.

He takes my hand and leads me to the lounge area near the fireplace, which is going given the weather outside.

"Here, let me take your jacket." He holds out his hands.

I get to work removing my jacket and beanie, then I pass

them to Bast, who sets them on the back of one of the armchairs, and finger-comb my hair.

"Are you going to tell me what's going on?" I set my hands on my hips and give him a playful smile.

"This is where we met."

I giggle. "Yes, I know."

"Because of that, it's special to me, even if we did meet because I was an emotionally stunted asshole."

We both laugh, and I shake my head. I've gotten over how things started between us, but sometimes I think Bast is still punishing himself.

"Do you remember what I said when you asked why I was in town?" He cocks his head and steps up to hold my hands.

"You said you were looking for a business to invest in."

He nods. "That wasn't true at the time, but it is now, so I bought the café."

"What? Really?"

"Really. I want this place to stick around for a long, long time, so I bought it so that I can be the one to preserve it."

That is so sweet. I squeeze his hands.

"The reason I want it around for so long is because I'd like to be able to take my kids here one day and tell them that this is where their parents met. That this is the first place I realized that my wife was going to change my life."

"Bast—"

Before I can say anything more, he drops to one knee.

I gasp, and my hands fly out of his to cover my mouth.

He slides his hand in his pocket and pulls out a ring box, then opens it to reveal a huge pear-shaped diamond ring. "Hattie, I love you more than life itself, and I cannot wait another moment to bind you to me. If it weren't for everything going on with your mom, I would have already done this, but now that she's doing better, I want to think about our future. Will you do me the honor of becoming my wife?"

"Yes!" I shout, my arms flailing above my head.

Bast lets out a whoop and stands to slide the monstrous ring on my left ring finger, then kisses me.

"We should elope. You're too good for me and I need to lock this down before you come to your senses," he says.

I laugh. "I'm a little bad, though." I waggle my eyebrows.

There's a glimmer in his eyes. "You know, you're right. You're just the right amount of good for me, and I'm just the right amount of bad for you."

"The perfect combination."

"Thank you, Hattie."

I run my palm down his cheek. "For what?"

"For showing me that all is not lost, even when it might seem like it is. That there's always an end to the storm, and that's when the rainbow appears."

We kiss again, and I say a little prayer of thanks. I may not spend all my time in church these days, but I know for certain that someone was looking out for me when they sent me Bast.

The End

ACKNOWLEDGMENTS

After we finished writing His Subordinate, we discussed what we might want to write next. Did we want to create a new world or return to an old one? Were there any secondary characters' stories we were interested in exploring? Bastion immediately came to mind.

When he first appeared on the page in his sister Ariana's story, he intrigued us, and we knew we had to explore his past and how that affected the man he became.

We started with revenge, knowing his story would somehow revolve around him wanting to make his mother pay for his childhood, but of course, a romance that does not make! LOL We had to figure out how to tie his love interest into that story, and that's when it dawned on us that he could have a stepsister he was jealous of but equally intrigued by. Enter Hattie.

She didn't know what she was getting herself into when she walked into that coffee shop and met Bastion for the first time, but she did know she was starting to feel like she was up for an adventure. And the rest as they say, is history!

As always, there are a lot of people to thank for getting this book into your hands...

The Valentine PR crew always keeps us in check and follows

up to make sure we're hitting those deadlines. Not only do we need it, but we appreciate it!

Regina Wamba did a wonderful job with this cover—so pretty!

Cassie, Ellie and Olivia—thanks for lending your talents to this project by way of editing or proofing. It would not be what it is without your help!

Big thanks to every blogger, influencer and reader who carved out time to read Bast and Hattie's story! We genuinely appreciate every review, edit, recommendation to your reader friends, rating, and social media shout-out you give us. We see you and are so, so grateful! <3

If you're intrigued by Bast's sister's story, you can check out His Subordinate. Or better yet, start at the beginning of the series with His Ultimatum and enjoy all four dirty-talking billionaire Voss brothers!

xo,

Piper & Rayne

ALSO BY P. RAYNE

Mafia Academy

Vow of Revenge

Corrupting the Innocent

Corrupting the Mafia King's Sister

Craving My Rival

Ritual Room

His Ultimatum

His Posession

His Obsession

His Subordinate

Standalones

Beautifully Scarred

Ruining Hattie

ABOUT P. RAYNE

P. Rayne is the pseudonym for the darker side of the USA Today Bestselling Author duo, Piper Rayne. Under P. Rayne you'll find twisty, forbidden and sexy romances.